MAN OF THE SWORD

By Paul Kenney

KINVARA
PRODUCTIONS

ISBN: 1500880841
ISBN 13: 9781500880842

To Billy

PART ONE
THE ENCOUNTER

CHAPTER 1

*I*n accordance with my orders, I waited on the platform of the Waterloo Station for the train to Southampton, surrounded by an oppressive crowd. Through an early morning mist I saw an old man heading toward me, holding a small, crimson text next to his heart.

His face and figure were pleasing to the eye and he seemed to glide among those he passed. Although he did not speak, the serenity of his disposition shone through his vibrant, violet eyes, bestowing kindness upon all that observed him pass. Whether it was providence or happenstance that occasioned our meeting, I am still uncertain.

September in the year of Our Lord 1918 brought with it a grim foreboding. Despite my youth and my apparent vigor, I was beset by the demon of my circumstance, for I had recently been a trained participant in the unrelenting savagery of battle. I was to report to Colonel Donovan at the regimental command post, South of the Argonne Forrest, within the week. I had not as yet completed the Colonel's assignment.

London had proven an ant hill of activity. Lives managed by uncontrollable fate seemed to shuffle past like specters lost in the rigors of war -- dark, inglorious war. I had spent what seemed like an eternity attempting to convalesce in Mayfair. Before the starched linen and cloying ether of my confinement could further besiege my mind and batter my soul, I advised my matronly nurse that I was discharging myself, for I could find no solace there. I had plummeted to the very depths of my being, tormented by notions that I had gone quite mad and nothing mattered after all. I had turned twenty four that spring.

Then there he stood beside me, removing his dark blue frock coat and revealing a sky blue shirt of the very finest linen, complemented by the most extraordinary pair of suspenders, pheasants in flight over a mountainside, as I recall. He spoke in my direction, but not to me, commenting upon the tardy arrival of the train to Southampton.

There was a certain timbre to his voice that was almost extraterrestrial. In fact, the term voice now seems a totally inadequate appellation for such an extraordinary faculty. He then seemed to focus his attention upon me and the telltale, damning tremor I was attempting to conceal, as the train signaled its arrival like the shriek of an enemy artillery shell.

"My travel takes me to the end of the line," he said. "Your company is welcome within my carriage."

Since he seemed in need of a traveling companion and his railway carriage appeared remarkably removed from the chaos and clamor of that place, I availed myself of his hospitality. It was September of 1918, during the war to end all wars, and I was in desperate need of an uplifting situation. Our sojourn began amid steam and smoke, as that serpent-like train departed, surrounded by the sights and sounds of anguished farewells, arising from those leaving and those left behind.

How old a man was he? I would not be able to answer with any degree of certitude, for he displayed a flexibility of carriage that was characteristic of a young man. His dress was that of a country gentleman. His dark blue coat and broad brimmed gray hat had been carefully laid next to him on the emerald seat that faced the emerald seat where I was situated. His crimson text was firmly secured within his manicured left hand. Immersed in his readings and his solitude, I refrained from any attempt at conversation, while observing the particulars of his person.

He wore butternut trousers and a ruffled blue shirt crowned by a starched formal collar that embraced a paisley ascot. His hair was almost entirely silver and his manly face displayed a broad gray mustache that curled tenderly over the corners of an expressive mouth. Of all his distinctive features, it was his eyes that drew and held my attention foremost. They were the color of English violets and they seemed to possess a piercing quality that was both beguiling and mesmerizing.

Recognizing the need to divert my attention from the uncertainty that lay beyond my destination, I retrieved pen and ink from my chestnut leather valise to return to the Colonel's assignment. At this, the old man put aside his crimson text and made inquiry of me.

"Is it to a lady that you write?"

"No," I answered. "It is a history of sorts, for my commanding officer."

"Then it is the war that brings you through London. I could not tell from your civilian attire."

"Yes, the war and a fortnight's furlough."

"Please allow me to introduce myself, Cornelius O'Keefe at your service."

"Captain Myles Sullivan," I replied, advising him that it was a distinct pleasure to make his acquaintance.

He then informed me that he was on his way to Southampton to visit with an old friend from his days in the military. As he spoke, I began to discern a slight brogue encased within a gentlemanly diction. He seemed particularly intrigued by the nature of my assignment. I advised him that because of my previous experience as a reporter and my position as the Colonel's adjutant, it had been determined that I should research and write a history of the regiment.

"And what regiment would that be?" he asked.

"The Sixty Ninth New York," I answered proudly.

My response provoked a faint smile from beneath his robust mustache. He then gazed out the narrow window at the panoramic expanse of the English countryside passing before us. For a moment he seemed enthralled by some reverie, as the train rumbled rhythmically over the rails.

He then reached beside him into his coat and retrieved a small golden flask from its breast pocket. He offered me a libation, which I saw no reason to decline in light, of my present circumstance. The warm and flavorful taste of the liquor was most enjoyable. It seemed to evaporate any need for formality between us. Continued conversation soon fortified the bonds that entwined us to the past.

He inquired further of me with the persistence and skill of one trained in the journalistic trade. Where had I enlisted? What counties in Ireland did my ancestors hail from? Had I served at the front? What was the nature of my experience as a reporter? When I advised him that I had covered the City's criminal docket for the *Times*, he again smiled. I also informed him of my aspiration to matriculate at Fordham and study for the law, once I returned from France, if I returned from France. This last remark seemed to disturb him, for he became suddenly subdued. He again partook of the flask and returned it to the pocket of his coat.

"Tell me lad. Do you believe in your generals?" he probed.

To this inquiry I had no ready response. For in truth I had seen the slaughter that resulted from the miscalculations of our General Staff and did not wish to expose my misgivings to the further inquiries of this mysterious old man. I then assumed the mantle of the inquisitor, emboldened by the spirits imbibed from the flask.

"May I make inquiry of you?"

"By all means, fire away," he replied, while reaching into another pocket of his coat and securing two cigars.

I could tell from their golden appearance that they were Cuban. He then quickly produced a tiny dagger-like knife from within his hat and prepared our treat with the skill of a surgeon. It was a pleasure to partake of my host's offering. The aroma from those delights reminded me of the newsroom at the *Times*.

"Were you a military man, Mr. O'Keefe?"

"Aye, at one time I was."

"What country did you serve?"

"I can say I served two countries, Captain, Erin, which is my home once again, and America, the land that adopted and nurtured me like a beloved mother."

"What was the manner of your military service?"

With this inquiry he paused and stood, rubbing the palm of his right hand with the thumb of his left. His eyes seemed to blaze forth as he stared at me, as if uncertain as to his next response. After positioning himself at the window momentarily, he turned and sat down once again. He then began the recitation that would help to complete my assignment for Colonel Donovan.

"I served in the Eighty-Eighth New York during the War of the Rebellion."

"Do you mean to tell me, that you were a member of The Irish Brigade?" I asked, astonished at this fortuity.

"Yes, that is what I mean to tell you, lad."

"My God, there can be but a handful of you left!"

My exclamation was without consideration of the old man's sensibilities. He stared once again at me, as if remembering those that had fallen beside him in battles that we of "The Rainbow Division" had only imagined.

He then closed his eyes and began to move the fingers of his right hand in a circular movement across the middle of his forehead. I apologized for the insensitivity of my remark. He didn't seem to take offense.

I knew that I must pursue the path that this strange encounter had presented to me. Relying upon the specifics of my historical research I delved into the flesh and blood of living history, appearing before me.

There was a figure from this old man's past that had always intrigued me. A legend revered by many of Irish descent who made their homes in Brooklyn, Manhattan and the Bronx. I had to learn of him, and I knew, I knew that the old man could teach me.

"Did you know General Meagher?" I asked, praying that he would be able to vivify one who had lived a life of adventure and become a telling footnote to the history of both Ireland and America.

The old man's eyes slowly opened and focused upon me. It was apparent that the mention of the name had conjured up some fond, indelible reminiscence within him. Slowly, he set down his cigar, sat erect and removed his ascot and collar, as if in preparation for what would ensue. He smiled and nodded his head.

"Indeed, I served with the General. Perhaps, I knew him as well as any knew "Meagher of the Sword". You see, I'm a Tipperary man. The Meagher's hailed from Waterford. When I was just a lad, I was in the courtroom when he and the others were tried for treason at Clonmel. Have you read much of Twain?"

"Yes, some."

"Twain insists that history is written with the ink of lies. Do you have the courage to write with the ink of truth, Captain Sullivan"?

"I do, Mr. O'Keefe."

"To understand the history you seek, you must understand Meagher and the times in which we lived."

He then blew a ring of smoke across the expanse of the compartment, while his piercing eyes were focused intently upon mine.

I knew at once that the old man was right. History that enlightens is not a lifeless recitation of dusty facts and deceased personages. It requires a vivid portrayal of life and times as they were, without the cobwebs and the distortion of apologetic hindsight. From what I had read and heard about General Meagher, it made perfect sense that the sheer power of such a person would have determined the nature of the fighting force that he helped create, a force that would perform legendary feats of valor during The Civil War, a force that included the Sixty Ninth New York Regiment, a force known as Meagher's Irish Brigade.

I knew that I would not soon forget that old man and our travel upon that train bound for Southampton, on that September day in the year of Our Lord 1918.

CHAPTER 2

*P*erhaps it was the impact of the drink. Perhaps it was the old man's engaging nature. At any rate I soon began to feel very secure in his presence. I had not felt secure in a long, long, time. I remembered how my dear, departed mother spoke to me of times in Ireland when the village storytellers would entrance the old and the young with tales of times and heroes past. That was the way it was on the way to my destiny in France.

"Tell me, Captain, will your pen write with fire?" he asked. I replied that I could not guarantee my prose would ignite, but only that it would display a certain style, a style that would entice those seeking enlightenment through the vessel of their imagination. This seemed to amuse him and mollify his concern for the quality of this recitation.

"I don't mean to be impertinent," he insisted. "The times of which I will speak were no ordinary times. Meagher and those who served and fought beside him were not men like we see today. They were a band of noble spirits, whose hearts were touched by fire, and from their flame a great nation was forged."

"Then, I will write with fire," I volunteered, recognizing a challenge from one steeped, I sensed, in the communicative arts. I suddenly felt as if I was in the presence of one who possessed some superior wisdom. One who could instruct as well as inspire. As O'Keefe began his recitation, I wrote as if it were my blood running through the pen.

"Thomas Francis Meagher was an Irish aristocrat, educated at Stonyhurst in Lancashire. By his twenty third year he had partaken fully of the salons, boudoirs and bordellos of Europe and been transformed by their influences. That is to say, as much as Meagher could be transformed by anything or anybody at that time in his life. It was then that he returned to Ireland and discovered that all had changed."

"Excuse me," I interjected. "In what year are we beginning this adventure?"

"Excellent, Captain," he responded, "it is indeed an adventure and I suppose I am your guide. But I too am a pilgrim, and before this tale is told, I shall discover as much as I shall describe. The year I would say would be 1846 or thereabouts. For that was long ago and I am quite old."

I did not wish to inject my inquiries into his recitation, for it delayed my transcription and it was becoming apparent that the old man was dispensing history as readily as the pulse quickens during battle. Yet the significant pieces needed some elaboration.

"You mentioned Stonyhurst, Mr. O'Keefe. What is the nature of that place?"

"Stonyhurst is a Jesuit college that has educated many from Europe's Catholic aristocracy over the centuries. It is said that Meagher excelled in drama and debate. Yet, he learned much more than the classics within those ancient walls. He became an ardent pupil of Father Christopher, a reformed member of a warlike clan. Before he received his Holy Orders, Father Christopher had been a master in the artistry of both the broad sword and saber."

"And did he teach Meagher the artistry you describe?" I asked.

"Yes indeed," he said. "Meagher became an exemplary pupil in many of the old priest's disciplines. In those days there would be competitions for the most superior swordsmen and *chevaliers* throughout Europe. The good Father taught young Thomas well and he soon took his place among the best in England. I have seen none who could ride with the self-same grace. It was as if he allowed his mount to run free and yet be devoted to his loving commands. I remember that bloody day at Antietam."

Suddenly the old man paused, as if some distant, dreadful apparition had come into focus. His vibrant eyes clouded over with a sorrowful glaze.

"Are you alright, Mr. O'Keefe?" I asked, alarmed by the pained expression that flashed across his face, like lightning crackling across the expanse of a rain swollen sky.

The old man stayed completely still for several moments before suddenly resuming his recitation. His voice was now a full throated blend of rasp and resonance. As I said, to give this gift the appellation of a mortally bound faculty was to do a disservice to its Creator.

"Meagher was a creature of the small segment of Irish who had somehow managed to survive and prosper within the dominion of the Crown. His father was a merchant of some considerable prestige, for a Catholic. They say the money his father made was honest and more than sufficient to establish his son as a gentleman of property. This was many years after his beloved mother's death. He ..."

"You spoke of a transformation," I interjected, attempting to return him to a straight and narrow path from which I could transcribe a worthy recitation.

"Ah yes, following his studies in England, the circles in which he revolved transformed him into an erudite libertine, nearly blind to all but self-indulgence. That is when he returned to Ireland. That is when he returned to Waterford and his beloved Suir, the river of his youth."

"As a lad, Thomas spent many a morning watching the golden sun sparkle across the Suir, from atop the hills confronting Waterford. When he returned, the time of the great hunger had begun. He wondered why his homestead on the river's quay had been deemed no longer suitable. His father was Waterford's mayor at that time and had once been its representative to the House of Commons."

"Meagher's father was a member of the British Parliament!"

"Yes, he and Daniel O'Connell, Ireland's "Great Liberator", were both members of the House of Commons. In fact, Thomas and O'Connell's nephew, John, had been classmates at Clongowes Wood, a Jesuit public school in Kildare. It was there that Thomas had grown to detest Daniel O'Connell's nephew. Alas, I will come to that shortly."

"It was upon his return to his father's newly chosen domicile, across the way from Waterford's beleaguered City Hall, that he learned the real reason for the change in address of the family Meagher."

"These are dangerous times, Thomas. The peasants are becoming desperate and I fear we have only seen the beginning of their suffering." That is how Meagher remembered his father's remarks on the blight that had begun to destroy the potato harvests."

"I once saw Meagher's father pass by in a carriage. I remember he possessed a noble bearing yet still displayed the common touch, as Brother

Kipling would say. He was a slender, refined man with a long narrow head of white hair. He would have been a man of sixty years or more at that time. A gentleman of considerable industry, he viewed the landlords and the British with suspicion but never disdain. For disdain was not good for his business of provisioning ships for the New Foundland trade."

"Thomas the senior, as he was called by those who knew the family well, thought it would be safer for his family and their servants to remove from the quay. You see the quay was where the desperate, malnourished wretches from the countryside came to beg for sustenance and pray for passage upon the coffin ships bound for America. They appeared like a sea of misery, sharing a desperate yearning to escape from the oppression of the landlords and the threat of death from famine and fever."

"Meagher was a student of Locke, of Jefferson and of Paine." He once told us before the battle of Fair Oaks that he and his father disagreed more than they agreed. You see, Thomas the senior had not resisted the British in their subjugation of Ireland. His son, on the other hand, would rebel against the Crown's tyranny."

Considering the eloquence of my aged companion and the meticulous nature of his recollections, I resolved to report accurately all that he described during our time together. It had become clear to me that his recitation of the life of Meagher and the lives of so many who fought beneath the green flags should be preserved for posterity. I trust I have done so.

O'KEEFE'S RECITATION OF HISTORICAL EVENTS

I wish to say that my life and that of General Meagher's took a similar course. He was older than I and the first time I heard tell of him was in the village at Clonmel. There was a story told of a young Thomas Meagher refusing to play his violin within the school orchestra at Clongowes Wood, in honor of the Prince of Wales. It was a scandal for those who admired the British and believed that they were our betters. Then there were the others, thank God, the ones who yearned for freedom from British rule. Meagher and I shared a common passion and perspective. We each dreamed of liberty and were willing to fight and even die to achieve it. I must not get ahead of myself, for Meagher's life was a wild and dark river. I ask that you submerge with me.

Meagher appeared a stylish sort at first blush, bearing the markings of a privileged upbringing. Compared to the hardened lads from Dublin and

Limerick, he seemed almost fragile. But he was like flint. His rebel soul was his sword and his manner of speech was inspired. He was taller than most men of that time, expanding with the years, but never losing a masculine sprightliness.

His hair was a dark chestnut, curling jauntily over his ears and his eyes were wolf like orbs of blue. He displayed a certain hop to his step and he loved the dance, almost as much as he loved the ladies. In his twenties, he appeared younger than his stated age. Later, the ordeal of war would line his face and streak his mane with silver.

He often spoke to me of his youth in Waterford and his heated debates with his father. They disagreed on both the plight of Erin and the blight of British rule. Meagher's father was a cautious man, ever mindful of appearances and circumspect in his discussion of such matters. Nevertheless, Thomas loved and admired him. I remember seeing his father after the treason trial. His heart had been broken by the terrifying fate that had befallen his beloved namesake.

Once again I have digressed from the presentation of events as they happened. Please, allow me to return to Waterford and describe what eyes that wished to see, beheld, during those dark and dreadful years.

CHAPTER 3

As I related, I hail from Tipperary. My father and his father before him worked in the mines. I received my education, however, in Dublin, under the tutelage of my uncle. He was a man of honest reputation within the Irish banking trade. At that time many of us were inspired by Daniel O'Connell and his passionate appeals for the repeal of The Act of Union, that dastardly legislation denying the Irish their God given right to live free and thrive in a free nation. O'Connell was our hope. In him, we of the merchant class saw a savior.

That was before Meagher, Mitchel and Smith O'Brien began to speak out for the young of Ireland. We were, alas, the young of Ireland, at a time when Ireland starved. At a time when ships with steerages full of the dying and desperate departed daily, leaving entire villages to the rain and the wind. At a time when other ships bound for Liverpool and Manchester were laden with the fruit of our fertile countryside. All the while, Irish children died and Irish mothers cried.

I remember traveling to Waterford on some banking business for my uncle. The sights and sounds of that place, as well as the other port cities of Cork and Galway, cannot be forgotten. That is when I first met Meagher. That is when I, who wanted desperately to lead, began to follow. I have never entertained either regret or remorse concerning the life I chose during those years of fear and famine. I believe it was during the spring, a time of beginnings, when Thomas set our course upon the rebel's path.

14

"Come along O'Keefe," he shouted, as he and Smith O'Brien departed from a dreary public house overlooking the river.

I had listened from across a heavy oak table, commanding a darkened corner of that smoke filled drinking establishment, as Meagher had lavished his impassioned attention upon two of Waterford's beauties. They had been conversing and caressing in a communal sort of way.

The proprietor, a small moth eaten man, took umbrage at the shameful nature of their display and demanded they acquit his premises forthwith.

I had become acquainted with Meagher that morning. We had been engaged in securing a line of credit for a shipment of wool from Glasgow. He had invited me to dine with him and his dear friend, William Smith O'Brien, and engage in the conquest of ladies of questionable reputation.

As we descended the hill toward the quay, I remember the sound of the city at that hour. A thick grey fog had enveloped the moorings along the Suir. It was as thick as soup around us. It muffled the sounds of the ships upon the river, attempting to signal their presence through the shrouded night. I recall Meagher fondling one of his lustful accomplices, just before we came upon the wretched creatures fleeing the famine that was spreading over the land.

They were as denizens of a nether world. At first we thought they were sacks of rags. Their emaciated figures were too weary to walk. They moaned for alms, beseeching us to save them from being gathered up by the wagons of death and spiriting them away. Their tortured faces were barely visible beneath the lanterns that spread an amber glow over the docks. There were hundreds of them, beckoning us like a hellish chorus. I remember my fears. I was terrified that their misery would be visited upon me and my family. I was afraid for my beloved Erin. Then she appeared like a specter in a shawl.

"Oh please, have mercy my fine gentle ones," she cried. "I was pretty once. Please, save my children. They are starving. Don't let the wagons take them from me, please."

It was Smith O'Brien who responded to her desperate appeal. She was barely eighteen years, as near as I could gather. Her pale skin was draped over her skeleton like face. Her bony fingers beckoned us. She seemed nearly mad with the hunger and the hopelessness of her state.

"Where do you take us, mother?" O'Brien asked, now diverted from more worldly pursuits by the entreaty of a sorrowful soul. She was my very same age, but yet so much older, too old for one so young.

"Let us leave from this place, my love, and you can have your way with me." O'Brien's now frightened companion offered through her crimson lips.

"Away girl, I will follow this mother. Will you come with me Thomas?" O'Brien demanded.

"Aye," Meagher replied. "I have seen the misery of Antwerp and climbed upon her barricades. Let us see where she leads. You need not come," he said, to his passionate accomplice. Then he gazed upon me. "What say you O'Keefe? Will you tarry with these tarts or abide with O'Brien and me?"

That was the first time I was challenged by him. There would be times ahead when his challenges would fire many a soul.

Meagher admired William Smith O'Brien immensely. It was as if Meagher was his younger brother. For those who have forgotten, Ireland exhibited many stars within her constellation during those tragic years. It is perhaps the troubled times that fashion the bravest hearts. I will speak to you of these brave hearts.

Smith O'Brien was a son of privilege and education. His ancestry could be traced to Boru himself. He was an Anglican by birth and belief. The fire of his disposition and the warmth of his heart caused him to soar above the rest. Like Meagher, he had been to the Continent and partaken of its wickedness.

He was a most eloquent spokesman, particularly with the written word. That was the trait that propelled him to become a member of Parliament. His appearance was that of a more formidable physical specimen than Meagher and he possessed the most unmanageable head of auburn hair, complemented by a resolute ruddy face and green eyes. A lover of music and manly pursuits, he and Meagher were worldly men in search of public acclaim.

You see Thomas Meagher loved the rhythmic rumble of his name. He was enamored of the crowd and played to them as they cheered his rise to prominence. I accompanied them on that night, the same night that we first encountered a saintly sort by the name of Brother Edmund.

The wretched mother led the way back from the quay and up a narrow alleyway to a great stone house surrounded by a fence of rusted iron. It was a dark, foreboding sort of place that was left in disrepair, perhaps by some failed member of Waterford's gentry.

As Meagher and O'Brien followed, their stagger from drink seemed to subside. We then came upon two of the constabulary as they made their rounds with a watchman's lamp. They surveyed us with seeming suspicion.

They seemed resentful of our privileged demeanor. After recognizing Meagher, they did not delay us with an inquiry as to our reasons for being about at such an hour.

As we drew closer, we heard children wailing from within that grim stone edifice. Except upon that bloody field of Fredericksburg on that dreadful night in the cold, I have not heard such a sorrowful din in all my days. The thick oak door of that place had been left ajar. As we entered, we beheld the unspeakable misery of a famine house. There were scores of emaciated, dying bodies upon patches of straw on its cold, stone floor.

It appeared to be a manor house devoted to the dying, devoted to dying children for the most part. It was then that his figure emerged, as if from a celestial visitation.

He was a small man, yet firm in stature. His face and manner were those of a refined gentleman. His age exceeded the half century and his hair was sterling silver. He possessed deep-set, pale, green eyes that displayed the most serene of expressions. He wore a dark brown cassock without the collar of a parish priest. His speech toward all within that terrible place was most benign. He was accompanied by two devoted young men. All three were tending to those passing beyond the reach of human kindness.

I shall never forget the wail of that misbegotten mother as she discovered her tiny, dying daughter, lying nearby, against a slate gray wall. Her sobbing was most unsettling to us all, but most particularly to Meagher.

I recall him drawing close to this tragic sight, his eyes brimming with tears. The child's decimated form was no more than a small sack of skin and bone. I remember Thomas removing his cloak. It was made of the finest red silk. Gently, he lifted the child and placed her upon it.

He was kneeling as he caressed that little one's anguished face. He was crying. We all were crying, crying for a mother and her children. Crying for our beloved Erin, amid the sorrow that had descended upon her like some Biblical pestilence. It was the beginning of the famine then, a famine that would soon sweep across Ireland and change our lives forever.

The old man then approached Thomas and spoke to him in the loving manner I have described. I was standing away from their encounter, next to Smith O'Brien. I could not hear all that was being said, because of the mother's weeping entreaties.

We soon discovered that the other of this poor soul's children had succumbed to starvation and was wrapped in a crude shroud nearby. This awareness caused the mother to fall into an unconscious state before us. It was then that the old man's words could be heard.

"Do you remember me young Meagher?"

"You have me at a disadvantage, Father."

"I am not a priest. I am a brother to the poor in spirit who have come to our beloved Waterford from the countryside. Your father and I have engaged in commerce. They call me Brother Edmund. Do you believe as we do?"

"How is that Brother?" Smith O'Brien asked.

"That the evil of this world can only be conquered by our love and our courage. Will you assist us in our mission?"

"What mission is that, Brother?" I remember asking him.

"To help heal the soul of the Irish people that now more than ever is in need, to educate the poor so that they may rise from their ignorance and servitude. This is the mission of our Christian Brotherhood. I ask you. Do you gentlemen have the courage to love those who have been forgotten? What say you? Do you have the courage?"

"I do, Brother," I remember Meagher crying, while he knelt beside that child and his manly voice echoed over the sorrowful din of that place.

We were to remember that night in the famine house, for it burned deeply into our souls and made us feel the pain of the peasants.

CHAPTER 4

*D*aniel O'Connell was a god who walked the earth, before that night at Conciliation Hall. As a boy, I recall reading of his exploits along with those of Wolfe Tone and Fitzgerald. His appearance, even without the customary adulation, was in itself inspiring.

At that time he was still a tall, imposing figure of a man with thick graying hair and fiery blue eyes. He displayed broad handsome features, a barreled chest and a booming voice that could resound across a crowd. By that summer, his devotion to the cause of liberating his people had begun to transform him into an old man.

A barrister by profession, he had developed an impressive reputation before the Queen's Bench. The blush of his skin and the hue of his hair were that of the black Irish. The dramatic gestures of his enormous hands combined with the deep resonance of his baritone voice in mesmerizing and mastering the devoted crowds that gathered to hear him speak. He was recognized as Ireland's Liberator. Yet his recent imprisonment at the hands of the Crown had caused his flame to begin to flicker.

Once, during a heated debate, he catapulted from the speaker's platform to confront a quarrelsome opponent attempting to shout down his thundering eloquence. Before their dispute was settled, O'Connell and his inner circle had battered the opponent and six of his cohorts into submission. The next evening O'Connell was seen in the company of his chastised adversaries, hoisting a pint to their health. Throughout Ireland, Daniel O'Connell enjoyed the zealous approval of the multitudes.

The night of the Repeal Association Debates had been long awaited. I remember sitting at my desk overlooking Grafton Street, unable to concentrate upon bills of lading and promissory notes in the sweltering July heat. For nearly an entire month, Mitchel's *Nation* had trumpeted the issues and described the accomplishments of those who would address the throng within that historical place.

I was able at some indebtedness to secure admission to the second balcony. I came to hear O'Connell. Yet I left inspired as never before by Meagher.

Since that night at the famine house, I had not seen Meagher. While I was immersed in matters of trade and commerce, he was traveling throughout Ireland, speaking to the peasantry of ambitious dreams of liberty, dreams that were unfettered by British dragoons and imperious landlords.

On the eve of the debates I passed by the location of the anticipated event. I recall receiving a handbill from a lad of promise who pointed out that Mitchel, Smith O'Brien and Meagher were to speak on the redress of Erin's pitiful predicament. There were so many of our young who longed for a free Ireland. I recall returning home that evening and dreaming of a new tomorrow.

The crowds began to gather and mill around that great Dublin hall since early morning. Carriages deposited the gentry upon its marble stairs, stairs that led through imposing columns to its spacious entrance. Horsemen from the constabulary kept the impoverished and the curious at a distance.

I remember the most violent thunder storm tore open the skies as I and others sought shelter beneath the hall's impressive Grecian architecture. This was immediately before O'Connell arrived in the company of his nephew John.

John O'Connell was the youngest of O'Connell's brothers' sons. Like his uncle, he was a man of considerable stature. Unlike him, he lacked substance, both in his manner and his mission. His features were dark and pointed, and his hooded brown eyes betrayed an indifference, indeed an avulsion, to the suffering of the peasant class.

His intellect, although superior, was not accompanied by his uncle's compassion. He was an opportunist without an ounce of devotion to noble causes. He dwelled beneath his uncle's shadow. Auspicious beginnings had proven his cross to bear.

During their childhood years, he and Thomas had been enrolled at Clongowes Wood. It seems a dispute arose concerning some youthful indiscretion on the part of a certain segment of the student body. As the result of information supplied by John O'Connell, Thomas endured the wrath and punishment of his Jesuit mentors, a wrath and punishment he would not soon forget. There was always the potential for an altercation when they met.

In the front of the hall nearest to the stage, the wealthy circulated in the finest formal attire. Among those in attendance were Lord John Russell, Lord Edward Drouen, the Marquis of Waterford, and many of the clergy, including the newly anointed Archbishop of the Dublin Diocese.

Amid the oppressive heat that rose to a fever pitch within the balconies, I waited anxiously for the commencement of the evening's events.

The first to make his appearance was William Smith O'Brien. His Protestant upbringing and election to Parliament had made him the acceptable choice for bringing decorum to that volatile atmosphere. He introduced himself amid polite applause and then introduced the array of speakers who would address the issues of repeal and reform.

When John Mitchell, the editor of the *Nation,* was introduced, the reception was enthusiastic. When Meagher was introduced, the response, to say the least, was tepid.

When O'Connell's introduction began, the crowd began to rumble with anticipation. As his name was finally shouted, he swept upon the stage to a thunderous ovation and took his place in its center. He wore a cranberry colored coat and tails. He displayed a congeniality and a dramatic presence that captivated the crowd.

The name of O'Connell was chanted again and again from the rafters. I remember joining in this adulation. With O'Connell to lead us, I believed we could prevail over our British masters. He seemed to dwarf the others upon the stage beside him. I recall staring down at Meagher, as he nervously reviewed the notes of his first political address, seemingly lost in the shadow of O'Connell. John Mitchel was the first of the speakers to make his address.

When the history of Ireland is written, the name of John Mitchel will echo forth along with the likes of Emmett, Davis and Boru. He was a devoted family man by then, who had written of Ireland and its quest for self-government within the editorial pages of his beloved *Nation*. He was a man of vision and purpose, who counted both the great and the lowly among his friends and admirers

Once, when I was hurrying across Phoenix Park, I saw him seated by himself reading the scriptures. At that time the deer and the birds of the air that inhabited that place verily surrounded him. He was a man of passion beyond his peers, particularly when it came to Erin's fate among nations.

Mitchel was possessed of a long slender stature and an angular face. He wore spectacles upon a prominent nose and his hair was a chestnut brown. His handsome face and sorrowful brown eyes signaled a genteel demeanor. If one had not known better, he could have been mistaken for a country pedagogue. His voice lacked the resonance so necessary for public discourse, yet his compassionate insight into the plight of Ireland's poor and propertyless was beyond comparison.

I remember him speaking that evening of the famine and the disregard of the landlords. It was upon the landlords that the British sought to place the burden of the desperate tenant farmers. A burden the landlords would reject. The next to speak was the champion of Catholic emancipation, himself, Daniel O'Connell.

As he approached the dark oak podium that commanded the stage, he paused, as if to collect his thoughts. Before commencing, he awaited the complete silence of the multitude within the spacious confines of that ancient hall. Only the sight of the ladies gently fanning themselves in the heat disturbed the reverence of his audience. He began softly and spoke in the following manner:

"My people, I come before you this evening to describe the means by which our beloved Ireland can achieve its freedom.

In Westminster, I have risen along with my noble friend and colleague, William Smith O'Brien, and raised my voice over and over against The Act of Union. I have taken my case to the Prime Minister and obtained an audience with Her Majesty, Queen Victoria. I have put forth our cause. I have most willingly endured the privation of a prison cell to signify our yearning for a free and independent Irish Nation."

"Our object is not the rupturing of our relationship with the Crown but rather a restructuring of that relationship to accommodate the will and well-being of the Irish people. We comprehend the bloody futility of the sword. We understand the inevitability of our extinction, should we take up arms against the Empire. Our recourse must be wise and righteous."

"We must continue to peacefully present our position through repeated protest and petition. We appeal to British reason and justice. We seek amelioration not confrontation. We seek Home Rule. We seek to be the masters of our own destiny. It is our fervent aspiration to take our place as equals beside our British partners, among the prosperity and promise of the Commonwealth of Free Nations. We firmly believe that this is our true destiny, so help us God."

The tumult was thunderous. The hall fairly shook with the eruption, as if of some volcanic upheaval. The "Liberator" had returned, unbowed, we prayed. Surely, we thought, such eloquence and magnanimity would redeem our people. Then we heard from Meagher.

At first he seemed almost cowed by his surroundings. He wore a coat of blue silk over amber trousers. His eyes were downcast at first, thus failing to display those fiery sentinels to the indifferent throng that attended his first political presentation.

Because of his peculiar diction, his speech at first seemed uncertain and was ill received. The crowd had determined that this was not the tongue of an Irishman, who delighted in the trills of a prominent brogue. No, this was the chirping of an imposter, a dandy, a privileged poodle. The hardened lads shouted their scornful remarks down upon Meagher from above.

It was then that O'Connell, himself, chose to intercede on Meagher's behalf. He quelled the crowd with the wave of his massive right hand, thereby sowing the seeds of his own public demise.

Suddenly, Meagher's intrepid nature seemed to blaze forth from his person. He began to speak with ferocity and facility, discarding the crutch of his detailed notes, thereby exposing his rebellious soul to the crowd.

"I stand before you humbly, as all Ireland is humbled in this hour of gnashing teeth. I recognize your contempt for my lack of the farmer's responsibility, the miner's fortitude and the "Liberator's" inspiration. Yet I must tell you that I am an apostle of freedom and a disciple of truth."

"Our Ireland is dying, while commerce among the favored continues unabated. I walk in relentless processions of mourning. I stand helpless over a generation of dying infants. I see the wisdom hidden in this hour of crisis. Time will not allow further delusion as to the design of our British brethren. Our history echoes with this response. We are enslaved. We will witness our extinction as a people, if we seek amelioration instead of rebellion."

"I learned it was the right of a nation to govern itself on the ramparts of Antwerp. I learned the first article of a nation's creed was freedom, a precious gift purchased with the effusion of generous blood."

"Abhor the sword, stigmatize the sword. No! For at its blow a great nation arose from the waters of the Atlantic. By its redeeming magic and in the quivering of its crimson light, the crippled colonies sprang into the attitude of a proud republic, prosperous, limitless and invincible."

"Such is the case in our beloved Ireland. We must rise as one, willing to endure the ultimate sacrifice, relentlessly seeking freedom for ourselves and Ireland's generations to come."

He stood there defiant and then turned away amid silence.

Then it sounded forth like a clarion call. It was the voice of a mother, sorrowful and solemn, bestowing God's blessings down upon him. Then the young and the powerless began to swell and shake, as if an epiphany had occurred. Like a river, they poured forth devotion to the one they christened, "Meagher of the Sword".

CHAPTER 5

ame can come at a fearful price. It allows for entrance to exalted places, yet bewilders with its siren's song. For one can fall victim to the belief that one is chosen. All that is worthwhile bears watching. There are no easy answers. The questions remain the same. Are the times constructed by those that live them or do the times the construction make? Those were times of horror in Ireland.

Meagher had made his decision before that fateful night propelled him to the forefront of the "Young Ireland Movement". He had come under the benevolent direction of Brother Edmund and thus was inspired into believing that he was called to lead his people to freedom. He was not alone in that belief. There were many of that creed. I have spoken to you of Mitchel and Smith O'Brien. There were others as well. I labored alongside them. I fought alongside them. I sobbed at their passing, as if a piece of my precious self was wrenched from me.

Their names were MacManus, O'Donahoe, O'Gorman, and Eamon Conley's enchanting daughter, Rebecca. They were Protestants and Catholics, some reserved and some boisterous. They were young and they were courageous. They were courageous most of all.

Rebecca Conley was a vision of loveliness that gently encased the iron of a miner's daughter. Her speech manifested both the lyricism of the poet and the bawdiness of the saloon. When I first saw her she was a lass of sixteen. When Meagher first saw her, he was smitten. It was during that night at Conciliation Hall. She remained behind the ornate scarlet curtain that cascaded from the rafters of the stage, separating the players from the play. The drama would now take a new direction.

Following his speech, Daniel O'Connell congratulated Thomas, as a score of others gathered around him like an adoring flock. As O'Connell departed from the hall, his nephew John appeared with the fangs of faction. You see, O'Connell's nephew was beside himself with outrage at having witnessed his childhood nemesis receive the adulation of the crowd. His disdain for Meagher and the others who had the temerity to confront and contradict his uncle was imbued with the green of envy. Such is the history of our people, faction and envy sewn with the thread of intolerance forming the fabric of the funeral shroud.

"You are no longer welcome at our meetings, Meagher," was how Thomas recalled the introduction to John O'Connell's attack. Insults soon followed that Meagher believed merited a more formal redress. You see, Thomas had become a duelist during his sojourn in Europe. I have already touched upon his prowess with the saber and the broadsword. It was not until later that I would witness his skill with a pistol. That would come on a mountain path in a howling blizzard.

It was Smith O'Brien who interceded this time, wrapping his manly arms around Meagher and ushering him outside into the rain that had begun to pelt Dublin.

"Are you in league with him, O'Brien?" O'Connell demanded, amid the soaking storm and the crowd that had gathered. "Do you also call for the overthrow of the Crown, you who stand elected within its House of Commons?"

"I call for a free Ireland. I call no man my better because of birth. Yes, I stand with Thomas," O'Brien cried.

That cry was echoed by Mitchel and the others. It was then that Rebecca Conley came forth in the storm to join them. She had the most exquisite raven hair and azure eyes. She possessed a fine firm figure oozing with passion and strength. She was Thomas Francis Meagher's first affair of the heart. On that night the Irish Confederation was born.

They retired to Mitchel's home overlooking the banks of the Liffey River. They spoke until dawn of things profound. From that day onward, John Mitchel, the scion of a Protestant father, became a devoted ally of Thomas Meagher. They inspired each other with notions of freedom and justice for all of Ireland, both Protestant and Catholic. They would pay a fearful price in British sterling for notions such as these.

I became a member of Dublin's contingent to the Irish Confederation by a sworn oath of allegiance, an oath of allegiance that called for a free Ireland, an oath that pledged my blood, to win that freedom. I would see Thomas at clandestine gatherings. Soon words would spread of Meagher and Mitchel, words that took shape in Mitchel's *United Irishmen,* words that inspired the brave and presented opportunity to the betrayer.

I remember that night at the Victoria Theater in Cork City when, we of the Confederation, came to present our cause. The meeting was organized by the Repealers, including among their number, one John O'Connell. He had advised agents of the Crown of our designs and our gatherings. Agents who were placed in strategic positions throughout that dimly lit location. Agents who sought to provoke a violent altercation that would justify the intervention of the constabulary, and the spilling of young Irish blood.

The crowd outside was full of hatred and hostility, as we entered. Oaths were shouted and objects of contempt thrown upon us. It was a perfect opportunity to extinguish the flame of rebellion that had begun to spread among our impoverished peasants, evicted farmers and desperate miners. These were the rank and file of our confederacy. Our opponents yearned for our demise. The Victoria Theater was as fine a place as any for an execution.

When Meagher attempted to make his address, there was no accommodation. I remember seeing John O'Connell, seated among his cohorts. He was stroking his pointed chin while displaying an expression of eerie delight, as Meagher was disrespected.

Sir Henry Baron, the Whig politician who would accommodate his way into the good graces of his British masters, was conspicuously present. I recall Thomas telling us that he had witnessed the cruel eviction of starving farmers and their families from Sir Henry's lands that very week. Sir Henry was a scorpion but John O'Connell, he was a serpent.

As I have told you, Michael O'Donahoe was one of us. He was a law clerk at the time, with flaming red hair, a hair trigger temper and an affinity for the drink. It seemed that he had been engaged by a group of ruffians near the rear door. They had maligned his parentage and spat upon his person. A donnybrook ensued that spilled into the alleyway outside. Although he battled bravely, he was beaten mercilessly by paid thugs. This was before Meagher and the others could render assistance.

It was then that Meagher's mettle was again tested. He had this most extraordinary composure at such times. I would often observe him in battle. He was imperturbable amid mayhem. This was his strength and his addiction. For Meagher began by loving battle. It was only later, after he had seen its face over and over again, that he became a peacemaker.

I will not forget how he withstood that mob within that place. I stood watching his every gesture as the venom spewed down and around him. He spoke to their souls through the din, biting into them with his manly courage.

I recall asking him whether he feared for his safety, during that overwhelming event. He informed me of a mystical occasion amid the dead and dying when Brother Edmund bestowed a solemn aspiration upon him. An aspiration that partook of the martyr's will. Such was the will of Thomas Francis Meagher.

By this time Rebecca Conley had become a trusted companion. She was the saving grace of our secret society. Thomas was not alone in his love for this exceptional creature. Later, I remember her weeping as the prison wagon transported Thomas and the others to their departure aboard a British Man O'War.

Concern for the well-being of O'Donahoe had become grave indeed. He had not regained his senses and appeared in desperate need of medical attention. Mitchel came forth and spoke for a cessation of faction in light of our shared oppression and the pitiful state of our people. He too was shouted down.

The Irish were the wretched of Europe then. To call oneself an Irishman during that time was to conjure in the minds of the many an image of squalor and subservience. They saw us as less than human. That was the artifice of their logic. It was used to perpetuate their injustice upon us. It was that way then. It is that way presently. The oppressor will often reason away his tyranny through a belief in his God given superiority.

We returned to a safe house that night and kept vigil around our companion's bedside. A priest had performed the last rites upon O'Donahoe. His family gathered for the tragic departure that we believed would soon occur. He had not regained his senses and his heart was barely beating. The doctor had come and advised us that Michael O'Donahoe was in the hands of his Lord and Savior, far beyond the reach of mortal men.

It was then that our lovely Rebecca came to his rescue. She spoke to him with that poetic love she brought to those she touched. I remember her kneeling beside his battered face, her words uplifting him, the bedclothes soaked with his blood. Meagher and Mitchel were praying nearby with tears and thoughts of retribution forming a fateful alliance in the dimly lit dawn.

I recall asking Thomas what assistance I could render at that hour. His response was clear. "Organize, prepare, the days of revolution and blood oaths are near." On that morning, while O'Donahoe struggled for his life, I saw a ferocity in Meagher's eyes that resembled that of a wolf. He had become a rebel through bloody words. Now was the time for bloody deeds.

The year was 1848, the year of insurrection. It had become a time of tumult and upheaval throughout the Continent. In Germany, Italy, France and Holland the people had risen up against the few. The American colonies had become a symbol of democratic aspiration. The declaration by Jefferson that "all men were created equal" was unparalleled in its threat to both the powerful and the privileged.

Before that time the people had been sheep, meek and resigned to their misfortune without a voice to protest their plight. Then suddenly the lambs were transformed into lions. Those with a press for printing could now spread the news and sway the multitude. Mitchel and Smith O'Brien published the truth to those in misery. Many chose to listen. A few chose to fight.

CHAPTER 6

O'Donahoe rallied and survived the vicious attack upon his person. Thereafter our spirit was indomitable. Smith O'Brien and Meagher soon began to formulate plans for armed revolt. Throughout the counties, in gatherings large and small, they plotted. In episodes minor and meaningful they represented the will of the Irish Confederation.

In retaliation they sought and caught the ones who had participated in O'Donahoe's beating. Pleas for mercy did not deter them from their bloody reckoning. They preached to the converted of revolution. They called for the manufacture of pikes to dismount the dragoons and the horsemen of the constabulary. By seeking to arm Ireland's dispossessed and desperate, they became the sworn enemies of the British Empire.

I must speak to you of one instance that etched the memory of Thomas Meagher deeply into my soul. A cold and unmerciful winter had descended upon Ireland in February of 1848. The famine had been raging for more than two years. The dead and dying had become too numerous to bury and to aid. Scores of corpses were being burned at repeated intervals to prevent the spread of the fever.

To see starving families thrust into the road by heartless, absentee land-lords was a common place occurrence. It was indeed the worst of times and it brought the demons themselves.

We called them the peelers. They were no more than thugs, hired by the English to inform and prey upon us like jackals. The worst of the peelers were stationed in Limerick.

Limerick City was a fertile field for the Confederation. I suppose you could call it our Command Headquarters. Ireland was an occupied country during that time. Between the formidable garrisons of British Regulars, the multitude of constabulary stations and the scores of paid informants infiltrating our gatherings, there really was no hope of ultimate victory for unarmed, famished, civilians. Yet we did win some battles and we did obtain some redress.

Slow starvation is beyond comprehension for most today. When one has no food; everything else is insignificant. In Limerick, the peelers used food to lure starving innocents into the bondage of their souls. They populated their brothels with Irish girls of tender years. They had the power of life and death over these children and they wielded that power fiendishly.

Meagher and the others had received numerous reports of perverse acts committed against Limerick's female population. Outraged fathers and brothers had beseeched the Confederation for revenge. Meagher along with Terrance MacManus, the recovered Michael O'Donahoe and Richard O'Gorman, became the avenging angels that justice demanded.

The peelers had three station houses in Limerick. The smallest of these was a wood and mortar roundhouse surrounded by sandbags and sentries near Limerick square. At the time it was commanded by sub-inspector Duane. It was said that Duane was the son of an Irish mother and a British color sergeant. We knew him to be a ruthless killer, who preyed upon the weak and the defenseless. Our attack was set to begin at dawn.

We, for I was a participant in this affair, had arranged for a diversion to occur. We set a wagon of wool on fire nearby, in the hope of luring the jackals from their lair. We placed that wagon in front of the Limerick offices of the British Trade Commission. A threat to the master's estate would beckon the master's servants, we believed.

Only a handful of our number had firearms. Meagher divided that handful and positioned them strategically for ambush. The rest of us were armed with the crude weaponry of our ancestors, sharpened pikes, scythes, pitchforks and axes. MacManus, O'Donahoe and O'Gorman were Meagher's lieutenants. They were devoted friends and they each had the heart of a lion when it came to a fight.

MacManus was tall with dark hair and eyes. He made his living as a merchant of wool and he despised the peelers with a near religious fervor. O'Gorman was fair and handsome with chestnut hair, and a ready smile. He was a young lawyer who possessed the most beautiful singing voice. We were enamored of his ways and delighted to have him join us in this reckoning. He had once served a clerkship for a Limerick law firm. He knew well the streets and alleyways of that city. Such knowledge would prove essential to our plan.

The alarm was sounded and the station house was alerted. A patrol of six was dispatched. There were five on foot with a leader on horseback. This was our expectation. They wore darkened blue uniforms with black leather helmets. Each bore a musket with a bayonet. Each had a sword and scabbard dangling from his belt. Within their cartridge boxes was enough ammunition to kill us all. There were only ten of us, brave and true. I had never confronted death before that morning. I suppose one never gets used to such an occasion. Our success required a sudden and lethal strike.

They came up the street at the double quick, their black boots sliding along the slippery cobblestones. Fate awaited them at the crest of the hill. There the street turned into the square.

We were concealed on either side of a branching alleyway, just before an ancient fountain. Our muskets were at the ready. Hearts pounding - breath in gasps - Meagher crying out for us to fire as they passed. Our volley shattered the stillness of dawn. Musket smoke floating thick and acrid. Then Meagher gave the command to attack. Oaths were screamed in agony and rage. It was a ferocious melee of hand to hand combat.

Suddenly he stood before me, dazed, yet quickly regaining his senses. He was as young and frightened as I. I struck at him with my axe, opening a wound across his breast. He slashed at me with his sword and then he was dead; shot by his own man, firing in a panic, a look of disbelief frozen upon his face.

It was then that I observed Meagher. He had waded among them with cutlass and dagger, slashing, thrusting, spilling blood everywhere. His eyes flashed forth with a wolf like fury. His vengeance was relentless amid the amber light of dawn.

Then there was the horseman. I remember he had long golden hair to the shoulder. He had felled four of our number before Meagher hurtled up behind him upon his charger's back. They struggled and tumbled off into that blood drenched alleyway, the horse running free from the carnage. Meagher made quick work of him, slashing his throat, while passing him through.

It was over as quickly as it had begun. All of their six were dead, while three of our number would die from wounds received. Limerick's outrage had been avenged. Such was my first engagement under Meagher's command. They would call it a massacre. We would call it a victory. That is the way it is in war.

In the weeks to follow the preparations for arming those willing to join the Confederation continued at a furious pace. The British, mindful of the insurrections now occurring throughout the Continent, began to reinforce their garrisons and tighten their control throughout the countryside.

Mitchel spoke openly of rebellion in each edition of the *United Irishmen.* He, Smith O'Brien and Meagher had become notorious thorns in the heels of the British Empire. Orders were issued from Lord Clarendon to round up the ringleaders of the Confederation, thereby severing its head. All three were charged with seditious acts.

They came at night. For tyrants use the darkness to their advantage. They tore each of them from their homes and shackled them hand and foot. Meagher was dining with his father when Waterford's sheriff, in the company of a score of deputies, arrested him. They were thrown into miserable jail houses in an effort to break their rebellious spirits. Each refused to bend. They carried on their defiance from behind prison bars.

At first, the power of an Irish jury protected them, refusing to convict in each and every instance. At least for a while, they were set free. Each of them knew that the time was nigh for a bloody climax. *The Nation* now joined with *The United Irishmen* in calling for resistance to British Rule. The Confederation grew stronger with MacManus, O'Donahoe and O'Gorman standing firmly by our sides.

It was then that revolution revisited France and brought renewed hope of a free tomorrow. Mitchel and the others had longed for an ally that could take the measure of the British Empire on land and sea. They saw in the French a worthy ally for throwing off the yoke of English Colonialism forever. Meagher, Smith O'Brien and O'Gorman were secretly dispatched to Paris, as representatives of a burgeoning Irish Republic. They were to meet with Lamartine in the fervent hope of freedom.

As Meagher related it, they met with France's wily minister amid the ruins of a palace revolt. Louis Philippe had fled with his servants and courtesans, leaving behind a legacy of excess and neglect. Lamartine was an amiable diplomat of advancing years. His mannerisms were peculiar and his preoccupations did not include the independence of the Irish people.

The timing for a French and Irish alliance had been premature. Meagher and his cohorts had searched in vain for their Marquis De Lafayette. Instead of arms and French warships, they received speeches and French sympathy. Lamartine urged caution and patience upon young Irish rebels who had forsaken of both.

Amid shattered dreams in Paris, Meagher, Smith O'Brien and O'Gorman wandered. Of course by that time the French had survived the deception of Robespierre and the destruction of the Napoleonic Wars. There was amongst the French a deep mistrust of those in power. Yet, there was also a fervent devotion to their beloved homeland. Their *amour de la patrie* was what Meagher admired most about the French. This love of country was symbolized in its flag.

The French flag was an inspiration to Meagher. He had seen it flying over the battlements of a French people, yearning to be free of despots dictating the course of their lives. He had committed himself to free his own people, even if it meant his death. His privilege and his knowledge had given him a vision, a vision of freedom's possibilities. To make this vision come to life required the utmost in courage. In this attribute, Meagher excelled.

He told me of that night in Paris. He and the others, sitting along the Seine in a café' near the Cathedral of Notre Dame. It was a night of brilliant stars. It was a night of devotion to a hopeless cause. On that night in Paris, Thomas Meagher, William Smith O'Brien and Richard O'Gorman collaborated in the creation of the Irish flag, that flag and others would guide Thomas and his brethren along paths of destiny.

CHAPTER 7

e met in the spacious upstairs room overlooking the quay, where a young Thomas had often prayed at the bedside of his dying mother. The three large windows that had afforded the young seeker the most magnificent view of the moorings along the River Suir were now concealed beneath curtains of gray muslin. On that night, the ornate chandelier suspended from the ceiling above us was without light. To all appearances from the street outside, the domicile remained deserted.

The mansion house had remained the property of the Family Meagher. It was used sparingly by the servants as a place of storage. The deluge of tormented souls that had beset Waterford in the famine's early years had now diminished to a stream. Death and forced migration upon seaboard coffins had taken their toll. There were twelve of us, as I recall, each a captain of an Irish Confederation Club. We spoke together by candlelight around a magnificent oak table, crafted in the Netherlands. It was a night of dashed hopes and solemn promises.

The meeting was convened to hear from Meagher and his cohorts on their mission of diplomacy to the French capitol.

Their report was a disappointment to us all. I remember the solemn expressions of those in attendance, as the candles cast exaggerated shadows upon the mansion's barren walls.

It was Mitchel who directed the course of the night's discussion. His angular face was wrenched with weariness and his speech was subdued. Although the Confederation had enlisted thousands in the cause of freedom, constructing a rebel army from the ranks of a starving people had proven a most daunting task.

It was then that Meagher, sensing our despair, rose to speak. He was wearing a brown frock coat and his dark brown hair was nearly touching his shoulder. His radiant eyes gave him a mystical appearance in the golden glow of candlelight.

He spoke without a trace of reservation. He had undertaken a mission and sworn to the Almighty that he would follow it through. You see, Meagher understood only too well the consequence of notoriety when armed rebellion was the game of choice. He welcomed the inevitability of his arrest and imprisonment. It was he who held us together when all it seemed was against us. He would make us swear to a blood oath on that night. It was the oath of a rebel brotherhood.

I recollect that he reached beneath his coat at a most appropriate time and removed the fruit of their endeavors along the Seine. It was our beloved tricolor. I loved its vibrant beauty at first sight. I believe I can relate the substance of what Meagher said on that night, the night when we became bonded together to the death.

"We bring to you this night a great deal more than the promise of a United Ireland. We bring to you the symbol of a nation that will rise from the ashes of faction and famine. We present to you a sacred cloth that signifies one land and one people. It is a flag of green to mark the hope of Ireland's Catholics. It is a flag of orange to mark the fervor of Protestant belief, and it is a flag of the purest white to mark the sanctity of our homeland, joining us one to the other in the promise of a free tomorrow. Let us go forth and raise this emblem above this city. Let us go forth and meet our destiny as free men, unbound by the chains of the past. Let the world know that we chose liberty and equality in the face of overwhelming tyranny. Let this be our legacy, so help us God."

We marched from that darkened place through the desolate streets of Waterford. It was then that we raised the flag of Erin for the first time over our country. As it ascended to the very highest point we could find, it seemed at first to flutter. Then suddenly, with the wind sweeping in from the Suir, it began to fly forth in all its glorious beauty. Each of our number gazed upon it beneath an April moon. We shared the same passion. We each whispered the same entreaty to the Almighty. It was not long before the might of the British Empire would fall upon us all.

The Crown feared an Irish insurrection, perhaps more than we ever imagined. Queen Victoria and her ministers had dispatched warships to the ports of Dublin, Cork and Waterford during that spring of 1848. Lord Clarendon, England's aging lord lieutenant of Ireland, had commissioned an army of spies and informants to infiltrate our Confederation and report upon developments observed.

Even our own clergy were in many instances agents of the Empire, delivering weekly sermons upon the evils of armed revolt. I remember reading of Meagher's despised adversary, John O'Connell, and those of his ilk, meeting in Dublin with England's representatives, in an effort to thwart the aims of our valiant movement. That was when the Treason and Felony Act was passed by a desperate Parliament. Thereafter, Ireland became subject to martial law.

We knew that the harvest time for our rebellion was fast approaching. In every county units of the Confederation were taught to march and maintain discipline in battle. Meagher was a student of Napoleon and he devised plans for a series of successive attacks upon British holdings. We published our intentions in The *Nation* and the *United Irishmen*, openly calling for the manufacture and sale of arms.

Lord Clarendon in turn, decreed that any inflammatory discourse or clandestine meetings would be considered treasonous activity. The Treason and Felony Act allowed for arrest and detention without habeas corpus. No longer was the Crown required to produce prisoners before a court and state the reasons for their imprisonment. Still we defied them.

Mitchel was the first of our number to fall. Again they came at night and spirited him off, away from his weeping wife and children. They dragged him to Newgate prison. Then, with a packed jury, they convicted him of seditious discourse.

I remember standing beside Meagher and Smith O'Brien in a Dublin courtroom when he was given the opportunity to speak before being sentenced, his long gaunt figure standing erect, his spectacles reflecting the May sun that filtered in through the courtroom, his thick brown hair now graying at the temples. With his wife and children seated behind him, sobbing, he delivered a speech that was clear and resonating. He rose to the occasion and preached to the world like a devout rebel minister.

"Neither the jury, nor the judges, nor any other man in this court presumes to imagine that it is a criminal who stands in the dock before you. My crime is that I yearn to be free, as others here today and throughout this land so yearn. I promise that after sentence is passed and I am taken from this place as a branded felon, hundreds, nay thousands, will take my place. You can imprison and kill our bodies. You can exile us to life beyond the seas, and yet our spirit will remain free. Ireland will overcome your tyranny."

As the sentence of fourteen years in transportation was pronounced, a rumble of outrage passed through the crowded courtroom. The reinforced peelers resisted the surge of the throng, while Meagher and Smith O'Brien vociferously registered their contempt for British justice. Yet the time to commence the rebellion was not yet at hand. The provocation of a violent episode was exactly what Lord Clarendon desired. He had concealed a regiment of seasoned dragoons behind the walls of Trinity College, hoping for an opportunity to be ruthless. British frigates were lying in wait in Dublin harbor, their cannons positioned to devastate the city.

Later, we watched as a prison wagon surrounded on all sides by British Regulars, armed to the teeth, delivered Mitchel in chains to a prison ship. He would never return to Ireland again.

In that year of tumult, the heat of a desperate July brought with it news that the blight would once again destroy the potato harvest. The ranks of the Confederation were now filled with more starving farmers and miners. Despite the fact that muskets and pistols were in short supply throughout our ranks, Meagher and Smith O'Brien believed that Tipperary and Kilkenny were the most strategic locations in which to light the fuse of revolution.

They had planned to throw up the barricades in the counties where the Confederation was strongest. They believed that this would divert the British to them and allow for successive attacks in Belfast, Limerick and Dublin. It was a wondrous plan, doomed to failure in a widow's yard.

The day rose with darkened clouds concealing the sun over the village of Ballingarry. I had gone there with O'Gorman, MacManus and Smith O'Brien, in final preparation for the insurrection. We came on horseback from Waterford.

The village was nestled in a valley, seemingly surrounded by the green of the Irish flag. Tipperary's fertile fields poured forth fruit for British trade but not for barren Irish tables. We met at Shay Healey's, a public house on the outskirts of the village. Shay was in his seventies. He had fought in '98 against the same oppression. The root cellar that penetrated an embankment of peat behind his pub was where our firearms were concealed.

There were hundreds of ragged, emaciated rebels awaiting our arrival in the village. We brought them four wagons of weapons, but there were only two wagons of firearms. I remember coming toward them. They were a rabble. Standing, sitting, lying in the road, they were a ghostly army of men and boys. Yes, there were females as well. Older sisters, mostly, looking after baby brothers.

Smith O'Brien was our commander. He held a musket over his manly head of flowing auburn hair and screamed his sacred duty to kill or be killed in the name of Erin. His crimson face and piercing green eyes displayed a fervor unmatched by his army. I knew that the day would tell the tale. We were to throw up barricades and lure the constabulary toward us. Our plan was to provoke sub inspector Trant and his fifty member garrison out into the open, then kill every mother's son.

We would draw them to us and attack their flanks. Then the cursed rain descended upon us. On that fateful day in the South of Ireland a great summer storm passed over the counties where the Confederation was the strongest. The torrent that ensued would alter communication and prevent coordination with Meagher's forces waiting in Kilkenny. To this very day I can recall the fury of that downpour, beseeching the Almighty to make it stop.

The peelers came as we had planned. There were fifty alright, with six on horseback. They were well armed and well fed. Their dark blue coats and trousers black with the soaking rain.

Trant was leading them with great flourish, urging them onward. His cutlass was extended in an erect right arm. He was a man of hefty stature with red chin whiskers and a stern expression. He galloped upon the back of a chestnut charger, following two of his advance guard.

Each and every one of those peelers must have been good family men, for when they saw our ragged rabble, installed behind makeshift fortifications, they veered off and retreated with their tails between their legs. We gave chase through the green hills surrounding the village of Ballingarry.

By midday the roads were thick with mud and our number had swelled to nearly four hundred. We were not to send word to Meagher unless we succeeded in our attack.

Trant had taken refuge in a gray stone house in the hills above the village. It belonged to the widow McCormack. She had left her five children in the care of a twelve year old girl. The peelers made these children their hostages, firing from the barricaded windows into our number, killing two and wounding many.

From the ranks of our number came the miners, carrying kegs of gunpowder, the tools of their treacherous trade. It was left to Smith O'Brien to determine the climax of the days' events.

I remember him cradling the head of a boy in his lap, while being pelted by the drenching rain. The boy's golden hair was covered in blood. He had been shot through the forehead and the breast by cowardly dogs taking shelter in a widow's house. They had fired on us with babies as their shields. They deserved to be killed for such cowardice. It was a time to be ruthless and to blow the widow's house to smithereens, killing fifty of the enemy, while sacrificing the innocent for our cause.

Then I recall the widow McCormack, being brought to Smith O'Brien in her agony. She was disheveled in appearance and sobbing uncontrollably, beseeching Smith O'Brien as if in prayerful supplication. She threw herself at him, hanging upon his neck, begging that he not be ruthless; that he not kill her innocents in the name of right and rebellion.

For our revolt to succeed, we needed what Meagher called the conviction of the crusader, the belief in the righteousness of a cause that justifies the dread of total war. We had ample reason, yet we were lacking in the instinct of the righteous killer. Smith O'Brien saw his own children shivering in that widow's house.

To win our freedom, we were required to be more ruthless than our oppressors, more cold blooded. It is that way with war. Make no mistake on it.

Well, Smith O'Brien spared that widow's children on that dreadful day and word was never sent to Meagher in Kilkenny. Our glorious insurrection was washed away in an unmerciful Irish rain.

After that, we became the hunted. They arrested all but three of the twelve that watched the tricolor fly over Waterford three months before. I was able to hide from their patrols, along with O'Gorman and the wounded Johnny Kavanaugh.

Later, I managed to book passage on the coffin ship, *Mary Kenny*. I gave my name as Aidan O'Leary, a village lad who had succumbed to the fever that spring. Before I would flee my beloved Erin, I would bear witness to the trial of Meagher at Clonmel.

CHAPTER 8

'Donahoe, MacManus and Smith O'Brien alighted from the prison wagon shackled hand and foot. Behind them came their shackled ringleader, the rebel who had spurned his privilege and fought fearlessly for freedom, Thomas Francis Meagher.

The noble spirits who fashioned the American Constitution knew well the significance of the right to trial by jury. Since the signing of the Magna Carter, men have fought and died for this right. It is the safeguard against the sovereign.

Justice for the four required a trial by a jury of their peers. Instead, they were tried by a jury of British lap dogs. Their convictions had been pre-ordained by Queen Victoria, herself. To spite her and her Empire, Meagher was chosen to speak before the Queen's Bench. It was a drama worthy of Shakespeare.

The village of Clonmel was the scene of this insult to justice. The court was a tribunal of Lord Chief Justice Doherty, Justices Blackbourne and Moore. They came in their red robes and powdered wigs, accompanied by a regiment of British Regulars, likewise wearing red. They were stationed in the village just to make sure that the Crown's justice would be meted out without incident.

An enormous, blood red, British flag festooned the wall behind the bench where the Queen's judges were seated. There was no mistaking it. This was a British show trial for those who had dared to defy British rule.

For that indelible episode, Meagher wore an emerald green coat and trousers, with gold buttons down the front. During the proceedings the rebels would be brought to the courthouse surrounded by a regiment of red coats.

After being unbound in the prisoners dock, Meagher would gesture reassuringly to those who followed his lead, telling them that he would not been broken by this ordeal. Before the convening of the court he would be forced to wear the powdered wig of a British barrister upon his black Irish head. Once at trial, his every movement would be accompanied by three of Her Majesty's soldiers.

They were all there in the overflowing courtroom. Thomas the Senior, the lovely Rebecca Conley, John O'Connell and Lord Henry Baron. O'Connell had come as a representative of those who chose to collaborate with the Empire.

O'Connell wanted to see his boyhood enemy receive his comeuppance once and for all. He wanted to see Thomas beg for mercy. He wanted to see him grovel before his British masters. He would be most disappointed. Lord Banberry had been brought in from London to present the case for the Empire.

Their jury was not chosen from the ranks of our weary miners, or from the multitude of our evicted farmers or our starving peasants. Instead it was chosen from the landed aristocracy, the gentry, and the landlords who sold their souls for the silver of British protection and privilege. It was a motley lot indeed. They were there to convict; not to set four rebels free. There are none so blind as those who will not see.

Banberry was the Queen's prosecutor. His skill was won in trials of treason where death was the punishment. He was a man of majestic bearing and booming voice. He was just beyond his sixtieth year and taller than most men of that time. He would display a slight limp as he walked slowly across the courtroom. It was said that he was not above exaggerating that limp when circumstances demanded. It was reported that he had been with Wellington at Waterloo and had ordered the battle surgeons to tend to others, before focusing upon his wounded limb. He would be the Queen's assassin at Clonmel.

Meagher was determined to put the Empire and its mistreatment of his people on trial. He had been a student of the law in Dublin, before he became a rebel and a spokesman for his people. He had served for two months as Malcolm Duffy's clerk. When Malcolm was not down with the drink, he was brilliant. He taught Meagher to cross examine witnesses against his case. Meagher took aim at the first witness to swear oath against him, Lord Henry Baron.

"Lord Henry, how many tenant farmers have been evicted from your lands during this famine?"

"Pray your Honor's judgment," Banberry cried with a noble flourish. "This has no relevance to the charge of treason."

"I submit sir, that it has all the world to do with the acts for which you label us traitors," Meagher replied, with a more exaggerated flourish, shooting a scornful glance at Banberry to the vocalized delight of his supporters. The Court, in the personage of Lord Chief Justice Doherty, conferred with his colleagues and made his ruling.

"Prisoner Meagher, this line of questioning is irrelevant and will not be permitted."

"May I be heard your Honor and present my proof?" Meagher argued, stunning Banberry with his skill as an advocate.

"Approach," the Court commanded to Meagher and Banberry. They came forward, Banberry with his limp and Meagher playing to his supporters, the men and women who believed in him and the rebellion. It is all reported in *The Nation*. You may read it for yourself even to this day. The words are true, as they will always be. Remember well, tyranny will always seek to silence the voice of freedom. Meagher delivered his proof in the most inspired tone of voice. It was an arresting performance indeed. The entire courtroom echoed with his words.

"Your Honor, we seek to show that it is the right of every man to pursue liberty. It is our right as men of free will. The Lord bestowed upon man, above all his creatures, the right to live free and to speak in defense of that freedom. My people have every right to be as free as the British, the same rights as the valiant rebels that have made America a refuge of freedom. When a government fails its people, it is the right of that people to throw it off, to plot and plan and yes, to bear arms if necessary, against the measure of the tyrant. I submit that there is no treason against tyranny. I submit therefore, that our acts and our deeds, of which we harbor no remorse, were justified."

Of course such a defense was not permitted. Lord Baron was allowed to testify concerning his observations of Meagher's treason at Conciliation

Hall in concert with the others. Oh but he was a most loyal servant of the Empire, that one.

He was a pasty faced mountebank who fawned his way to the pinnacle of human disregard. He recalled Meagher's speech and his call for a free Ireland. He told the Court of that night in Cork when Meagher, in the presence of his accused accomplices, preached rebellion to those in attendance. How he could have heard Meagher above the din of O'Connell's brigands was beyond comprehension.

He then enlisted by oath and affirmation the corroboration of John O'Connell, seated conspicuously upon the church bench bordering the advocate's arena. He was the reasonable, acceptable Irishman, acceptable to British domination that is. The jury returned their verdict after a cursory retirement. After all, when the play is the thing, one must keep up appearances. They brought all four of the rebels together for sentencing.

It was a golden October morning. I was standing in the back of the Clonmel Court, a slate gray, heartless sort of place where many a wretched soul had been sentenced to the work house. They had placed bars upon its windows fearing an insurrection. I recall looking down its narrow aisle to the Queen's Bench that commanded the entire edifice. The bench, with its white wigged servants, and its overhanging British flag, nearly obstructed two tiny windows of stained glass. The press of the crowd had caused these windows to be opened, providing a glimpse of our green Irish hills outside.

I remember seeing the Lord Chief Justice arrive in a gilded coach, surrounded by a company of dragoons. He was a regular servant of the people, alright. My passage was set for that evening upon the coffin ship, *Mary Kenny*.

When the Chief Justice inquired of the prisoners whether they wished to make a statement before the sentence of the Court was pronounced, Meagher rose to speak for them all.

They were a fine company of rebels, dark MacManus with the scarred face, fiery Smith O'Brien with the green eyes, the rotund O'Donahoe and his flaming red hair, and Meagher of the Sword.

He spoke with the wit of a fearless Irish rebel. He spoke in defiance of British Rule and in disregard for the fate that awaited them all.

"My Lord, this is our first offense, but not our last," he began.

The others were standing when he looked to them. All of them had been the recipients of British justice. He smiled in their direction and they responded in kind. In a galling instance of contempt, Meagher's words gave notice to the world that he and his band of rebels would never surrender their spirits to British tyranny.

"If you will be lenient with us this once, we promise, on our word as gentlemen, to try to do better next time. And next time, sure we won't get caught."

The reaction of the Queen's Bench was one of outrage. The Chief Justice in his flowing red robe, beneath the blood red British flag, pronounced this sentence upon each and every one.

"You are to be taken from this place and hanged by the neck, but not until you are dead, for your bodies will be taken down and drawn, then quartered and your remains will be delivered to the Queen's ministers, to do as they wish. May the Lord have mercy on your souls."

They took them away with an army surrounding them. I remember the face of Meagher's father. I remember the tears of Meagher's devoted Rebecca, tears that told of a love that would never be consummated. Tears that would drive her to take her life.

All four were lodged under guard at Mountjoy Prison. They were allowed no visitors during that confinement. They awaited their fate on gallows they viewed from their prison cells.

It is said that a plot was devised to free them before their execution. I heard tell that it was a priest who betrayed their conspiracy and informed upon them. I cannot say whether this was in fact the case. I only know that from that time forward, Meagher exhibited the deepest distrust for political prelates.

Throughout the world the word spread. The Irishmen who dared to defy the Empire on freedom's behalf were to be executed. From the Continent, the Colonies, and America, a resounding protest arose. As the result, Queen Victoria met with her ministers and decided that the penalty of the Queen's Court, sitting at Clonmel, was too severe. The sentence of death would be commuted.

By the Queen's mercy, these Irish rebels would not be drawn and quartered. Instead, they would be exiled beyond the seas to the place called Van Diemen's Land, for the remainder of their lives. Their voyage upon the *Swift,* a three masted sloop of war, would begin from Dublin Harbor in June of 1849.

CHAPTER 9

They were prisoners, torn away from all that they loved and cherished and thrust into a dungeon, down into the darkness of human cruelty. This was the sacrifice they had chosen for the cause of freedom.

All four would face their fate intrepidly. All four, who had failed in revolt, were to be imprisoned at the mercy of an Empire. An Empire they had dared to defy. An Empire they had dared to condemn. An Empire that now held them helpless in its tightened fist.

Some make the choice to accommodate, to look away while the weak are enslaved. Some exist in a place of indifference and self-indulgence, busying themselves with trivial affairs. Others cry out for justice. Others fight back with a righteous fury.

Smith O'Brien, MacManus, O'Donahoe and Meagher were courageous souls. Like Jefferson, Adams and Franklin before them, they banded together as brothers in an open defiance of British Rule. They were believers and seekers of a new way. Some say men like these are bestowed upon us by the Almighty. I am not certain of this. Yet I must admit that from time to time I have taken great comfort in such a notion.

Thomas related to me the ordeal of his exile and I spoke to him of the coffin ships. There was a choice, I suppose. One could have groveled in Ireland and died a slave, or resist and embark upon a most harrowing voyage.

47

Meagher, O'Donahoe, MacManus and Smith O'Brien were at first chained below the deck of the *Swift*, a Man O'War brig, as it cast off from Dublin harbor. Later, in the lice filled issue of the Crown's prison garb, they would be lashed to its heaving deck and exposed to the elements of the Atlantic.

They would be cuffed and cursed by a motley crew of British seaman. They were "the rotten Irish scum" who dared to defy the Queen. They were prisoners under life sentence, their fates twisting slowly in an unmerciful British wind.

I asked him once about thoughts of desperation; whether he and the others in their anguish had surrendered to a hopeless state. He responded that not one of them despaired during their ordeal. Although they would suffer, they would not succumb. They sought solace in each other and in the Almighty. Such is as it was on the coffin ships.

I did not return to my concealment following the sentencing at Clonmel. I had been warned by a village lass that the Brits were on my trail and I too would be imprisoned and exiled beyond the seas, should I not depart with haste. I stole a landlord's horse and rode through the countryside at the gallop. I had prepared a rucksack of meal and biscuit that would last at most a week. I had the clothes on my back, a brown wool suit and worn leather shoes, unfit for a voyage of six endless weeks.

I posted letters to my father in Tipperary and my sister living in Cork. I cannot say whether these were ever received, for both would succumb to fever that winter. I would set sail upon the *Mary Kenny* with one hundred and eighty seven others. An October tide would carry us from Waterford. Our only hope was the freedom of the New World.

The Captain of Meagher's floating prison was a taciturn, stunted sea dog by the name of Oldham. He had served her Majesty nary forty years and had received his commission while battling pirates in the South Seas. His wrinkled, sallow face resembled a decrepit ship's map and an assortment of pock marks ran downward like tears from his lifeless brown eyes. He spoke with a bluster when presiding over burials at sea and the disciplining of a twenty man crew of brigands, impressed from the alley ways of Liverpool and Birmingham

It was said he had survived shipwreck twice before his twenty first birthday, once off the coast of Tortuga in a summer squall and once in a typhoon near Madagascar. He was amused by children who would bow and scrape and intolerant of women who spoke their minds. He despised Meagher and the others for their traitorous ways, until an incident occurred in Bermuda that gave him cause to question his convictions.

Convicts for delivery to Van Diemen's Land, now known as Tasmania, were not the only cargo of the *Swift* on that voyage.

The brig was heavy in the water with timber from the Maritime Provinces, along with barrels of salt pork and nutmeg. Under a cloud of sail, it traversed the turbulent North Atlantic and made its way toward warmer climes.

It was in Bermuda that molasses and rum were to be procured for the markets of Rio de Janeiro and Cape Town. It was in Bermuda where Meagher, O'Donahoe and MacManus were released from their leg irons for the first time and allowed under guard to roam the torrid marketplace that ran alongside Hamilton harbor.

The sea was an azure blue as the natives turned out in force in a frantic effort to persuade the crew of that three masted vessel to part with two months wages.

By that time the crew was more interested in rum and whores than making life miserable for a band of Irish rebels on their way to exile. Oldham had extracted the solemn promise of all but Smith O'Brien to not attempt escape, if released from their chains. Once the word of Meagher and the others was given, it would not be disavowed. That was the way of gentlemen then, even gentlemen who had been beaten and starved as they had.

As Meagher recalled it, there was a stone gray bawdy house of two stories overlooking the harbor. There, coffee colored ladies along with others of the Caucasian race, displayed their comely attributes from its spacious window settings. Around a corner and down a narrow cobblestone lane, Meagher, O'Donahoe and MacManus traipsed in the company of two of the crew.

Oldham had ordered that their prison rags be burned, supplying them with an issue of seaman's clothing. The condition of their haggard bodies, however, could not be concealed beneath their attire. Each of the exiles would drink his share of rum within that steamy port of call.

It was there that Meagher observed horse and carriage, wagon and coach. All were gathered around a stone block with steps leading up either side. In the center of the block there appeared an additional step with a rusted iron ring affixed to a wooden stake. Meagher and his accomplices approached a gaily clad citizenry, milling around in a most festive mood. They presumed an execution or some such attractive event was soon to occur. In the crush they became separated from the Captain's escort.

Suddenly there were just the three. The uncompromising Smith O'Brien was still in irons on board ship. It was then that they observed the cause of the occasion that had drawn the crowd. It was a scene most memorable indeed. The throng had gathered in anticipation of a slave auction.

England had prohibited the outrage of human bondage within its territory years before. Yet, Hamilton Harbor on the island of Bermuda was a way station for Arab slavers on their voyage from Africa, bound for New Orleans with the sweltering steerages of their sailing vessels overflowing with men, women and children of the black race. Meagher would describe this miserable spectacle in chilling detail, years later.

There were children being torn from the arms of their desperate mothers, men and boys chained by the neck, row upon row, as overseers from Carolina's plantations examined teeth and limbs to determine fitness for lifelong servitude. From the depths of their desperate state, the rebels saw their likeness in the faces of those abject slaves. It was MacManus who first told me of Meagher's outrage and his violent reaction to the conduct of a certain slave trader, within that broiling marketplace.

There was no mistaking it when Meagher became incensed by an act of overwhelming injustice. He would grow increasingly somber and his eyes would glaze over in a most frightful manner. It was the look of the righteous killer. He wore that look during that bloody episode in Limerick. He would wear it when the Brigade made its desperate attack upon Bloody Lane. I understood well the look that MacManus described during that auction of the enslaved.

There was a terror stricken young girl, perhaps fourteen years or less. Her mother sobbed as she was placed upon the auction block. MacManus spoke of this in a most memorable manner years later while we lunched at the Metropolitan Hotel. That was before he met his ending in California. He and O'Donahoe were devoted companions to Meagher

***

At this, O'Keefe paused as if in reflection. There was a sadness that seemed to pass over him and cause him to become distracted. Just then we heard the steward coming to present the menu for our luncheon. O'Keefe remained pensive during this intermission. The steward treated him with deference and a degree of familiarity that seemed to signify that he was a gentleman of considerable prominence, worthy of much respect.

After our repast, O'Keefe continued to be distracted from the matter of his recitation, reading instead from his crimson text. He then closed his eyes and there came over his face the most serene expression. Then suddenly he emerged from this serenity and appeared more vibrant, more vital.

I wondered about the text. What it contained. What wisdom it revealed. There was something very peculiar about this old man, something mysterious, his age for instance. To have been in Ireland at that time, he would have to be at least ninety years of age. Yet, he appeared so much younger.

"Tell me of the front, Captain," he abruptly demanded.

I knew he would eventually come to my reasons for being away from my regiment when the pitch of battle was rising to a climax in France. The world was awaiting an allied victory. Our troops had arrived in the nick of time to reverse the tide of battle. The allies needed one more thrust to gain the prize that had eluded them and cost them so very much, and I was in London. O'Keefe simply sat awaiting my recitation of the things of war. I felt compelled to reply.

"It is a place of horror, wholly lacking in honor and glory, Mr. O'Keefe. I have had a belly full of the front and in truth I fear for my sanity. Who wouldn't have such fear after what I have witnessed? Men mangled and blown to bits by their own shells, boys buried alive and choking to death on mustard gas, their skin peeling from their tortured faces, dying boys, crying out for God's mercy, crying out for mothers and sweethearts they would never see again. That is the front as I know it."

I was ashamed I had spoken so freely. Then I suddenly felt myself beginning to tremble, first just above the knees and then from behind, like some beast was holding and shaking me. I recall O'Keefe standing over me, his hand suspended above my head, as if administering an absolution.

When I awoke, he was standing at the window, staring, sipping from a snifter of brandy. He approached and provided a crystal glass containing a most beguiling golden liquid. I drank and at once felt enchanted. Then I was at peace.

He sat down across from me. He was now wearing a deep green jacket of the finest velvet and trousers of black silk. On his manly feet were a pair of the most finely crafted leather boots.

"I believe we were speaking of the episode in Bermuda, were we not?" O'Keefe remarked in a matter of fact manner.

"Yes, that is what my notes reflect."

"Before I continue, Captain, may I provide you with a lesson from my own observations of the face of war."

"You may."

"You are correct that there is no honor and glory in war. Yet, war is a grim necessity when men seek to enslave other men. The glory and the honor rests in the love of one's fellow man. The love that causes a father to sacrifice all for his child is the self-same love. To be willing to lay down one's life for another brings its own honor and glory, beyond the bounds of this world. Such was the love that we of the Brigade possessed. Such was the love of Thomas Meagher."

CHAPTER 10

O'KEEFE RESUMES HIS RECITATION

There are those who prey upon the weak and defenseless; those who have the instinct of the predator; those who lack the quality of mercy. Such was the swarthy, sweating, bastard conducting that slave auction in that broiling Bermuda marketplace. His prey was a vulnerable child, condemned by nothing more than the color of her skin. Terrified and trembling, a chain connecting her slender neck to a wooden stake, she became the object of a crude display.

The auctioneer was a master at playing to an audience accustomed to the oppression and enslavement of the black race. He was a walrus like brute with an expansive waist and a massive, balding head covered by a tattered yellow fedora. His fleshy brown arms were decorated with crude tattoos and his boisterous voice rang out above that raucous gathering, as he plied his devilish craft. He too was from the Dark Continent. He had a whip and a ring of keys dangling from a wide leather belt. He was a master at getting his price for human flesh.

The display of the girl was designed to arouse the passion of the slave holders who had come to Bermuda in search of a bargain. Further transportation to New Orleans would increase the price of the unfortunates forced to endure further confinement in that slave ship's suffocating hold. The auctioneer had positioned himself behind that whimpering child and used the handle of his whip to reveal her privates to the crowd. Meagher stood watching as she was mauled by the bastard.

MacManus told me of Meagher's actions at that point. He was dressed in the red and white issue of a British seaman. As the auctioneer circled from behind the innocent, he ran the whip's handle beneath her ragged clothing, exposing the child's breasts. Meagher could stand no more. He bolted forth and leaped upon the block. In one fluid motion he was upon the auctioneer. He wrested the whip from his grasp, then pummeled him mercilessly to the ground before the block. Like a wild animal, he roared his outrage toward all in witness to that inhuman display.

"Are you blind to this child's pain? Dogs have more decency!"

With that he consoled the sobbing girl then directed his wrath upon the auctioneer, prone before him, unleashing his fury with the whip, directing the lash at that yelping coward's face and eyes, screaming with a vengeance that scattered the crowd.

"Since you are blind to suffering, I will make you blind to all things."

That was when the guards assigned to watch over the convicts forced their way to the block and interrupted that auctioneer's reckoning. They cracked Meagher's skull with a club and returned him senseless and in irons to the bowels of the *Swift*. There he would await Captain Oldham's judgment. There a reunion with an old friend would take place.

I must speak to you now of the journey upon the coffin ships, for the ranks of the Irish Brigade were filled with boys and men who survived those harrowing passages in search of freedom. There were one hundred and eighty seven upon the *Mary Kenny* when it set sail. A cruel, winter voyage across the North Atlantic awaited us. There were so many instances of suffering and sacrifice that I can recall from that dreadful passage.

Most came over with responsibility thrust upon them by famine and fever. Some were as young as fifteen, who had survived the death of parents, setting sail in charge of younger brothers and sisters. There were young widows traveling with helpless children, attempting to comfort them in that fearful darkness below deck. There were desperate fathers seeking to preserve what was left of their starving families and solitary figures making the journey alone. Most were ragged, hungry, terrified and cold, a multitude of nameless victims of that great hunger. Their misery still disturbs my rest.

I thanked God I was alone and in care of only myself. You see fugitive warrants had been issued and I was fearful of arrest and exile. It was said that Boston had many Irish born who had worked their way into the Emigration Service. It was said that they were not as particular to the detail of classification as they were in New York.

I recall viewing all uniforms with the same suspicion, for any one could make of me a prisoner. I took care to speak only when spoken to and to become inconspicuous in the preoccupied crowd. My hope of freedom resided in my concealment beneath a dead boy's name.

There were many routes taken by those fleeing Erin during the great famine. Most sailed to Liverpool first, and then booked passage upon a larger, faster packet ship, bound for the South Street Seaport in New York or Noddle's Island in Boston.

Others sailed to those ports directly.

We were loaded like codfish upon these "coffin ships", with disease and death stalking us during the entire voyage. Some sailed from Cork, some from Limerick, and some from the other Irish seaports to Quebec. From this Northerly destination, entry into America was achieved by days of travel across a border wilderness, and then by booking a water passage down into the teeming cities of New York, Philadelphia, and Detroit. A winter passage brought the added risks of ferocious ocean storms and collisions with icebergs, floating like frigid beasts upon the merciless North Atlantic.

During the six years that the famine raged across Ireland, near to a million Irish entered America through New York. Tens of thousands more sought refuge in Boston and Philadelphia. Still others would sail further south to Savannah, Charleston, and New Orleans. We would meet these Irish again. When we did, it would be a reunion most bloody.

I joined the line that stood in the pelting rain and darkness on the quay in Waterford. I recall staring across toward the mansion house of the family Meagher, now boarded and abandoned. It was there that we had taken our blood oath.

Suddenly the name of Aidan O'Leary was bellowed from the interior of a fishing shack, which served as the site of all medical inspections. By his appearance the doctor was a drunkard with a pince-nez perched precariously upon his long boney nose.

His examination was limited to looking at my tongue and the palms of my hands and inquiring whether I was sound of body and mind. I advised him of a fictitious relative in Boston from whom I intended to secure employment. He stamped my papers and handed me a tin pail for my ration of drinking water. I felt relieved once I came aboard.

The *Mary Kenny* was a barque of 458 tons with three square rigged masts and single top sails. She was commissioned in Quebec for Grant and Sons Shipping and had a copper hull meant to withstand the pounding of a six week winter voyage. There were twenty two in her crew, some from America, some from the provinces, some on the run from either heritage or history.

The Captain was a God fearing Presbyterian by the name of Owens. This would be his second voyage as the master of his own ship. He was boyish in appearance, yet reasonably seasoned in the nautical trade. He would display both his caring and his courage to all who survived the ordeal that was about to commence.

There were two classes of passengers aboard the *Mary Kenny.*

There were the few who made up the cabin class and the many who were to make their journey in steerage. To the few the crossing was an opportunity to dine upon fine linen in the shipboard saloon and to make interesting acquaintances.

Scores of pigs and sheep were brought on board as a source of fresh meat for the cabin class and the crew. There were also goats who would eat almost anything and a cow for the Captain's milk and butter. All livestock was kept between decks. Their stench would add to the misery of those confined below in steerage.

My sleeping accommodations for the voyage consisted of a rectangular berth, made of pine, two feet in width and five feet in length. There were row upon row of these berths arranged in tiers of two and three. Shortly after coming aboard I received the number ninety-four. It was to be displayed prominently upon my right shoulder. It signified the location of my berth as well as my appellation when receiving rations or discipline from the captain and his crew.

I recall looking into the faces of my fellow passengers and wondering how many of us would survive that winter voyage. I remember there was this boatswain's mate by the name of Lowery. He took great pleasure in abusing those of us confined to steerage. We would endure his transgressions for that entire crossing.

The first night we remained in the harbor at Waterford. The dispossessed who would make that perilous journey had not yet lost all semblance of gaiety. I do believe that from their sad and sorrowful state there arose a strength of purpose and a sense of the significance of song. Sure and if we didn't kick up our heels on the eve of that awful voyage to freedom.

For those who had seen loved ones shake and perish from fever, the presence in the crowd of a fiddler and two who could play a tune upon the pipes seemed a gift from the Almighty and a harbinger of a safe journey. I too shook off my burdens on that occasion and took part in a fine succession of reels below the decks of the *Mary Kenny*.

The following morning the sun broke through the clouds, as we set sail upon the Suir and glided out toward Saint George's Channel. We stood in lines that ran up from steerage to the main deck. There our day's rations were distributed under the supervision of the first mate. He was a barrel of a man by the name of Montgomery. Not a kind word was ever uttered by this miserable son of the sea during that entire voyage. Yet he would prove his mettle when crisis fell upon us.

I received a ration of a solitary herring, a slice of cheese and a moldy biscuit for that day. There were also two pints of water. Even with the provisions I had brought with me, I knew that hunger would be my cruel and constant companion. Some had the temerity to complain about their allotment, only to be abused by Lowery's blows.

I shall never forget standing with the others on deck, watching as the white limestone lighthouse on Hook Point faded across the horizon. Farewell, my beloved Erin, farewell.

Soon thereafter the sea and a strong westerly wind carried us into the teeth of an October squall. We could see the approach of the drenching storm from across the horizon. We were ordered below into the darkness.

Candles and lanterns were not permitted in steerage, for fear of a fire below decks. All of us had heard of the disaster that had befallen the *Ocean Monarch*. Fire aboard ship and fog banks that covered shipping lanes were treacherous adversaries to a voyage at sea. A winter journey across the Atlantic was terrifying enough, without the added complication of those enemies to bedevil our quest for freedom.

During the first week there was much seasickness. The stench and human filth that permeated the pitch black steerage caused us to escape to the deck whenever the weather permitted. Many chose frostbite over the misery of that darkened confinement.

When foul weather forced us below deck, the timbers of the ship would creak and groan as she pitched mercilessly upon the swells. During those intervals we remained in our berths for days on end; most often being thrown about like marbles in a shoe box. It was as if we were all ghosts being battered about in a world where light had been extinguished, ghosts of all ages and sizes, moaning with sickness in the darkness. The calm would bring different perils.

You must remember that there were barely enough provisions to last through that six week voyage. To lose precious days, because the wind had suddenly disappeared, was a source of great concern to Captain Owens. He addressed us during the second freezing week.

He advised us of the fact that we were behind schedule and in need of a more drastic rationing of food and water. A child of six and a man of forty five years would die that night. There would be many of our number who would perish upon that voyage. All of the dead were wrapped in sacks, weighed down and committed to a watery grave.

During the third week we heard the seaman cry out from his perch upon the mizzen mast. "Icebergs dead ahead, icebergs dead ahead!" Then we spotted them. There were half a dozen of them and they were headed directly toward our battered hull.

I cannot explain our feeling of helplessness in the darkness, the freezing sea pouring over the sides and down the hatch into our miserable living quarters, all of us beseeching the Almighty to spare us from a collision with one of those monstrous denizens of that merciless sea.

The Captain attempted to alter course to avoid being surrounded by those treacherous adversaries. Again and again we felt the impact of the ice banging upon our hull, like a cursed landlord demanding his arrears.

On the fourth day of the third week we began to take on water. The sea had managed to gain a foothold among us, through a leak in our copper covered hull. It was not long before the bilge pumps were in place, displacing us from our berths and our belongings.

With everything we loved and owned at peril, a community began to take shape among the passengers confined to the steerage of the *Mary*

Kenny. We took turns using whatever we could to arrest the sea water from submerging our domicile. Pails, barrels and even chamber pots were employed to evict the watery invader. Ice soon formed throughout the hold, compounding our misery. Six more would succumb to the rigors of the journey during that third week, and yet two were born to give us some sign of hope. Then the fever came into our midst.

It was the fever that we feared the most, more than fire below decks, more than the freezing sea. We had seen it kill too many and knew its face well. The Doctors called it the Typhus. It was a dreaded killer that stalked us upon our forsaken island and hid among us as we sought to escape by sea.

Its symptoms were a wrenching, blinding agony of body and mind that brought an unquenchable thirst. The thirst is what I remember most vividly. During the fourth week the fever caught up with the *Mary Kenny*, her passengers and her crew.

It was a child who brought its scourge upon us. I had seen her during the second week. She had a small pink face with a shawl wrapped tightly around it. When that face became the color of rice water, we knew.

At first she grew weak and cried out from the relentless throbbing in her tiny head. Then she began to shake and vomit over and over for hours on end. In her delirium she howled from the thirst, like a creature from the nether world. Then her eyes seemed to retreat deeper and deeper into her skull. Then her skin became dry and wrinkled. She was gone in less than two days' time. Soon we saw the signs in others. A man of thirty or so who wore a gray stove pipe hat and a herring bone coat was next. His ordeal was endured in silence. His corpse was found floating face down in the knee deep sea water.

I remember many miserable nights, shivering in the cold and the darkness. We were beyond hunger and left to the mercy of the angry Atlantic that battered our vessel. My fellow prisoners were above, behind and beside me in the torment of that place. Their moaning was like a chorus from the depths.

Fever would claim six more of our number, before we learned that two of the crew had been infected. During a frigid calm, the Captain called all who could stand to the main deck for a terrifying pronouncement.

The captain was a shy man in his twenties. He wore the burdens of that voyage like a jagged scar upon his ruddy pock marked face. He was devoted to his duty. He believed that our only chance of survival was to decrease the rations of food and water and quarantine the sick in the saloon adjacent to the first class cabins. It was there that I witnessed his compassion. He and the first mate would soon become unlikely angels of mercy.

There was a widow by the name of Haggerty. We spoke once, while awaiting our daily rations. She was a tall dignified mother who would read to her three children, whenever she could. She fell to the fever during the fifth week. When the Captain learned of this he brought her children into his own quarters. He enlisted the assistance of an aged spinster to provide solace to those orphans.

He ordered Montgomery to dispense laudanum to the caretakers of all children under twelve. Its purpose was to help provoke sleep and ease the pain from the hunger that now tormented us all. I remember watching, as the Captain and his stalwart first mate passed among those infected, both of them risking their lives in service to their calling. Both would become infected before we reached Boston. One would succumb and the other survive.

It is that way with crisis. To some it poses danger, for most are weak and afraid of adversity. To others it presents an opportunity, a chance to exhibit courage, a chance to rise above this mortal prison and by example blaze the way to a release. The Captain and his first mate Montgomery were such as these.

Why did some succumb to the fever on board, while others survived? The same inquiry applies to death in battle. Once upon the plain at Chancellorsville, a shell burst near our position, killing all around but myself and an eager child who was our drummer boy. The toll inflicted by that canister was without rhyme or reason. Such is the way of fate in the lives of men. I suppose we are all upon a perilous voyage in this life, the uncertainty of our destiny lying hidden from view.

I spoke to you of the Captain of the *Mary Kenny* and his compassionate courage. There were others on the vessel, however, who exhibited the darker side of human nature. As I related, the boatswain's mate was a belligerent by the name of Lowery. He was a stocky gargoyle of a man with coarse raven hair that covered his person. His laugh was reserved for ridicule and he used the thirst to have his way with the weak, the young and defenseless.

When it was light, Lowery would beat and degrade us with a thick vinegar soaked rope's end. "Irish scum," he called us. With the darkness, he would pass through the steerage with a lantern and a dirk knife. He threatened all of us with his hulking presence. He advised us that he was the Captain's representative to the filthy, rotting Irish. We had grown to know the face of the oppressor only too well.

There was a boy of eighteen by the name of Shaughnessy. I believe his first name was Liam. He was a red haired, ragged lad who had become the guardian of two younger sisters. Their parents had perished in the first year of the hunger. The girls were twins with golden hair and fiery blue eyes. They appeared to be descendants from the Viking tribes that conquered Erin centuries before. They were proud and beautiful, yet vulnerable to the viciousness of that bastard, Lowery.

Lowery lusted for these children and used the thirst as a means of having his way with them. It was succumb or die, for in that last week we were all dying aboard the *Mary Kenny.*

When you have been degraded for so long, you begin to believe in your own unworthiness. You begin to surrender, to bend and scrape, to grin and bear injustice and brutality simply to survive. Such is as it was aboard the *Mary Kenny.*

I shall never forget the darkness of that last week in Steerage; blown off course; the Captain and much of the crew down with the fever. It was a time of untold distress.

Indeed, it was a flag of distress that brought out the paddle steamer, *Covenant,* to rescue one hundred and forty one of our number. Among that number was our valiant Captain. He would live to command a naval frigate during the battle of Vicksburg. For his courage and his caring during that conflict, he would receive the Medal of Honor.

Now let me turn to Lowery. For his reckoning is a lesson in the wages of cruelty. After my arrival in the port of Boston and the completion of my quarantine, I obtained employment from a tavern keeper by the name of Vaughn. He had women of the street who would frequent his establishment, located within a stagger from the East Boston docks. I was working behind the bar on the night that Lowery happened by. He was feeling no pain, at least at that time, at least long enough for justice to be meted out.

When I saw him, I knew that this was opportunity knocking. I told the lads to let Lowery remain and act as rowdy as they could stand. I ducked out the back door and sent a boy to hustle up Liam Shaughnessy. He was working nearby in a foundry. He was now a grown man. He had been a blacksmith's apprentice in Ireland. In America he would become his own master. His sisters had survived their ordeal aboard the *Mary Kenny* and would marry others who came over on the coffin ships. On that night he would settle his score with Lowery.

The word had been spread about Lowery. We had told of his cruel laughter in the darkness of steerage. Six of us removed him from the tavern when he was down with the drink. We took him to a shack near to the docks. There, rats as big as dogs roamed.

We strapped him to a pine chair, like the pine of our berths upon the *Mary Kenny*. We sobered him with buckets of freezing sea water and kept him away from the light. Shaughnessy then emerged to administer a most proper punishment for one so cruel.

With a bucket brimming from a nearby outhouse, he made him drink and drink, asking in the manner that Lowery used to violate innocence. "Do you thirst? What will you do for a drink?"

When Lowery was fished from the harbor, the rats and fish had made him faceless. Good riddance to the bastard was the righteous sentiment of all he tormented aboard the *Mary Kenny*.

CHAPTER 11

*L*et me return now to Meagher and his voyage upon the *Swift*. After his assault upon the slave trader, Thomas was thrown in irons in the hold of the *Swift*. Like the steerage it was dark and without pity. His head reeled from the blows at the block. He was in the nether world of the nearly conscious, a ghostly galleon floating on a turbulent sea. There he came upon more than a friend, more than a brother. It was his kindred spirit, William Smith O'Brien.

In chains himself, Smith O'Brien sought to give Meagher hope, for the blows upon his head had twisted him. Indeed, they had nearly defeated him. He had begun to surrender, to concede to overwhelming injustice. The free spirit that was Thomas Francis Meagher began to succumb to tyranny, and to contemplate his demise as the sole means of egress from its cruelty. Before he fell victim to this hopeless state, Smith O'Brien came to his rescue.

"What is your name?" he demanded over and over again. "What is your bloody name, you Irish bastard?"

Meagher's failure to acknowledge Smith O'Brien's inquiries only increased his resolve to revive his devoted friend's spirit, to become one with his soul and rescue him from his desperation. He berated him, then reinforced him with caring words, calling to Meagher in his stupor, while his own face was bathed in tears.

"You are Meagher of the Sword. You are Meagher of the Sword. You are a free man even in chains. We are free men even though they beat us like dogs. We will be free Thomas, because we see and know of their fear. Hear me, Thomas. Hear me my brother. We will be free because we know their fear of our being their equals. Swear this oath, Thomas. They will not enslave us, as long as our souls are free. Swear it. They will not enslave us, as long as our souls are free."

On the third day, Meagher came to the full possession of his senses once again and the fire in his soul was rekindled, rekindled by a devoted friend. Then fate turned the kind side of its face toward him. It was a storm that would release him from his chains. For when a Man O'War is about to be lost at sea, it is the concern of all aboard, even the despised, even the imprisoned.

The gale rose in an instant. They were five days out from Rio de Janeiro when the torrid west wind made a mountainous horror of the sea. Three of the crew were washed overboard before the alert rang out from the polished bell below the captain's quarters.

The imprisoned were brought before the Captain one by one. He would not allow them into his private quarters in chains. You see, he despised the idea of being a seaboard jailer. He spoke to Meagher the last, for he recognized the cut of a leader. He had come to admire the power of his person. He would speak to Thomas like an angry uncle.

"I have been informed of your exploits in Bermuda, while under my arrest. What have you to say for yourself?"

"My acts were justified, sir," Meagher said unflinchingly, as he stood respectfully before the seafarer. "I am not a man, if I allow such behavior to occur, without a proper punishment."

"You, who are a prisoner under life sentence, would suffer this ordeal for a slave?"

"What makes a slave?" Meagher asked. "Is it the master or the slave himself? A friend has made me see that there can be no masters, as long as our souls are free. I have fought against enslavement in my homeland and will fight against it wherever it appears. My only regret is that I failed to blind that dog with his own whip."

With that the Captain stared at the roaring sea that appeared outside the portal of his cabin. He had a bulbous nose and small green eyes that darted back and forth in the recesses of a long narrow skull. His brown hair had begun to gray and his chin whiskers were flecked with specks of gray and white.

He was wearing a tattered blue sea coat with braids upon his sunken shoulders. He was once a tall man but years of stooping aboard ships at sea, in fair and foul weather, had hunched his back and bent his knee. He would often stammer when required to speak to the crew. He did not stammer when he spoke to Meagher.

"You are a man of honor, then?"

"Aye, sir. My word is my bond."

"I am in need of your assistance and that of your friends. I fear the loss of my ship in this storm. I am in need of your word of honor that you will aid us in this ordeal and I will release you from irons."

All but Smith O'Brien would vow upon the captain's bible. All but Smith O'Brien would be released from their chains to lend a hand in saving the *Swift*. The sails on two masts would be damaged by the gales that marked the storm. Another mast would break in two, plummeting down upon the deck, killing two of the crew.

The three convicts would perform valiantly during that peril at sea, helping to save the lives of all on board. For two days and nights the *Swift* was adrift in the calm that followed the storm. Then the coxswain cried out with a joyous relief "land ahoy! land ahoy!"

The gratitude of Captain Oldham was manifested in his granting leave ashore, without restraint or guard, to all but Smith O'Brien. In addition, he bestowed ten pounds from the ship's coffers upon each of the three. The repairs to the *Swift* would take nearly a week to complete. During that time three Irish rebels and most of the crew were allowed leave ashore to partake fully in the worldliness of Rio de Janeiro.

Brazil's major seaport was a place without rule or law. There, right was determined by might and disputes were settled with the thrust of a sword To MacManus and O'Donahoe, it was a haven, full of rum and riotous release. To Meagher it was where he would meet another love. Her name was Esmeralda and her eyes were dark like blazing sapphires.

As long as I knew Meagher, he had always been a man for the ladies. They seemed to revel in his company and delight in his yearning to be free, free not only from oppression, but from propriety as well. His pleasure was in the pursuit of women who challenged him, in and out of the boudoirs.

When Thomas was bent upon seducing a female he would make of her a jewel and give her significance. He would whisper to her of moonbeams and meteors and lead her to amorous places where only romantics reside. When we first met in Waterford, Meagher seemed more of a rogue than a romantic, yet as the curse of the famine continued and his passion turned to the liberation of the Irish people, his appreciation of the mystery that is the female was ignited.

One night in Chattanooga he spoke to me of Esmeralda. She was a descendant of a Conquistador who had settled in Rio de Janeiro, when it was no more than a fishing village. He was a colonel in the army of Cortez, whose heart had been captivated by an Aztec princess. He was a warrior chief, who had ceased his wandering upon discovering his one, true love. In Rio de Janeiro they would live by the sea and partake in the rapture of each other. Their progeny were creatures of bearing and passion.

Thomas would never forget his encounter with the exotic Esmeralda, for she persisted in haunting his dreams until the very end of his days. It was Esmeralda who would test Meagher's allegiance to his oath.

The others had taken the usual course of men removed so long from the company of women. MacManus and O'Donahoe would purchase companionship amid the celebration taking place. That entire port city was alive with the revelry of a saint's holiday. There were seamen of many nations who came to that place in search of its assortment of worldly pleasures. Most came to drink and chase the women who relied upon the seafaring trade for their survival. Others came to gamble for gold.

Meagher's intent was to sample all of the wares of that sultry place when he descended the gangway in the company of his cohorts. During the course of his sojourn, however, he discovered one he would always remember. His eyes beheld her as she was leaving an ancient mission.

She was wearing a mantilla of white over gleaming tresses of ebony. She was crossing herself with holy water at the time their eyes met. It was her smile that made him linger. His search was not for love, for he knew well that he was bound by his oath and his exile. Yet love brought him to the beauty that was Esmeralda. It was she that spoke first. It was in the Spanish of the Castilian dialect that Meagher had mastered at Stonyhurst.

"Do you come to visit the Mission of Our Lady, senor?"

"Yes, I am in need of a lady's guidance," Meagher replied.

"Have you lost your way then?"

"I have been lost for so very long a time." Meagher answered. "I have traveled far but the way is covered in clouds and fog."

"Are you a gentleman of the sea?" she inquired, moving close enough to caress, her dark eyes burning from within her sensuous brown face.

"No senorita, I am a gentleman of the land they call Erin and a prisoner of the sea."

"A prisoner, senor! What was the nature of your offense?"

"I sought freedom for an enslaved land. Now I am bound for a place beyond the seas and in desperate need of a lady's guidance."

"Come then, senor. If you are truly a gentleman, I am certain that this lady can help you find your way."

That was the manner of their meeting, as Meagher described it. She took him from that place in a brown leather carriage. A spirited Appaloosa mare transported them through a maze of narrow jungle pathways. She resided in a hacienda on the outskirts of the city. She lived with an invalid father and a dozen devoted servants. She made Meagher welcome in her home.

Her mother, he learned, had died giving her life. They would soon become inseparable, riding together at daybreak and learning each other's secrets in the warmth of wild secltuded places. Each moment together was precious, for they would soon come to an end. She begged him to stay with her. She advised him of places of concealment and avenues of escape. He embraced her and loved her desperately. Through their passion he sought release from the burden of his oath. Yet his word was a bond he would not break.

Their parting was heartbreaking for them both. He composed a farewell that spoke to her from the depths of his loving heart. He left it in a special place that he knew she would visit in her solitude. The words told much of the man that was Meagher.

This is how they read:

My Dearest Esmeralda,

My word as a gentleman was given, before my heart surrounded thee in love. With each breath I take, I yearn for thee. Our souls will one day meet, where prisoners are free.

All my love,

Thomas

CHAPTER 12

*I*t was Meagher's intrepid nature that elevated him above the rest and made of him a leader. Again and again, he would rise to the occasion in times of crisis, while others would waver, beset by fearful misgivings. He would expose his own neck to the noose of frightful circumstance again and again, before enlisting others to enter the fray.

He could project a fearless emanation that commanded allegiance. By doing so, he gave to us a sense of duty and a sense of purpose, a higher, selfless purpose that bestowed a spirit of brotherhood upon those who served within the ranks of the Irish Brigade.

It was this spirit that caused so many to perform acts of the utmost sacrifice. Time after time, I witnessed its presence in many a terrifying episode. It was a camaraderie, a community of concern for each other and the cause of freedom.

In its highest form, it manifested itself as a disregard for the darkness of death. For those were times when a man was measured by the magnitude of his courage and the keeping of his word. Those were times when Meagher and others like him, blazed the way for legions to follow.

He returned to the *Swift* having been tested. Few would have faulted him had he escaped into the arms of Esmeralda. How easy it would have been to remain and revel in her warmth and affection, bringing an end to his confinement and loneliness within her embrace. Her abiding love had capti-vated him and bestowed a replenishing solace upon him, only to be forsaken.

With an aching heart, he abided by his oath to a man who imprisoned him. At first he was sullen, unwilling to share his sorrow with his trusted companions aboard the *Swift*. Then, suddenly, he was required to turn his devotion toward caring for a dying Smith O'Brien.

The continued brutality and contempt of the British crew had begun to wear upon his cherished friend. Alone in irons for weeks on end, in the damp, dank hold of the *Swift,* Smith O'Brien had begun to wither. Because of his stalwart refusal to give in to his jailers and to cooperate with their Captain during that voyage, the crew had taken pleasure in scoffing and mistreating him at every turn.

He was given just enough food and drinking water to hang on as a shadow man. Then came the scurvy. His limbs and joints beginning to throb with pain and stiffen. His face turning sallow while he fatigued from the most elemental of exertions. When the bloody boils welled up beneath the skin of Smith O'Brien's chest and arms, Thomas knew that he was in the grip of a fatal adversary.

Thomas spoke to me of the meeting he arranged with the Captain dur-ing his friend's cruel ordeal. At the time, he and the others had been re-leased from their shackles and removed to berths at the other end of the hold where Smith O'Brien remained in irons.

At every opportunity he would ask permission to visit with him in his agony. When that permission was denied, Meagher petitioned the Captain for an audience in his cabin. After the *Swift* weathered another squall, the Captain agreed to see him.

"I come to intercede for Smith O'Brien, Captain," he began.

"I have afforded him ample opportunity to lessen his pain Meagher. It is not my preference to punish so severely, yet his rotten rebel heart will not surrender. What choice does he leave me?"

"The choice of being merciful, Captain-that is the choice that presents itself to you."

"Shall I show mercy to a man who betrayed Her Majesty and dishonors the Union Jack that I serve and defend? I ask you?

I called upon him to give his oath and he has refused me. The Empire cannot endure, if it is not ruthless when threatened by such contempt. Just as a captain cannot keep command of his ship, if he allows a mutineer to poison its crew."

"A captain who has won the respect of his crew fears not the dialogue of mutiny," Meagher argued. "Yet an unjust captain is always subject to its threat."

"I have heard much of your eloquence, Meagher, and observed the manner in which the others look to you for direction. Perhaps you can convince your friend to concede and the conditions under which he suffers will improve. I tell you, I am not by nature a harsh man."

"My friend is dying." Meagher pleaded. "He is not a threat to your ship or your bloody Empire. He is a man in need of your mercy. I cannot prevail upon him to concede. My hope is to prevail upon you to spare him. Please Captain, allow his rotten, rebel heart to continue beating. Please, Captain.

That evening the ship's doctor tended to Smith O'Brien. With the administration of lemon water and fruit, brought upon board in Rio de Janeiro, he began to emerge slowly from his agony. By then they were well upon the latitudes of the South Atlantic, wending their way toward Southern Africa. It was of these torrid climes that Coleridge wrote, "Water, water everywhere and not a drop to drink." When the wind no longer blew and the sea surrounding the *Swift* turned a dead calm-that was when the thirst came, bringing madness and death

They were three days voyage from the port of Cape Town when the air that filled their sails seemed to suddenly vanish. As any sailor knows, the Southern Atlantic can swell with the gale of a hurricane at one moment and then fall silent and motionless in the drift of the doldrums with the next. To a captain and crew used to such a voyage, both were dreadful hazards to survival at sea.

A sailing vessel can become a ghastly graveyard when the wind departs and the sea becomes as smooth as glass. Their water soon began to dwindle, as the *Swift* lay motionless for days on end. It was not long before mortal fear began to rise among the crew.

When water is in scant supply and a blazing, savage sun seems fixed in the center of the heavens, discipline must prevail or a sailing ship will be lost at sea. All of the crew had been through the doldrums before. All dreaded each dawn without wind. Three swallows a day was the ration commanded by the Captain for all on board. The thirst began to twist the minds of those whose survival became an obsession. Meagher heard their remarks and knew that they were meant for hearing. "Those bloody Irish pigs are stealing our water. Why should we ration with them? Why not throw the bastards overboard and be done with them."

Every throat was parched, their bodies blistered and seizing with the thirst when the Captain reduced their ration of water to two swallows a day. Each scorching, windless hour would bring with it even more desperation.

During this interval Meagher and the others endeavored to stay out of sight, remaining in their berths, thereby seeking to avoid the ire of those who despised them. When death began spreading its boney fingers over the vessel, there were those who resolved to eliminate a band of rebels to save their sun blistered skin. Smith O'Brien was now back among them, weakened yet relieved to be in the company of his brothers.

Meagher saw the signs growing more clearly. There were a dozen or more who had gone to the Captain and demanded he restrict the dispensation of water to those crew members remaining alive. The Captain's courageous refusal provoked a more sinister scheme.

Their design was to fall upon the Irish and slash their throats, thereby salvaging what was left of the drinking water for the Captain and his crew. It was a plan produced by the thirst and the threat of a miserable death.

Meagher learned of this plot and used a cabin boy to get a message to the Captain. The Captain summoned him to come to his quarters at dawn. That old sea dog had grown fond of his proud Irish prisoner. The Captain had seen the signs as well. He could rely on a loyal following of fifteen to resist the threat. If it became every man for himself, without discipline, without order, he knew they all could perish.

Those who stood by the Captain were loyal British seamen who had fought and bled under the Union Jack. The dead calm and duty would make them the allies of Irish rebels. At that moment all were shadow men upon the *Swift*. Three had already died from the thirst, raving mad before the end. More would succumb before day's end.

A bevy of sharks were seen off the bow. Suddenly there were more than two score of those dreadful predators circling the ship. They seemed to sense the approach of more carrion.

The Captain spoke, this time without ceremony. He knew that the command of his ship was in peril. He had his spies among the bastards. He wished to concentrate his forces around his cabin and the ship's magazine.

Word had been received that they were to commence their deadly endeavor that night.

Both he and Meagher knew that straws had been drawn and plans had been laid that would mean the end of his command. He was determined to retain control of his ship. He had decided to arm Meagher and his comrades against the threat.

"Can I count upon you and your men, Meagher?" he asked.

"I have given you my word, Captain. We are your prisoners. We will follow your commands. The arms you supply us will not be used against you or your ship, I swear it."

"I will speak to them in Hobart of your cooperation, Meagher. I do believe it will not be so terrible after a while. There are many in Van Diemen's Land who have adjusted to their fate."

"I have given you my word that I will not attempt an escape. I have rendered assistance when your ship was beset by storm. Now I have sworn to defend it to the death. Yet, I will never adjust to being a prisoner. I will never lose hope of one day being free. I must go now and speak to the others. Good evening"

The Captain stood surrounded by his loyal following. They were armed and at the ready for what they thought would soon occur. Each stepped aside as Meagher passed through them. They seemed to sense his power and at least for that moment seemed to admire his courage.

Meagher, MacManus and O'Donahoe were prepared to defend their floating prison, while Smith O'Brien would remain below decks, too weak for mortal combat. It was then that the blessed wind suddenly returned, bringing with it the means of survival.

There would be no force of arms, no need to quell a threat at sea. There was simply a British Man O'War under a cloud of sail, heading toward the Port of Cape Town, with four Irish convicts on board.

CHAPTER 13

*I*n Cape Town, Meagher arrived, as a shadow of himself. The journey had already lasted nearly three months and the Tasman Sea was still thousands of miles away. At that time the quest for ivory had brought every manner of man to the most southerly of Africa's ports. The Captain had commanded that the rabble from his crew be thrown in irons, preferring charges against them for insubordination and conduct unbecoming of British seamen. Perhaps they too would become prisoners bound for the colonies of New South Wales and Van Diemen's Land.

Of the rebels aboard, only Meagher was permitted to go ashore this time. Within the marketplace that ran alongside the port, he sought to disappear, while the *Swift* was provisioned for the voyage that remained.

At that time he was desperately searching for some divine intercession, longing for some supreme guidance that would make straight the course of his life and make sense of his suffering.

He sought refuge within an ancient mosque. Falling upon his knees and prostrating himself in the manner of a Bedouin devotee, he prayed. While in this state the eyes of a certain adventurer focused upon him. As Meagher searched for his salvation, the one known to the English as Richard Francis Burton was searching Cape Town for men of destiny.

Burton was an agent of her Majesty, engaged in preparations for another hazardous expedition into the belly of Black Africa. He admired the cut of Meagher's manly figure and was intrigued by his mystery. He was in the company of a dozen African tribesmen, Zulus mostly, when his eyes first fell upon Meagher entering the Mosque of Thalasaam.

It was a subterranean place of worship, a refuge from the scorching heat and dust carried on the torrid winds of the Tropic of Capricorn. Its interior was a maze of chambers and cells, designed to provide its congregation with a place of solace and devotion.

Meagher believed that there were many paths to the presence of the Almighty; that the Buddha, Mohammed and the Christ were all worthy messengers of the Divine. Meagher, like Burton, had become the master of many languages with the knowledge of many faiths. Burton dispatched Matuto, his devoted guide, to make the appropriate introduction. Matuto had become Burton's devoted companion, since slaying a lion that was poised to devour one of Burton's bearers, by means of a shield and spear. Time would tell that Burton had chosen well.

Matuto was not only fearless; he was wholly without guile. He stood well over six feet in height with a deep brown complexion and sad yet serene ebony eyes. His forehead had been scarred with a ritual three stripes, closer to the brow than the hairline. He spoke a score of languages and wore a multi-colored robe that flowed majestically from his sinewy person. He made his introduction, after Meagher had completed his prayerful sojourn within the Mosque.

"Sir, are you a man who savors adventure?" he asked.

"I am a man who savors freedom", Meagher replied.

"Please come to my Captain. He wishes to speak with you."

Meagher followed him to Burton, seated within a spacious open air room at the top of a winding stone stairway. He was protected by the native members of his expedition. He too was a tall sinewy man. His hair and broad mustache were coal black and his handsome, manly face wore a warm, receptive expression as he introduced himself with a confident shake of Meagher's hand.

His appearance reminded Meagher of MacManus. Yet, Burton was older and displayed a certain refinement in his bearing, while MacManus was more a man of the people.

Burton saw in Meagher a worthy recruit for his upcoming adventure into the darkness of the Congo. After their cordial introduction, Meagher and Burton retired to a small chamber overlooking the harbor. It was there that Burton shared his brandy and inquired of Meagher's station.

"I seek men of character and courage to accompany me upon my next expedition. I saw the manner in which you passed among the worshipers at Thalasaam. It was a bold gesture for a solitary white man. It speaks of a fearless heart. What brings you to this place?"

"A prison ship on its way to Van Diemen's Land."

"Are you in the service of Her Majesty?"

"No, I am regrettably, Her Majesty's prisoner, bound for a life in exile."

"What was the nature of your offense?"

"High treason," Meagher answered unashamedly. "I fought for the freedom of Ireland. I have been condemned by Her Majesty's ministers for defying British rule. I am a rebel by choice and conviction and will never abide tyranny, no matter how refined or ruthless it may be."

"Do you despise all that is British?" Burton probed, his manly figure rising, then standing above a seated Thomas.

"No," Meagher replied, rising to confront this agent of Her Majesty's might, this agent who would one day help discover the Victoria Lake and the source of the Nile River. "I mark each man according to his measure and not according to an accident of birth."

"I admire a man who has the courage of his convictions. Perhaps one day we will meet, when both your course and mine have been run. Let us drink to destiny." Burton offered, reaching for his glass and raising it toward Meagher.

"I prefer to drink to freedom."

Burton paused and stared, straight into the fire that was Meagher's eyes. Without speaking, he reached for Meagher's glass and handed it to him. With his expression softening from resistance to acceptance, he acceded to Meagher's wishes.

"Freedom it is, then."

At that, Meagher and Burton downed their brandy beneath a blazing African sun and the watchful gaze of Matuto. Meagher would never see Burton again. He would, however, see Matuto. He would happen upon him years later, during a game of chance in a land worlds away from that place.

It was nearly another month before the port of Hobart appeared upon the distant horizon. By that time Meagher and the others had survived even more hardship. Fever had broken out aboard the *Swift,* while crossing the Indian Ocean. Two of the crew would die and O'Donahoe would nearly succumb, before the green wilderness and sun bathed cottages of Van Diemen's Land were sighted.

Each of the four rebels stood on the deck as land drew nearer, each of them wondering whether that forsaken prison colony was where they would grow old and die. Their voyage had lasted one hundred and eleven days. Their exile now began in earnest.

At first their welcome appeared warm and inviting, as dozens of small boats containing exiled well-wishers sailed out to greet their arrival. In a land where time and circumstance passed with a snail's pace, the arrival of these infamous Irish convicts had been an eagerly anticipated event. Their welcome, however, would be short lived.

Without apology or even the slightest hint of gratitude, each of the four exiles were shackled and chained one to the other. A Captain who weeks before had relied upon them and their word to help save his ship and his command delivered them like tethered beasts into the cruel custody of the Assistant Comptroller of Convicts.

His name was Nairn. He was a small foppish sort with an insidious tone of voice and an absolute predilection for dreadful methods of redress and repression. His loathing of all things Irish, especially Irish rebels, was the keynote of his control over that forsaken land. In October of 1849 Meagher and the others were brought before him, after spending three days confined alone in putrid huts of mud and straw. Each one of them was starving and parched from the thirst.

Nairn wore a powdered wig along with a red tunic and blue trousers. He carried a black leather riding crop that he would use to torment the exiled and the imprisoned, brought in chains before him. Discourse by a prisoner while in his presence was forbidden. Nairn was determined to prevent all discourse among all rebels, while in exile upon Van Diemen's Land.

Meagher rarely spoke of this pain filled episode. Only once did he disclose its agony. The manner in which he described his ordeal was both vivid and indelible. It was still an open, oozing sore years after it had transpired. It was an occasion that Meagher would always remember with a galling mixture of hostility and regret.

"You are all traitorous dogs who deserved to be hanged." That was the manner of Nairn's introduction to the four rebels who knelt nearly naked before him, their hands bound behind them. "Your filthy carcasses are in my charge now, and I will do with them what I see fit. There is no hope of escape. The sea and the sharks will assure your imprisonment for the rest of your miserable lives."

"You will be taken from here this day," he continued, "brought to the fields where you will be worked like the dumb beasts you are. Should you complain or give voice to any utterance, except compliance, you will be lashed, lashed until the marrow of your bones appears through your rotten Irish skin. Should you twice defy any rule or any order given by Her Majesty's ministers while indentured thus, you will be hanged and left for the beasts to devour."

He then stood above Meagher and paused. He wore a sneer on his powdered face, bloated from drink and dissolution. He too was a prisoner of Her Majesty, condemned to the confinement of others in a prison surrounded by a cruel sea. He beckoned those that brought them to him, the brutal, willing ones who did his bidding. They knew well what would come next. Their pleasure was another's pain.

Nairn was standing near a hearth, its embers flickering, casting the shadow of his person upon the limestone walls of his quarters. From that hearth he brought forth a blazing iron and ordered those that followed him to hold Meagher steady. He then brought that white hot iron to within a hair of Meagher's terror filled eyes, his voice exhibiting an eerie delight as he spoke.

"I have been to your God forsaken Ireland and seen how the landlords mark their sheep. It is our custom here to press this mark so that all may know treason by its face. There are many who have written to me on your behalf, Meagher. The Captain of the *Swift* and others in the England you betrayed. They have implored me for mercy. Shall I show you mercy? Shall I refrain from marking you? Answer me, you Irish bastard. Beg for mercy from Her Majesty or your face will bear this mark forever. Beg now or feel this iron upon your flesh."

"Have mercy," Meagher cried out amid his despair, succumbing at last to the commands and the cruelty of the Empire.

Nairn chose not to brand Meagher's face, for he was mindful that others were aware of Meagher's exile and concerned with the manner of his treatment. Instead he blazed the mark on the palm of Meagher's right hand, searing his flesh with a *T*, a *T* that would always remind Meagher of the evil that is tyranny.

CHAPTER 14

For six months they labored unceasingly. Forbidden from speaking, except in compliance to shouted commands, they were little more than slaves, divorced from all human discourse. To such men as these, this was the cruelest punishment. The days and nights were endless.

In solitude they worked and slept, dragging their weary bodies through the rigors of mindless, back breaking labor, without merit, without care. Clearing land of timber; working chest high in swamps under blazing heat; burrowing in mines like forsaken moles. This was the fate of exile for life. This was the plight of three of the rebels.

Meagher, MacManus and O'Donahoe suffered and survived this mindless misery, while Smith O'Brien endured an even crueler fate. His refusal to comply with the commands of Captain Oldham during the voyage had labeled him an incorrigible. As such, his exile would transpire amid solitary confinement upon Maria Island. This was the bleakest hole of that darkened universe of loneliness and hopelessness.

Smith O'Brien had indeed escaped the noose, but now was forced to endure a more sinister form of punishment. He resided in a tiny thatched hut on a wind-swept, barren hillside, damned by the alienation of that place. His heart would ache from the torment of being completely cut off from the world he once knew.

Without warning, Meagher was suddenly summoned to appear behind the walls of the place where he had been branded. He knew not, what punishment awaited him. He had passed beyond pain at that point, prepared to meet his fate with more fortitude this time. He was resolved to confront his next ordeal without cries of mercy. It was March, 1850 and Thomas Francis Meagher was about to begin a new chapter in his life of exile.

In Tasmania, it was the autumn of his twenty sixth year. He was hickory hard from his labors and his skin had been bronzed by the sun of the Southern Hemisphere. His dark hair, so often soaked with the sweat of his brow, now gleamed with golden highlights. He was clean shaven, and his piercing eyes were like that of a wild animal.

His dress was the customary fedora of woven straw and a blouse and trousers of the lightest cotton fabric. His calloused bare feet were encased within sandals of hemp. Despite the circumstance of his indenture, he had regained his dignity. Fate would take a novel turn and lead him to a new beginning.

Nairn had been replaced, given the sack by certain of Her Majesty's ministers who had grown tired of his methods and his manner. It was said that he had been caught *in flagrante delicto* with a certain servant of the Crown who preferred the dress of the female and the lift of the cocoa plant. A new regime had been instituted within Van Diemen's Land and a new approach to the convict population begun.

Meagher, MacManus and O'Donahoe would soon receive another brand of confinement from their British jailers. A solemn promise to not attempt escape would win for them tickets of leave. Tickets of leave that would allow them to remain within certain specified districts of that untamed wilderness; free from forced labor, yet forbidden from engaging in discourse with each other. Smith O'Brien, however, would continue to endure his exile upon Maria Island. There he would plot in making a reckless escape by sea. When this escape failed, he was transferred to Port Arthur and confined to a cottage surrounded by a sea of informers.

Meagher's word was given under oath and his ticket of leave was to remain upon his person at all times. His location separated him from the others who had chosen the rebel course. Any information received of clandestine meetings among them would mean a return to their indenture and the hardest of hard labor. He was required to report every fortnight to his overseer.

Meagher was exiled to the mountainous region of Campbell Town, an area of strange birds and beasts. There he fashioned both bow and spear. There his first task was to survive the winter that had begun to blast its bone chilling breath upon the landscape. There he would make the acquaintance of others who had adapted to their exile; others who were tethered by their circumstance; others who were victims of British injustice.

He would construct a cottage in the Lake Sorell region. There he would learn to hunt and to fish, and trap game along its banks. He would barter pelts for provisions in the settlement of Ross, thousands of feet below his refuge. He would be divorced from the company of men for months at a time. In his solitude, he would write poetry and read, whenever circumstance permitted.

With much effort he tamed a wild grey hound that became entangled in one of his traps. Later he managed to secure a flintlock musket and trade for a chestnut stallion whom he named Elijah.

He rode with grace and purpose through the misty mornings and the wild windy nights. He had become a man of the wilderness. It was a lonely, loathsome existence for one like Thomas, who so enjoyed the company of the crowd. Then she appeared on the road to the settlement of Ross. In the spring of a September morning, he came upon a disabled carriage and a beauty by the name of Catherine Bennet.

After Meagher was gone, I read his letters about her. She was a redeeming drink to one dying from the thirst. She was a vision to an infidel. He loved her from the moment their eyes met. He admired her spirit and her love for children. Perhaps it was the time of season, or the seasoning of time. She was a delight to one whose heart had been broken. She was his absolution and his reason to remain. She would haunt his dreams and bear his child. Catherine, his beloved Catherine, was how he would always remember her.

Before the storm of battle, during America's darkest nights, he would retire to his private moments and whisper her name. Although there would be others he would love and lose, none more than his beloved Catherine would steal his heart and keep it.

She was eighteen and in need of a man like Meagher. She was tall for a lady and she spoke with innocence bubbling through her radiant face. Her eyes were hazel pools into which the romantic Thomas would plunge.

Chapter 14

On the morning of their meeting she was dressed in white and her chestnut hair gleamed in the sun. Her face wore an unblemished blush and her fertile form made men stop and admire. Her father was Eamon Bennet, a former highwayman and willing participant in the rebellion of '98. Thomas began by being of assistance to her. To those who give much; much is given.

The rocky road to Ross had broken the wheel of the carriage she was conducting. She was caring for a doctor's children, while he was in New South Wales on matters of business. Thomas came upon them rounding a bend in the road. He was upon the gallop and Elijah's sinews were lathered and glistening. He too was dressed in white, wearing his broad brimmed fedora. There was no expectation that such a beauty would meet his gaze and alter his ways.

"May I be of aid to you and your company?" he began, his throat becoming parched, upon beholding her loveliness.

"The spokes have given way and I fear being in this place when night falls. I am the nurse for Dr. Hall's children. We came here from beyond the Three Stones. The children desired a day in the town."

Meagher dismounted and removed his fedora. He then brought Elijah toward the children, congregated upon the roadside. Meagher delighted in the company of children when his mind was free. On that day, he would make a conquest of them all.

He tethered the chestnut to a nearby tree, removed his blouse and began to repair the broken wheel. His strength and his gentle manner attracted Catherine to him. She sought to assist and he welcomed her contribution.

He could tell that Catherine was a woman of resource and respectability. She was trained to care for the children of the gentry. She asked his name and he replied politely. She had been told of him by her father. He was surprised that there was a notoriety that still attached itself to the name of Thomas Francis Meagher. He rode behind them toward the settlement of Ross while the children stared and waved to their gallant *chevalier.*

As they neared the outskirts of the settlement, he reared Elijah back and galloped away. In an instant he returned, sliding from the saddle and bounding momentarily upon the road, then catapulting on to the animal's back. I tell you Geronimo, himself, would have admired the manner of his horsemanship. On that day he resolved to court Catherine Bennet.

Repeated rendezvous would be arranged in settings wild and beautiful. They would navigate the crystal green of Lake Sorell in a skiff he called Esperanza. It was within this skiff that he told her of his passion and she of her's. They would wander together upon magnificent mountain trails; he reciting Browning and Shakespeare, while she dreamed of a life together forever. His romantic heart was captivated by her loveliness. After their first embrace, he requested a meeting with her widowed father.

In 1798 the green fields and villages of Erin had run red with Irish blood. The United Irishmen yearned for independence and died by the thousands in the fury of battles named and numerous. There was Wolfe Tone and his failed effort to win freedom with the aid of the French Navy. There was Fitzgerald and the power of his person. There was Vinegar Hill and New Ross. It was civil war, and it was awful in its savagery.

Eamon Bennet stood with them, fought beside them and became an exile to the land beyond the seas, after resorting to a life among brigands and cutpurses. He loved a lass whose own exile arose from stealing bread for starving younger brothers. In Van Diemen's Land they would become as one. She would die from consumption on a mud filled road, winding through an endless forest and tear his heart apart. With his fire fading, he became reclusive. His love for his daughter, Catherine, was all that kept him alive.

He was seated in a great wicker chair, his body wracked by disease. His voice faint and eyes dim, he was a white haired stocky sort with arthritic hands and a distracted manner. His garden had become his universe and he called his plants and ferns by name. To his beloved Catherine he was her Da. She brought Thomas to his garden and asked him to remain, as she climbed the path to her Da's wicker perch. There he sat like a bird of prey with a broken wing, while she whispered to him of her love for another exiled rebel. Then she beckoned Thomas to come and introduced him.

At the time he was smoking a crude pipe and gazing across the mountains to the Tasman Sea. Wearing the tattered dress of a destitute country gentleman, his illness would not allow him to stand. He was honored with the visitation of one as renowned as Meagher of the Sword. He gestured with a gnarled right hand to have Thomas sit beside him and converse. He relished the excitement of a novel experience. In the lassitude of that place, where time was marked in decades, manly conversation between such as these was a rare occurrence indeed.

"I have read of your exploits, Thomas Meagher," the old rebel rasped. "I am honored to make your acquaintance. I am curious as to your intentions. Will you make a home of this island or will memory and the wanderlust make of your days a misery?"

"I know no misery when I am in the company of Catherine," he answered, looking squarely into the faded green eyes of the old man."

"Will you have tea with me?" Bennet implored. "We can speak of many things. It has been so long since I have spoken to other than my daughter. Perhaps you will stay the night and tomorrow we can ride beyond the Three Stones and watch the albatross soar."

He acquiesced in the old man's request. The next morning they rode out to a mountainous plateau that overlooked the Bass Strait. They spoke in torrents. They sat alone in a carriage and watched free birds fly above them. In the blaze of sunset, Thomas made the request that would bring him and Catherine together as one.

"I am in love with your daughter, and my love will last forever. I ask your blessing to make her my wife."

The old rebel stared into the sincerity that simmered within Meagher's passionate eyes. He said nothing. He seemed to be fixed upon an image, a will of the wisp reminiscence. Suddenly a torment seemed to seize him and then in an instant subside. With a doleful smile he spoke, measuring each and every syllable as if it were powdered gold.

"Let us not speak of forever, Thomas, for forever is much the longer within this land. You have my blessing and my hope of a joyous tomorrow."

CHAPTER 15

Their love was an elixir, a soothing warm melody that entranced them both. Catherine was his redemption and he, her saving grace. They were inseparable in spirit and determined to survive and prosper on an island of exiles. Their marriage was the subject of much anticipation. They exchanged their vows on the same plateau where he had asked her father for her hand.

They made a cozy home of Meagher's cottage on Lake Sorrel. She would persist with her duties as the nurse for Dr. Hall's children. He would continue his trapping and fishing. They would visit her father each and every Sunday. He would await their arrival anxiously and grow sad with every departure. In November of 1851 an envoy from Meagher's past would make his appearance and bring with him the winds of change.

It was while Catherine was with child that his wanderlust began to take hold. One morning while securing provisions in Ross, Meagher was advised by a haggard old man who knew much of the occurrences in Campbell Town, that a certain John Phelan had been making inquiries toward securing a rendezvous. He had told the old man that he had news of Mitchel and Smith O'Brien.

At first, Thomas rejected the overture, not wishing to infest the circumstance of his simple life with notions of escape and the promise of freedom. Instead, he returned to his cottage by the lake and his beloved

Catherine. Later, while dining together, she noticed his distraction. Her love detected in him a gnawing restlessness.

"What is the matter, my love? You seem out of sorts this evening."

"It's a melancholy, nothing more," he said, not yet comprehending the yearning for freedom so deep within his Irish soul. Thomas would endeavor with all his heart to deny his nature and hold fast to the precious love of his wife. Yet, the promise of freedom was a jealous mistress indeed.

A rendezvous was eventually arranged through the haggard old man. Phelan along with another would visit Meagher through a round-about route. They made a circle through the wilderness and came upon Lake Sorrel from the North. Their journey was meant to avoid detection, since their discourse could mean the gallows. Phelan would never forget his first encounter with Meagher of the Sword.

Phelan was a firebrand who would fight at the drop of a hat. He was the seventh son of a drunken father and a mother who feared he was destined to be lost, along with so many of her other boys. He was exiled for striking one of Her Majesty's officers and not showing remorse during a lashing. He survived the fever, as well as the voyage to Tasmania, while still a lad of seventeen.

His hair was the color of the orange and his face bore the call of the wild. His eyes were most peculiar, one blue and one hazel. He resembled a very dangerous and cunning cat. Meagher had been his icon since his older brother told him of the speech at Conciliation Hall.

Phelan and his companion were lost and fearful of night fall, high in the mountains above the settlement at Ross, when they first encountered Meagher. Suddenly the baying of a hound sent chills up their spines. Then they were confronted with the echo of the aborigine howl, *coo eee! coo eee! coo eee!*

As darkness drew nearer, they were filled with dread. Then Thomas galloped upon them, carrying a pistol at the ready. When the hound appeared baring his teeth, Phelan drew his dagger and his companion scampered up the nearest tree.

"Come down from there and state your business," Meagher shouted.

They could not see his face beneath a hooded cloak. His voice piercing their persons from the darkness. Toward Phelan, he then directed his attention. "Why do you trespass upon this place? Speak or I will blow a hole through your insides and allow this hound a feast?"

"We come in search of Thomas Meagher. Can you guide us to him?" Phelan implored, as his companion complied with Meagher's command and joined them within the darkening glade.

"Why should I assist you?"

"We bring with us news of his friends, Mitchel and Smith O'Brien. I carry a letter from Mitchel himself; smuggled here by those who believe in a free Ireland"

With that Meagher slid from the saddle. The movement caused his great gray hound, *Brian,* named for the hero, Boru, to heel at his side. In the darkness his voice demanded that Phelan deliver his proof; the flintlock pointing at his heart. Phelan hesitated at first. When Meagher drew nearer, he caught a faint glimpse of his features from beneath the hood.

Sensing he was in the presence of the one he was seeking, he reached beneath his shirt and produced Mitchel's letter. Meagher recognized Mitchel's hand and ordered them to follow him along a narrow mountain pass.

Upward they traveled, winding their way through a treacherous wilderness in the dark. They came upon a clearing and suddenly lost all sight of their guide. They fell upon the earth, seeking a respite from their travel. After a while they saw a distant light making its way toward them.

Suddenly, Meagher appeared in their midst, carrying a torch to light the way. He was on foot this time and without the hooded cloak. He beckoned them to follow once again, leading them onward to a rustic cabin, across the lake from his cottage.

There he entered a room with a fireplace, fashioned from the stone of the surrounding mountains, a candle in a glass on the mantle. The hound stood as his protector, until Meagher commanded the devoted beast to heel. It was there that they began the discourse forbidden by the Crown.

"You are Meagher, then. My brother William told me of you. I am John Phelan and he is Eamon Corbett. He says little, yet he is one of us. We are at your service."

"May I see the letter?"

"Before I do, Mitchel asked that I make this introduction," Phelan offered. "We were on the same ship, sailing from Pernambuco. I am afraid your friend endured a rough passage, filled with fever and asthma. He survives to see you again. He told me of Smith O'Brien. He told me that you were the one to lead us. These are his words."

"Thomas, I have been kept alive by thoughts of our reunion.

I have petitioned the heavens on hands and knees to give us redemption, to take us away from this wilderness. I have had a vision of America. I have a dream of our salvation in America, in the City of New York. You must make your escape and you must make straight the way for countless others. I have seen this, as I see the sunrise over the mountains. In America, our people will one day be free."

As young Phelan finished his recitation, Meagher's eyes were flooded with tears. He was seated at a simple wooden table, when he was given the letter. He made his way to the mantle of the fireplace. There, beneath a lamp, he read Mitchel's message to him. It spoke to him of times past and blood oaths made.

Meagher's refuge rested on the side of a great, green mountain, overlooking a lake of breadth and beauty. When the clouds were gone and the sky was a majestic blue, he would sit for hours and stare across the lake. It was a wondrous prison house, a wondrous prison house, indeed.

He cherished the letter from Mitchel. He would read it and read it, over and over, in the days to come. It was his talisman, his reassurance that the path he was about to follow was righteous. He knew what it meant to follow Mitchel's direction; just as he had followed the direction of Brother Edmund after that night at the famine house.

In the days that followed his heart would ache as he watched his beloved Catherine swell with their child. How could he leave, when it meant deserting her in her time of need? He wrestled with an answer, wondering if there was an answer at all. He prayed, as he prayed in the Mosque at Thalasaam. That is when Smith O'Brien likewise spoke to him through a letter smuggled from his cottage near Port Arthur. It was brought by a mute boy, who knew well the trails and passes of that part of Van Diemen's Land.

In his letter O'Brien advised Thomas that his eyes were failing and his hopes for a free Ireland were dim. His blaze was becoming an ember. Meagher heard the voice that once echoed within the walls of Parliament and promised his people freedom. It seemed without vigor, a distant echo of the past.

Meagher would sit at his oak dining table, after Catherine retired for the evening. There, a tallow candle cast its light upon the letters from his friends, friends who had always been faithful, brothers of different blood who had endured so much together. Smith O'Brien and John Mitchell had indeed been given the same vision.

They called to Meagher like a haunting chorus, presenting their proposition squarely before him. Their words were ready reminders of nobler purposes and grander designs. He could not resist them, no matter how hard he tried.

"You must depart from this place," they cried. "You must depart and ride the summer wind to America. You must depart and lead our people to freedom."

He would make his decision to return to the rebel's path under the stars above his mountain lake. He lay in the belly of the boat, named *Esperanza,* staring at the constellations, seeking direction from above.

He saw again the anguished face of his father, after his conviction at Clonmel. He saw it all within a haunting vision. Smith O'Brien calling to him in the bowels of a prison ship, beseeching him with manacled hands, Mitchel, surrounded by a company of redcoats, being led away from his weeping wife and children. Then finally, the benevolent face of Brother Edmund appeared like an angelic guardian from a place of serenity. Above all the rest, it was he who spurred Meagher to his destiny.

CHAPTER 16

*F*or weeks he cared for her, as the time drew near for the appearance of his firstborn child. He tried to speak about it but the words would not come. After searching his soul, he resolved to send word to his father. Thomas, the Senior would be relieved that his son had married and was about to become a father, thus easing the ordeal of his exile.

Thomas earned from every imaginable labor to prepare for Catherine's confinement. He arranged to have her cared for by a nurse and a trusted advisor by the name of Damien. Damien had been an accountant and had become a missionary of sorts, before he was exiled for engaging in seditious discourse.

Before the time for Meagher's leaving arrived, he had begun a correspondence with the Governor of Van Diemen's Land, a scoundrel by the name of Dennison. He reminded Her Majesty's servant that his father had been a Member of Parliament, enamored and esteemed by Edmund Burke, himself. Meagher wrote to him, not as a prisoner but as an equal, pleading on behalf of those exiled with him, seeking their pardon based upon the teachings of Locke and Jefferson.

With a change in British Rule, Smith O'Brien would eventually receive a conditional pardon and be freed from his exile. Thereafter, he would take up residence in Brussels and finally return to his beloved Ireland, dying a broken man.

As to Mitchel, after being confined to the prison ships for so long a time, he remained in seclusion gathering his strength. After years of exile, he would escape to the promise that was America in the garb of a prelate.

MacManus was the first of their number to make his escape, sailing forth from Melbourne Harbor. He would travel first to San Francisco and then settle South of San Jose. Although O'Donahoe's delivery from exile was delayed by the vigilance of the Crown's agents, he would arrive in America years later.

Then there was John Connel, a broad brush stroke of a man with red chin whiskers and a hulking physique. He was a thief who had been sentenced to Van Diemen's Land from Liverpool. Fond of games of chance and ladies of the evening, he had acquired a reputation of sorts in the handling of a knife. At their very first encounter, he would challenge Meagher and nearly pay with his life. He would later become his ally in making an escape.

For Thomas there now remained but two orders of business. The first was the most onerous: to inform his beloved wife of his decision to escape. The second was to advise the magistrate of police for Campbell Town that he was resigning his ticket of leave, thereby inviting his hot pursuit by a company of Her Majesty's dragoons. An unrepentant Irish rebel was about to throw down the gauntlet once again.

His last occasion with Catherine would be etched into his breaking heart. They were standing together on the shore of their lake, silhouetted against a setting sun.

"Catherine, I must speak to you of a sorrow that is about to enter our lives."

"What is it, Thomas?"

"I am to make my escape from this place. I must depart and prepare the way. I will make a home for us in America."

He fell at her knees with this promise upon his lips. He kissed her swollen belly while she sobbed uncontrollably and fell into his arms. Through his own tears he recited his reason for leaving. He had undertaken a blood oath to lift the Irish from their oppression. He would leave before he could share his exile with his first born child.

She did not beseech him to stay, for her love for him was boundless. She knew the restless river of his soul. The birth of his child would force him to remain and die in that place. She believed his promise and prepared herself for a season of suffering. Her devotion was directed to her unborn child.

She would watch as Thomas rode off through the night, a torch lighting his way to tomorrow. She would watch with tearful eyes as that torchlight faded and suddenly disappeared.

A sense of honor and a sense of betrayal can be interwoven into a painful quilt. To many an outward appearance, Thomas Meagher was a gallant leader of men, instilling in his followers principles of duty and courage under fire. Yet in his private moments he was not at peace. He was tormented by his forsaken love for Catherine Bennet. This torment would bring his ending.

He believed that he had failed her, deserted her in her time of need. He would tell himself again and again, that a nobler quest required his undivided loyalty. Yet he would be haunted by her tears, when confronted with the pronouncement of his leaving. In the years to come there would be many that followed a similar path, leaving their homes and the ones they loved in the quest for the freedom to be found in America.

Over the years that I knew him, Meagher would often hearken back to events in his life that fashioned his character and fired his soul. Perhaps the most significant of these was a certain mystical encounter with the one we knew as Brother Edmund, an encounter that determined the direction of his life, an encounter that shaped him and set him apart.

He would speak of it in a voice of eerie resonance. It was during the darkest days of that great hunger, long after that night at the famine house. The Irish who endured those terror filled times would remember them well. There were thousands who had suffered an agonizing death, making them a feast for the worms.

They were being buried in pits, without cross or marker, to prevent their rotting flesh from infecting the living, and dragging others into the abyss. Thomas was laboring in the dark. It was then that he slipped upon a muddy slope in his exhaustion, sliding down beneath and among those being buried.

While drowning in the mud of the dying, his heart filling with mortal fear and dread, he insisted that he was lifted. This was the manner of his description. As he lay screaming, overcome by the madness of that terrifying moment, he described being transported to a serene glade, beneath a flowering tree and beholding the face of Brother Edmund.

He would see that face in Cork City, before addressing a hall of strangers and enemies. He would see it in Limerick, before slaying savage men. He would see it at Antietam, before leading The Irish Brigade into Bloody Lane.

CHAPTER 17

His letter resigning his ticket of leave was delivered by his friend and confidante Damien. Damien was at one time the accountant to many of the leading merchants of Dublin. He had become acquainted with Thomas through the provision trade. It was said that he became mad in a debtor's prison and began to preach the gospel.

One St Patrick's Day, during a sermon in front of a Galway workhouse, he accused Queen Victoria of subjugating the poor and profiting from their misfortune. He would be exiled for words spoken against British Rule.

In Tasmania, he would preach less and counsel more, becoming a missionary to a most irreverent flock. When he learned that Thomas had been exiled, he traversed savage rivers and snowcapped mountains, first to encounter and later to serve the one they called Meagher of the Sword. He would care for Catherine with the loving heart of a devoted older brother. It was he who delivered Meagher's challenge to the magistrate of Campbell Town. The notice read thus:

TO THE MAGISTRATE OF POLICE FOR CAMPBELL TOWN. I, THOMAS MEAGHER, HEREBY RESIGN MY TICKET OF LEAVE. I WELCOME THE PURSUIT OF MY PERSON. I WILL NO LONGER BE IMPRISONED AND SUBJECT TO BRITISH TYRANNY.

YOUR MOST DISOBEDIENT SERVANT
THOMAS FRANCIS MEAGHER
ERIN GO BRAGH

A company of dragoons was assembled with orders to bring Meagher back, either dead or alive. He soared on the back of Elijah, caressing that golden stallion's neck and whispering his aspirations into his ear. Their manes intermingled; their hearts entwined; fashioned together by their proud natures. He wore a cape, a rapier and a slouch hat. He was armed with a dagger and a flintlock pistol. He had secured his provisions in a rucksack and tied a bedroll to the back of Elijah.

He waited along a mountain pass under a summer moon. He waited for his accomplice, his partner in that desperate endeavor. Connel was tardy and time was running against their bold escapade.

The plan was to strike northeastward over the mountains that loomed ahead in the darkness. A crude compass and the stars would guide them along their path. Thomas watched with dread as the wilderness below him flickered with the torches of the approaching dragoons.

Then the sky drew dark with a hellish fog. It resembled that dreadful night on the quay, when a dying mother beckoned him toward his destiny.

When Meagher heard the hounds approaching he began to despair. Suddenly the burly, red haired Connel came roaring toward him on a spirited spotted mare. They then galloped away without salutation. The hounds of hell, itself, snapping at their heels; the fog descending upon them, making their journey over mountainous trails a numbing nightmare. Yet the fog would dull their scent and delay the approach of their pursuers.

In the third hour of their escape they came upon a swollen river that fell off into the torrent of a waterfall. By torchlight they examined the map they were to follow. There was no indication upon it of such a treacherous impediment.

"We must decide which way is best," Meagher urged. You're the gambler, Connel. Chose quickly, for I fear it means our lives."

Connell was paralyzed with indecision. The hounds baying through the muffled fog. He swore oath after oath at the miserable mist that blanketed the night and extinguished the guiding light of the moon and the stars.

"Make up your mind, man, or all is lost," Meagher cried.

"This way," Connel shouted, as he plunged from the bank into the swiftness of that raging river. Meagher readied Elijah for a moment, reassuring him that all would be endured together. In an instant they were soaring, then submerging into the depths of that swollen torrent. Meagher broke the surface gasping for breath. His heart throbbing from the chill of those mountain fathoms. At one, he and Elijah rode the current. Up ahead was the hulking figure of Connel, hanging on to the neck of his terrified mare.

Suddenly there was a rumble of thunder. It then began to pelt rain, adding to their ordeal. Then falls could be heard roaring in the distance. How would they survive? Meagher wondered. How would Catherine and his child learn of his demise? He and Elijah were swept by the river's current over the falls; the sound of Connel's screams ringing in his ears.

Both he and his stallion would survive the descent into the maelstrom that swirled below. Connel's mare would not fare as well. She would become impaled upon a protruding ledge and be swept away into the deep. The dawn would bring the conviction that two men on one horse would soon be caught by a disciplined company of dragoons. Concealment by day and travel by night would offer their only hope of escape.

While Meagher lay exhausted along the bank of that swollen river he heard the rustle of a pack of those dog like devils that inhabit that forsaken land. They had been drawn to that place by the scent of bloody horseflesh. Their prey was Elijah, lying beside Meagher in the thickets. Their attack would be repulsed by Meagher's fury, as he wielded his rapier and dagger like a creature possessed. Thereafter he and Connel would discover a darkened cave on a ridge above the river. There they would rest and conceal themselves from their pursuers.

Much of Van Diemen's Land is harsh and heartless wasteland. During that first night, away from the loving embrace of his beloved Catherine, the misery that made of Meagher a man of sorrow raged.

In vain, he attempted to forget, endeavoring to extinguish all notion of his forsaken wife, during that desperate flight from exile. Finally, a fitful sleep would fall upon him. It was Connel who awoke him with the fearful news that a band of riders were nearby.

By then the dragoons had lost their scent and forsaken the chase. Now a more sinister brand of pursuer had taken up the hunt. With a price on his Irish head of one hundred quid, Meagher now became the quarry of more mercenary predators. In the furor of that moment, Connel began to wonder, why so many seemed aware of their leaving.

"How did they know that we were gone?" he whispered.

"I informed the Magistrate," Meagher replied unashamedly.

"Are you a bloody fool?"

"I had given my word that I would not attempt escape. I was required to warn them of my leaving. It was a matter of honor."

"There is no honor in this place, Meagher. Your word may just bring us to the hangman."

Later, Meagher would keep watch, as Connel slept, while the ones who hunted humans for British pounds searched in vain.

After nightfall, they set off once again. This time the moon and the stars pointed the way toward their destination. In the distance they heard the echo of a musket, knowing that their pursuers had discovered the place of their concealment. Meagher had managed to save the rucksack that contained his hope of sustenance. This he shared with Connel, without a thought of his own famished state.

Then they were required to scale the jagged peaks that rose above them; daunting obstacles that made their deliverance seem futile. That was when Connel fell to the ground, crying out in his exhaustion.

"It's hopeless. I can't go on."

"We are not done," Meagher screamed. "I will make this escape or die. You can take your rest on the back of Elijah. Now mount up, man, or I will run you through where you lay."

They made their way upward, with a band of killers following behind. For four nights they trekked, cold, wet and hungry. By daylight, they rested, their meager provisions barely sustaining them. Both were beyond fatigue, yet they continued to climb, with Elijah carrying first one and then the other.

On the fifth night, they rounded a narrow mountain pass. The rain again began to drench them. It was here that Connel fell from Elijah, sliding downward and arresting his descent upon an overhanging sapling; his screams echoing across the canyons toward their pursuers.

Connel's rescue meant chancing a fall from a windy, rain drenched precipice. Meagher acted with dispatch, dangling his upper body over the edge, while his legs were anchored around the trunk of a tree. With all his energy he pulled the flailing Connel toward him, demanding that he cease his screaming and attend more closely to saving his neck. Once that rescue was made, their journey continued, as Connel pledged his undying gratitude for his deliverance.

On the seventh night they saw the Tamar River shimmering below them. It reminded Thomas of the times as a child when he would sit in the hills confronting Waterford and gaze upon his beloved Suir. Upon his knees, he prayed that this river would mean their redemption.

They would make their descent in the darkness, searching for a signal fire from the aborigines who were to be their allies. Suddenly, their eyes beheld a most welcome sight. There below them were three torches arranged in a line.

At that time, Meagher knew he must say farewell to Elijah, his faithful friend. He brought the stallion to a secluded jungle path, beginning to brighten with a blazing morning. It was a place well suited for such a farewell. With the utmost care, he removed both saddle and bridle and used his blanket to rub Elijah's sinews to a glistening warmth. Whispering words of devotion, then slapping his right flank, he set Elijah free.

CHAPTER 18

They were fierce in their appearance and they despised the British. The relocation and slaughter of their people by agents of the Empire had made them receptive to the overtures of a burly thief and gambler by the name of Connel.

He had encountered the two as they were readying their nets for another foray into the treachery of the Bass Strait. They were noble specimens of a people pitted against the winds of change. They used an open boat with a ragged sail to traverse the rapids of the Tamar and descend into the swirling strait that separated Van Diemen's Land from New South Wales. For a price they had agreed to assist in the escape of two convicts.

They were father and son. The elder's name was Vincent. He was reed thin with long leg and sinew. His skin was the color of chestnut and his hair that of pitch. His nose was spread across his face and his mouth seemed to extend from ear to ear on a hound like head. He wore a loin cloth of green and carried a blow pipe that could kill at fifty paces. His age was unknowable, a guess would make him forty.

His son was perhaps fifteen and of the same stature as his father. He had black, braided hair that touched his shoulder. He too was a chestnut shade of brown. He played a primitive flute and his nearly naked person was at one with the wild. He spoke only when spoken to and then very little. His father had named him Peta. Both of them knew how to navigate the shark infested waters of the Bass Strait.

By this time, Meagher was obsessed with the notion of escape. He believed he could will his way to release. He had somehow passed beyond the sorrow of his separation from Catherine and become one with the natural. In moments of meditation he would envision the promise of America and pray that he would be allowed to partake of it.

They shoved off from a misty lagoon, Connel and Meagher concealed under fishing nets in the bottom of the boat. There were British outposts upon the Tamar. They would send frequent patrols out to secure provisions and harass the natives.

Down river, they were swept, on the back of a relentless current. Then their boat approached a stretch of violent water. Vincent beckoned his contraband to rise and assist in preventing a collision with the jagged rocks that seemed to protrude at every bend. With sharpened poles, they pushed away from these obstacles of death and destruction. Once they passed that treacherous stretch of water, they came to a place of serenity.

It was there that they speared fish and retired to an inlet beneath an overhanging tree. There they would eat and speak to each other of matters beyond their present circumstance. Vincent spoke first, crouched in a wild animal way, licking his fingers from the remnants of the freshly cooked fish. He had a sing song way of speaking with just the hint of a French accent.

"How do you come together to this place?"

"We come to escape, to escape to America, the New World,"

Meagher said, while lying against the bow of the boat. The meal had made him drowsy.

"America, I have heard of this place. Tell me of America,"

Vincent demanded, while staring intently at Meagher.

"It's a bloody place without peelers and overseers," Connel offered, while lying in the grass. "A place where Old Jack Connel can walk down the street with a tart on each arm and a jingle in his pockets. Meagher here, he wants to save the world. Me, I wants to save me arse and give it to the landlady up the duff."

A look of incomprehension flashed across Vincent's face. It made Meagher chuckle.

"What my brother Connel means is, he wants to be a free man. Free to do as he pleases with whomever he pleases. Within reason that is. This is why we escape; why we come to this place together."

"Can my people be free in this place, you call America?" Vincent asked, staring over at his son, engaged in removing all signs of their meal. He was the sentinel to their party. He was trained well in the ways of survival, placing berries of a most delicious vintage before his father and the two exiles.

"He is a fine lad. You should be proud," Thomas said, with an appreciative smile.

"Can my son be free in America?" Vincent pressed, moving closer toward Meagher.

Meagher pondered his inquiry, remembering the block at Bermuda and a brutal overseer bringing anguish to the face of a child. An innocent child, chained like a dog because of the shade of her skin, a child whose skin was the shade of Vincent's skin. "When we come to America," Meagher promised. "When all of us wanting freedom come to America, it will become the place we can make of it. We must make it free."

With that, Vincent reclined along the banks of the Tamar, staring through the leaves of the overhanging tree at two black swans floating free. He and Thomas would soon become as brothers and Peta would become as Meagher's son.

There was a way about Meagher that made him a guide to the young and the brave, the ones who displayed the spark that he would make a flame. I can remember the lobby of the Metropolitan Hotel, filled with eager young men who wished to serve in the Brigade. Meagher would sit across from them, close enough to see the sweat roll down their necks. There he learned of their mettle and searched for the qualities that he could fashion into courage under fire.

It was their third day dodging British patrols along the river, when they came upon a view of the Bass Strait. It was still some night's travel away. They would conceal their boat just before dawn and remain in that place until sunset. In that place the snakes were waiting.

Legend says that St. Patrick drove the snakes into the sea. It seemed to Meagher that they took up residence within the mouth of the Tamar River. Snakes of size and dimension, snakes that could slither next to the sweating skin of a man and strike in an instant, their venom coursing through human blood.

It was Connel who would be stricken. It was while he was cursing his infernal bunions, standing in a knee deep pool on the bank of the river. It was an asp that sank its fangs into his leg.

His scream was muffled by Meagher in an instant. Then he began writhing as the venom began to course through his system. Vincent was on him like a hound, demanding to know the color of his attacker. Connel's response was not forthcoming.

Aborigines almost always carry machetes when traversing the jungle. Vincent slashed an X upon Connel's calf, then sucked and spat the poison into the bush. Peta climbed a majestic tree and descended with a jungle leaf. He rubbed the leaf within his palms and spread its residue upon the wound. They would hunt for game while Connel rested. Meagher was left to tend to the thief he had made a friend.

Meagher first met Connel among a crowd of ruffians in the market at Campbell Town. At the time, Connel was full of the drink and spoiling for a fight. He had heard of Meagher and sought to test his mettle. In the crushing boredom of that place such encounters were a sport of sorts.

At first, Meagher dismissed his rude address. Not satisfied with this rebuff, Connel began to follow him along the planks that formed a crude walkway on the muddy street. He alleged that Meagher had given offense and demanded satisfaction. A spate of insults finally caused Meagher to halt and confront Connel.

"What manner of fool are you? Do you provoke a deadly response to pass the time of day in this swill hole?"

"You're a cowardly dog," Connel slurred. "You insult me with your manner and your speech. They call you Meagher of the Sword. I call you a bastard, fearful of a fight."

"Then it's a brawl you want," Meagher whispered, drawing close enough to kiss his tormentor. "Then let's have at it."

By this time a crowd had gathered hoping for a notable occurrence. Connel grabbed for Meagher's throat. Thomas smashed his knee into the bear's groin. Connel tumbled backward and came to rest in the mud of the street. The ridicule of the rabble who were observing the spectacle incensed him. He rose slowly, dropping a dagger from his sleeve into his burly right hand. His game had now turned to mayhem.

Meagher was equal to the challenge. From his waist he drew a knife and beckoned Connel in his direction, backing down an alleyway that afforded a more concealed location for a duel to the death.

Connel rushed at him, seeking an opening to deliver a fatal thrust. Meagher parried then slashed, catching Connel above his right wrist, causing him to drop the dagger into the mud. It was now Meagher's turn to play the tormentor. He leaped upon Connel, from behind, placing his knife against the bear's pulsing neck. He was a breath away from killing and he seemed to welcome the event. His mind soon arrested his passion. Instead, he delivered a well-deserved lesson to a bully boy.

"Tell them you are a braggart and a drunkard," Meagher ordered, spinning Connel toward the crowd and drawing blood from a slice to his neck. "Tell them or you're a dead man. Tell them."

Connel complied, while his band of ruffians began to disperse. He would encounter Thomas again when sober. He would then tender his apology. Before long he became an ally that Meagher could rely upon.

While locked in a battle with the venom coursing through his veins, he spoke to Thomas of his life in Liverpool. Then he focused upon more pressing matters.

"Speak to me Meagher, for I fear I am finished. "Do you believe in a world beyond this place?"

"I believe you will survive and the world beyond will await your arrival. Now rest and forget the notion of dying."

"Are you not afraid of death, Meagher?"

"I fear living as a slave even more."

"You are a friend to me then? I have few friends," Connel confided. "My brother Terence, he was me' friend. He was hanged with a dozen others, after a trial in the Old Bailey. He chose the life of a thief over the workhouse. Are there no workhouses in America, Meagher?"

"I pray there are none."

"Will we make this escape? Or is it all a bloody dream?" Connel's inquiries beseeched Meagher for a meaningful response.

"A dream can become a great notion, my friend. Dream of being free in America."

They remained there awaiting the return of their savage guides. Praying for deliverance from their imprisonment. On the night of the eleventh day they made their way into the swirling treachery of the Bass Strait.

CHAPTER 19

By then that bastard Dennison had enlisted an army to hunt down one Irish rebel. Riders had been dispatched to every settlement with news of Meagher's escape. Red coated dragoons and mercenary cut throats were everywhere, searching, spreading the word that Meagher had given the Crown the slip.

Catherine had seen her beloved's crude likeness nailed to a tree on the main street of Ross. Her confinement was fast approaching. That evening she remained with Da, once again crying herself to sleep, while he sat beside her bed, stroking her head.

O'Donahoe learned of Meagher's escape while engaged in securing provisions. That night he would down a dozen pints in a smoke filled public house and stagger to his domicile in the company of a local tart. John Mitchel, on the other hand, was immersed in his scriptures, while seated within his garden, when the word reached him. He simply smiled and prayed silently that his devoted friend would find his way to America.

Smith O'Brien was sleeping, still weakened by his years of captivity, when awakened by the report from a fellow prisoner that Meagher had once again given the Crown a pinch for their punishment. O'Brien arose, went to a chestnut desk of drawers and removed both pen and paper. There he would write of that fateful night in Waterford, beneath a tricolor flag.

The swirling currents that churned the waters of the Bass Strait, along with a summer squall, had carried the aborigine's boat hither and yon in the darkness. The passage to Waterhouse Island would take all of that black night and most of the early morning. With the sun they came upon the sharks.

At first they saw a solitary whale breeching in the distance. Then their eyes beheld a terrible sight. It was a group of fins, barely visible above the surf, fins that were making their way toward their open boat. Vincent had warned them. The warmth of the water and the multitude of fish that inhabited the Strait would attract the beast that all men of the sea fear. Peta gave to Thomas a spear. They were to strike for the lifeless eyes of the menace, while Connel and his father heaved upon the oars. Meagher would recite the chilling details of that shark attack, again and again, on the eve of battles to come.

There was a frenzy about them, as they passed beneath and beyond the battered boat. It seemed as if the sharks had increased in numbers to nearly two score. It seemed their design was to swamp the boat and feed upon flailing flesh defenseless within the deep. Each followed Vincent's directions, as he struggled to stay the course. Waterhouse Island was visible in the distance.

Again and again they came, while Meagher and Peta plunged their long crude spears into their midst, blood spurting and staining the water about them. When all seemed lost, they were suddenly carried on the surf to the shore, leaving the shark to search for other prey.

Waterhouse Island was a desolate wind-swept rocky place inhabited by platypus and pelican. It provided access to the shipping lanes of New South Wales. It was from these lanes that a rescue had been arranged.

It seemed that Connel had become the acquaintance of a certain seafaring man during a game of chance in Hobart. The man advised Connel that his Captain was an old pirate by the name of Hollingsworth. He had plundered his share of galleons and was not opposed to transporting exiles to Pernambuco for a price.

The ship was the *Elizabeth Thompson* and it was due to set sail from Melbourne Harbor during the third week of January, in the year of our Lord 1853. They were to rendezvous at twilight. They would recognize the vessel by its distinctive sails of scarlet. There was naught to do but wait, concealed by day and afoot by night.

Vincent and Peta had showed them an inlet where an open boat lay beneath the flora that grew in that lonely place. Their provisions were meager and each day brought increased hunger. The aborigines had given Connel their word. They had agreed to keep vigil alongside their contraband for five days and nights.

The rain and wind would soon become relentless, making their means of concealment a muddy mess. At night they shivered, soaked to the bone.

On the fourth night Connel's manner turned dark. He had been railing against the fates for failing to produce a rescue. He then began to despair and vent his spleen toward the others, saving his most odious remarks for Peta. The circumstance of their predicament had made of him a most disagreeable accomplice. Soon he began to make wild accusations, cursing the young aborigine and accusing him of pilfering his rations and plotting behind his back.

He was lying amid the rocks. The darkness and a downpour dangling him near the end of his tether, when Peta passed nearby. Without the hint of a provocation, Connel stood and kicked the lad upon the small of his back, sending him sprawling upon the sand. Vincent retaliated on his son's behalf. Before Meagher could intervene, Connel fell, striking his head upon a rock, the blow rendering him senseless.

During the following day, he lingered, lapsing in and out of a nightmarish nether world. Meagher and the aborigines remained by his side, attempting as best they could to give him comfort. Suddenly he came to and cried for Thomas to hold him. It was as if he were a child seeking the solace of a father's embrace. With a sincere entreaty, he delivered his farewell.

"Forgive me, Meagher. Forgive me, Father, for all..."

With the crude spears that repelled the sharks, they buried Connel beneath the sand on Waterhouse Island. To the world from which he had been exiled, he was a brigand and a common thief. To Meagher, who watched as he died, he was a misguided ally. He would say the words that ushered Connel into eternity. In the years to come, Thomas Meagher would say the words over many who were forsaken and forgotten, many who had been his companions and his allies.

On the morning after the death of Connel, Vincent and Peta prepared for their leaving. They had each grown to respect and admire this white man with the eyes of the wolf, this white man who spoke to them of freedom and America. They walked together to the inlet from which they would depart. Words were not enough to describe their feelings at that moment. They had given their word and kept it. They had kept a vigil of five days and nights and the ship that would bring Meagher his rescue still had not arrived.

For Vincent and his son, it was a time for returning to their primitive world, along the Tamar River. For Thomas, it was a time for continuing his journey alone.

As a red dawn spread across the sky beyond them, their shadows were cast upon the sand. Three shadows cast by the light of a new day, three souls facing the uncertainty of a precarious tomorrow.

Before they pushed their boat into the surf that crashed upon the shore, Meagher embraced them and thanked them for their guidance. With the wave of his right arm, he bid them farewell.

For three more days he remained marooned upon that desolate island, like a pilgrim fasting in the desert. As the sun was descending slowly in the sky on the afternoon of the third day, he stared across the Bass Strait toward Melbourne Harbor one last time. He was at the end of his rope. He knew that he could not last through another day.

It was then that he beheld a most glorious apparition. It was then that his heart leaped within his chest. It was then that he fell upon hands and knees and beseeched the Almighty, praying that his eyes were not deceiving him, that what he beheld was not a mirage. Again he stared and observed the scarlet sails of a ship heading toward him from across the Bass Strait.

It was not a mirage. What he beheld was altogether real. It was the *Elizabeth Thompson,* a three-masted barque bound for Pernambuco, Brazil. Its sails were filled with the wind of promise, filled with the wind of freedom. It would carry him toward a land of liberty a land where slaves and exiles could be free.

CHAPTER 20

*I*t was the promise of liberty and the land that drew us to America. Before their conquest and their servitude, the Irish had been a proud people, in possession of the land and the means of their own destiny. Through force of arms and years of deception their land was taken from them; torn from their grasp by the powerful and their ruthless minions, leaving them to the mercy of the landlords and their overseers.

This was the Ireland of my birth. This was the land that the famine descended upon, causing countless clans to wither and die upon it. Despite our leaving, despite the bitter harvests that drove us away, we remained a people with a yearning for the land. Some have said that the Irish derive their nature from this historical influence of land and clan.

I must speak to you now of the America we entered. By the hundreds of thousands we came, along with the others who had been dispossessed and driven from the land, the others who came in search of liberty, all of us fleeing from the old ways, the oppression and despair of the past. Yet the old ways were sewn deep within the fabric of those who wielded power, even in a land that promised the blessings of liberty and justice for all of its citizens.

We did not dream of cities of gold; nor did we find them. What we found was the same as before; a powerful few seeking to control and oppress a powerless many, their arsenal of weapons included the control of commerce, intolerance and of course, brutality. Yet in America the powerless possessed a powerful promise to combat and defeat this oppression and tyranny.

It was written in the blood of those who had fought and died in America's Revolution. It rang out across a darkened world and awakened it to a new beginning. America had been born with the promise that within its boundaries all men were created equal. It was this promise that would cause so many exiles to fight and die in the fearful carnage of civil war. It was this promise and land enough to make it hold true, that drew us to America.

In Boston, we arrived to find the descendants of the colonists fearful of our difference. The divergence of our native tongues presented a din of babble to their unaccustomed ears.

At first, they sought to ignore us, to restrict our movements to areas that were well within their firm control. Yet our numbers soon overflowed these geographical boundaries and caused them to resort to more sinister means of oppression. These were the means used by those who called themselves Nativists and Know Nothings. They despised our difference and spread lies about our beliefs.

It is the irony of man that he will strive and achieve for himself and his progeny and then through that achievement seek to control and oppress those whom he can master. In the cities of America, we began to gather like locusts, presenting a persistent problem for those concerned with maintaining their hold upon the reins of power.

Yet others saw themselves in us. Others who had come to America with the self-same hopes became sympathetic to our plight and our yearning for liberty. These were the ones who had opened their eyes to our identity of spirit and their hearts soon followed.

We, who came to America during that time, were exiles from the old world. A world we had grown to despise. In that world we had never been given the promise of liberty. Our history had never been blessed with a fervent belief in the Natural Rights of Man. Our institutions were based upon privilege and inheritance, excluding the teeming masses from that which makes life upon this earth fruitful and free.

In America, the sacred documents that brought that Nation into being, echoed with this promise, filling us with the hope of a life where happiness could be pursued. This was the promise that caused those in power to fear us. For they had believed in the same promise and saw in the expanse of America a means of making that promise hold true.

They were haunted by the spirit of their own cherished beliefs, yet disposed to deny the blessings of liberty to those who had come like the flow of the tide to their shores. Our dissimilar origins, cultures and colors became ready excuses for the denial of liberty's promise within their dominion.

In order to thrive in the America we found, it was essential that we work and that we learn. Those who opposed our betterment understood well that through these avenues, we could become a force to be reckoned with. That is how they sought to thwart our advance. At every turn they were there to block our employment and our education.

Yet our numbers and our clannish ways would prevent them from the achievement of their ends. Soon we began to form secret societies and organizations that fostered employment and the education of those unable to read or write. Soon more and more of our people began to gain entry into areas of commerce and politics that brought money and power to the places where we lived and worked. Through our religious devotion and the priests and nuns that ministered to our people, we grew strong in spirit, believing that we would one day become the equals of those determined to oppress us.

I suppose it all started with the clan after all. In the valleys of Erin the Dominican Friars discovered a tribal people possessed of a valiant spirit, a people who shed each other's blood with a ruthless fervor. The Dominicans and later the Jesuits focused this fervor upon the story of Jesus and the sacrifice of hanging upon a cross. This was a powerful change in the history of our people.

In Ireland, the Dominicans built their monasteries and the Jesuits their schools. Still the clans continued to make war upon each other and then seek atonement for their bloody ways. It was our nature, I suppose, to be warlike, then return to more righteous ways; to be wayward, then find our way back home.

I recall a time during the Peninsula Campaign when they labeled General McClellan a coward and Lincoln a fool. All at that hour seemed to have forsaken us. That was when the spirit of the clan arose within our ranks, our flags, our fidelity and our ferocity, emerging like specters from the Dark Ages, rising from that time when the clan was all. Our fervor was rekindled from our past.

We would come to revel in the fighting and killing ways of our ancestry. That was the spirit of the regiments that comprised the Irish Brigade. In battles most harrowing, we closed ranks and fought as of old. We were a fierce clan indeed, and we were led by men of strength and purpose, men who believed that our valor would demonstrate our worthiness as Americans, men like our one and only chieftain, Thomas Francis Meagher.

"Would you permit me to speak to you of other matters, Captain?" O'Keefe suddenly requested.

He was standing at the window of the railway carriage, watching the mist descend upon the English countryside. It seemed I had dozed off during his recitation and wrestled with a fitful sleep. His entreaty had awakened me and caused me to tender my sincerest apology.

"It is I who should apologize," he said. "I sometimes become lost in the memory of times past. Shall we have another drink," he offered, again passing his flask and focusing upon my person.

This time I partook of his offering in greater detail. I knew that with each passing hour, I was drawing closer to my destination and dreaded the thought of returning to the front.

"There are no demons as devilish as those of our own creation, Captain. Don't you agree?" he said, as he sat across from me. "I suppose the imagination can be our greatest ally, as well as our most formidable adversary."

"I suppose," was my anxious reply, for I was unwilling to share my torment with a stranger on a train, no matter how familiar we had become. Yet, he seemed at all times to comprehend my sentiments and to address them without my elaboration.

"Courage is a mysterious quality indeed, Captain. Who knows from whence it arises. We are all mortal men with mortal fears. Fear is as natural as birth and death and the love of a mother for her child. It causes us to be vigilant and directs us toward our means of survival upon this earth. From time to time, all of us question whether we are weak and more inclined to give way to our fears than other men. It is a misgiving that is particular to those who have seen the horror of battle."

"Be not afraid, Captain. Courage will flow from the belief that only the dead are without fear and war is a most unnatural circumstance. A recognition that fear is a natural state of being will aid in its conquest by courage. Add to that an unselfish dedication to your men and you may find yourself able to control, but not eliminate this natural state of fear. In this life there are many lessons to be learned. Each day provides us with the chance to learn more and by that learning rise above the form that confines us here."

"Is that why you read so diligently from that crimson text?" I asked.

"No," he replied. "That is another lesson. It will make itself known in good time, all in good time, Captain."

"Did you ever doubt yourself? Did you ever fear for your sanity?" I heard myself asking against my will.

"I do not envy you your youth or your demons, Captain. War by its very definition is depraved. Killing another for a cause or a country is against all laws of nature. Be not so hard upon yourself, and search inside for that which is eternal. Therein you will find your serenity, even in battle most bloody. Now let me return again to my tale of Meagher and his Irish Brigade."

PART TWO

THAT SPLENDID
GREEN APPLE

CHAPTER 21

*I*t was in New York City, when I saw Meagher again. It is said he landed first in San Francisco and tried his hand in the gold fields outside Sacramento. It is said that he struck it rich and after working his claim, happened upon a pair of scoundrels having their way with a dim witted girl. He despised cruelty toward the weak and the defenseless. He made those scoundrels pay and pay dearly for their transgression.

Their uncle, who called himself the sheriff, came for Meagher that night with a mob in tow. When they tore up the backstairs of his boarding house, torches ablaze, brave with the drink, Thomas was long gone and hard to find. He had grabbed a sack of the amber dust and made his way to San Francisco upon a spirited mare. He was armed with a dirk knife and a dueling pistol. He was dark and dangerous during those years. The disorder of that time required such a disposition.

San Francisco was the perfect city for an Irish rogue to make up for years of exile and deprivation. There was a saloon and a brothel called the *Barbary Coast*. Meagher became a silent partner to a French Count who fled Marseille with the family's fortune. He enjoyed the company of an assortment of characters, quite beyond description. There were bully boys from Mayo and Roscommon, a half breed by the name of Quill and a dwarf that once bit a landlord's private parts in a dispute over the payment of rent.

Meagher was a rare breed to them all. At one moment he would recite verse. At the other, he would threaten a brigand who had given offense. He spoke to me often of that time, admitting that he was wholly without restraint and inclined to earthly pursuits. Meagher would never wear the pretense of the plaster saint. Like many of us, he was a man of passion with feet of clay.

Meagher's arrival in New York was a most momentous occasion for those of Hibernian stock. He arrived in the middle of the night; his ship bound for the South Street Seaport. He was on route from New Orleans, finally making his way to his long prayed for destination. He wondered why the shores seemed to shimmer with fire as his ship weighed anchor.

Unknown to him, the Irish immigrant population of New York had been awaiting his arrival. *The Boston Pilot* and other Irish newspapers had kept his legend alive. Bills had been introduced in Congress to petition the British to set the exiles of the "48" uprising free. The tale of Meagher and his cohorts had been described on city sidewalks and in the pubs and halls where the sons of Erin gathered. There were thousands of his countrymen who turned out to bid him welcome; their torches lighting his way through the darkened streets.

It was a time of shooting stars and blazing rockets. It was the time when Meagher came home to his City; a place where his legend and his legions would grow. By the fall of *1857* he would become engaged in the newspaper trade. That would be his thirty fourth year.

I must speak to you of our meeting, for it leaves a lesson of loyalty's reward. From necessity, I departed from Boston. I had fallen in with a desperate lot that soon turned to schemes and events that were criminal in intent. I had been drinking on a regular turn and losing hope of finding a suitable occupation. I had arrived that morning by rail, my pockets as barren as my cupboards back in Boston. I had read Meagher's writings in the *Irish News.* Before I set eyes upon his manly figure and face, I was met by the resonance of his voice. As the sun was sinking slowly over the city, he was engaged in a grand performance on a platform in the center of Madison Square.

The leaves on the trees that festooned that park were ablaze with hues of gold and scarlet. In reaching that location, I had traversed that magnificent thoroughfare known as Broadway. It was a city alive with hope and promise. There were carriages and riders bouncing about, and a vibrant mixture of foreign born. Meagher was dressed in a green frock coat. His angular face now exhibited both mustache and manicured chin whiskers. His hair fell almost to his shoulder in dark brown ringlets. His violet eyes blazed as before, while the soaring passion of his melodious voice delivered words of wit and wisdom. He was addressing the thousands that had gathered to hear him speak, telling them of the courage of a cherished friend.

"My friends, I come before you to speak of one who remains a prisoner. One whose character and devotion to the cause of Ireland's freedom became the flame that ignited a relentless fire. You, who have come to America in the hope of freedom, must not forget the man whose courage and sacrifice stood out as a beacon light, shining forth toward the promise of this tomorrow. We must give notice to the world. We must petition our leaders. We must expose the injustices perpetrated upon the people of Ireland and cry out in one irresistible voice that John Mitchel must be set free."

The multitude that had gathered was a melting pot indeed. As I made my way toward Meagher's ringing address, I saw Celtic visages throughout. They were young and vital, whitened and bent. There were sweethearts and families. Some were dressed in finery, but most were not. There were Irish children everywhere. Yet, this was more than an Irish occasion. Many came to hear Meagher's words who had never heard of the Irish Sea or the shops in Dublin Town.

There were the Poles, who stood together in rows, their eager faces turned toward the sun. Perhaps they did not comprehend the meaning of his words, yet they fully understood, that they were playing a part in a free assembly. They too had fled oppression and enslavement to the landlords.

I saw a Russian family of six. They were a proud and comely group. The oldest son was carrying a balalaika at the ready. He was preparing to play a tune and pass the hat for pennies. His performance would allow his family to eat.

There were German acrobats and an aspiring operatic soprano, awaiting her debut before that festive audience. There were Norwegians and Dutch in wooden shoes and hats like nestling butterflies. And, there were two coffee colored freedmen, standing beyond them all, watching warily from a small hill, attracted but not encouraged by the crowd.

The crowd was Meagher's instrument, his emanation. The Irish shouted his name again and again, while the others chimed in. There was a delirium, a sincerity of sentiment for Thomas that made my heart leap. In

New York, Thomas Meagher had found his loyal following. I resolved there and then that I too would follow him, wherever the fates would lead.

I made my way toward him, buffeted by the crowd. It was as if I was an open boat, adrift in a surging sea. I saw his figure passing beyond my reach and cried his name. He was surrounded by a phalanx of companions. He did not hear my call. I fought my way closer, as he was swept away toward a waiting carriage. I reached his proximity as the carriage door closed. Suddenly he was gone, and I was left alone.

It was there that I encountered the one we called William Herbert. He had become a loyal friend to Meagher in San Francisco. His name at birth was Yuri Friedovich. A Russian Jew, he changed his spots and his name on many an occasion. He would become a Lieutenant in the Sixty Ninth Regiment.

Herbert was standing near to Meagher's carriage as it departed. A handsome man with a long, slender frame and face, his eyes were gentle orbs of brownish grey and his chestnut hair shone in the sunlight. He was impeccable in a blue frock coat and trousers. Sensing my despair in failing to reach Meagher, he spoke to me with an engaging kindness. His speech bore the trace of the Ukraine.

"You appear disappointed. Is there message I may convey on your behalf?"

"I am an old friend. We fought alongside each other. My name is O'Keefe, Cornelius O'Keefe."

"You may reach him in care of Metropolitan Hotel. You may use my name as introduction. I am William Herbert."

"Pleased to make your acquaintance. When would a meeting be convenient?"

"There is little ceremony among us. Please, come this evening. I convey your message upon my return. I am certain he will enjoy the company. Come tonight... Metropolitan Hotel."

With that, he too was transported by carriage from the crowd that had gathered at Madison Square. I recollect the feeling of warmth that swept over my person on that occasion. As the sun set over the City of New York, I traversed its thoroughfares and squares, content in the knowledge that I had finally found a home.

CHAPTER 22

*I*n the lobby of the Metropolitan Hotel the fragrance of the ladies provided an entrancing bouquet. The formally attired gathering was making its way up a sweeping staircase; embroidered it seemed in a sea of flowers, when I caught sight of the one called William Herbert. He was at the entrance to a sumptuous ballroom, wearing an amber coat and trousers. His violin greeted the invited guests with a Mozart Sonata.

Our eyes met and his welcome was warm and apparent. I entered and made my way to a most delightful table, where punch was being served and young ladies courted. I would await the finale to the violinist's salute and accompany him to a suitable location, a location where I might share a moment with Meagher.

It seemed I had arrived in New York at the time of the Harvest Ball. In the crowd were luminaries and Archbishops, Fenians and "Free Soilers." It was a representative gathering of New York's Irish elite. I was placed at a table near the far door. Herbert told me to wait and he would bring Thomas around for a visit. There was a vibrant infectious air that permeated that celebration. Perhaps it was the punch, but more likely it was the personages who were drawn to that place and time.

Meagher soon arrived in the company of a striking young woman with the earmarks of a cultured upbringing. He was attired in a black coat and tails. He wore a broad emerald sash across his manly chest, as did several of the men in his company.

For two years he had served as a law clerk to Justice Robert Emmet in the Manhattan Court of Common Pleas. By the time of the Harvest Ball, he was a barrister of considerable promise and influence, as well as a contributing editor to the weekly publication of the *Irish News*. He was a man who had made his mark and the shepherd of a loyal following. Years later he and I would remember those days before the Rebellion with fondness.

I was advised by William Herbert that Meagher had been the recipient of much suffering since his escape from exile in that land beyond the seas. A son named Patrick was born in Tasmania but his beloved Catherine had not survived. The child would be brought to Waterford and raised under his father's direction.

After three sorrow filled years as a widower, Thomas met and married the lovely Elizabeth Townsend, the daughter of a wealthy New York merchant. Her father had opposed their union from the outset, believing that Meagher was lacking in property and suitable prospects for the future. Through her love and her charming ways, she softened the old man's heart. Begrudgingly, he gave them his blessing.

Elizabeth was Meagher's equal in intelligence and his superior in custom and grace. On that evening she was totally radiant in a gossamer gown of blue, her golden hair and sparkling hazel eyes perfectly complementing a slender womanly frame. One could tell by the way they responded to each other, that they were joined in love's embrace.

There was a full orchestra of brass and strings that performed a succession of reels and waltzes under a dozen candled chandeliers. I watched with admiration as Meagher swept his sweet Elizabeth off her feet again and again. In an effortless, manly way he took the lead on that occasion, urging others to follow them in that merry display.

I reveled in the fragrance and the flavor of that evening, returning repeatedly to the table where the punch was dispensed. It was while I was so engaged that I became acquainted with the lady who would become my wife. Alas, that is another story, too detailed and meaningful for inclusion within this recitation.

As the evening wore on, I noticed that Meagher had retired to a spacious veranda overlooking that vibrant thoroughfare known as Broadway. At that time he was in the company of the others who wore the emerald sash. Although William Herbert was supposed to arrange a rendezvous, he seemed more involved in the conquest of an alluring coquette who fluttered a lavender fan above her heaving breasts.

Thereupon, I decided to make my own introduction to the one I would later follow into battle. As I made my way toward him, he was seated amid a crowd of nine. These were the men around whom the Sixty Ninth Regiment of the New York Volunteers would be organized. They would become the core of that splendid green apple, known to history as The Irish Brigade.

I will introduce you to them now. For their tale of courage and camaraderie is the essence of the history you seek. Still today, I marvel at the deeds I witnessed. The valor of the Brigade would be displayed again and again, upon fields that ran red with blood and became the subject of legend. I suppose it was our heritage that determined our destiny.

Meagher was engaged in a heated discussion of the *Dredd Scott Case* when his attention was drawn to my familiar face, coming toward him from across that spacious veranda. I must admit that I was fearful of him not recollecting our times together. After all, the passage of nearly a decade had occurred and we had each been transformed by the years and their trying circumstance. He did not forget me, however, and rose in a joyful manner to renew our companionship. He raised that unforgettable voice in an allusion to one of his favored biblical passages.

"Set another place at the table. He who has been lost is now found. Gentleman, a brother from before has arrived among us. I introduce you to an old and valiant friend of our cause, Cornelius O'Keefe."

Each of them stood, as if I were a brother to be embraced. Each was directed by the presence of Meagher. His warmth and genuine affection for a stranger had transformed that stranger into a sibling. In that circle there would be no pointed angles, no lone wolfs or Judas goats.

I remember it as if it were last evening, their faces so vital and indelible. They were at the summit of their lives and they believed in a higher destiny. The rattle of sabers had begun throughout the Union and young Irish men were about to perish on a scale never seen. In a war none dared to imagine.

I believe it was Michael Corcoran who most impressed. Like his father before him, and the chivalrous Earl of Lucan from whom he was descended, he was a lighthouse of strength and magnetism. His stature soared above the others. He was a reserved and reverent man with a broad forehead and drooping mustache.

The features of his manly face were angular and prominent, while his teeth and his dark hair were straight and strong. At that time he was a major in the Sixty Ninth Regiment of New York's Militia. When not in uniform, he was the proprietor of the Hibernian Hall, the location of many a rousing Fenian gathering. In Ireland, Corcoran had been a postal clerk and a member of the Constabulary. During the insurrection of "48" he resigned these positions and threw in with our Confederation. I recalled observing him at Clonmel during the trial. He had fled, before the peelers could catch up with him.

Like many others, he lived by his wits upon entering New York. He was without peer in gallantry, and displayed a firm resolve to one day free his beloved Erin by force of arms. He and Thomas were our archangels. That was the first month of his thirtieth year.

Next to him was Robert Nugent. Like Corcoran he was a tall man of great dignity. A native of County Down, he was a modest, loyal companion, content to follow the lead of those who could fire the crowd. He was a fine judge of brave men and sturdy horseflesh with a high narrow forehead and an unruly set of coarse black chin whiskers. I remember most the manner of his gait. With his long thin legs and erect posture, he exhibited the slow, deliberate ambulation of a whooping crane.

As I recall, Nugent had lost his mother and brother to the fever before boarding a coffin ship bound for Quebec. He arrived in New York with both wife and child. Like so many of his countrymen, he took up residence in the borough of Brooklyn.

Nugent was a man of considerable learning who enjoyed fine literature and poetry. I believe he was the manager of a dry goods emporium before joining the Old Sixty Ninth. He and I were born within ten days of one another. He and I were about to embark upon our twenty ninth year. I admired his strength of purpose and his courage under fire. In the blood and agony of Fredericksburg I would watch him fall.

Laurence Reynolds was a surgeon with a keen wit and a steady hand. Born in Waterford, he was educated in London. It was there that he became a famous Chartist. A poet and a scholar, he would write of Erin and the Irish Brigade with an ear for the essence of thoughts eternal.

Reynolds was a small and slender man in his forty first year. With the years his chestnut hair had become streaked with silver. On occasion he would wear spectacles upon his cherubic face, thus resembling an erudite school boy. His pale blue eyes signaled a nature of kindness and serenity that encouraged the disclosure of intimate details.

A confidante to us all, he had a youthful vigor that surpassed that of men half his age. He had a notable tenor singing voice and was known for his repertoire of bawdy jokes. He too had joined in the uprising of '48', fleeing from Dublin with little more than the clothes upon his back. A most sincere man, it was he who would assist Meagher in writing so many of the sorrowful letters to mothers and fathers whose sons would depart for war, never to return again.

The next to make my acquaintance were Jack Gosson and Charles Lucky. Captain Jack, as he was called, was a barrel-chested mountain of a man, with hands like banjos and wavy black hair. The son of a Dublin Solicitor, he was an adventurous, incorrigible rogue.

Fearing that his son's wayward notions would lead him to the gallows, Gosson's father prevailed upon Daniel O'Connell to arrange for his appointment to the Austrian Army. Once enlisted, he fought with distinction in Syria and used his manly charms to seduce one of the Caliphs' concubines.

Before his twenty first year, he became a color sergeant and fought in the Alps of Italy under the command of Graf Radetsky. Once, while engaged in a skirmish on the outskirts of Brescia, he was thrown from his horse and rendered senseless. It was then that a stalwart corporal within his regiment came to his rescue, thereby winning his undying gratitude.

The corporal was the second son of a Milanese noble, a small muscular man with dark aquiline features and a magnificent head of black hair. His name was Carlo Luchesse. After their service with the Austrian Army had run its course, he and Luchesse made their way to America. Upon their arrival in New York, they made a name for themselves among the immigrant population in The Five Points. It was there that they became associated with Boss Tweed.

When Thomas Meagher arrived they saw an opportunity and volunteered their services as his guardians. It was Thomas who bestowed the name of Charles Lucky upon Luchesse. Captain Gosson and Lieutenant Lucky would become the bravest of the brave within the Irish Brigade.

They were each in a merry state indeed, when Meagher introduced them to me.

Among the officers who would provide distinguished service in the War of Rebellion, there were many who received their baptism of fire within the Papal Brigade. Daniel Kirby was one of these. He hailed from Kerry, receiving his commission through the intercession of a Jesuit who had studied in Rome and taught him at Clongowes Wood. He excelled in mathematics and knew well the principles of Newton and the astronomy of Galileo.

He was an elegant gentleman and a favorite of the ladies, with golden hair, dark brown eyes and a small straight nose that turned up in an attractive sort of way. Like Meagher he was a master swordsman who gravitated to danger and hopeless causes.

It was said that his father was robbed and murdered by a band of drunken ruffians during the time of the Great Hunger. Upon his return from service on the Continent, he swore revenge and killed each and every one of those bastards in a most frightful manner.

Kirby made his way to America through Quebec. At first, he built a home in Philadelphia and began to make his mark. Later the wanderlust caused him to travel by river boat to the Port of New Orleans. There he would meet and marry a southern lady of much allure, yet little common sense. While in Louisiana, he applied himself to matters of commerce and secured a spacious homestead near Baton Rouge.

His business pursuits would eventually bring him to New York. There, at a Fenian gathering, he made the acquaintance of Michael Corcoran. It was Corcoran who introduced him to Meagher. On the veranda of the Metropolitan Hotel, it was Meagher who introduced him to me. On that evening he was in his thirty first year and a proud son of the State of Louisiana.

I had become acquainted with Johnny Kavanaugh long before that evening. On that dark rainy day in the village of Ballingarry, I watched as a fifteen year old Kavanaugh was carried from the widow McCormack's yard, wounded in the leg by the discharge of a coward's musket. I was told that he escaped to France and remained with friends in the Port of Le Havre. I heard the British placed a generous price upon his head. I was pleased to see that he was now a fine figure of a young man.

At twenty four, Kavanaugh was the favorite of the group. He had deep set green eyes, golden hair and a slight limp to his left leg. Of all the members of the Brigade, Johnny Kavanaugh is the one I miss most. My fondest wish would be to see his smiling face once again.

Felix Duffy was a captain in the Sixty Ninth Regiment of the New York Militia when we made acquaintance. He was a veteran of the Mexican War and an able leader of men. Although short of stature, he possessed a strong sinewy frame that could withstand the most extreme duress. He was a devout, church-going man with orange colored hair and pointed features who adored his wife Mary and doted upon his five children.

Although he had passed his thirty fifth year, he too seemed much younger. It was Duffy who would keep his promise to the mothers of the boys he led, making sure they attended Mass and wrote home every week. It was Duffy who would snatch the colors from the enemy at Malvern Hill and save Meagher's life in the battle before Bloody Lane.

James Quinlan was an engineer by trade and likewise a member of the Old Sixty Ninth. He was a personable man who made his living by the erection of bridges and buildings throughout New York and Brooklyn. A thirty year old native of Galway, he could sketch the most glorious landscapes in the blink of an eye. He was a portly man with bright blue eyes, a fine head of golden hair and rounded shoulders.

On rare occasions he would partake of too much whiskey and relate prodigious tales concerning his prowess as an engineer. He was a wonderful foil for the pranks of Captain Gosson. It was Quinlan who would assure the boys that our General Staff would never order us to cross a river under fire and engage the enemy by a frontal assault on Marye's Heights. Many a brave lad would pay the ultimate price during that incredible act of folly.

As I mentioned, Meagher had engaged the gathering upon the veranda in a heated discussion of the *Dredd Scott Case*. Not having heard of the matter, I watched with a keen interest as this fiery disciple of Jefferson and Paine stood among us, wrestling with the beast that would soon tear the Union apart.

"Have we not learned the lesson of our own sad history? I say that the enslavement of any man diminishes us all. I fear it will prove our undoing, gentlemen. I fear it will."

"These blacks are not men like us," Kirby argued. "It is the will of God that has made them slaves."

"Are they not born like us, suckled like us?" Meagher asked. "The Nativists say that we are less than they, fit only for a life in the gutter."

"This is Abolitionist talk!" Kirby cried, rising to confront Thomas, his face flushed with the anger that welled inside him. "Do you side with those who condemn men from my state, men who care for their slaves and put them to work in the fields?"

"The Abolitionist and the Nativist are both serpents," Corcoran shouted, standing between Meagher and Kirby. "I say enough with this talk of slaves and masters. Let us not fight over matters such as these. Let us unite for the Fenian Cause. Gentlemen, here's to a free Erin!"

I recall that we all stood at that point and raised our glasses in the hope of Ireland's freedom. Yet, I remember feeling uneasy, uncertain about the matters that Thomas had mentioned. In The Declaration of Independence, there was no accounting for the slave. Only war could bring a balance to America's ledger.

CHAPTER 23

Three years would pass. Years that resounded like a terrible thunder with talk of slaves and masters. Years that saw the poison of human bondage infect every organ of the Union.

In Ireland, we had witnessed the famine spread its misery over the land of our birth. In America, we witnessed the shadow of slavery spreading its darkness over our adopted land. There was a cataclysmic clash of wills in the wind. The old ways of the aristocrat would die hard. A reckoning was sweeping towards us like a relentless river. The Irish Brigade would be created to help stem its torrent.

I suppose I should tell you of Meagher and his exploits during this period. As a barrister in the Law firm of Meagher and Campbell, he engaged in the trial of infamous cases. It was Meagher who assisted in the defense of the impulsive Daniel Sickles, after he shot his wife's lover. This was the same Daniel Sickles who would lead his men to the slaughter at Gettysburg.

As a lecturer, Meagher told of Ireland's heroes and his sojourn in Costa Rica. It was there that he envisioned a canal that would link the Atlantic to the Pacific. In Philadelphia, Boston and New Orleans, he wove his spell over the crowds, thrilling them with his wondrous speaking voice and his glorious allusions.

I accompanied him on many of these occasions. You see, following that night at the Metropolitan Hotel, I was able to secure employment within the

125

offices of the *Tribune*. There I would deliver reports on matters of interest to our readers. The comings and goings of Thomas Meagher and the others who had been tried for treason at Clonmel were always a noteworthy subject.

During those years that preceded the war, Thomas had kept the cause of his fellow exiles alive, traveling throughout the Union and lecturing tirelessly upon the injustice of their imprisonment. As I have told you, MacManus, Mitchel, and O'Donahoe would all live to breathe the free air of America. William Smith O'Brien, however, would never partake in its promise. After a sojourn in Brussels following a pardon by Queen Victoria, he would die in seclusion. William Smith O'Brien was an Irish patriot and a man for the ages.

Terrance MacManus was the first to make his escape from the exile of Tasmania. After making his way to California he would enlist in the Union Army and rise through the ranks.

It was through Meagher's efforts that both Mitchel and O'Donahoe were enabled to gain their freedom. After much adventure they each arrived in the city of New York. It was a joyous occasion for Meagher to be reunited with these loyal companions. They each had suffered much hardship in exile without losing their devotion to the cause of a free Ireland.

In America, Mitchel would once again follow the rebel's way. Through the power of his pen he would gather support for the Southern Cause and eventually move his family to the Virginia countryside. It was there that his three sons would enlist and fight beneath the Stars and Bars.

As for O'Donahoe, I believe he succumbed to the drink and died a pauper under suspect circumstance. I recall that Meagher was deeply saddened, when he learned of his passing. It was Meagher who penned his touching obituary within the *Irish News*.

I particularly recall one occasion during that period, when Meagher and I traveled to New Orleans. He had been asked to lecture a gathering of Irish born on the matter of The Young Ireland Movement. I remember a hall packed to the rafters with those who had fled the famine and made their way to the Southern ports of Savannah, Charleston and New Orleans. All were enamored of Meagher. At a dinner in his honor thereafter, he was asked his position on the subject of secession. Meagher was diplomatic in his response, respecting the views of those who favored the Southern cause, yet insisting that the preservation of the Union was essential to the freedom of the Irish people.

While making our way back to the hotel, we passed through Jackson Square. It was there that Meagher suddenly ordered the driver of our carriage to stop and await our return. With that, he grabbed me by the arm and led me down an alleyway to a courtyard covered with vines and wild flowers. It was a steamy September in the year 1860 and the storm clouds of insurrection were gathering over the land.

We came to an ornate door that bore the head of a wolf upon it. It was apparent that Meagher had been to that location before. He then proceeded to rap a gentle tattoo on this door with his walking stick. It was as if it were a password of some sort. I remember asking him. "What manner of place is this, Thomas?"

With the wink of his eye, he rapped this peculiar tattoo once again. At that point the door slowly opened and a dwarf with a disfigured face bade Meagher welcome. He then beckoned us to enter, holding a lantern.

He led us through a damp, dark catacomb with chambers on either side. I recall the walls being covered with murals that made me strangely uneasy. It seemed as if we had entered some nether world. I was about to speak when we stopped.

The dwarf had motioned to us to remain. He then proceeded onward toward a small door which was the color of the orchid. He seemed to whisper an incantation and then beckoned us toward him. I followed Meagher as the door opened from within. It was necessary to stoop in order to gain entry to this coal black chamber.

Suddenly, a candle was lit and we beheld an old woman seated before a circular table of varnished oak. She was neat in appearance with a regal bearing. She wore a bonnet upon her hoary head and an emerald necklace around her wrinkled neck. Her face was narrow, with tiny spectacles covering sorrow filled azure eyes. She commanded Meagher to draw closer, as she handed him a set of peculiar cards. Meagher shuffled them and laid them upon the table. She looked upon him and then upon me. Her whispered voice bore the trace of a brogue.

"Have you come to seek what lies ahead for thee?

"Yes mother," Meagher answered respectfully.

"Why do you bring a stranger to this place?"

"He is an old friend, mother."

"He must not hear what the cards tell us. This is for your ears only. Draw closer, my wild one, and I will reveal what you seek."

As she turned each card over, she whispered in Meagher's ear. I will not forget the sadness that passed over his handsome face, as she spoke. It was as if his heart was wounded by her words. Why he had come to that mysterious place; I cannot imagine. You see, Meagher was a breed apart. Like a wild, dark river, he possessed depths and passages that none could fathom.

I have often wondered if this ancient creature had truly given him an insight into the terrible times that were ahead, for he was a man who spoke often of his destiny, as if he had been given a vision of such things.

As our carriage made its way toward our hotel, we passed by the levee. There beneath the light of many torches, we happened upon a most distressing event. Meagher commanded that the driver again come to a halt. There upon the docks, we beheld a mass of nearly naked slaves being unloaded from a sailing ship. I recall the terrible crack of the whips and the baying of tethered hounds.

I had never seen such a sorry sight. There were men and boys shackled by chains. There were women, wailing with sorrow, wailing over terrified children of tender years. I remember Meagher staring from the window of the carriage, his face now filled with rage and shame. He spoke in a near whisper. It was the same voice I heard before that bloody morning in Limerick.

"I once thought that the rebel's cause would always be my calling. I tell you O'Keefe, rebellion in the name of this evil endangers us all."

I would remember that night in New Orleans. For it was the time of my own awakening. I would recall the words of Lincoln. Our Union had indeed become a house divided. The blight of black slavery was certain to cause that house to crumble and fall upon itself. Within its ruins there would be no safe haven, no adopted home. We could not let that occur.

Upon our return to New York there was much anticipation of the upcoming Presidential election. Lincoln was not the popular choice among the Irish. They were in favor of the Democratic Party and their feisty candidate, Stephen Douglas. To the immigrant, the Tammany ward bosses were their source of jobs and their only chance to escape from hopeless poverty. To the Irish, the Republicans were Abolitionists and Nativists.

We believed that the ones who clamored loudest for the end of slavery were the same ones who despised us most. As Corcoran had said, the Abolitionist and the Nativist were both serpents. In Boston and Philadelphia, it seemed that the powerful men who championed the Republican Cause reserved their condemnation for the slave traders and the Irish.

To them we were fit only to live like beasts. It was our loyal compatriot, Richard O'Gorman, who helped to revise the manner of our thinking. As a lawyer, he would champion the cause of a free Ireland and speak out against black slavery.

I had always admired O'Gorman. In Ireland, he was one of the first to rise up against the oppression of the British Empire. He was a handsome man, with fiery blue eyes, chestnut hair and a strong sinewy frame.

His intellect and his courage were exemplary and his laugh made others feel joyful, even under the most trying of circumstances. He, along with Meagher and Smith O'Brien had traveled to Paris in a vain effort to enlist the French as allies in our rebellion. He would remain our loyal friend to the end of his days.

I remember an afternoon in New York when Meagher and I encountered O'Gorman as he was making his way back to his law office. He had just succeeded in winning a verdict for a desperate client accused of embezzling funds and he was in the mood to make merry with some old friends.

I remember entering a drinking establishment filled with cigar smoke and Irish rogues. I don't believe we were required to purchase a single drink, once O'Gorman announced that he had just won his case. I recall waking up the following morning in O'Gorman's office, with Meagher asleep on the floor. There must have been a fine time had by all. I only wish I could remember more of it.

Thomas was living on Fifth Avenue during that period. By then he had grown tired of lecturing and the practice of law. He had even given up his position with the *Irish News*. As I recall, he was being considered by President Buchanan for a diplomatic position in Nicaragua or some such Central American outpost. In truth, he was a man in search of himself. The wanderlust within his rebel soul had once again taken hold and become a source of discontent for his devoted wife, Elizabeth.

I remember we were all there one evening, Corcoran, Nugent, Dr. Reynolds, William Herbert, O'Gorman and myself. There was an abundance of drink and spirited conversation. I recall a discourse by Corcoran concerning matters near to his heart.

"We must make ready for an incursion into Canada," Corcoran declared, standing in Meagher's study. "I can at this time raise a force of three thousand men. With your help and support my friends, England will be forced to defend her dominion to the North. This is our means of ridding Ireland of its oppression."

"I have heard this all before, Michael," Meagher responded.

"It is not the time for such an attack. A force of three thousand is no match for the might of the British Army. Your Fenian Brotherhood will be cut down like ripened corn."

"Tell them, Richard," Corcoran cried to O'Gorman, his voice rising with the blood in his manly Irish face. "Tell them all. Have we not the support of thousands here and at home? With proper training and sufficient arms, we can become a force to be reckoned with. Tell them."

O'Gorman had been sitting in the corner of Meagher's spacious library, texts and classics of every description surrounding him. Unlike the rest of us, he had not partaken of the household's brandy. He was the brightest of our group. He rose and stroked his chin, as if in contemplation. As soon as he spoke, we knew that his thoughts about the future of our adopted nation were most profound.

"No man is more devoted to the Fenian Cause than am I. In my darkest solitude the hope of a free Ireland is what sustains me. I am proud to call the Fenians, brothers unto death. I am devoted to the overthrow of British rule by those trained in the military arts. Yet, the time for such an undertaking is not nigh. I have heard Lincoln speak at the Music Hall in Boston. I was inclined to reject his remarks due to my political preference, yet I was taken by his words and swayed by his conviction."

"This Union is our last best hope of freedom, gentlemen. The flag that flies over this fair city has become our flag. I am certain that some of us have looked upon the Southern cause as a noble and righteous one. For we all have the blood of the rebel running through our veins, for we all have friends and relations residing among the Southern States. Yet the matters at hand are far beyond those of faction. This Union and this flag must not be scorned and desecrated by those who preach secession. Before all other causes, we must first preserve the Union against those who would cause it to fail. This is our solemn duty, gentleman."

They say that certain men have the gift of prophecy. On that November night in the year 1860, an Irish rebel by the name of O'Gorman spoke to us of things to come. Before the election of Lincoln, before the cannons fired upon Fort Sumter, our band would become one in the defense of America.

CHAPTER 24

efore they could court-martial Corcoran for refusing to parade the Sixty Ninth in front of the Prince of Wales, the Confederates fired on our flag as it flew over Fort Sumter. To Meagher this was a sacrilege.

He had abided the slavery of the black race. He had even been entertained by slave holders upon their plantations, without uttering a protest to their practice of that "peculiar institution". But firing upon Old Glory was another kettle of fish. The Tricolor and the Stars and Stripes were Meagher's sacred cloth. When Beauregard and his bunch of strutting peacocks blew holes through the flag, the killing season commenced.

Lincoln knew what the Union needed. It needed an army, an army that could protect Washington and carry the scourge of battle into the states who had dared to secede. The Civil War was commenced by those who sought protection for the old ways, the ways of the aristocrat and the slaveholder. Many an Irishman would fight beneath the Stars and Bars. Many more would join the ranks of the Union's army. Rivers of Irish blood would be shed to make of us a nation where all men could be free.

Corcoran and Meagher were among the first to rally to the colors. I resigned my position at the *Herald* and enlisted as a color sergeant in Meagher's Zouaves. I remember well the day the Sixty Ninth departed from New York. It was early spring. The ladies cheered and showered us with rose petals. Flags and banners flew from every window along Broadway as the strains of *Garyowen* resounded on the pipes. *Remember Fontenoy, Erin Go Bragh* and *On to Richmond* were our slogans and our rallying cries.

I recall the lovely wife of Judge Daly presenting Corcoran with a glorious flag of green silk and Meagher vowing it would never be lowered in defeat. We were all so young and brave as we departed. We held the belief that Mr. Lincoln's Army would crush the rebels and march on Richmond before the winter wind could whistle down Fifth Avenue. We were ignorant to the horror of modern warfare then and the cost of making America one.

The uniforms of Meagher's company of Zouaves demonstrated this ignorance. Our tasseled turbans, short jackets and baggy pantaloons of bright blue and red became burial garb for many a brave young man. When shot and shell rain down upon you, it is wise to be inconspicuous and under cover. This was a lesson that would be written in blood and gore during the early years of that terrible conflict.

The tents and huts of the army spread like a majestic blanket across the rolling green hills of Arlington Heights, Virginia. From that location, one could partake of breathtaking views of the Potomac and Georgetown. We joined the Sixty Ninth at Camp Corcoran. We were restless to begin our noble destiny and anxious to exhibit our courage under fire.

I recall encountering Captain Quinlan after my arrival in camp. He was engaged in the perusal of a great map that depicted the Warrenton Turnpike and a railway bridge near a place called Manassas Junction. He was smoking a long black pipe while his bright blue eyes attempted to fathom what lay ahead. His company of engineers would lead the regiment's line of march at noon. It was a glorious July day in the year of Our Lord, 1861.

On the march southward, we could see the wagons and buggies of Washington's gentry, trailing behind us as if on a holiday. It was then that our regiment was ordered to join the brigade commanded by Tecumseh Sherman. Meagher had told me of his meeting with this disheveled red haired colonel and the fiery tongue and disposition that were his hallmarks.

Meagher and Corcoran were wary of Sherman. They believed he lacked a proper appreciation of the soldier's sacrifices. To them he was a man of melancholic temperament and little loyalty. Sherman would often speak of bitter enemies and seldom of devoted friends. In the battle that would soon take place, his life and his glorious military career would be saved by Corcoran and a band of brave lads from the Sixty Ninth.

We spent that first night encamped near a foul swamp with mosquitoes buzzing and biting us relentlessly. On the following morning we resumed the march. Quinlan and his engineers again led the way with our drum corps close behind. They were followed by Colonel Corcoran, Captain Meagher, and Lieutenant Colonel Haggarty, the gallant young officer who had taken Nugent's place, after he fell from his horse.

By ten o'clock we came within view of Fairfax Courthouse. It was here that the regiment received orders to swing to the left and flank the rebels who were making their retreat.

Upon an open field, behind that picturesque village, we beheld the enemy for the first time. They were a mile or so in front of us. They looked to be of regimental strength and they seemed to be drawn up for a fight. They were ragged in appearance as they stood in formation amid a cloud of Virginia dust. They wore butternut and grey. I remember Meagher and Corcoran riding out in front of the Sixty Ninth. Both were mounted upon spirited chestnut chargers. Each was a perfect target for a bold sharpshooter's aim.

I remember Meagher riding back towards us and drawing his sword, his voice ringing across the field like a church bell. "There they are boys. If it's a fight they want, it's a fight we'll give 'em."

We all cheered and watched with an awful delight as the rebels fled from the shells of the Eighth New York Artillery. We followed close behind their line of march, raising the colors over Centreville and Germantown along the way. It was then that several of our militia regiments, including the Eighth New York, retired from the field. Their enlistments had run out and they had followed suit. To the credit of the Sixty Ninth and the other Irish regiments, we chose to remain and fight even though our enlistments had run their course as well.

Beauregard was in command of the rebel forces that withdrew from the Federal advance into the forest that ran along the stream known as Bull Run. It was here that he positioned his infantry and artillery in strategic locations to slow the progress of our forces and await reinforcement from Jackson and Johnston. Their plan was to link up outside the railway station known as Manassas Junction. It was there that the first major engagement of the war would take place. It was there that the world would first hear of the Sixty Ninth's courage under fire.

On the eve of battle we were encamped in the woodlands that ran along-side the plains of Manassas. In the distance we could see the campfires of the enemy. Both sides were awaiting the fury of the following day, Sunday, the twenty first of July.

I recall being summoned to Colonel Corcoran's tent by a drummer boy of tender years. Drummer boys were often company mascots. Some were as young as twelve. It was a sorry sight indeed to see one of these babes struck by a .58 caliber minnie ball. Once one of those deadly messengers found its mark amid flesh and bone, life as you knew it would never be the same.

I remember speaking to that bright eyed lad, as we made our way toward Corcoran's tent.

"Are you afraid of what will take place tomorrow?

"No sergeant", was his reply. "I have made my confession and received Communion. The Lord will take care of me."

"That's a good lad," was all I could say.

You know I envied that fearless boy on that night. I remembered the scripture of Jesus and the little children. How he preached about having to become as a little child in order to enter paradise. I do believe that a child-like faith gave many within the Brigade their courage, and made them a force to be reckoned with in battle. Some others resorted to the drink.

When I arrived at Corcoran's tent he was seated out in front with Meagher and Lieutenant Colonel Haggarty. The sun was setting. The mountains stood before us in the distance, bathed in a golden light. Meagher was the first to speak.

"Are our boys ready for their bloody baptism?"

"I believe they will do their duty," I replied.

"Do you believe that this war will be over before Christmas?" Corcoran asked, as he puffed upon a fine cigar. His manly figure was dressed in Zouave attire of red and blue. His large head wore a red turban.

"I hope and pray that it will," I said. "I hope and pray that it will."

"I never believed that they would fire on our flag," Meagher remarked. "Damn their rebel souls to hell. Sherman says that we must destroy their army and their will for making war, before this will be over. What do you say, Michael?"

"I believe Sherman is mad," Corcoran replied. "Did you see the look in his eyes when he spoke of this war? I thought for a moment that we were in the presence of Lucifer, himself. There is no honor in the war he foresees, only murder and destruction.

"What of that old woman in New Orleans?" I asked of Thomas, remembering that eerie episode in the catacombs behind Jackson Square. "What did she foretell about this war?"

Meagher seemed particularly perturbed by the question. He shot a surly look in my direction, as if to convey that I had betrayed a confidence between us.

"Have you resorted to fortune tellers now, Thomas?" Corcoran teased. "I tell you sometimes I worry about you."

Meagher focused upon Corcoran without making a response. He then shifted his gaze to James Haggarty. He was a fine figure of a man with chestnut hair and a ready smile. I had seen him kissing his wife and babies before our departure from New York Harbor.

"I paid no mind to her predictions," he muttered, while turning away from us. "Nothing is preordained."

CHAPTER 25

*B*efore dawn we were on the move taking up our position upon a plain encircled by verdant woods. The line of battle for our army extended for miles to our left. In among the darkened forest before us, columns and batteries of the enemy awaited our advance. A glorious sunrise brought with it a day of reckoning. The thunder of cannons and the scream of canister and shot signaled the beginning of that memorable engagement.

To our left we saw clouds of smoke billowing from behind a ribbon of wood. Soon the pop of musketry was heard in the distance, growing louder and more pronounced. Then volley after volley was heard. It was then that Meagher appeared before us on horseback, his wild eyes on fire above his Zouave attire. The boys cheered and he saluted them with a flourish.

McDowell had commanded that an attack be made upon the enemy's left. The Sixty Ninth was soon ordered to move to the right and attend to their formation. Captain Duffy and his Company G passed by us in order of march. His expression seemed so serene. It was as if he were about to take a stroll through Phoenix Park. I remember reassuring my boys, telling them to aim low and mark their targets well. There were over a thousand of us who rallied to the colors of the Sixty Ninth on that fateful morning. The enemy appeared through the wood like a brown horde.

Corcoran then galloped front and center and drew his saber. He sat tall in the saddle when he gave the command to advance at the quick. As we drew closer to the wood where the enemy waited, we received a volley from a line of rebel skirmishers. I saw at least six in Company A fall. Some of them screaming and moaning.

We halted and returned fire, felling near to a dozen rebels. One was shot through the right eye and writhed on the ground before turning still. Another had his throat explode from the impact of a minnie ball. He gurgled his notice that he was killed and fell on his face dead.

Then Meagher reappeared. He ordered us to discard our coats and haversacks and form up to move forward at the double quick. It was then that their artillery found its range. Shell and shot screaming through the trees. Death and devastation visited upon us. All at once the battle seemed to rage around us like a whirlpool of mayhem. In the melee that followed, we fought like demons, until the rebels captured two of our batteries.

It was then that I recall seeing Meagher out in front with his saber above his head, as a shell exploded nearby, killing his gallant charger. He was lying there dazed, before regaining his senses. The boys cheered him wildly. I recall that he ordered me to bring up the colors. I came up at the double quick, unfurling our emerald green flag on the run. He smiled and slapped me upon the back, then seized the flag and waved it for all to see. The air was thick with smoke and fire; our men were falling all around.

"Boys, look at the flag!" Meagher screamed. "Remember Ireland. Remember Fontenoy. Give them the bayonet. At the sprint, charge!"

Together we bounded into them with an infernal clash. The batteries seized by the enemy blowing holes in our ranks. Our boys rallied. They rallied to Meagher of the Sword. I saw Haggarty fall while leading his men. He was shot through the chest. I saw Keefe fall with the regimental colors. Two of our boys ran to him; only to be cut down by an enemy volley. Three rebels then set upon Keefe, wresting the colors from his grasp and making him their prisoner. In the next instant, I saw him pull a pistol from his boot and kill his captors. He made his way toward us, wounded, but protecting our regimental banner.

The battle raged on. Our valor and our volleys were now joined by our artillery. The rebels began to fall back. We sensed that a glorious victory was within reach. Then Kirby Smith brought the rebels their reinforcements. They soon began an attack upon our right flank. An attack marked by that shrill piercing war hoop, known as the rebel yell.

Our teamsters were the first to break and run. Their drop soon became a deluge that swept victory away. Through it all, the Sixty Ninth of Meagher and Corcoran held fast, trying to rally and form a redoubt against the enemy.

Then the rebel cavalry came cutting and slashing like a bevy of sharks. Meagher saw that the rout was on. He searched for Corcoran. He was not to be found. He ordered our buglers to sound the retreat. We fell back in an orderly fashion, all of us searching amid that maelstrom for a sign of our beloved Colonel.

It seemed that Corcoran had rallied approximately fifty of his men upon the turnpike. He was determined to fight to the death, rather than surrender to the rebels. Then he saw Sherman and his aides falling back. He observed the rebel cavalry heading straight for them. With the colors in hand, he signaled across the battlefield to his commander, advising him of the imminence of his peril. Sherman soon made his way at the gallop toward him. With the protection of a perimeter created by Corcoran and his valiant following, Sherman and his aides were able to make a safe retreat. Corcoran was not so fortunate.

His men were falling around him. There was no hope of evading death by further resistance. Both McIvor and Connolly convinced him that discretion was the better part of valor. He surrendered to the rebels with the tender of his sword.

While aiding the wounded that surrounded him, he discovered that he too had been struck. Thereafter, he and his men would be transported back to Richmond. It would be a long and trying ordeal before Michael Corcoran would set his eyes upon Thomas Meagher again.

The first battle of the Civil War, known to history as Bull Run, had been fought. The Union Army had suffered a most humiliating defeat. Yet from the ashes of that defeat, both the Irish Brigade and a Grand Army would rise.

Close to one hundred and fifty members of our regiment had fallen upon the plains of Manassas. During this ignoble rout the Sixty Ninth had done itself proud. Not one of our green flags had been captured. Not one of our brave lads had failed to perform his duty. McDowell, himself, commended our gallantry, asserting that an army with the fighting spirit of the Sixty Ninth could storm Richmond within a fortnight.

Poems of praise and eloquent eulogies, however, would not soothe the bitterness we felt at having been betrayed by our General staff. We knew the truth and we spoke it around our bivouac campfires. Our army was poorly trained and poorly led. The preservation of the Union would require a drastic change in the manner of Washington's war making or the rebels would reign victorious.

Soon after the disaster of Manassas, General McLellan was summoned to Washington and given command of the army. Now we who had rallied to the colors after Fort Sumter began to believe that the army had a commander who merited our confidence and courage under fire. I tell you the lads of our Brigade loved the one they called "Little Mac."

After Manassas, the regiment returned to New York amid a welcome for conquering heroes. Yet those who returned had been transformed by the baptism of battle. Heroism amid defeat was not a cause for celebration. Since most of our enlistments had run out, we were able to reside at home and reflect upon the sights and sounds of that, our first engagement. It was far different from what we had imagined. The weaponry of that war had made it different. The gallant tactic of marching in ranks toward a fusillade of shot and shell would soon reap a horrid harvest.

I remembered most the childlike face of that drummer boy I had encountered on the eve of battle. I remembered him crouching behind a massive oak tree, amid a group of our lads firing their smoothbore muskets. It was then that one of our own shells screamed and burst among them, leaving his headless torso to keep an eerie vigil against that tree; his boyish hands beseeching the Almighty in prayer.

There was a commemoration of the dead and wounded of Manassas held some months following our return. It was an autumn day and thousands gathered in Jones Wood to pay their respects and assist the loved ones of those who had fallen. Many of our dignitaries were there, Archbishop Hughes, Judge Daly and William Seward. Each of them spoke of the brave men and boys who would no longer muster in our midst; the brave ones who had fallen in the gallant tradition of Irish hearts, rallying to distant drums.

It was Meagher alone who spoke of the task ahead and the need for an Irish Brigade. It was the same eloquence and the same magnetic voice that I had heard at Conciliation Hall. And yet it was a different Thomas Meagher. The defeat at Manassas and the loss of Corcoran had visited an agony upon him. His tone was no longer that of a firebrand. He spoke as a father who had witnessed the death of his beloved sons.

It was a golden afternoon. The trees of Jones Wood wore their finest fall attire. The speakers' platform was covered in red, white and blue bunting. Meagher was seated between his lovely wife Elizabeth and his law partner Malcolm Campbell. He was introduced by his devoted friend Richard O'Gorman. He strode to the podium amid a torrent of cheers and applause, resplendent in the blue and gold coat and trousers of a Union officer.

His chestnut hair and robust mustache bearing just a trace of silver, his violet eyes appeared like burning embers above his ruddy angular face. He stood with his hands behind him, waiting for the exultation of the throng to subside. At that moment he was an undisputed leader of the Irish Immigrant Class. He spoke with passion and eloquence on that occasion.

"My dear friends, I am touched by your affection and humbled by the occasion that brings us together. As I stand here before you and gaze upon the faces of those I have had the honor to lead into the tumult of battle, I know that Divine Providence has bestowed its grace upon me.

I have received many blessings from the Almighty during my time upon this earth. Chief among these are the love and affection of so many who stand here today, so many who have come to this great land in search of freedom and liberty. Now our home of freedom and liberty is threatened by those who have forgotten the promise of this democracy.

I speak to all who have come to America from the Old World, to all who have fled from the tyranny of the past and endured that harrowing voyage from across the turbulent sea.

Now is the time to answer the call to arms. Now is the time to honor the dead and wounded who so valiantly served in the battle now past. Now is the time to defend our Constitution and rally around our glorious flag.

I have received authority from the War Department to form an Irish Brigade. I will commence recruitment this coming Tuesday at The Metropolitan Hotel. I intend to raise three regiments of brave and temperate lads from our beloved New York. I will then raise two more regiments from the cities of Boston and Philadelphia.

This Irish Brigade will fly the green flags of our noble ancestors. This Irish Brigade will teach those who seek to oppress us that we are their equals. In the noble defense of our beloved Union, may God bestow His blessings upon us all."

CHAPTER 26

*I*n a multitude they came. They were lads of all shapes and sizes. Some arrived from the countryside with the straw of the haystack and the smell of the barnyard clinging to their persons. Others came from the city, hardened by the sting and soot of the back alleys and dock sides. Many were survivors from the coffin ships. Some were outlaws. Some were schoolboys. All were eager to follow Meagher of the Sword and go down in history as the bravest of the brave.

In the first instance they were to give their names and place of residence to Corporal Kavanaugh. He was seated in the lobby of the Metropolitan Hotel at a small folding table beside Major Quinlan, above them hung the emerald flag of the Brigade.

Upon it in gold was a sunburst over a harp and a garland of shamrocks. Both men wore the bold colors of Meagher's Zouaves. Both had distinguished themselves for gallantry at Manassas. Their role was to greet the eager recruits, perform a quick inspection of their demeanor and provide them with a number for further examinations.

While the lads awaited their turn in the barrel of recruitment, they congregated and conversed in small groups. Some had made the journey alone. Others had arrived in the company of a friend or three. Many spoke of Erin and their aspirations for the task ahead. All professed a fervent desire to risk life and limb in the service of their adopted land. Their first obstacle was to appear before Dr. Reynolds and pass muster.

On that occasion the good doctor was assisted by James Purcell, a refined, bespectacled surgeon. He was a lanky man of thirty one years, with a large head of coiled black hair and a kind and affable manner. Like myself, he was a Tipperary man who had lent a hand in the '48 uprising. It was Purcell who would defy death again and again during the slaughter of Cold Harbor. Both he and Dr. Reynolds were a credit to the Brigade as well as their noble profession.

Jack Gosson, Charles Lucky and I had been given our own parts to play in the selection of those who would become members of the Brigade. Gosson and Lucky were to test their mettle and agility, while I was called upon to assess their brains. We were situated upon the second floor, seated at a long mahogany table within the hotel's spacious ballroom. The table was decorated with a gold and green embroidered cloth. We each wore the dress blue uniform of a Union officer.

By then, I had been brevetted to First Lieutenant. As I recall Gosson had retained his Captain's bars and Lucky his lieutenant's stripes. After the once over in the lobby and the passing of muster by the medical staff, the recruits were sent one by one to us. Of course Captain Jack and his Italian partner had long before devised an initiation. They would each send the lads a message that was loud and clear.

The ritual was the same for each and every one. Lucky would walk to the entrance of the ballroom and bark the recruit's number down the stairway. He would then stand at the threshold, while the lad made his way toward us. No matter how quickly the lad came, Lucky would command that he move quicker. "On'a the double," he would bellow. "You think'a we have all day to wait on'a you," he would cry, the lieutenant's thick Milanese accent often surprising and unsettling the lads.

You see most of these boys came from homes that spoke only Gaelic. Then Lucky would draw his small muscular body next to the recruit and begin the attack, his tenor voice and dark aquiline features tearing into him.

"Stan'a straight. Say'a your name."

"Thomas Kelly"

"Well, well, Thomas Kelly," Gosson would begin, from his seat in front of the lad, his blue eyes staring menacingly from his ruddy face, his thick brogue bringing some sense of familiarity to the youth before us. "This here is Lieutenant O'Keefe and I am Captain Gosson. So you want to join the Brigade do ya? Do ya know what will be demanded of ya?"

"No," the youth would reply.

Then Gosson would jump up, his enormous chest and shoulders heaving with feigned outrage, while Lucky would shake his head disapprovingly next to the lad.

"What manner of fool are ya?" Gosson would scream, while making a bee line for him. He would then stand over him and continue the joust while staring down into his eyes, his coarse beard and mustache touching the boy's face.

"I tell ya Lieutenant what are we to do with such as him? T'inkin he can waltz in here and take up our time wit'out even knowin' what we demand. Tell 'im, Lieutenant. Tell 'im so he will not forget."

"Is'a no use, Captain. I know think he wann'a learn 'bout such'a things."

"Is the Lieutenant right, Kelly? Are ya a hard case, comin' here wastin' our precious time? Do ya suppose we accept any guard house soldier int'a our Brigade?"

"No, sir" the youth would reply.

"Would you like to know what is demanded of ya?" Gosson would ask.

"Yes sir."

"To join up wit' us lad, you'll need a steady hand, a stout heart and a willing mind. Now, do ya now know what is demanded of ya?"

"Yes, sir," the recruit would answer.

"That's a good lad. Now come with us upon the veranda and we'll see what you're made of."

Overlooking Broadway, Gosson and Lucky would give a demonstration of the proper techniques for fighting hand to hand. There were two bales of hay that were used for bayonet thrusts and a blanket covered with straw for tumbling and falling. Those who were agile and quick to learn the lessons taught were passed on to me. Those who were clumsy and slow to follow were not.

My task was to pass only the bright ones on to Meagher and Nugent. You see, the youths who became members of our band of brothers were sifted and selected with great care. The intent of those who organized the Brigade was to form an exemplary unit, courageous in battle and chivalrous in behavior. It was a noble design and a worthy aim. Much preparation was needed to ready the lads for the horror that awaited them.

There were three regiments of recruits sent for training to Fort Schuyler. I remember my first visitation to this our *alma mater*. The Fort possessed a fine formidable facade with slate gray casements and at least twenty separate mounts for large caliber guns. Behind its ten foot walls was a spacious esplanade for parades and drills, as well as rolling hills for tents and houses. It was situated on a promontory that reached like a boney arm outward toward Long Island Sound

While stationed there, the boys would be instructed in the fine points of soldiering. On the esplanade, in weather fair and foul, they would march and drill. On the rolling hills they would muster for bayonet training and musketry practice. By the campfires, the more seasoned soldiers like Gosson and Duffy, would dispense their wisdom and instill their discipline.

All of the Brigade could read and write. All were expected to care for their gear and their hygiene like gentlemen. All were trained in military tactics, army regulations and Irish history. Those few whose vagrant ways could not be reformed were sent packing back to the places from whence they came. In the Brigade there was no place for shirkers, slackers or those who would skedaddle when the air was filled with lead.

Meagher preferred the smooth bore to the rifled musket. He was a student of Napoleon, Caesar and Genghis Khan. He believed that the charge of valiant men, trained in hand to hand combat, was a weapon that could overcome even the most stalwart rebels. In the fury of battle at close quarters, a well-trained force with a mystical tradition could silence the most blood curdling banshee yelps.

Meagher was our example and our inspiration. Out of the mist when least expected, he would appear on a golden charger, sometimes alone, sometimes accompanied by his faithful aide de camp William Herbert. Often he made his rounds by the light of bivouac campfires, speaking fondly to the lads and inquiring of their homes and loved ones. They loved him like a father and he returned their sentiment, as if each and every one was his beloved son.

On Sundays the men and boys of the Brigade would receive visits from wives and children, parents and sweethearts. On special occasions there would be concerts by the regimental band, picnics, three legged races and steeple chases.

I recall sweet afternoons, walking along the banks of the Sound in the company of my loved ones; each of us swelling with pride; each of us feeling that we were a brother in arms among a host of comrades. Fort Schuyler was where the Irish Brigade took its shape and received its purpose.

Meagher's aim was to form and train the Brigade, then to make a written request for General James Shields to lead it into battle. Shields was a grizzled veteran of the Mexican War who had earned the love and admiration of his men and enhanced the reputation of the Irish soldier in America.

He was stationed in California when presented with the honor of Colonel Meagher's request. He would respectfully decline the invitation, pointing out in his reply, that there was another better suited to lead the Brigade in battle. Shields insisted that the only man who was worthy of the honor was the one who had drawn the recruits to him, the one who molded them into a fighting force to be reckoned with, the Man of the Sword, himself, Colonel Thomas Francis Meagher.

We all were in accord with the recommendations of General Shields. Each and every one of our number was proud to serve under the man who had always been faithful to his friends and his beliefs, a man who personified the qualities that the Brigade possessed. It was Meagher and Meagher alone who should lead us in battle. He was the promise of whom we wished to be.

There were many outside the Brigade who opposed such a course of action. They were for the most part small, envious men, who resented Meagher's eloquence and accomplishments, men who sought to thwart Meagher's ascent and thereby deny to us the chance at liberty.

Yet we had learned the ways of politics and power by then. We knew that our strength was in our numbers and our unity. We petitioned our legislators to act on our behalf and sought an audience with the man who had been elected to lead the Union during its darkest hour, Abraham Lincoln.

CHAPTER 27

By the time the Brigade was stationed at Camp California, outside of Alexandria Virginia, there were seven hundred and forty five men and boys whom Meagher had chosen to serve within the ranks of The Sixty Ninth Regiment. In addition, he had selected eight hundred for The Eighty Eighth Regiment and hand-picked nearly a thousand more for the Sixty Third.

Before we were joined by the others from Boston and Philadelphia, there were two thousand five hundred and forty who had volunteered to march beneath the glorious green flags of Meagher's Irish Brigade. They were Green flags of silk, embroidered at Tiffany's with Gaelic slogans that read *Ireland Forever* and *They Shall Never Retreat from the Charge of Lances.*

I became a Captain in Company B, of the Eighty Eighth New York. There were twelve of us selected from the Brigade to accompany Thomas in his meeting with the beleaguered President.

We rode into Washington with Meagher and Nugent in the lead. After stabling our horses, we enjoyed a dinner at Willard's Hotel and awaited the summons from the leader none of us had met. William Seward, Lincoln's Secretary of State, arrived at the hotel shortly after six. His close association over the years with Archbishop Hughes had made of him a trusted friend to the New York Irish.

Meagher became acquainted with Seward while at work for the *Irish News*. Seward was a tall man in his sixties with silver hair and a booming voice. A shrewd businessman with his finger firmly positioned upon the political pulse of the country, he had once been the leader of the Republican Party. Seward had seen something extraordinary in the rough-hewn "Rail Splitter" and sought to assist as well as influence him. I must say there was something extraordinary indeed about Lincoln.

I cannot say what I expected when I met him. We were in the foyer of the White House, beneath a magnificent chandelier, when he appeared. He was carrying his youngest son, Tad, upon his back and galloping about like some large misshapen dray horse. One could tell at once that he was without pretension and deeply devoted to this precocious child. He bid us welcome and begged our indulgence, while he and the lad scampered upstairs to say goodnight.

We were shown down a hallway and into an enormous drawing room with portraits of Washington and Jefferson adorning its walls. We stood before a fireplace of white marble and examined the interior furnishings that manifested an unmistakable refinement. We were honored to be in such a majestic place.

When Mr. Lincoln returned, Seward introduced him to Meagher. He seemed genuinely honored to make the acquaintance of Thomas and in turn pleased to meet each and every one of our band. His long thin figure towered above us. He was wearing a black coat and trousers with a white shirt and blue frontier tie.

His face was care worn with sad gray eyes, a long nose and a high forehead. His coarse, unruly hair was a deep brown and he wore a manicured dark beard running from ear to ear. The handshake and manner he displayed were straight forward and firm. His voice at times was high pitched, yet by no means offensive. There was a certain presence about him that both disarmed and charmed.

A black man servant in formal attire appeared with a silver tray. Upon it were a decanter and goblets of the finest crystal. From a cherry wood cabinet beside that ornate fireplace he produced a bottle of Irish whiskey. As I recall, Lincoln abstained from the spirits yet encouraged us most strenuously to partake in this libation. Little encouragement was needed for such an undertaking among our number.

Lincoln then sat upon a hand crafted rocking chair located in the center of the room. He invited each of us to pull up a seat and take a load off the floor. It was as if we were his sons returning home for a holiday visit. It was then that he began to speak of the state of our Union and the war that brought us into his living quarters.

"Colonel Meagher, Seward advises me that you have raised three regiments of Irish soldiers and hope to raise two more.

"Yes, Mr. President, our lads are ready and willing to serve and more are on the way."

"That's the spirit, Colonel. That's the spirit. We will need as many as you can muster for the times ahead. I am determined to see this through to the bitter end and I need men who have the will to fight. Your men showed their will at Bull Run, Colonel. Please accept my gratitude on behalf of the Union for their valor under such trying circumstances."

"Thank you, Mr. President."

"Has there been any word of Colonel Corcoran and his men?"

Seward asked, standing behind the President.

"Colonel Nugent received a letter two days ago," Meagher answered. "Tell them the news, Robert."

"A letter was smuggled out from James McIvor, one of Colonel Corcoran's lieutenants," Nugent advised. "They are being held at a tobacco warehouse somewhere in Richmond. Corcoran was wounded and without medical attention for some time, but his spirits are good and his men have not despaired."

"I will see what can be done to assure their safe and swift return, gentlemen," Lincoln promised, as his sorrowful eyes fell upon each and every one of us. He then stood and made his way toward the cabinet where the liquor was kept.

Removing a silver pitcher he poured himself a drinking glass full of water. After draining it, he wiped the back of his left hand across his mouth, like a parched field hand.

"They tell me your Irish Brigade is in need of a leader. What do you say to that, gentlemen?"

"We say that Colonel Meagher is all the leader we need", Quinlan volunteered.

"Is that the sentiment of all the men, Major?" Lincoln probed, standing in the middle of the room, focusing upon each of our faces, like a barrister probing a jury.

"Yes, Mr. President" was our unanimous response.

"What about you, Colonel Meagher?" Lincoln asked. "Will you serve the Union and follow the orders of your superiors, even if you disagree with them? Are you the man for this job?"

"I believe that I am, Mr. President." Meagher answered, his eyes staring upward into the eyes of Abraham Lincoln.

The President smiled and then spoke in a backwoods way.

"Maybe you're right. Let me take a little while and turn it over in my head. Maybe sleep on it. You know when I was just a young pup studyin' Blackstone and makin' a nuisance of myself around the Illinois Circuit, I swear my brain would get plum chock full from time to time."

"There was this old lawyer by the name of Cyrus Poole who used to say to me, "Abe, when you get all bollixed up with too many notions, just find a nice shade tree and have a snooze for yourself and sure as shootin' sweet sleep will make some sense of it all." I suppose I'll have an answer for you boys right quick. I sure do appreciate what you and your people are doin' for the Union, Colonel. I surely do." With that, he bade each and every one of us farewell.

As we were making our way back to our horses, across the rolling field leading from the rear of that place called the White House, I recall that there was an enormous moon, shining in the night sky. I remember glancing back over my shoulder and seeing the tall gaunt figure of the President, watching after us, from an upstairs window.

In the moonlight I could make out his features as clear as day. I turned and waved to him. I will never forget the sorrow and the concern that was written upon his face, as he waved back. He waved back, just like he was one of us. I suppose that was his greatness. He saw and understood so much more than we did, and yet he never stopped being one of us. I tell you, Old Lincoln was one of a kind, alright.

The next afternoon we received the news. Lincoln had made his decision. He had agreed with General Shields and the men and boys of the Brigade. Thomas Meagher was indeed the man for the job. He would be commissioned a Brigadier General and given command of The Irish Brigade at Camp California.

The following night I attended a banquet in Meagher's honor. Many of the Army's General Officers were present. It was a rousing celebration marked by fine food and drink. The regimental bands had combined to form a magnificent orchestra. They delivered spirited renditions of many a fine Irish melody.

Time and time again the voices of our brave lads were raised in song. Their youth and their vigor bound together by a joyous camaraderie. We were brothers in spirit, unafraid of death. We would march into hell with an Irish rebel leading the way. We were a fighting force that would prove faithful to its promise. The spring would bring the Peninsula Campaign and the summer the slaughter of Antietam.

CHAPTER 28

A relentless rain soaked us to the bone, as we shivered upon the transports off the coast of Fortress Monroe. To many, the misery and seasickness of the coffin ships was revisited. The plan was to move up the peninsula between the James and York rivers and attack Richmond with an army of more than one hundred thousand men.

For months we had trained and drilled while General McClellan molded the rabble that turned tail at Bull Run into a formidable fighting force, a force that could take the measure of the Confederate Army and make them pay a frightful price for their treason.

In Washington, scores of armchair generals had demanded that the army engage the enemy and bring a quick end to the rebellion. Yet, for those career soldiers who had witnessed the bloodshed of Vera Cruz and laid siege to the fortress at Chapultepec there was much detail required for such an undertaking. Lincoln repeatedly demanded that the army commence its attack, doubting whether the people he governed had the stomach for a protracted conflict.

Although history has proven unkind to McClellan, we who served under his command believed in his leadership. We, not they, were the ones who would fight and die for the Union. We, not they, saw the wisdom in the delay of detailed preparation.

Like an enormous serpent, tens of thousands disembarked and marched toward the outskirts of Yorktown. The Brigade had become a part of Fighting Dick Richardson's Division and Bull Sumner's Corps. I had been introduced to Richardson at Camp California. He was a fearless, fighting soldier with a commanding yet disheveled appearance. Since he wore no epaulettes beneath his slouch hat, on many an occasion the men mistook him for an enlisted man.

Like Grant he could curse and drink with the best of his subordinates. Like Grant, he understood the dirty business that was war. Many of our lesser generals demanded spit and polish in the ranks. Both Dirty Dick and U.S. Grant demanded only that we fight like hellcats and then fight some more.

Yorktown and Williamsburg were the initial objectives of our advance. The Brigade was held in reserve in the muck and mire that was Camp Winfield Scott. The rain had made of the peninsula a quagmire of oozing stinking filth. Men, horses and caissons sank deeper and deeper into the mud of that Virginia Spring, while Lee and his band were busy as beavers, constructing redoubts, rifle pits, breastworks and entrenchments upon every road and along every river leading to Richmond.

Night and day we listened to the sounds of skirmishing around us. The sight of blood drenched men, returning with tales of a determined enemy, lying in wait out there in the storm, was commonplace. We were anxious to begin and steel ourselves to the sting of battle. We inched forward, passing by places of history, where Patrick Henry cried for liberty and Cornwallis surrendered. Another bloody chapter in the history of America was about to be written by men in blue and butternut.

When the rain finally stopped, Meagher sensed that the men needed a welcome diversion from the ordeal that awaited them. He called us to his quarters and proposed that a steeple chase be conducted on the following afternoon. Leave it to him to display a disregard for death and disaster. Here we were on the road to Richmond, within striking distance of Johnston and Lee, and we were about to engage in a rousing celebration. I tell you this is what the men truly admired about Thomas. By God, he had a flair for fearless events.

The steeple chase commenced on the same day that the bloody affair at Fair Oaks began. All morning engineers under Major Quinlan's command constructed hurdles and sunken water jumps for the event. It was decided among the officers that the winner's purse would be the coveted tiger skin that was prominently displayed within the tent of the Brigade's commander. It was said that Meagher had bagged the beast on one of his mysterious forays into the jungles of Costa Rica. Of course the losers, as always, could expect a pint of whiskey for their pain and perseverance.

Before the riders appeared, Meagher called upon little Johnny Fleming and his father to provide a spirited medley of Gaelic airs upon their fiddles. I tell you this lad and his Da could make the angels themselves sing and dance. There was much merrymaking among the men as they cavorted to the music.

Gosson and Lucky were commissioned to commandeer three barrels of whiskey and twelve barrels of beer from a sutler's store. Father Corby, the chaplain of the Eighty Eighth Regiment, gave a solemn blessing to the festivities and Timmy Concannon delivered a heartfelt rendition of *Kathleen Mavourneen*.

The sky on that day was a magnificent blue. At the outset, Meagher made his official introduction to the Chickahominy Steeple Chase. Upon the reviewing stand beside him were Generals Richardson and French, two favorites of the men, chosen to serve as judges of the event. Then the jockeys and their mounts were introduced by Quartermaster O'Sullivan, a burly, bearded son of Erin with a pie face and a clownish manner.

Each of the jockeys were resplendent in colors arranged from makeshift attire. I will always remember the arrival of Captain Gosson, adorned in a flaming red blouse and jodhpurs, derived from the curtains of a Confederate Hotel. He wore an officer's coat turned inside out and an enormous smoking cap, festooned with buttons and beads. I tell you the men roared when they took note of his appearance. On that day, he was the clown prince of the Brigade. On horseback, he was a marvel to the men. In battle, he was the bravest of the brave.

As was his custom, Meagher would engage in a spirited repartee with his roguish captain.

"Captain Gosson," Meagher would bark, his speech assuming an exaggerated brogue. "You appear too taken with the drink to engage in this event."

"In truth, General, I have sampled the nectar provided and am able to report that it is fine Irish stock, as am I."

"I shouldn't want you to break your fine Irish neck while in such a state, Captain. If you can demonstrate your fitness for this event, you can continue on as a participant."

"Does the General demand a show of formal horsemanship, like that displayed by the Seventh Hussars? Or would he prefer a display of riding, Indian style?" Gosson slurred.

"I suppose a demonstration of both would be in order, Captain."

With that, Captain Jack catapulted upon his black gelding's glistening back, pulling upon the reins and unleashing a display of the finest horsemanship the men would ever see. He commenced with a formal prance and curtsey. Then he took off at the gallop, twirling and somersaulting in the saddle, like a wild Indian.

Finally, while doffing his cap, he soared effortlessly over a most treacherous water jump and came to a halt back before the reviewing stand. With that, Gosson dismounted to the cheers of the assembled Brigade and received the General's permission to put his skills to the test within the Chickahominy Steeple Chase.

There were twelve horses and men that took their place at the post. The race was run at a fever pitch, with the riders flashing around the half mile track like a heavenly host. Gosson of course was the early favorite, clearing each of the first five hurdles with a fury and flair that made it seem that he could not be vanquished. Next came the water jumps and a dead heat around a series of stumps arranged in a figure eight. Then there was a gallop around Tyler's farmhouse and finally a mad dash across a plowed field for the home stretch.

It was there that the speed of Major Kavanaugh's mount outdistanced the rest. As I recollect he wore emerald green colors and a tricolor cap. Upon the back of the lightning quick "Katie Darlin," the little major managed to snatch a narrow victory from the grasp of Gosson and Major Warrington.

With much ceremony and a series of toasts, the prizes were dispensed. Then Johnny Fleming and the singers of the Sixty Ninth performed a rendition of ballads. These brought vivid thoughts of home and memories of sad, sweet days gone by in our beloved Erin. I tell you there was many a tear shed by those brave men on that occasion.

It was then that the final event took place, before the sun set over the Chickahominy. The drummer boys from each of the three regiments were assembled and provided with a mule for a mount. The race that ensued was a hilarious sight to behold. The lads were so young and full of joy as they made a valiant attempt to turn those stubborn jackasses into noble chargers. I tell you the laughter and delight of the Brigade on that day was an event that I shall never forget. I swear I can still hear them even today. That night, Meagher received orders for the Brigade to begin its march toward the railway line at Fair Oaks.

As we drew close to the place the rebels called Seven Pines, the rain began to pelt us once again. We came upon a foreboding swamp more than a mile in width, amid the chill of darkness. We were somewhere in the backwater of the swollen Chickahominy river, as best I can recall.

Nugent was in command of the Sixty Ninth and I was the Captain in charge of Company B within the dear old Eighty Eighth. I shall not forget the ordeal of crossing that swamp when not a hand could be seen before your face. There was many a fear filled Irish voice, whispering the Our Father, as we began that treacherous crossing, including my own.

We of the infantry slid in first, up to our breasts, our muskets held above our heads. The horses and artillery soon followed. Snakes and swamp rats of every size and shape were swimming among us. Fallen trees, submerged brambles and sink holes caused us to stumble again and again in the putrid stink of that bug infested mess.

I recall two of our lads becoming lost in that forsaken swill hole, dragged down by their sopping wet knapsacks beneath the surface, never to return to this life again. I tell you the air was blue with the oaths of our men as we made our way onward toward uncertainty. Cursing the dark, cursing the wet that chilled us to the bone, cursing the rebels who awaited our advance like spiders within a web.

We emerged from the grasp of that swamp, as an orange dawn spread across the sky like a quilt. The birds and bull frogs brought a welcome chorus to our ears, as we dragged ourselves up the embankment. After an hour more of marching, we ascended toward a magnificent grove of cedar trees that commanded a view of the river. Before long a camp was erected on this site.

We congregated in half naked circles, drying ourselves and hanging our sopping wet attire near the campfires. Before the sun had reached its zenith in a cloudless azure sky, our spirits had been revived. As I made my rounds, I was greeted by a chorus of grateful voices. The smell of coffee and salt pork was everywhere. We were half a day's march from the railway at Fair Oaks. It was there that the Brigade would have its mettle tested and prove more than equal to the task.

CHAPTER 29

By noon we were on the march again. We followed Howard's Brigade across a grapevine bridge that spanned the raging waters of the Chickahominy. It was there that an aide de camp of General Sumner caught up with Meagher and delivered a revised plan of attack.

The Sixty Third was ordered to fall out and guard the approaches to the bridge, while the Sixty Ninth and my Eighty Eighth were to proceed down the turnpike and into a wood that ran along an open plain. As we marched through that wood, we began to hear the thunder of cannon in the distance.

The Sixty Ninth with Colonel Nugent in the lead, was the first to arrive upon the scene of the previous day's battle. It was a ghastly sight indeed.

Everywhere across an expanse of forest that faded from view, were the dead and dying. Cries for mercy and water made a hellish din that echoed among the dismembered trees. We could hear the shrieks of men being tied down, while shattered limbs were sawed from their heaving bodies. I recall a lad of no more than fifteen, with a gaping hole in the middle of his chest, begging to be put out of his misery.

The carcasses of two slaughtered horses were scattered around an overturned caisson. A congregation of dead were locked together among those remnants of mortal combat, the last expressions upon their gray, frozen faces signified the fury of the fighting that had taken place the day before.

Indeed, it was a haunting, charnel house for men to pass through on the way to their own encounters with the angel of death.

Meagher ordered our surgeons to tend to the wounded. There was many a bloodied rebel among that sorry lot. I spotted a Confederate Officer in butternut and gold, seated upon a tree stump. Half his face had been shot away. As our column made its way across that horrid landscape, his remaining green eye stared at us from beneath a makeshift tourniquet. He seemed to smirk, as if in possession of a hidden truth, a superior wisdom that would soon be revealed to one and all who wore Union blue.

Meagher approached, riding Dolly, his magnificent ebony mare. When he saw the condition of this rebel officer he dismounted and inquired as to his regiment. With a manner that was matter of fact and refined, he replied that he was a Major in the service of Virginia. When asked if there was any comfort that could be provided, he replied that his preference was to remain where he was, since his men would be back that way shortly. The dash and defiance of this remark disturbed us.

There was another rebel, lying by the side of the road as we passed. His gray jacket was opened to reveal a scarlet stained shirt. He had been gut shot with a minnie ball. It was clear that a wound in that spot meant a slow and agonizing death. I remember the feelings of pity that rose up inside of me at that moment.

Even though he was an enemy and a traitor to his country, I could not despise him in that sorrowful state. The imminence of his death had somehow lessened my enmity. He was holding a letter in his blood drenched hand. He seemed to be reading it over and over, while he waited for eternity to arrive.

I spoke to him as I passed and soon discovered that he too was Irish. He too had made the voyage to America in search of a new tomorrow. Alas, he wished me well and gave to me the letter. He asked that I write to his wife about the circumstance of his passing. I should have refused such a request, but I could not. For some reason I believed that his letter and my promise would somehow protect me in the battle about to take place. Such are the superstitions of war.

As the sun broke through the clouds, we made our way to the edge of the wood. Nugent and the Sixty Ninth was to our right. Meagher was riding back and forth behind us, urging us to ready our guns and bayonets for what was to occur. At that point Sumner appeared, accompanied by four of his aides. He saluted Meagher and asked if he could address the men. He was riding a chestnut charger and seemed so much larger than life itself.

Shot and shell soon began to scream through the trees above us, showering our surroundings with the debris of falling branches and limbs. We could see the rebels massing for an attack upon our left. We watched as Hogan's batteries found their range, tearing gaping holes in the enemy formations, while others moved up to fill their ranks.

The smoke filled plane before us was more than a mile long and twice that in width. Our drummers were furiously beating the call to arms. The fifes and pipes brought our blood to a boil. Sumner's voice rang out above the din. His fleshy face was the color of crimson and his hoary hair and beard made him seem like Prometheus himself.

"Boys," he shouted. "I am your General. I know the Irish Brigade will not retreat. I stake my reputation on you."

It was Captain McMahon who yelled a response from the ranks of the Eighty Eighth, the same McMahon whose courage under fire would inspire us on that day. "We have not run yet, General. And we will not run now."

"I know boys, God bless you all," Sumner shouted, as he saluted us with a tip of his slouch hat.

We all cheered as he and his aides galloped off to our right, disappearing back into the wood. The yell of the rebels commenced the attack to our left. There were thousands of them, whooping and hollering, as they fired and charged across that open plain.

Shells were falling everywhere by then. Their bugles echoed as red and orange flashes spewed forth from the barrels of their rifled muskets. Smoke was rising in the air. The sky and clouds above the battlefield were serene and indifferent to the fury of the scene below.

Their charges would be beaten back again and again by the bravery of the lads on our left. Then the rebel batteries were moved into position for a withering cannonade. With this deadly accompaniment, they charged again and broke through those lines of blue.

With Meagher on Dolly urging them forward, Nugent and The Sixty Ninth advanced from the wood and on to the plane. Our green flags were unfurled and tilted like lances in the hands of stalwart knights.

I then saw Meagher riding toward us at the gallop. His saber was flashing above his head, while calling us to him with those wild eyes and that manly voice. I screamed for my men to follow, sword and pistol at the ready, bayonets fixed. First a volley, and then we charged into a mass of grey and brown enemy.

The Eighty Eighth uncoiled and struck like a jungle beast. It was a clash of wills. It was a fight to the death.

My Colt shot two of them as they lunged toward me like snarling dogs, my sword, slashed through flesh and bone. The whine of minnie balls filled the air around us, like a thousand angry bees.

The splat of bullet into flesh, the groan of those struck down filled my ears. Mortal fear and savage screams became mingled, a spectacle of hate and death accompanied by cannons roar. They fell back. We cheered. Again it recurred. Dead and dying were all around, brave men lying on bloody ground.

By late afternoon we were fighting around a white farmhouse. There were so many who fell from my company, at least two score by that time. I remember seeing Captain McMahon with his boyish looks and pink cheeks. His face was black with smoke and powder. His blue eyes burning like coals. He led an attack over a stone wall and into a farmyard. Lieutenant Turner was behind him, crying like a wild Indian. He shot three rebels dead as they charged from the right. Poor Timmy Concannon, he was shot through the throat, never to share his song with the living again.

I ran toward the farmhouse. I recall retrieving a rifle from a dead Johnny and leading a band of six or so lads to a rail fence. From there I saw one of our drummer boys, little Seamus Riley. He held a musket bigger than himself. He was no older than fifteen years of age. He was a mite size man of steel on that bloody day. He was hiding beside the remnants of a wagon, blown apart by a shot from our batteries.

There was much close quarter fighting near that place. The rebels were massed beyond the railway. One of their officers with a plumed hat directed them toward us at the double quick. We fired into their ranks. Soon we were no more than ten rods apart; the blaze of muskets dropping the dead in piles.

That damned rebel in the plumed hat was relentless. His valor commanded our respect. We vaulted the rail fence and charged into them. Blood and gore were everywhere. Oh, what a killing field we made of that cow pasture. Then, we saw little Seamus emerging from the smoke with that plumed rebel before him, a musket trained upon the small of his back.

He had made him his prisoner. I tell you. I cried with joy to see such a sight. It was as if that little lad were my very own son.

Then it was that I saw Meagher and Nugent fighting amid a horde of the enemy. Duffy was there and Lieutenant Lucky too. They seemed to be swimming in a pool of rebels. Lucky was waving the colors of the Sixty Ninth back and forth. I recall screaming at our color bearer to rally the men toward Meagher. I feared he soon would fall.

He was conspicuous upon horseback and a prize for a rebel marksman. I swear he had the lives of a cat and the luck of the Irish on that bloody day. From upon the back of Dolly, he slashed his sword and fired his Colt. The reins of his mount were clenched between his teeth. I saw a rebel leap upon the mare's hind quarters only to be shot through the face by Captain Duffy. I swear I never saw Duffy rattled, even in the most trying circumstance.

Two rebels then fell upon Lucky, fighting like jackals to wrest the colors from his manly grasp. Suddenly a rebel's rifle butt crashed against my skull. I believe I shot him before I fell. When I came to, there was Meagher hovering over me.

He was smiling and shaking his head. Father Corby was beside him. For a moment, I believed that all of us had been removed to a heavenly place. Then my head began to throb like blazes. I shall not forget Meagher's words to me on that occasion. It was at that time that he addressed me by my Christian name.

"You gave us a scare Cornelius. We thought you were lost for sure. Now you can tell your grandchildren that a thick Irish skull can come in handy."

I recall him handing me his flask and me taking a pull like there was no tomorrow. The battle at Fair Oaks claimed over a hundred of the Brigade as casualties. We would learn later that Joe Johnston, the rebel commander, had also been killed.

To this day I cannot say who the victor was. I only know I was proud of our boys. Proud to play my part within that splendid green apple that would come to be called The Irish Brigade.

CHAPTER 30

*I*t seemed an eternity before the throbbing pain of my head wound allowed me to stand erect without becoming ill. During my convalescence I became a disciple of Father William Corby, the stalwart chaplain of the Eighty Eighth.

Although a man of the cloth to be sure, Father Corby was known more for his bravery than his piety. He was both two fisted and hard-nosed, with a twinkle in his eye and a tale upon his lips. He would live to found a Catholic University in an Indiana cornfield and dedicate it to the Mother of Christ.

Hailing from Michigan, he joined up with us sometime in 1861. He was of average height and a muscular frame with bold blue eyes and a dark flowing beard that seemed to have a mind of its own. Like Dr. Reynolds, his closest companion, he was a man of letters, often quoting Virgil or the writings of Saint Thomas Aquinas. Yet when the battle raged, he would rise to the occasion, ministering to the wounded while shot and shell exploded around him.

It was the manner of his manly consolation to dying lads, wearing both blue and gray that set him apart in my eyes. In the period of my own recuperation, I witnessed the sweet soothing milk of his kindness and the honey of his boundless compassion.

He once spoke to me of war and the reasons why human history is so full of killing. At that time we were no more than ten miles from Richmond. It was shortly before the battles of the Seven Days submerged the Brigade in a series of furious bloodlettings.

We were camped near White Oak Swamp. Both McClellan and McDowell were busy seeing Stonewall Jackson in their nightmares, while Meagher was spending his nights writing heartfelt letters to the mothers and fathers of our dear departed lads. The heat of that Virginia Summer was like a hellish furnace.

I remember my longing for a cool autumn night and a stroll with my wife through Washington Square. I was dosing in one of the convalescent tents when I was awakened by the sound of Felix Duffy's voice.

It seemed Duffy had been grazed by a minnie ball, while leading Company G of the Sixty Ninth on night picket duty. Since he was in no condition to ride back to the line in the dark, Dr. Reynolds had insisted that he remain there throughout the night. Duffy was as bull headed as he was fearless. I remember interceding on the good Doctor's behalf, just outside my tent.

"Duffy, will you stop making a royal nuisance of yourself and listen to what he says"

"Well I'll be damned. Here's another country heard from," he cried. "It will take more than a nick like this to make me leave the line, O'Keefe."

"What if your chaplain requests it?" Father Corby asked, as he emerged from the darkness into the light of the campfire.

He was on his way back to his tent after a night of blessing the sick and wounded. I recall that a handful of our lads had filled their empty canteens with swamp water some days before, and come down with the malaria. Some brand of sickness was always with us, it seemed.

Since Duffy was a church going man, he attended to the good father's wishes and immediately ceased his protest. He soon apologized for any disturbance he may have caused and began to make his way to a convalescent tent. At that moment Father Corby asked us to join him for a pot of tea. Such an invitation was an honor and a privilege. Besides, I had grown weary of the same conversations of soldiers that passed my days of recuperation.

We walked together by the light of Dr. Reynolds lamp. I would see many such lamps on the battlefields where the Brigade would fight and fall. It was within the Chaplain's tent that the conversation turned to thoughts profound in nature. I believe we had finished listening to one of Dr. Reynolds lyric poems when the bandaged Duffy spoke

"You know Doctor your poetry will make The Brigade immortal someday."

"Immortal, you say?" Father Corby remarked, with the wink of an eye. "You'll not be finding immortality in mere words Captain, but in your everlasting soul."

"For sure, Father," Duffy replied. "I only meant that the Doctor's poetry will remain long after we are all dead and gone; ashes to ashes like the Good Book says."

"What is the purpose of all this misery, Father?" I remember asking, while seated on a cot inside the tent, seeking his perception on the reasons for life and death on earth.

"We live and then we pass into oblivion," Dr. Reynolds offered, as he gazed into the flickering light of the lamp, hanging above us. "It is a process that follows scientific principle, nothing more."

"You know that is not your belief, Laurence," the Chaplain remarked, while pouring a spot of tea into my cup. "Please, excuse my friend this evening. The sight of our boys dying around him has darkened his mood and shaken his faith, I fear."

"You're a better man than I, William," Reynolds remarked.

"When a dying lad grabs my hand, soaked in his own blood and demands to know why, I'll be damned if I'll speak to him of pearly gates and celestial beings. Man's bloody history is full of young boys dying for noble causes. I am weary of the whole bloody business, goodnight, gentlemen." With that he rose and exited the tent, making his way across the darkened compound.

As I watched our forlorn friend depart, I could not help but notice how he had grown so much older since that night on the veranda of the Metropolitan Hotel. I suppose all of us had grown older with the madness and the mayhem that swirled around us. I still sought an answer to my question from the one whose calling had brought him closer, I believed, to the source of my uncertainty.

"Father, what do you say? What is the meaning of our life upon this earth?"

He stared at me, and then closed his eyes for a moment, as if in some prayerful meditation. I can still recall his words to this day.

"This life is a crucible, a place of suffering and decay for the body and the mind. Yet man is more than flesh and blood. He is more than an intellect. He is by nature divine; as the Christ was divine. It is only through his time in the crucible of life that he learns. It is only through suffering that he is able to attain his divinity. This is what my faith tells me, Captain. It has been this way since the very beginning of time."

I thought often of that night with Father Corby. His words would return to me during the days and years that followed. You see, I was truly blessed by the circumstance of my life, blessed by my association with so many men of vision and noble purpose. I tell you sometimes it is as if it were a dream, a reverie arising from a flight of fancy. It is then that I think of Meagher and I know that these were not shadows, but real beings who walked the earth. No, it was not a dream. It was the flesh and blood of life with all its drama and disappointment.

I returned to my command the following evening. The lads seemed genuinely happy to see my Irish face once again. They gave to me a cherished gift. It was the gallant young Lieutenant, George Ford, who made the presentation. It was an officer's sword from the Papal Brigade. It was magnificently crafted and inscribed in Latin with the words *Vince in bono malum*. Father Corby advised me that the words meant *conquer evil by doing good*. From that night onward I would wear that sword proudly. On many a bloody plain it was all that stood between me and death in battle.

The following week Company B was assigned to picket duty in the wood outside of Gaines Mill. It was a moonless night and the lads were uneasy as they took their positions within their rifle pits and behind their fortifications. It was along the picket line that we made contact with our enemies in gray and butternut. As I recall, the company positioned across that wilderness from our own was part of A.P. Hill's division.

Those Virginia boys were crack shots alright. I swear they could see in the dark. Before we arrived on the line they had picked off two careless New Jersey lads. It was the clang of their coffee cups that betrayed them.

We spoke only when concealed and out of harm's way. I recall a particular encounter that took place on the eve of battle. It was one of the enemy who initiated the discourse. He had a sweet, sonorous Southern voice and manner. It was Sergeant Grainger who spoke from the ranks of the Eighty Eighth.

"Hey Yank, where y'all from?" the rebel called, his voice echoing through that black, humid night.

"The Irish Brigade and we have your Richmond surrounded," Grainger called back.

"Well, why you over there then? Come on in and join us. We'll give y'all a right warm welcome."

"We'll be there shortly, reb, after we finish up eatin' and smokin' our tobacco. No point in fightin' on an empty stomach now, is there?" Grainger yelled from the bottom of a rifle pit.

"You sound like a right smart fella, Irish. Why you comin' round here anyway. Don't y'a know you only gonna' git yerself killed,"

"We came to steal your women. We hear they're partial to lads from the Auld Sod."

"Ya better watch out Yank, or we be the ones stealin' yo' womenfolk, fo' this here war's over. I hear tell Old Stonewall is on his way to Washington right now. You best hightail it back home, 'fore it's too late."

"We want to see Richmond before we do. You'll save us a place at the table, now won't ya?"

"Surely will, Irish. Only, don't keep us a waitin!"

While encamped near White Oak Swamp, the Brigade received reinforcements from the Twenty Ninth Massachusetts Volunteers. We had hoped that an Irish regiment under the command of Irish Officers would join us from Boston. Yet the time was not ripe for such an event.

It seemed old Governor Andrew and his Abolitionist brethren had opposed the notion of Erin's own carrying the colors of the Commonwealth into battle. Those of us who had lived in Boston advised the others what to expect from the sons of Boston's aristocracy. At first, we saw The Twenty Ninth as a regiment of blue bloods with names like Chase and Choate. In the battles to come, both their blood and our's would be shed for the Union.

CHAPTER 31

The fear of failure has been a pox on many a powerful man. One can speak with confidence and be equipped to succeed, but if nagging doubt lingers, it destroys.

It was this fear that plagued General McClellan. He was a master of preparation, an expert at organization and a proper example of military bearing. With a fine head of auburn hair and handsome features accentuated by a robust, red mustache, he was much admired by the men of the Brigade. Yet he lacked that intrepid spirit, so essential for decisive endeavors.

It is not a hardened heart that causes me to criticize the weaknesses of the man, but rather a desire to speak the truth. The fault for the failure of the Peninsula Campaign can be found in General McClellan's quaking apprehension of defeat.

The plan of attack for the Campaign was to have McLellan join up with McDowell between the James and York Rivers and sweep into Richmond with the fury of hell itself. Instead, the Army became bogged down in the mud and the delay of McLellan's preparation, which to him seemed forever inadequate to secure success.

After Stewart harassed us with his cavalry, and Jackson made fools of Banks and McDowell in the Shenandoah, Lee divided his army and struck at Mechanicsville. It was then that General McClellan began to succumb to his fear. Instead of pushing forward and crushing Lee's army in detail,

McClellan's fears made boogie men of the rebels and allowed Lee to grab and hold a bold initiative. In truth, the Confederacy possessed a greater number of capable Generals. Had they possessed the resources of the North, we would have lost the war.

From the very outset of the Seven Days Battle, Meagher began to have misgivings about McClellan. When the Brigade was finally brought up to attack the rebels at Gaines Mill, much of the Army was already deployed to assure a safe retreat. Before the battle of Savage's Station, Meagher and Sumner met with McClellan. Both of them believed that a persistent advance could drive the rebels back into Richmond and overwhelm the city. Both of them believed that the tactic of the attack was the only way to assure a conclusive victory for the Union. General McClellan, however, was of a far different disposition.

Their meeting took place within the General's Headquarters, overlooking the Chickahominy River. It was a torrid June afternoon, as the tempers of two powerful men flared like wildfire in sun dried grass. It was Sumner who provoked the dispute, following McLellan's monologue on the need for the Army to pull back from their positions around Richmond.

"Are we retreating, General, with the church bells of the rebel capitol close enough to sound in our camps?"

"We are redeploying General Sumner. The enemy is massing in superior numbers as we speak. I will not attack entrenched positions of overwhelming superiority. I care too much for these men to order them to the slaughter."

"How reliable is your reconnaissance, General? Sumner blustered, as he stared at the map of the Peninsula set forth upon the table in McClellan's quarters. "The rebels are stripping our dead of their clothing. I believe we can deliver a decisive blow, if we have the will."

"Pinkerton has spies throughout the city. They tell him that Jackson has arrived from the Shenandoah with sixty thousand men."

"We need to strike and strike now, General," Sumner insisted, pounding his fist upon McClellan's table, his white beard and florid face giving him the appearance of an angry Father Christmas. "If we can bring our siege guns closer, we can wreak havoc upon the rebels and regain the initiative. Give me two divisions and a plan of attack and the war will be over by the Fourth of July."

"Are you questioning the wisdom of my strategy?" McLellan roared, his face wrenched with fury. "I have been called upon to save this Union and I will conduct the operations of this Army in the manner I see fit. We are falling back. I want the Second Corps to redeploy. Meagher's Brigade will hold and provide the cover for the movement of your men."

"General McClellan," Meagher interjected, attempting to defuse the situation. "I am certain that General Sumner meant no disrespect. I believe we all have a part to play in preserving the Union. I know that the President has..."

"Do not speak to me of the President," McClellan cried. "He is a baboon who knows nothing of military matters. I know the proper course for this campaign, General Meagher. Your Brigade will remain in its forward position while we redeploy. Is that clear, gentlemen? Good day."

It was a sobering event for Meagher to witness. He had seen authority exercised in many a varied way over the years. He had looked into the eyes of McClellan and saw that he lacked the courage of his convictions. A creature of self-importance, he was openly disloyal to his President. Meagher felt then that the Brigade was in the hands of a General whose disposition would not permit a bold victory.

The Army would withdraw from its position within striking distance of Richmond and begin its retreat back down the Peninsula. Emboldened by this circumstance, Lee's Army followed in hot pursuit. At Savage's Station, White Oak Swamp and Glendale, the fates would unleash the dogs of war.

I must relate an episode that occurred during the battle of Savage's Station. We were falling back beyond the Chickahominy and the enemy was hot on our tail. I recall that the rebels had transformed a train into an ironclad and mounted a thirty two pounder upon it, spewing its shells in a line of fire that fell among our retreating forces.

At Savage's Station our wounded were abandoned in misery.

We passed by them and saw so many of those brave soldiers bleeding and dying along the road. We did not want to leave them there. We helped them as best we could, knowing that their fate would soon be a rebel prison or a shallow grave. Meagher was enraged at the thought of leaving those gallant boys to the mercy of the enemy.

Our stores were burned by the ton and billowing clouds of smoke darkened the horizon. The miles were filled with marching men desperate for food, forced to eat snakes and insects to survive, while the devil darkened the door of our escape. It was a most sorrowful time for all who were present.

We of the Brigade had never left our dead and wounded. We were ashamed by the sight of so many from the other brigades bent upon saving their filthy necks and fleeing past their brothers in blue.

During the battle of the following day, a bayonet charge and hand to hand fighting gave us the trace of a reckoning. For a while we struck back at our damned tormentors. Again, Meagher was out in front, rallying the men in a series of attacks that broke the rebel ranks.

An artillery duel soon filled the plain with shell and smoke, a thunderous shattering for man and beast. I remember Major Quinlan leading the Eighty Eighth on that occasion. He was mounted upon a golden charger. I was leading a company of lads when a sea of screaming rebels swelled around us. At one point the boys from the Sixty Ninth seized two flags and two rebel batteries. In the smoke and fire of that moment I could no longer see Meagher. I feared his death or capture.

I made my way toward the place of his last sighting; a band of twenty lads following my lead. At that time, two rebel horsemen leading a ragged company of killers charged us from the left. Suddenly, William Herbert grabbed the colors of the Sixty Ninth and rallied what was left of his regiment to us. With his revolver he dropped two rebels who had drawn a bead on me. I would not forget his valiant intercession on our behalf.

Finally, the enemy broke and ran, leaving their dead. We searched the battlefield high and low for signs of Meagher. He was nowhere to be found. All the men were forlorn at the thought of his loss.

Late that night he reappeared under a shroud of mystery. His jacket and cap were riddled with bullet holes. His face was battered, and he had no recollection of where he had been. He only knew that his faithful mare, Dolly, had made her way back to our lines and a corporal from French's Brigade escorted him to the camp of the Sixty Ninth. It was not uncommon for many to be separated from their regiments in battle, when so many thousands were engaged.

Time and time again the Brigade was called upon, and performed with distinction. After each engagement, Meagher would retire to his tent and write to the mothers of brave sons who would never return home again. Like Lincoln, he began to wear the weight of this responsibility upon his person. Like a father grieving over the loss of his own sons, he would grow solemn and disheartened whenever one of our lads would fall.

I recall an occasion when I along with others of our band were visiting with him in his tent. We were west of White Oak Swamp and the rebels were all around. Dr. Reynolds, Nugent, William Herbert and I were present. After joining Meagher in a modest repast, cigars were distributed. It was clear that Meagher was not himself on that stifling hot evening. His head was downcast and his manner distracted, his elbows on the table.

"Will we engage the enemy again tomorrow?" Dr. Reynolds asked. "We have little chloroform left and our men need a rest."

"Would you like me to work a miracle Doctor, and transport them back to Fort Schuyler on the clouds?" Meagher snapped.

"Perhaps we are in need of a miracle, right about now," Reynolds answered, from across the table where Meagher was seated, his face signaling his irritation with this rebuff.

"Well you've come to the wrong place, Doctor. I have no miracles to muster. Nugent, where is the brandy?" he cried, as he pulled away from the table. He was wearing a soldier's shirt, open at the neck and his suspenders dangled over his trousers. His thick dark hair was disheveled and beneath his dispirited eyes were sacks of worry and weariness.

"You've polished off the last of it, Thomas. I'll send to the sutler for some more in the morning."

"The morning is it? I'll not wait for the God forsaken morning. Herbert, go to Duffy's tent. He always has a pint."

"I think you need some sleep, Thomas," Dr. Reynolds counseled. "The ordeal of this campaign is beginning to tell upon you."

"Sleep you say! Will you tell me how, with the faces of our dead lads haunting me when I close my eyes? I tell you, this place reminds me of Waterford, with the dying all around."

He sat down at the table once again and placed his head within his hands. None of us spoke. We all had seen too much dying. Boys so young and so full of life's promise, killed like hogs in an infernal slaughterhouse.

"Never mind me lads," Thomas moaned. "Forget the drink, William. I'll not be needing it. Doctor, I'll requisition the chloroform you need. I'm sorry that I burdened you with my melancholy. I'll catch some rest and be a new man in the morning. Goodnight to all of you."

The next day the Brigade was gathered together for a roll call. Among our four regiments almost three hundred had been killed and wounded at

Savage's Station. These losses would soar higher and higher as we fled that cursed Peninsula. Each day, as we stood in ranks, we would make our own account of the faces of those left. Haggard and starving in that scorching Virginia sun, we were laid low by the ordeal of our retreat.

Then the sight of our battered leader, back from his bout with his demons, suddenly brightened our passage through hell. At that moment, when all seemed lost, it was Meagher who gave us our will and our yearning to deliver a blow that Lee would not soon forget.

It was a cloud filled, late June morning, with a hint of sun appearing over the trees to the East. Meagher gathered the lads that remained, in a clearing behind a line of tents. He promised that they would get their chance to strike at the serpents that slithered around them. He told them to bide their time for a bold maneuver.

He swore vengeance on the bastards that fired on our flag at Fort Sumter. He vowed that those slaveholding peacocks would get their due. He did not fear the enemy. He knew that they were men and nothing more. He would make of us hounds from hell at Malvern Hill.

CHAPTER 32

etreating, fleeing, bridges to our rear burning to slow the pursuit of the relentless rebel army, we crossed White Oak Creek and sought a respite from our forced march near an old farmhouse. The Brigade was spent, with many a wounded brother in arms hanging on by the skin of his gritted teeth.

Father Corby passed among us where we lay, dispensing his blessings along with the residue from his canteen. We had not eaten a hot meal in days. The dust and heat of that place added to our misery.

Then the enemy moved his cannons to the wood before the swamp. Soon death and terror were visited upon us, as shot and shell landed everywhere. In some units panic reigned, causing a stampede of teamsters and wagoners. Most were turned back by the fixed bayonets of our reserve units. Many brave lads, deafened by the roar of the rebel batteries and the scream of their shells, cried like children in a brutal storm.

Then it was that our gunboats steamed up the James River near Turkey Bend and began to add their horrifying chorus to the spectacle before us. The sight and sound of their exploding missiles in the wood where the rebels mustered caused us to cheer wildly.

By late afternoon the enemy attacked at the Charles City Crossroads. They were determined to destroy us before we could escape from the Peninsula. After we were called up to support Hazzard's batteries, a most spectacular artillery barrage ensued. I recall huddling upon the heaving ground and praying that a rebel shell would not finish me. I saw Hazzard himself, carried from the field, his foot blown off by a rebel missile.

At that time, Sumner dispatched a rider to General Meagher. We were to move up along with Sickles' Excelsior Brigade. As we passed the hundreds of weary and wounded lads retiring from the front, you could hear their thankful voices crying and cheering. "Here come the Irish." And "thank God, it's Meagher's Irish Brigade." We were once again a splendid green apple as we marched by in battle formation.

By early morning the fight at White Oak Swamp was over. Exhausted, we made our way toward Malvern Hill and a long overdue reckoning with the forces of Robert E. Lee.

Along a nine mile front that extended across a barren plain one hundred and fifty feet above the surrounding countryside, we waited. McClellan had ordered a formation of one hundred cannons hub to hub across the crest of Malvern Hill. A flotilla of gunboats, floating on the James River secured our right flank.

The Brigade was held in reserve along the center and left of our lines. The enemy artillery began to bark at or about ten on that broiling, July morning. The enemy's tactic was first to shell, then skirmish, then attack a smaller force with superior numbers. This strategy had served them well during the battles of the Seven Days.

Lee and his generals had gambled again and again that McClellan would not stand and fight. That he would fall victim to his nature and fail to seize the day. Lee's gamble failed at Malvern Hill. McClellan's Army would play its trump and deal a blow to the bastards that had made that Peninsula a living hell. The Brigade would play a conspicuous part in that reckoning.

Earlier that morning, Meagher had been summoned along with Sumner to McClellan's quarters. "Little Mac" was resolute as he spoke on that occasion. He was confident in the knowledge that his line of supply was now intact and his flanks were secure. If there was a lesson that McClellan had learned from the Mexican War, it was that an entrenched army with superior firepower and a strategic position could hold firm against the most determined enemy. Perhaps Malvern Hill was Little Mac's finest hour.

"Well gentlemen, this is where we begin to give the devil his due" he declared, as he unrolled a detailed map of the battlefield upon a table within the shade of a spreading oak tree. He then ordered his aide to distribute Cuban cigars to each of the General Officers in attendance.

As the plan of battle was explained, it was apparent that the Irish Brigade was to remain in reserve until the appropriate time; then march into history with their green flags unfurled. This was the day that Meagher had been waiting for.

Upon his return, Meagher summoned all of his officers to a farmhouse less than a mile behind the lines. It was at that moment that he spoke with the fire we had learned to love. All of us listened attentively, yearning to do our duty.

William Herbert passed among us dispensing a wee drink as Duffy and Quinlan sat beside each other, Duffy's elbow resting upon Quinlan's rounded shoulder. Meagher's words still ring within my ears.

"General Sumner has just addressed me in the presence of our Commander, General McClellan. All of the General Staff were present as he spoke of the Brigade. "General Meagher," said he, "I rely upon the Irish Brigade more than any within my division. Again and again I have called upon them in the most extreme circumstance and they have never failed me. I commend them."

"Lads, on this day the Brigade will have its chance. All of you have seen too many of our brave boys fall, giving the last ounce of their young lives to the cause of freedom. Today we can strike with the power of their valiant spirit. Today on this field of battle lead your men as never before. Lead them with the knowledge that those who have gone before make us invincible. Lead them with the belief that through this bloody ordeal a new nation will be forged. Lead them with the conviction that God Almighty bestows his righteous power upon us."

It was then that we drank a toast to each other and received the blessings of Father Corby. Like a proud Irish clan, we were prepared and poised to kill or be killed upon Malvern Hill.

The battle began, as the enemy, true to form, commenced a barrage up and down the line, then sending its skirmishers out to probe for an advantage. By three o'clock the enemy began to concentrate on the left, mounting attacks against the positions of Kearney and Couch. At the double quick they came, ragged waves of brown and gray, their war whoops met by the oaths of our lads in blue.

Couch's men remained under cover until the rebels were nearly on top of them, then delivering volley after volley into their faces. All up and down the line of battle, brave men fought and died, while shells fell like rain from the heavens.

I remember resting in a wood surrounded by two score lads from B Company. One of the boys had captured a sheep and we were about to enjoy our first hot meal in more than a week. The sun was descending in a cloudless sky, as the smell of lamb brought thoughts of peaceful times to all that came near. As we remained in reserve, the fury of the battle wafted over the stifling air.

I remember pondering upon the courage of the lads that I would lead into the fire of that battle. They were boys mostly, with childlike faces. Their dust covered uniforms concealed boys' bodies and hearts. Most had not reached their twenty first year. Drummer boys of twelve and fourteen nestled among them like younger brothers, prepared to beat a tattoo that would cause all to rise once again and descend into the abyss of war.

I suppose it has always been the young who do most of the fighting and dying in war. Perhaps age brings with it a reluctance to follow, a resistance to forsake all that one cherishes in the fury of battle.

During those terrible years of the Rebellion, I witnessed many an act of cruelty and many a deed of the utmost devotion. Again and again I would see boys clubbing and killing the enemy like fallen angels, possessed with the blackest of hearts. Yet when the tumult subsided, they would return once again to their lost youth and their fealty to each other.

I do believe that those who perform deeds of valor in war do so for their fellow soldiers. They fight and die for their lads, determined to persevere despite the consequence, rather than forsake their companions in the ranks.

It was close to seven in the evening when the call to arms came for the Brigade. The enemy was massing fresh troops in front of Porter's position on the left of the line.

The men admired Porter and his adventurous spirit. Many had watched, as he had flown within a battle balloon weeks before; his field glass searching for the deployment of the enemy outside of Fair Oaks. His men had been at it all day. We traveled at the quick in battle formation, drums beating, fifes wailing; the sound of heavy firing drawing closer.

Colonel Kelly had replaced the fever-ridden Nugent at the head of the Sixty Ninth. Major Quinlan was in command of the Eighty-Eighth; his blue eyes shining above the grime of his face and his tawny beard. As we came over the hill, the spectacle ahead made us quake. The entire plain was ablaze with battle, shells landing, smoke rising, muskets volleying over and over. Thousands were engaged in a death struggle.

Suddenly, Meagher appeared to give us strength once more. He called to the lads by name, telling us to be brave and wreak revenge upon the rebels that had slaughtered our brothers at Manassas, Fair Oaks, and Gaines Mill. Father Corby blessed us as we passed. He was tending to the brave lads of the Ninth Massachusetts, who were being pulled back so we could meet the enemy head on. Then we headed into the thick of the horror.

Meagher rode out before us at the gallop. Herbert was beside him, along with Kavanaugh. I remember him raising his sword to Captain Hogan, as ten parrot guns were brought behind us, just beyond the crest of the hill. The rebels were charging us from the ravine that ran in front of Malvern Hill. Their strength was at least two divisions and they were led by a score of mounted peacocks. Our fifes and drums rang across the hillside and then grew silent. Then Meagher ordered the charge.

We swept into them like a tidal wave, firing at will and thrusting with bayonet and sword. It was a sea of killing, oaths and groans, the smell of powder filling our nostrils, the smoke and blaze of musket fire stinging our eyes. Two boys fell beside me, each shot in the chest. I saw another lad slashed by a rebel saber, his face cut in two.

I emptied my Colt and reloaded again and again. I cannot recall the number I killed. A rebel with a full white beard and Captain's bars came for me. He was an able swordsman, until shot through the back of the head; his brain showering my face; his gore tasting sickening sweet on my tongue.

I saw Duffy, his carrot hair flowing from beneath his forage cap. He was a dervish of destruction and death, his small sinewy frame wading among a score of rebels, cutting, slashing, firing furiously into their faces. He was like a scythe in ripe wheat. The boys of the Sixty Ninth followed his lead, battling the rebels upon the face of Malvern Hill.

Then I saw Duffy fall. He was in a melee with a bevy of rebels. O'Toole, the color sergeant from Kerry, rallied to him in the company of eighty or so lads from the Sixty Ninth. A gang of rebels met them with a volley and then charged into them with sword and bayonet. I saw O'Toole stumble, shot in the throat. As he fell, two rebels snatched the colors of the Sixty Ninth and made for their lines with the prize.

Suddenly, Duffy reappeared like a tiger, passing one through with his sword and blowing the other away with his Colt. He grabbed the colors from the grasp of the dead and held them aloft for all of the Brigade to see. The lads cheered. I tell you he was a man for the moment, that Duffy.

The rebels brought up more troops. They came at us from every direction, screaming and cursing like creatures possessed. I saw Joyce O'Connell, the handsome young captain. He was shot through the ear and the lung, his golden hair and green eyes filled with blood. O'Donaghue too would fall, his face shot away by a rebel cavalier. He was a brave lad and much devoted to the Fenian Cause.

There was Sergeant Haggarty, his insides full of grape shot. He would linger for days, before he passed. He rests now with his brother, the valiant Colonel who died at Manassas.

As the tide of the battle began to turn in the enemy's favor, Meagher reappeared and ordered those who could walk to make for the crest of Malvern Hill. "Pull back, lads. Pull back to the crest."

He was riding back and forth behind us, waving his bloody sword above his head. I heard bullets whining all around him. I saw a rebel leap upon the neck of Meagher's charger, only to be slashed to the quick. He was a man of the sword on that murderous day, I tell you.

As we retreated up the hill, three brigades of rebels were at our heels. Meagher was firing his Colt back over his shoulder when he reached the crest. It was then that I understood his signal to Hogan and the placement of the parrot guns.

With the skill of a gallant *chevalier,* he laid his charger down and ordered us all to fall to the ground. Then in a simultaneous maneuver, Hogan's men pulled the lanyards on those guns, delivering death to the bastards giving us chase, our prone bodies feeling the shock of that cannonade. Our faces buried in the dusty soil of Malvern Hill.

Again and again the rebels attacked, only to be shot to pieces by our volleys of musket and cannon. Twice more we would charge them. Our blood drenched bayonets sweeping them from the blood drenched face of Malvern Hill.

A reckoning was had at a fearful cost. The Sixty Ninth alone sustained one hundred and fifty five dead and mortally wounded. Young Lieutenant

Frank Hackett was killed along with O'Toole, Butler, and Carr. Burns, Maroney, Whitty and Leddy were sent to the transports as walking wounded, while Turner and Major Kavanaugh were dazed and carried from the field when their horses were shot from under them.

The circumstance of battle did not allow us to bury our dead with ceremony. At daybreak of the following day many a crude grave was constructed upon Malvern Hill.

I recall standing at the crest and observing the debris of the battle. Dead and wounded men and beasts were everywhere. The smoke billowed and the stench of death was unbearable. It was an apocalyptic monument to Mars. When asked to describe the conflict at Malvern Hill, D.H. Hill, replied "It was not war. It was murder."

My last recollection of that battle and the blood drenched Seven Days was witnessing James Hackett, a Lieutenant in D Company, scooping out a shallow grave for his younger brother in that blood drenched soil. I cried as he kissed his beloved sibling and wrapped him in an overcoat, placing him to his rest in a coffin made from the wood of a demolished farm house.

I would make my tally of the dead and bring them to Dr. Reynolds. He and Thomas would then write more sorrowful letters to Irish mothers.

On the transport to Harrison's Landing, a quartermaster reminded me that it was the Fourth of July. With all that had occurred, I was in no mood for a joyous celebration.

CHAPTER 33

I accompanied Meagher upon his return to New York, in order to replenish the depleted ranks of the Brigade. The Peninsula Campaign had taken a fearful toll upon each of the regiments. The pageantry of marching bands and bouquet showers had been replaced by requiems for fathers, sons and brothers who would never again see the dawn.

Along the back streets of Manhattan, and atop the hills of the Bronx and Brooklyn, the Irish grieved for the ones who had been their hope of a free tomorrow.

I was given the task of consoling the bereaved. I visited with the families of those who had died in battle. They would ask about the last moments of their lads. Did they suffer? Were they brave? Did they receive the sacraments before they passed? I must confess I told many a lie to ease the pain of those sorrowful souls.

Life was harsh indeed for those left behind. It was harsher still for widows with babes to care for. I tell you on more than one occasion I wept openly at the thought of so many fatherless children; not to mention the multitude of the maimed who hobbled back to their homes with their bodies broken by the blight of war. In many an Irish saloon, hats were passed in an effort to ease this endless suffering.

The bloom was off the rose of valor by then. Greeley's *Tribune* told of the slaughter upon the Peninsula and condemned the President for his handling of the war. I suppose the bane of a free press is a demagogue with a bully pulpit.

In many a quarter there was talk of an armistice and an ignoble end to all the killing. Still, Lincoln and others like Meagher and O'Gorman held fast to their belief in the Union. It was the last best hope of earth and it had to be preserved, despite the terrible carnage.

As a lawyer and a cherished friend, O'Gorman was much involved in the providing of assistance to the widows and orphans of our fallen comrades. All throughout New York and Boston, he and Meagher lectured on the need for a Union victory. Their devotion to the cause of freedom was exemplary. Yet the crowds that came were diminished and the Brigade's enlistments dwindled. The prospect of marching into the mouth of a voracious beast and returning without a limb or not returning at all, discouraged many a lad from rallying to the colors.

This was not as it was in the South. There the rebels could talk of defending their homesteads and preventing the damn Yankees from taking away their rights. In the North the aim of merely preserving the Union failed to excite and ignite the populace. Both Meagher and Lincoln knew that the North needed a new cause worth fighting and dying for. Passionate appeals, rousing tributes and the mastery of the moment were met with a muted response.

Among the Irish, the threat that the British Empire would enter the fray on behalf of the Confederacy would turn many a lad away from their fealty to the Stars and Bars. Such was the case with Daniel Kirby.

Kirby was a lieutenant in the Louisiana cavalry when he returned home from an engagement of his regiment to find his wife in the arms of a certain river boat gambler. A duel to the death ensued. Disgraced by the affair and disturbed at the prospect of becoming an ally of the British Empire, Kirby secured a surreptitious passage up the Mississippi and then over land to New York.

Kirby had a way about him that others admired and imitated. Like Meagher, he possessed a certain flair for the dramatic. His golden hair and dark brown eyes enamored him to the ladies, despite his recent misfortune in that regard. His walk was distinctive and his manner refined. He was impeccable in his dress and his pride made him quick to respond to the slightest affront.

An expert with the sword and the pistol, he would prove a most valued recruit during the bloodiest days of that war. The summer of his thirty fifth year would be a time of reunion for old friends and enemies alike.

We were gathered at the Hibernian Hall when he appeared among us. We were there to recruit and receive the news that Michael Corcoran had been released from the hellish ordeal of his confinement. It was a joyful interlude amid a dreadful year.

Meagher had succeeded in signing only seventeen lads from the Boroughs while four more had traversed the distance from Boston to take the place of friends who had fallen. A pouring summer rain brought a measure of relief to a sweltering Manhattan on that August night. Suddenly, we saw a figure in a yellow duster and broad brimmed black hat, skulking near the door.

It was Johnny Kavanaugh who called to him across the expanse of the Hibernian Hall.

"Come into the light and state your business.

"Is this the place of recruitment, gentlemen?" The shadow queried with an unmistakable Southern accent.

"Step up man. Come out from the shadows and let us take a look at ya," Kavanaugh demanded.

With that, Kirby emerged from the darkness and removed his hat. His golden mane tumbled to his manly shoulders, and he threw his head back, revealing the face we all knew and admired.

"Tell me," Kirby cried, as he saluted Meagher with the pomp of an officer trained within the Papal Brigade. "Is this an Irish affair or one reserved for Yankees and Abolitionists?"

"Have you come to join us, Daniel?" Meagher asked.

"I figured it's time you blue bellies learned to stand and fight. I suppose I could teach you."

"Will you give us your word to serve and defend the Union?

"I will, General.

"Then it would be an honor to have you, Lieutenant",

Kavanaugh, Herbert and Meagher then welcomed Kirby back with open arms. He would take his place within the ranks of the Sixty Ninth Regiment and prove to be a devoted friend and ally.

In the week that followed, news of Corcoran's release and return to our midst was the subject of much anticipation. I recall that Thomas was scheduled to address a gathering at the Music Hall in Boston, when he received the telegram. He ran down the hallway of the hotel to my room, in order to break the news. Corcoran had returned to New York and a hero's welcome. Meagher was as anxious as a schoolboy to see and speak with his dear friend once again.

Once again that magnetic smile reappeared upon his manly face. It seemed that nothing could darken his mood. That night he spoke to the gathered throng with the same fire as before. After his address we were invited to dine at the Copley Hotel with a score of Boston's leaders.

Thomas was accompanied on that occasion by his lovely wife. She was a vision to behold, as she nuzzled next to him. I recall that all of our party was introduced to the distinguished Governor Andrew, the freedman, Frederick Douglas and a little known writer from Concord by the name of Emerson.

Kavanaugh and I had managed to invest the punch with just enough Irish to bring a smile to even the most reserved of the Mayflower Colony. We were seated at a great table with blacks in formal attire serving us dinner. Meagher was aglow with the news of Corcoran's deliverance, as well as a goodly portion of the hotel's brandy. After dinner we spoke of the task ahead of us.

"How is your recruitment faring, General?" the white haired governor asked. He was seated across from us at the table. He was a tall, aristocratic looking man in his later years with piercing blue eyes.

"It could use a regiment of Boston's Irish, Governor," Meagher answered, while lighting his cigar from an ornate table lamp. "You do believe that an Irishman is every bit the equal of one of your home grown lads, do you not?"

"Why of course I do, General. Are you not content with the men of the Twenty Ninth?

"Indeed I am, Governor. In fact, I have resolved to make them honorary Irishmen upon my return to Harrison's Landing. Perhaps the next batch will include a few more with the names of Murphy and Reilly."

"I am told the President has made plans to organize a black regiment, General. Are you in favor of such an enlistment? Douglas asked, his voice and manner manifesting the dignity of a man who had risen above his own enslavement. He was a powerfully built figure of a man, with fiery brown eyes, a full head of coiled gray hair and broad African features.

"I am in favor of an end to this bloodshed and the preservation of our Union, Sir. If the enlistment of the black race will help accomplish these ends, I support it."

"Why do the Irish make such fine soldiers?" Emerson asked in a sonorous voice. He was a refined, handsome man in his middle years, with a prominent nose, a farmer's shoulders, and chestnut hair. He had been studying Meagher throughout the dinner and appeared an admirer of his spirit and his service to the Union.

"Just as the Bedouin craves the desert, since it is where he finds his refuge; the Irish crave a cause to fight and die for. Our history, I suppose, has made us this way."

At that moment Meagher stood and proposed a toast to his friend Colonel Michael Corcoran. All at the table raised their glasses and joined in the salute.

On the train back to New York, we reminisced about Corcoran and the fateful day of his capture at Manassas. Meagher had seen what the confinement of a valiant spirit could do. He spoke to us of Smith O'Brien and how the darkness of his confinement and exile, removed from all that he loved and cherished, had diminished him. He asked us to pray that Corcoran had retained his spirit during the ordeal of his own imprisonment.

We would know before the sunset of the following day, whether the old Corcoran had survived or a lesser being had returned to take his place.

CHAPTER 34

The lighthouse still stood erect. It was a joy to see our brother in arms once again. Michael Corcoran had returned to us from the depths, battered for sure, but not broken. His gait bore the trace of the wounds he endured at Manassas.

His confinement had indeed been harsh. At first, he was taken to a Richmond tobacco warehouse which had been transformed into a make-shift prison. There he was held along with thirty or so lads from the Sixty Ninth. It was a place where the minutes passed like hours and the days like months. What there was for food was alive with maggots and the guards were inclined to be cruel and vengeful.

Thereafter, Corcoran was taken to Castle Pinckney in Charleston Harbor. There he and his men suffered much privation. They were exposed to the elements, without the benefit of shoes and the means to remain sanitary. It was McIvor who advised us of Corcoran's courage while so confined.

The war they thought would last but a few months had dragged on and on. All the while their captors grew more resentful of their burden. On one occasion the despised captain of the guards discovered that some peaches had been pilfered.

From the ragged ranks of the imprisoned he selected a lad of seventeen for prison punishment. He was blonde, blue eyed, and vulnerable to that bastard's venom. He was stripped to the waist and tied to a post for flogging. That is when Corcoran interceded on the lad's behalf. He would pay dearly for that charitable act.

He would never speak to us of his ordeal at the hands of that beast or his sojourn at the Charleston Jail amid depraved criminals. Yet, afterwards, the manner of his speech acquired a certain stammer.

We had gone to Corcoran's home and been told that we could find him at Jones Wood. It was an August afternoon and storm clouds were closing in. The reunion that would take place would be bittersweet and would be eclipsed later by an encounter with a near forgotten serpent.

When Meagher and I came upon him he was seated on a bench, feeding an eager congregation of sparrows.

He seemed to be savoring the simplicity of this endeavor as we approached. He was wearing a pale blue shirt with a formal collar and a pair of herringbone trousers. His dark hair had recently been cut and his drooping mustache was now complemented by a close cropped beard.

I must say he appeared much older than he did before his capture. The boney angularity of his manly features seemed drawn and forlorn. He appeared a most solitary figure as we drew near. Suddenly, Thomas interrupted Corcoran's solitude with the exuberance of his greeting,

"Sure and if it's Corcoran, himself, back home among the birds of the air. My God, Michael, it is a joy to see you safe."

Startled by Meagher's approach, he was reserved in his response. Although they embraced, it was Meagher who appeared to cherish the moment more. I could see the tears streaming down his face, while Corcoran's eyes were dry and dim in their appearance. I too embraced him and felt a certain distance about his person.

"Have you seen any of the lads, Michael?" Thomas asked.

"Some" was his reply.

"Will you allow me to buy you dinner? I am sure a leg of lamb with all the fixings would be to your liking. What do you say?"

"I'll be s..staying here for a while. I enjoy the company of the wee birds. They are blessed creatures who neither kill nor hate."

He continued to feed the sparrows, while we sat on either side of him. He then glanced at both of us and seemed for a moment to be at a loss for words, a look of melancholy passing over him. He then managed a sorrowful smile and spoke as if to a priest within the confessional.

"I missed the pleasure of your c..company, Thomas"

"Oh Michael, my dear," Thomas moaned, "My heart is heavy with the sadness of these days." His tears choked his manly voice to a whisper. "I pray this war will end before all of our brave lads die."

"How many are left from the Sixty Ninth?" Corcoran asked, as he looked into Meagher's eyes for the first time.

"Of the thousand we mustered at Camp California, there are but two hundred and ninety five to answer reveille this day. I have returned to gather more lads for the slaughter, I fear."

"We must play our part, Thomas," Corcoran declared. "This war has been visited upon us for a reason. From the darkness will come the light."

"I pray that it will, Michael. I do. Now what do you say to my dinner invitation?"

"I'm famished," Corcoran answered, as he put forth his hand to Meagher and embraced him once more. This time it was Corcoran's eyes that glistened with tears.

We secured a carriage and traveled down Broadway toward the Metropolitan Hotel. During the ride we spoke at length, telling Corcoran of the travails of the Brigade upon the Peninsula. We also spoke of those two rascals, Lucky and Gosson. Like a sponge he soaked up our conversation, delighted to be removed from the ordeal of his confinement.

The meal we had was heavenly, and the company of Corcoran made our interlude unforgettable. We were seated at a sumptuous table located in the corner of the Hotel's spacious dining hall. Chandeliers, candlelight and the hotel's finest wine bestowed a glow upon the entire affair.

Word soon spread that Meagher and Corcoran were there and together. Visitor after visitor came to pay their respects and join in toast after toast. The melancholy displayed at Jones Wood was caused to disappear amid that joyous celebration.

Meagher's desire was that Corcoran would return to the command of the Sixty Ninth Regiment. Yet, during his confinement Thomas had become his superior in rank and been deemed by the General Staff to be the unrivaled commander of the Irish Brigade. This change in circumstance made Corcoran reluctant to become Meagher's subordinate, feeling that it might prove a detriment to their lasting friendship.

"Will you be joining us soon, Michael? The lads will be wondering when their old Colonel will be coming back."

"I'll not be c..coming back, Thomas. Sure and if it's your Sixty Ninth now. You're in charge of the Brigade, my friend. You are its heart and its soul. I've resolved to gather my own legion of lads to fight shoulder to shoulder beside you. When all is said and done in this war, we'll take up the Fenian Cause and free our beloved Erin. This is the way I have chosen to s..serve. Will you not be wishing me the best?"

"If that is the way you've chosen, I'll not be opposed. You will always have my loyalty and my friendship."

As we stepped through the ornate mahogany doors of the hotel, the rain began to pelt the city in torrents. A thunder storm, it seemed, had come to cleanse the cobblestones and drive away the stifling summer heat. We were sheltered beneath the crimson awning that marked the entrance when an elegant carriage pulled in front. From its interior five gentlemen in cloaks of black and stove pipe hats alighted. Their conversations and their manners were decidedly British. The chimes from a nearby church signaled that midnight was upon us.

It was said that there was a delegation of trade that had arrived from London the night before. I could tell from the librettos they handled, that they had spent the night at the Opera.

There was one among them who appeared a most familiar figure from our past. It was none other than the unworthy nephew of an Irish patriot. It was the traitor who assisted in the injustice and imprisonment of his own at Clonmel. Standing before us in the rain was John O'Connell. He was a visitor to a city where the boot of power was upon the other foot.

As soon as I made the recognition, I shot a glance at Meagher. He was speaking in cordial terms to the uniformed lad at the door, whose task was to offer greetings and secure transportation for the hotel's guests. The flattery of his manner and the vociferous nature of his address to Meagher of the Sword caused O'Connell to pause and turn slowly upon the sidewalk. There he was, face to face, with his nemesis.

There are none like the Irish for recalling a past transgression and securing revenge. Meagher's face became crimson with rage. His eyes focused their terrible light upon his old adversary. It was his practice during those dangerous times to conceal a weapon of one sort or another upon his person. I could not prevent him from drawing a rapier from the body of his walking stick and placing it against O'Connell's throat.

He spoke in that near whisper that always signaled a resolve to kill or be killed. O'Connell's companions were stricken speechless by the sudden nature of Meagher's violent salutation.

"I thought I would never lay eyes on you again. Have you come here in the company of your masters to sell more Irishmen into bondage? Or are you in league with the Confederates and an enemy of the flag that flies over this City?"

O'Connell did not speak. His face was ashen with terror. It was Corcoran who intervened, his words reaching into the depths of Meagher's vengeful spirit. I shall never forget how he towered beside his cherished friend, turning away the hand that was positioned to strike down one who had betrayed his people.

"Thomas, this is not the time or the place for such a reckoning. Allow me to serve as your second and call upon this person in the morning. If he is truly a gentleman, he will s..select a second from among his companions and agree to meet us upon a field of honor. The choice of weapons will be left to him. Now let's take our leave from these British bastards."

A most notorious bloodletting was avoided on that night. True to his promise, Corcoran appeared at the hotel the following day, only to find that John O'Connell and the rest of the British delegation had departed at dawn.

The following week a formal protest was registered by the British Government with Secretary of State, Seward. The response from Seward, one of Meagher's closest allies in Washington, was most appropriate.
My Dear Sir,

Following an investigation into the circumstance of your protest, we have concluded that your subjects were engaged in behavior that was both inappropriate and provocative at the time of their encounter with distinguished citizens of New York City. I must remind the Ambassador, that we expect any delegation from the Empire of Britain to conduct itself in a courteous and dignified manner while guests within our borders, and not engage in acts that detract from the relations between our two independent Sovereigns.

William Seward

Secretary of State

I believed we would never see or hear from John O'Connell after that occasion. I presumed that he would slither back to where he resided, among those of his kind. The future, however, would prove me incorrect. There would be one last encounter between O'Connell and Meagher. But first, Thomas and what remained of The Irish Brigade would be required to book passage through the fires of hell.

CHAPTER 35

*D*espite his best efforts, Meagher could entice but two hundred and fifty lads to join the Brigade before Antietam. Of that number, a mere forty took their place alongside the two hundred and ninety five still standing beneath the flags of the Sixty Ninth. The Sixty Third, Eighty Eighth and Twenty Ninth were likewise depleted by death, disease, wounds and desertion. Such was the state of our strength before the season of killing began in earnest.

The summer of 1862 was a time of darkness for Abraham Lincoln and the Republic he sought to preserve. He had grown tired of McClellan's resistance to his designs for a Union victory and he searched for a general who would fight and lead the Federal Army to victory. In the West, Ulysses Grant had fallen into disfavor, after the carnage of Shiloh Church and Tecumseh Sherman had yet to overcome the troubling perception that he was quite mad.

Attentive to his Republican supporters from the New England States, Lincoln settled upon John Pope as the man to lead what was then called the Army of Virginia on to Richmond. By the end of August and after the defeats of Cedar Mountain, Second Manassas and Chantilly, the President recognized that Pope was both incompetent and insufferably vain.

Once again he turned to General McClellan to win the war and preserve the Union. As I mentioned, the men of The Brigade were much enamored of "Little Mac", for it was their belief that he cared for them deeply and despite his dilatory ways, was their best hope for a Union victory.

Lee and his band of peacocks had a far different design in mind. The rebel invasion across the Potomac into Maryland had scared the daylights out of the armchair warriors in Washington. It was upon the terrain outside of Sharpsburg that rivers of blood would turn that landscape crimson.

Never has there been such a day as that of seventeen, September, 1862; nor such a slaughter as that known to history as Bloody Antietam. I suppose I should tell of it all and describe the sights and sounds of that terrible engagement. I must confess that the memory of that time and place still disturbs my rest.

The orchards and rolling hills of western Maryland presented a magnificent summer canvas through which columns of blue, wagons of white, and horses of chestnut and ebony made their way. From barn and homestead Union banners flew, as the Army marched to the martial syncope of fife and drum.

At every bend in the road, it seemed a pretty girl beckoned, with a pitcher of buttermilk and a plate of sweet cakes. As I recall, we were surprised by the warmth of our welcome, for it was said that Maryland was in the camp of the Confederacy. It was within the confines of Frederick, Maryland that a most propitious event occurred.

Those who saw the Union as the last best hope of freedom had been beseeching the Almighty for an occurrence, one that would benefit the North and alter the course of the war. The discovery of three cigars wrapped in Lee's plan for the Maryland campaign, dropped a golden opportunity into McLellan's lap.

On the 13th of September, he knew that Lee had divided his forces and sent Jackson on to capture Harper's Ferry. This discovery would afford McClellan the opportunity of using his superior numbers to defeat the rebel army in detail. What was required was a decisive plan of attack carried forth with the utmost dispatch. Although McClellan reveled in his good fortune, his delay in deployment allowed Lee and his army to escape destruction.

It is said that he who hesitates is lost. That fortune smiles upon the bold of heart. Had McClellan been possessed of the intrepid spirit of his Virginia adversary, his name would now blaze forth from the afterglow of history as the valiant leader who saved the Republic. Instead, he would command The Army of The Potomac during the bloodiest single day of that momentous conflict and forsake his chance at a decisive Union victory.

Lee was determined to stand and fight amid the rolling hills and bluffs of the Maryland countryside between Antietam Creek and the village of Sharpsburg. Over a three mile front he positioned his army of nearly forty thousand to withstand the assault he knew would come. McClellan deployed his army of seventy thousand across the creek from the rebels, and made plans to engage the enemy in a series of attacks, as dawn arrived on the seventeenth. It began as a dark, gloomy morning with pockets of mist hanging over the hollows and fields that would soon be visited by the horror of war. Many a lad in blue and butternut was unable to stomach his breakfast on that fateful day. The hardened ones were grateful that a scorching sun would not add to their agony, but they were mistaken, for I cannot remember another day when the blazing sun appeared and remained fixed in the heavens for so long.

It was just about six when the cannonade began. I recall climbing to the top of a rise as the sun began to burn off the mist. Father Corby was leading the Eighty Eighth in prayer and you could see from the faces of our lads that they knew a terrible day was at hand.

Lee's army was deployed with Jackson and Stuart's divisions facing us on our right, D.H. Hill and his North Carolinians held the center, while Longstreet was opposing us on our left, guarding the turnpike to Sharpsburg. Walker's regiments were held in reserve.

Lee directed his army from a hill overlooking the entire field of battle. I could see their forces moving to meet our men, massing on the right. They were like two seas of gray and blue positioning themselves for a cataclysm.

McClellan had deployed Hooker's forces to our right, facing a Dunker Church and a forty acre cornfield. I remember how white and peaceful that church seemed, framed within the green and gold of the woods and corn that stood nearby. The Brigade was again part of Sumner's Corps, positioned to the left of Hooker and facing a rail fence that stood before a farm.

The Sixty Ninth, Twenty Ninth, Sixty Third and my dear old Eighty Eighth were in place from right to left. Our ranks in columns of four, stood at the ready with bayonets glistening in the now scorching sun. The drums, fifes and green flags now steeling us for what lay ahead.

To our left were Franklin's forces followed by those of Butcher Burnside. His divisions faced a wee bridge that spanned Antietam Creek and led up the hill to Sharpsburg. Fitz John Porter's forces were held in reserve.

From where we were located, I could see Hooker on his milk white charger, using a glass to observe the movement of the rebels within the cornfield and the wood across the Hagerstown Turnpike from the Dunker church. From the hills beyond the cornfield Jeb Stuart's artillery began to find the range of our lines. Hooker in turn concentrated his batteries upon the rebels hiding amid the cover of the corn and wood.

Methodically, shot and shell began to cut the corn like a scythe, revealing companies of dead and wounded rebels within. I remember watching as their officers collared skulkers within their ranks and used the flat of their swords to beat them back into their positions. The slaughter was terrible.

I recall reading recitations from historians of the battle, telling how the men were eager for a fight on that day. I can only say to those who have seen the face of war and been called upon to do the fighting and dying during such an occasion, only a damned fool would be eager to engage in such an event.

To the generals and the ones who observe the killing from a distance, there may be thoughts of glory and honor. To the soldiers whose hearts beat with a furious tattoo, while shells and bullets fly around them, there is only the desire to be someplace safe and to survive. Killing and valor are often the necessary means of enduring such circumstances.

We moved off toward the rail fence as the enemy shells fell among our boys, limbs and torsos detached and hurtling through the air. Our lads were screaming, as the dull thud of grape shot tore into their flesh. It was a terrible hailstorm bringing death and destruction everywhere. I kept yelling to the lads to close up and to make their way toward a farmhouse and barn, now set ablaze up ahead.

I remember seeing Duffy tending to a lad who had been his corporal. His face was black with the smoke that filled the air about us. I saw a drummer boy from the Sixty Ninth, his drum demolished and his boyish belly torn open from the fragment of a shell. He was so young, with a babe's face, so full of fear.

Suddenly I spotted Meagher, riding back and forth to my right. I watched as his trusted Dolly, black as night, leaped the rail fence, as if engaged in a steeple chase. He was shouting. He was cursing. Calling to the men to fire on the rebs who had gathered to the rear of the farm's out buildings. His face was aflame as before. "Come on lads. Come on lads. Shoot them down. Shoot them down," he kept crying.

The rebs wheeled and volleyed toward Meagher. I thought for sure he was killed. He was not. His cap and cloak were riddled with bullets but he remained in the saddle. I cried to the lads of the Eighty Eighth, falling and firing around me. Our flag had been torn to shreds by the rebel fusillade; our drums and fifes no longer echoing across the valley. "Look at the General. Rally to him boys."

We ran up to that cursed fence, men in front being shot down as they climbed upon it. There were at least fifty of our lads dead and dying around that damned obstacle. The men behind, handing their muskets to those in front, assisting in the killing of those who were killing them.

With my glass, I looked up to our right and noticed that Hooker's batteries had suddenly fallen silent. I knew what that meant. I saw a mass of bluecoats, as numerous as leaves on the trees, sweeping down into the bloody acreage of the head high golden and green corn, roaring forth with a terrible chorus of screams. Oh, what a killing field that became!

I saw men firing and tearing their cartridges with their teeth. Stalks of corn on fire, smoke rising from that field and blackening the faces of those engaged in the killing. The sky for miles around was covered in the smoke of that tumult. It was then that I spied the sun, beating down upon us, immovably fixed in place, it seemed. The whole world seemed to stand still as that horrid day dragged on.

The thirst for all who fought on that field was unquenchable. Off to our right I could see the Dunker church; its white washed walls were now riddled with shot, shell and minnie balls. All at once a rebel brigade charged forward from the wood to our right. They were a tidal wave of hate and ferocity. They looked like haunted scarecrows come to life, yelping and cursing as they volleyed then attacked, their bayonets glistening in the sun.

Quinlan and Meagher were still in the saddle, the Sixty Ninth and Eighty Eighth surrounding them. They rallied the men in lines of fire, one kneeling, one standing above and one with muskets at the ready in the rear. "Front rank fire!" Meagher cried, as the men kneeling delivered a withering volley into the faces of their attackers. "Rear rank fire!" as rebels came and died in a storm of lead. They were decimated by the volleys that poured forth from our smooth boor muskets.

Then we were called to strip off our sacks and packs and drive them back toward the wood with the bayonet. I tell you I never saw the lads so crazed with the fury of that attack. They were crying and laughing like demons from hell itself. I saw Nugent on a charger snorting blood.

Meagher and Quinlan rode forth, hacking at the heads of the fleeing gray backs. I was chasing a haggard looking rebel with a torn slouch hat and no shoes. I took aim with my Colt and discovered it was without bullets. He turned with me at his heels and lunged with a Bowie knife in his fist.

He cut me across the chest and then sought to drive the weapon through my heart. In mortal fear, I somehow managed to wrest the knife from his grasp and slash his bearded throat. Dying and bleeding like a pig, he dragged me to the ground; his crimson hands now fixed around my throat, his face black with powder.

His eyes were like a firestorm of green. His gasping breath was upon my face. He was choking my life away, when Kavanaugh appeared and finished him with his pistol. For the remainder of that attack, Kavanaugh was by my side. I will never forget him.

It was Kavanaugh who fell wounded a life time before at Ballingarry. We had become the best of companions while recruiting lads for the Brigade. There was a pleasant way to him as well as a strength. I tell you, on the bloody field of Antietam, he was a man possessed by the god of war. I witnessed his valor again and again.

Always leading, always intent upon securing a noble victory, I saw him fall for the first time when a fragment from a rebel shell tore into his left calf. He then bore a limp in both legs, one from an Irish uprising and the other from that dreadful day, wounds that became badges of honor in the cause of freedom.

Back and forth the battle raged in that horrid cornfield. I remember cheering as Hooker's forces drove the rebels from their position and across the turnpike to another wood. It was then that Lee sent in Hood's division as reinforcement for Jackson's troops. It was a slaughterhouse of such proportions, it defied description.

Dead and dying of blue and gray were everywhere. The turnpike was strewn with corpses; their body parts torn asunder by horses and caissons charging back and forth. The cornfield was a living nightmare of gore and blood, a forty acre harvest of death. Men fought hand to hand to the death in scores. Muskets fired and reloaded so furiously they became white hot and incapable of being held, a sweeping panorama of mayhem and misery.

While positioned to the left of the Dunker church, I witnessed another event that sent shivers up my spine. McLaws' men drove Hooker from the cornfield about eight in the morning and delivered a fearful slaughter upon them near another rail fence. It was then that Brigadier General John Gibbon and his black hats of Wisconsin's Iron Brigade came to the rescue.

Like Meagher, Gibbon was a fearless leader, admired by his men. He possessed a calm and deliberate demeanor under the most terrible circumstance. Like Meagher, he inspired his men to deeds of the utmost valor. Gibbon saw that a breakthrough by the rebels at that point could turn the tide of battle against us once and for all. With the training of an artillery officer, he ordered the deployment of three batteries beyond that rail fence; then rallied the fleeing forces of Hooker around him.

Marsena Patrick's New York troops were sent in to reinforce this position. The batteries soon barked at the rebels, but their aim was too high. Double shot canister flew over the heads of the advancing enemy and landed in the vicinity of the Dunker church. With my glass, I watched as Gibbon, mounted upon his gray charger, directed the men to lower the muzzles of the cannons to meet the rebels headlong and point blank

I recall watching as that gallant soldier finally sprang from his saddle and adjusted the elevation screws upon the guns. The enemy was swarming across that rail fence as the lanyards on those fearful guns were pulled. With that thunderous volley, men and fence posts were blown to smithereens.

After three more hours of slaughter in the cornfield and woods beyond the Dunker church, the conflict to our right subsided. Thousands were already dead upon the field of battle; entire columns stacked up like so much lifeless cordwood.

I remember being told that Fighting Joe Hooker had been carried from the field, shot through the foot, while old General Mansfield was shot to death. The sun had not yet risen to the middle of the sky, when the fight for Bloody Lane commenced.

CHAPTER 36

eyond the crest of a hill in the center of the battlefield there was a sunken farm road that would become the scene of the most fearful slaughter I have ever witnessed. D.H. Hill had ordered his North Carolinians into this natural rifle pit that broke off from the Sharpsburg road and ran between rolling hills to the Hagerstown Turnpike. There the rebels were massed behind a barricade constructed from a rail fence. Gordon was in command and determined to hold the center of Lee's lines at all costs.

After the attack on the right, McClellan launched a frontal assault on this entrenched position. Calling first upon French and then Sumner to carry the battle to the enemy and break the backbone of Lee's army. We were in the forefront of Sumner's Corps. The valor of the Brigade during that bloody engagement was a testament to Irish soldiers everywhere.

In an open field, under a constant barrage, we mustered. Our task was to sweep up a hill and reinforce the beleaguered forces of General French, fighting a losing battle with the rebels near the crest.

With fife and drum sounding forth, the green flags flew over the remnants of our noble Brigade. We gazed upon each other, believing it would be our last day upon this earth. We started at the double quick, and then broke into a sprint. Meagher was riding out with his sword swinging above his head. It was the race of our lives.

The fire from the crest of that hill was murderous. I watched as scores of our lads fell in rows. It was as if they were dropping under a deadly rainstorm. I was beside Kavanaugh when he received his second wound, a shot below his collarbone. I ran to him as minnie balls whined around me. Then our torment was multiplied with the arrival of swarms of angry bees. By the hundreds, they buzzed and stung us; evicted from their hives by the infernal weaponry of man.

I will not forget the sound and the fury of that assault, the cries, the curses, the prayers and the thunder of it all. It was a whirling, swelling torrent that swept us upward toward the enemy. How many reached the crest? I do not know. I remember our banners and flags falling again and again, only to be taken up and carried forth into history by our brave lads.

Tennyson has written eloquently of the bravery displayed by the six hundred horsemen of the Light Brigade. On that day at Bloody Antietam, the Irish Brigade raced upward into the jaws of death, beneath the glory of their green flags. All were tried and true to the colors, upon that frightful day.

Upon reaching the crest, we fired a volley into the faces of the rebels fighting there, driving them toward the refuge of their lads positioned below. As the smoke cleared, we took up position on the crest. It was then that we observed the sunken road and all its terror.

Regiments of enemy infantry were massed in columns like ants swarming over a butter cake. We fired upon them and they returned fire over and over again. Slowly our forces began inching closer toward the enemy, bringing a slaughter to that blood drenched lane. In the front ranks their boys and our's fell by the score. They were so young and brave.

I remember at least a dozen lads fighting around me, firing as fast as they could, while attempting to repel the ferocious attacks of the few enemy soldiers who hurtled over the dead and landed in our midst with sword and bayonet. Arms grew weary from the slash and thrust of such close quarter killing.

I saw Shanley fall, shot through the forehead. Then Clooney was there with his knee blown apart. He stood with his sword as a cane and was cut down by a shot through the lung. At least eight of our color bearers fell in that deadly duel.

Meagher suddenly appeared on horseback. It was McGee who rallied to his calls to raise the colors and follow him toward the slaughter pen of that sunken road. I remember McGee waving the banner for all to see, screaming for the men to sweep onward toward that deadly sea of gray and butternut.

It was then that Meagher's trusted Dolly was shot from under him at the gallop. Amid the smoke, I saw Thomas lying lifeless on the slope leading down toward Bloody Lane. That was when the indomitable Felix Duffy began to make his way over the dead and dying to rescue his beloved General.

Amid a hail of enemy lead he crawled, bullets penetrating his stalwart person, his carrot red hair now blackened by the smoke of battle. I watched while pinned down by a murderous fire, as he lifted Meagher and dragged him up from near the lane. His mission accomplished, he died with his wife's name upon his lips.

Soon after Meagher and Duffy fell, I saw Johnny Kavanaugh fall. He was leading a band from the Sixty Third when a rebel volley killed every one of their number. A wife and seven children would mourn his passing.

For an eternity we blazed away at the rebs pitted against us. Then our ammunition began to run out. Fighting Dick Richardson, seeing our peril, called up Caldwell's Brigade to bring us relief. As we pulled back from the killing, we threw ourselves upon the field beyond the crest; exhausted by our ordeal and crazed with the thirst. We were lying there, attempting to catch our breath in the stifling heat.

I remember seeing Gosson being carried past me, stunned by a fall from his murdered mount. From all around the minnie balls flew. Then Caldwell's Brigade came toward us amid a storm of bullets and shells, company by company in the heat of that withering fire. We moved off from the crest of that awful hill. It was a brave and orderly maneuver under the most harrowing of circumstance.

More men were thrown into the fire as we pulled back. I saw Colonel Cross and his brave lads from the Fifth New Hampshire, rubbing the soot from their cartridge boxes across their faces like war paint, then fighting their way down toward that sunken road, screaming like wild Indians.

It was then that Daniel Kirby, late of the Louisiana Cavalry appeared near us. He was carrying a lad from the Sixty Third across his back. I prayed that he would not be killed during that errand of mercy. Although shot and shell were everywhere, they did not claim his life.

On the slope of the valley behind me knelt Father Corby, administering the last rites to a multitude of our lads. Close by this valiant priest, crouched Dr. Reynolds. He had enlisted six or so boys to load our wounded into wagons. I cried at the sight of their kindness.

Toward midday our caissons and batteries were drawn close to Bloody Lane. The fire from McClellan's siege guns had silenced the rebel cannons, positioned upon the hills beyond Sharpsburg. Then some brave New York boys worked their way into position to fire down upon the rebels swarming upon that road. Finally, a barrage at close range drove them from that now terrible trench of dead and dying. As the rebels were routed and fled into a nearby cornfield, a cheer arose across that valley of death. Still the sun was fixed in the center of the heavens.

At that time, McClellan sent an aide to Sumner, seeking his counsel as to whether his forces along with Franklin's reserves could pursue the fleeing gray backs. This deployment could well have cut Lee's lines in two and brought about the destruction of the entire rebel army. Such was not to be the case. Sumner, the Old Bull of the Mexican War, had never seen a slaughter like that of Antietam. His dispatch to McLellan advised that his command and that of Hooker had been cut to pieces, making their further engagement impossible.

Now the battle shifted to our left. It was there that Butcher Burnside was readying his forces to cross the stone bridge that spanned Antietam Creek. All morning McClellan had been imploring his reluctant comrade to commence an attack upon the left.

On the bluffs beyond the stone bridge rebel batteries were positioned to deliver murderous volleys into nearly twelve-thousand of Butcher Burnside's men. The slaughter of those stymied attacks would write a most bloody lesson on the folly of a frontal assault upon entrenched positions. This lesson however, would soon be forgotten by Butcher Burnside.

At first, Burnside ordered General Crook to the attack. He and his Ohio Regiments emerged upon a ridge that ran above the stone bridge and beneath the commanding knolls from which the gray backs soon began a deadly target practice. We watched as Crook's men moved forward toward the bridge; only to be driven back again and again by the enemy fusillade.

In the years to come, Crook would win acclaim upon the frontier as the wily Indian fighter who returned Geronimo to the reservation at San Carlos. Perhaps the ferocity of that day ignited a flame in Crook's heart that would later cause the western prairie to blaze like a wildfire. Yet, on that day, his bravery and that of his men were no match for the enemy gunners. His attacks would fail even to reach that cursed bridge.

Again McClellan demanded that Burnside press his assault on Lee's left. This time Sturgis was called to lead the charge.

A tall, undisciplined soldier, with a marginal appreciation of what lay ahead, he led his brave boys from Maryland and New Hampshire into a murderous fire, while attempting to cross that damned bridge.

It was another scene of dying boys and dismembered corpses. Over and over again they pushed forward as shot and shell fell upon them. I recall seeing scores of the brave being blown to bits, as they swept forward in that deadly storm. After two fruitless hours, those attacks likewise ended in failure.

By this time, McClellan was beside himself with Burnside's failure to progress. It is said that he dispatched an aide from his inner circle to challenge the Butcher's manhood in a most offensive sort of way. It was a Colonel by the name of Ferrero whom Burnside chose to mount the next of these fateful attacks.

Ferrero was a lady's man with raven black hair, dashing good looks and an agile muscular frame. His forces hailed from the rough and tumble streets and alleyways of New York and Philadelphia. It was said that the Fifty First New York and the Fifty First Pennsylvania were two of the rowdiest regiments within McClellan's Army.

I know of one occasion when Gosson and Lucky set up their own sutler's store, within hiking distance of these unholy lads. Their aim was to dispense homemade rotgut and secure a small fortune from men who drank and fought like a horde of demons.

It was Gosson who told us that many of the lads in service to the Fifty First New York had been enlisted straight from the jails of the City and given their parole as an inducement. I do believe this was an exaggeration, yet not without a grain of truth.

In bold blue lines of two plus two, they marched then rallied to the double quick. Amid the wooded hillside, directly beyond the bridge, there were four hundred or so Georgia sharpshooters under Toombs'command. They delivered a murderous fire down upon those charging bluecoats, dropping them in rows, as they fought their way across that cursed bridge.

I watched a shell strike the stone borders of that span, showering granite fragments upon those brave lads. After what seemed like an eternity, our guns finally found their range upon the hillside and bluffs where the enemy field pieces were positioned. After another hour of savage assaults, Ferrero's men finally made it across and began to fight their way up the hill into Sharpsburg.

It was about this time that troops under the command of Rodman waded across Antietam Creek down-stream from the stone bridge and ran smack into Lee's right flank. Again the fighting was furious. Then the luck of Lee once again hastened to the rescue.

It was then that A.P. Hill and his foot sore regiments arrived upon the battlefield in the nick of time. Those ragged sons of the devil had just captured Harper's Ferry and many were wearing the stolen blue coats of the Union forces. Suddenly, those rebels, dressed in blue, began attacking Rodman's Connecticut boys, while screaming like banshees. Rodman's forces hesitated, then faltered, then fled in a rout.

This was the time for McClellan to throw caution to the wind and deploy Porter's forces held in reserve. Once and for all he could seize Lee's Army by the throat and throttle it for trespassing into Maryland. At that point, however, the apprehension of defeat reappeared within his heart. He had wildly overestimated the strength of the enemy forces marshaled against his army. His hesitance of purpose would not permit him to commit all his forces to the fray.

They say that twenty six thousand fell on that fearful day.

We of the Brigade suffered more than five hundred casualties. I recall lying amid the remnants of the decimated Eighty Eighth, looking out over that horrid place, watching the surgeons' lamps flicker, as they made their way through the multitude of wounded, hearing their desperate cries for mercy, water, and an end to their ordeal upon this earth.

I pondered upon the events of that frightful struggle and told myself that a victory of sorts had been gained. Lee had not carried the day. In truth, his army had not been destroyed, yet it had been deterred. This, I reasoned was an achievement. Our army had not been chased from the field by those ragged sons of the South. This in a sense spelled victory.

I could not help but admire those who wore the gray and butternut of the Confederacy on that day. They seemed to possess dash and a strength of purpose that far exceeded our own. I wondered whether we would ever truly defeat such an army, ever really vanquish such a foe and return to our homes with the war won.

I knelt and prayed for our dead. I recalled their faces and was overcome with a profound regret. There they appeared before me, Duffy, Clooney, Shanley, Kavanaugh, Mansfield, Richardson and so many thousands more.

I could not help but think that somewhere across that place of slaughter knelt another captain, wearing the rebel colors, praying for his dead and likewise wondering whether the war would destroy all that was good and worthy on both sides. It was Lincoln who would give to those who wore blue a new cause worth fighting and dying for.

CHAPTER 37

Throughout the ranks of our devastated Brigade there was an abiding concern for our leader's welfare. As I made my way from campfire to campfire with our weary men lying beside their stacked muskets, again and again I heard the inquiries. "Any report on the General, Captain? Is the General still with us? Have you heard tell of General Meagher?"

I must confess that my heart bore a wee trace of envy at such a showing of love and affection among the men, and yet I too was beset with the same sentiment.

The Brigade was the child of Meagher and when its father was carried from the field at Antietam it seemed diminished, bereft of its beating heart. My love for the man I had followed along the quay of a dying Waterford and through the dawn of a Limerick bloodletting would not allow me to sleep on that night. I secured a horse from a protesting quartermaster and rode out for an answer. Did Meagher still reside among the living or was he at rest among the dead?

As I rode behind our lines, I shall not forget the sights to which I was witness. Everywhere I traveled, there were wounded and dying. It was as if the Almighty had become incensed with humanity itself and was bent upon an apocalypse that would consume us all.

I wondered what awful transgression had merited such a dreadful retribution. My mind was too disturbed to deliver a response. I was focused upon another inquiry. Where in that world of misery was my General? It was in an old church with a whitewashed steeple where I learned the answer.

There was a congregation of officers milling around the courtyard of that place of worship, when I arrived. It was, I learned, the site of McClellan's headquarters during the early morning assault by the forces of Hooker and the struggle in the cornfield. It was now a field hospital for commissioned officers.

As I dismounted, I saw Dr. Reynolds descending the church's stairway. He was wearing a leather apron, drenched with blood. His once cherubic face seemed drawn and his hair was now a snowy white. His spectacles were perched upon his head and he seemed to drag his weary figure along, as if his narrow shoulders were the recipients of an enormous burden. I could only imagine his ordeal in ministering to the dead and dying from that unmerciful killing field.

"Doctor Reynolds, it is a joy to see you alive and well," I cried, as I tethered my horse upon a nearby picket fence. He looked up and seemed at first unable to recall my identity. His pale blue eyes were distant and distracted in the torchlight.

"Oh my boy, I thought you were lost along with our dear Kavanaugh. Have you come to inquire of the General?"

"Yes Doctor, I saw him fall and watched as Duffy was killed, dragging his body from before the sunken road. Tell me, is he alive?"

"It will take more than a tumble from a horse to kill the likes of him. God bless Felix Duffy. God bless all our brave lads. They did themselves proud on this bloody day."

"Where is he? Can I speak with him?" I asked, my heart filling with a joyful relief.

"He is resting inside. He'll have a whale of a headache and I removed some grape shot from behind his knee, but he should be his old self in a week or so. Go in and say hello. He was asking for you. It's good to see you in one piece O'Keefe. I must tend to the others. Good night, now."

"God bless you, Doctor," I whispered, overcome by the depths of his caring nature. I watched as he crossed the road toward a farmhouse filled with more wounded lads. He would labor in the awful vineyard of his calling until dawn. Oh, what a giving soul he was! Oh, what a credit to a noble profession!

As I entered the church, I could smell the stench of death and chloroform. There was a large wooden cross that was nailed to the wall across from me and at least a dozen officers lying upon gray army blankets draped over pews of white oak. There were three nurses dressed in blue and white linen moving about among the wounded who suffered there. Lanterns and candles cast shadows upon the walls and gave the interior both a solemn and a celestial appearance.

I approached one of these angels of mercy and asked her the whereabouts of General Meagher. She pointed me toward a small room toward the front of the church. Within that room I saw him, lying upon a blanket on a large oaken table. He seemed to be sleeping. His left leg was bandaged at the knee. His bullet riddled cloak and forage cap were laid beside him upon a cane back chair. A large window allowed the moonlight to shine into the room. Upon a nearby table, there was a small white porcelain pitcher and basin, next to a flickering candle.

As soon as I drew close, he opened his eyes. I cannot describe the joy of that moment. Neither of us could speak. Tears were in our eyes and in our throats. He raised a trembling right hand and placed it in mine. I kissed him for the first time and tasted the salt of his flowing tears. As he held my hand, he smiled a faint smile. There are none so close as brothers in battle.

"I feared you were lost," he whispered. That was all.

On the night of the following day, we heard what seemed to be the sound of a mighty river echoing across the distance. In a sense, it was a river, a river of men and horses, wagons and caissons. It was Lee and all that remained of his bedraggled gray army, marching back across the Potomac toward Virginia.

There were no fifes or drums, no rousing anthems to raise the spirits. There was simply the thunder of those weary legions, abandoning all their dead and many of their wounded upon that blood red battlefield. As dawn spread an orange stain across the heavens, thousands of grotesque apparitions populated that valley. It was as the psalm says, a valley of the shadow of death.

There were multitudes of bloated corpses, blackened by the sun. Swollen carcasses of horses and mules with grave expressions that signaled their incomprehension of that inhumane habit of man, known as war. The Antietam flowed with a rusted hue, painted by the bloodied dead, bobbing like corks within its waters.

Over a three mile swath, in every imaginable contortion, lay the rotting remains of the brave who gave their lives for a cause or colors that would fade. All around were burial details of blacks, enlisted to hide the remains of those who were once young and gay beneath that fertile blood drenched soil. A myriad of flaming pyres fanned by a September breeze brought the greasy stench of slaughtered horseflesh to the nostrils of all who roamed over that horrid cornfield, those merciless pastures, that terrible sunken road and that grave stone bridge.

I wandered with William Herbert. His face was wrenched with the agony of one who had played a part in that indelible episode of murder. I recalled the song of his violin and wondered if he would ever slide his bow in a joyous reel again.

He seemed stooped as we walked beside each other. His blue jacket and trousers were covered in blood and his cap was gripped firmly between his hands, in honor of our noble dead. His handsome face was mired in soot. We did not speak. Words were no match for the sights and sounds of that dreadful valley. We watched them shoveling scores of dead rebels into a massive trench, known now only to God. I looked away, fearing I would see a quiver or a shake from those whose hearts still beat while being buried alive.

We came upon Father Corby overseeing the placement of tiny white crosses upon the graves of our dear departed lads. I asked of him the number of those who had fallen within the Eighty Eighth. He stared at me for a moment, his face bespeaking a profound sorrow. He then recited from rote, twenty eight killed outright and another seventy seven wounded and carried to the surgeon's tent.

It was Herbert who inquired of the Sixty Ninth's roll of dead and wounded. The response was forty four killed and one hundred and fifty seven to endure the surgeon's knife. Oh how fleeting are the joys of this earth. Oh how imminently hovers the angel of death over those who take up the warrior's lot.

Near the Dunker Church we spied them, like vultures swarming near carrion. Their implements were cumbersome and their design callous. His name I learned was Brady. He made his living as a purveyor of photographic displays. He was a short mole-like man with dark unruly hair and pointed features. He was wearing a surgeon's coat of white and he was surrounded by a bevy of fawning assistants.

As we approached he called to us in an irritating voice, inquiring whether we wished to become a part of history by striking a noble pose amid the dead of Antietam.

It was Herbert who shouted the oath that spoke of our shared outrage. I suppose there are always the greedy ones who seek to feather their nests by making spectacles of human misery.

I remember seeing a prominent piece in the *Tribune,* upon my return to New York. It touted the gruesome nature of that mole's handiwork. I tell you I was repelled by this morbid fascination.

I wanted to stand outside that detestable side show in protest.

As one who had fought and killed on that terrible day, I felt lessened by the disregard of such a display. To most, Matthew Brady was a pioneer, a historian who brought the personages and horror of the War of the Rebellion to the world. To those who bore witness to the dreadful slaughter that was Antietam, he was a jackal who cared but little for our noble dead.

CHAPTER 38

It is said by some that life is like the sea, a perpetual series of ebbs and flows. I know now, but did not know then, that from the conflagration of Antietam, a bright new blaze of liberty would be ignited. I know now, but did not know then, that the War of the Rebellion was the crucible that would make us a nation of free men. Redemption is always a painful ordeal.

I recall gathering together in the village of Sharpsburg; our band of brothers had been reduced in number and our resolve to fight and die for the preservation of the Union diminished. Duffy and Kavanaugh were gone and more than five hundred of our brave lads had been killed and wounded alongside them.

Meagher, himself, was among the casualties. The absence of his fiery spirit seemed to remove the torch which blazed our path through the dreadful darkness of that war. We were lost and in need of a new beginning.

Lee had returned to Virginia and McClellan had decided to leave him be. Meanwhile, the Army of the Potomac licked its wounds and sought a renewal of its will to win the war.

Like a messenger from the Almighty, Abraham Lincoln came forth to fortify our hearts. Within a week, he would lift up our souls as well. I recall standing upon the dusty streets of that village, still stained with the blood of the brave soldiers who had fought and died there. The stench of decaying flesh was still in the air on that warm September afternoon.

As Lincoln passed, we cheered him as our true and exalted leader. He then climbed the stairs to a makeshift speaker's platform, while all who congregated nearby awaited his address.

I do not recollect his words, for I was far removed from the place of his pronouncement. It was the aura of his presence that seemed to lift us from that valley of death. Later, he walked among us, his statuesque figure apparent above the crowd. We could tell that he cared deeply for us all by the pained expression he exhibited and the manner in which he offered both solace and counsel to all who approached.

I remember happening upon Quinlan on that occasion. He too had been made weary by the sight of so many of our lads falling around him. I was in the company of Herbert and Kirby when we spotted him, seated upon a stone wall near a rusted gate, bordering the Sharpsburg Road.

"Quinlan, come along with us," I called.

He sat there stationary and acknowledged my greeting. He then motioned for us to join him at his place of rest. It was shortly after Lincoln had departed in the company of McClellan and the others from the General Staff. As I drew near to Quinlan I determined the reason for his fixed position. He was three sheets to the wind and incapable of removing himself from his perch near that rusted gate.

"Quinlan, you're as drunk as a lord," Kirby remarked in a soft syrupy Southern way.

"You're damned right I am, and I plan on stayin' so, for a long time. 'Tis a soldier's prerogative to grab a snoot full after a battle such as this. I tell ya, I never saw such a fight. I swore the sun was fixed in the heavens above us."

"Aye," I replied. "Did you hear Lincoln's speech?"

"Indeed, and they were fine words that were said. I do believe I'd follow such as he down the barrel of a rebel cannon. I've not seen his like upon this earth, and that's a fact. I'm told he plans on freein' the slaves now that Lee has left his dead and hightailed it back home. I tell ya, the worm is about to turn. You mark my words, lads. The worm is about to turn alright, and a new day is comin'. A new day is comin'."

We were camped upon Bolivar Heights when we heard the news. Lincoln had done it. He had freed the slaves and raised the hymn of battle to a higher, more meaningful octave.

I must admit that I was uncertain whether this was the righteous course to follow. Most who fought beneath the green flags were opposed to

Emancipation. We looked upon it as the unholy province of the Abolitionists and against the interests of the immigrant Irish.

It was Lincoln who would help convince us that the freeing of the slaves was indeed a noble endeavor. But it was the black soldier who would help to win our respect, by shedding his blood in battle. And finally, it was a glorious hymn, written by an aged New York woman that would help to capture our souls and lead us to fight and die for a new birth of freedom.

In October Lincoln would pay an unexpected visit to our camp. By that time the lads who had managed to survive the fiery ordeals of Malvern Hill and Bloody Lane had warmed to the serenity of their new surroundings, and began once again to work and play in the forgotten joyfulness of their youth

It was not that way with Meagher. It seemed the blow to his head and the task of writing even more sorrowful letters to family members at home had taken its toll upon his nature. He had lost interest in manly conversation and began to resort to the drink at a regular turn.

For days he would be down with the melancholy, locked in his quarters alone, foul of mood and profane of speech. The ordeals of his storied life had begun to weigh down upon him. He was a man beset by a yearning to break free.

We soon began to talk among ourselves regarding his behavior. There was a sea of concern for his well-being. Just before Lincoln arrived, we managed to corner Thomas and reach out to him. It was Father Corby, Dr. Reynolds, Nugent and I who resolved to take matters into our own hands and resurrect his spirit from the depths.

At first he refused our overture, unable or unwilling to look into our faces for fear of what we would see. It seemed that he was determined to drink himself into an early grave. While he was down with the drink, we managed to gain entrance to his quarters. He was without hope and in desperate need of a helping hand.

It was I who seized him and attempted to bring him to his senses, while Dr. Reynolds administered a concoction that sent shivers through his system and rendered him adverse to the sight and smell of the drink. It was then that he lashed out, fighting and cursing every one of us. Even Father Corby received his venomous abuse. Then we watched him wretch and cry, wrestling with his demons. I tell you it pained us all to see him in such a lowly state. Then, after days of despair, he began to emerge once again as the one we were proud to follow.

"Is that you, Doctor?" he whispered.

"It is I, Thomas." Reynolds answered. "You've had a rough time of it. You need to take your rest now."

"I was chained upon a ship with our lads," he moaned. "All were corpses, shot full of holes. Their mothers kept asking me why. I lacked the means to give them solace, Doctor. Their words were echoes over and over. What has become of my loving son? Why did you lead him away to be killed? I could give them no reply. Their sorrow sealed my lips."

We drew around him. Each of us feeling the agony he was under, each of us yearning to remove that awful cup of misery from his breaking heart. We would each take our turns at his bedside, ministering to his needs and partaking of his company.

In the hope that the salve of an Irish melody would soothe him, I summoned the regimental fiddler, Johnny Fleming. It was then that the old Meagher seemed to reappear. The blush soon returned to his manly cheeks and the light of his violet eyes again shone forth. That was the day before Lincoln arrived.

As I recall, we were engaged in a game of rounders between the lads of the Sixty Ninth and those of the Eighty Eighth. Gosson was in rare form with the shinny stick on that sun splashed October afternoon.

On each of three occasions the swing of his manly arms had launched the ball far beyond the reach of two of our swiftest lads. With each of these missiles, he would shout and cackle, and make the rounds of that diamond shaped field, bare-chested and breathless upon his return to the markings called home.

At that time two riders approached, advising us that the President and an escort of officers were making their way to our camp. I then spied Meagher, galloping in from the East. He was mounted upon a snow white mare with Herbert and Nugent riding alongside. It was upon that field that he and Lincoln encountered each other once again.

The manner of their greeting manifested their respect and admiration for one another. Meagher was flattered that Lincoln had taken the time to seek him out and renew the acquaintance made at the White House the year before. Both spoke of the times and the trials that lay ahead. I recall Lincoln passing among us. He wore a black coat and trousers, with a stove pipe hat. His voice seemed to crack when he spoke and yet his words touched our hearts.

As I grasped his hand, I reminded him of our farewell in the moonlight of a lifetime before. He seemed to recollect the occasion and patted my shoulder in a fatherly way. He told us that the war had now become a crusade. He assured us that the emancipation of the slaves was the righteous course to follow. Time would prove to all of us that Lincoln was right.

CHAPTER 39

While the Brigade remained at Bolivar Heights, it was joined by the 116th Pennsylvania Regiment. Soon thereafter word was received that McClellan had been replaced and we were now under the command of Butcher Burnside. That was a dark day indeed for the Army and most especially for the Brigade. It seemed that the politicians in Washington had hounded the President into the removal of the only commanding General, before Grant, who enjoyed our confidence.

I recall the last time I saw McClellan. It was a blustery cold day. The wind was whistling across the plains and valleys surrounding our camp outside of Warrenton, Virginia. As McClellan approached, Meagher ordered the Brigade to throw down its flags in tribute. In a gentlemanly gesture "Little Mac" ordered the men to refrain from such a display, reminding them that the green flags should not be desecrated by such an act, no matter how well intentioned the sentiment.

We knew that McClellan lacked the killer's instinct; that his hesitance in times of crisis and tumult was a most unfortunate burden for a President whose supporters demanded a bold victory. Yet, on that day, as that proud and comely man passed into history, I must admit that the mood of the men he molded into a fighting army was melancholy indeed.

We were in desperate need of more recruits for the ordeal ahead. The Twenty Ninth Massachusetts had been transferred to the Ninth Corps and the all Irish Twenty- Eighth took its place within our ranks. They were a fine company of fellows, enlisted for the most part from the streets of Boston, with names that were familiar to those who hailed from Cork and Galway. After we moved our camp to Falmouth, Virginia, Meagher dispatched a delegation from the Brigade to make its return to New York City.

When we reached New York, emancipation was upon the lips of all we passed. Lincoln had understood better than any, his people's yearning for a higher purpose to justify the sacrifice of war. While we walked the streets of The City, we began to sense that the spirit of the people had somehow been uplifted by Lincoln's proclamation.

We of the Irish Brigade knew well what it meant to fight for freedom. It was Lincoln who taught us that fighting for the least of our people would help secure the blessings of liberty for all of our people. Such was the greatness of the man. We were soldiers in Mr. Lincoln's Army now, an army whose purpose was to make men free.

Meagher had selected our delegation from the ranks of each of the original regiments that comprised the Brigade. He placed Lieutenant Colonel James Kelly in charge. I tell you when the twelve of us walked down Broadway, three abreast, the blue and gold of our crisp new uniforms turned many an admiring head. Sure and if we were as proud as young men could be. We were battle hardened veterans, now standing in the forefront of a noble cause.

Our mission was threefold. We were to visit with the families of our dear departed lads. Then we were to attract as many as we were able to an enlistment within the Brigade and last we were to retire our bullet riddled flags for pristine banners of silken green and gold.

Along the way we were permitted to return to the arms of our loved ones and to toast a pint or two to the causes and companions that had made our service worthy. It was while we were engaged on one such occasion that we became embroiled in a most glorious donnybrook.

Each of us had been supplied with the names and personal effects of comrades who had fallen on the field at Antietam. We were to seek out their families and deliver their cherished articles, along with a letter written by either the General or Dr. Reynolds.

My task was to visit with the bereaved of the courageous Felix Duffy and the beloved Johnny Kavanaugh. As part of my preparation for these sad encounters, I was required to read the heartfelt letters labored over by our leaders and recall in my own words the essence of those departed.

I had rehearsed my tragic lines over and over again. I knew that once I saw the tears of the loved ones I had met during those glorious days at Fort Schuyler, I would be in dire need of a recitation to rely upon.

Meagher firmly believed that the members of the Brigade were brothers in life and in death. He would tell us that the deceased were still with us in spirit and that we could call upon them in times of tribulation. By believing that our filial devotion eclipsed the boundaries of flesh and blood, the loss brought about by death was lessened.

Duffy lived in the Borough of Brooklyn. Because he had served in the Mexican War, he could speak to us in intimate detail of men like Lee and Longstreet, Sherman and Kearny. When my thoughts turned to Duffy, I recalled his carrot colored hair and the manner in which he saved the life of Thomas Meagher.

Duffy was a Christian gentleman who loved to raise his tenor voice in the joyous strains of an Irish melody. Like Meagher, he was enamored of the dance and the gallop of fine horseflesh. He commanded Company G of the Sixty Ninth with a firm but forgiving hand. I once saw him speaking like a caring father to a lad who had turned tail and run at the battle of Savage's Station. That self-same lad would die while carrying the colors into Bloody Lane. Duffy would be placed to rest beside him on that day.

Duffy loved his men and sought to safeguard both their bodies and their souls. His wife and four of his five children were present when I climbed the creaking back stairs to their domicile. As soon as I appeared, she knew my purpose. I comforted her with my recitation; rendering my service with a breaking heart, yet managing to refrain from crying aloud. Her tears fell like rain.

It was the youngest, a lad of no more than seven years, who called after me as I made my way toward my horse. He shouted in a quaking voice that he too would be a soldier someday, just like his Da. On the ferry boat that made the crossing to Manhattan Island, I prayed fervently for Duffy's wife and children.

The Kavanaugh's lived with three other tenant families in a house of stone and wood. I had known Johnny Kavanaugh since our days together in the Irish Confederation. He was a handsome man with golden hair, green eyes and a noticeable limp, obtained in our fight to free Ireland from its oppression.

I also knew his wife, Nannie. She had been Johnny's sweetheart since childhood. I tell you they were devoted to each other and neither rebellion nor war could keep them apart for long. Together they brought seven children into the world. As I walked up the hill leading to their home in the Bronx, I recited again the words of my heartfelt eulogy.

I came upon Nannie and her children just after their return from Sunday Mass. I told them of their beloved John's valor and the nobility of his sacrifice. I delivered a lock of his golden hair and the bible he kept next to his heart. I was nearly finished with my recitation when his little girl climbed upon my lap and asked why her father had not returned. I tell you I could not hold back my tears. I will never forget her sorrowful face. Oh, but war is a most inhuman state of affairs!

In those days there was a significance to our flags that brought fire to our hearts. Again and again the most enduring acts of manly courage would take place in seizing or protecting the sacred cloth we called a flag.

To Meagher and to almost all who fought on both sides of that conflict, flags were symbols, relics to be cherished and honored. They stood for the glory of a country, a state, a brigade, or a regiment. They spoke of devotion and a nobility of belief. They gave meaning and remembrance to the sacrifice of so many brave men who shed their blood in that war. The ceremony in which our war torn flags were retired was a most memorable occasion for our band of twelve.

Following this ceremony we were the guests of honor at a most sumptuous banquet. There was music and a display of step dancing by a dozen colleens of tender years. Most of their parents had come to America at the time of the Great Hunger. It was a delight to observe the bloom of their cheeks and the radiance of their smiles.

Thereafter the crowd was treated to a spirited rendition of the Battle Hymn of The Republic. It was reported that the composer was a woman of advanced years who awoke from her slumber with the lyrics ringing in her ears. I was told the singer was attached to the Opera. He was a barrel of a man in a burgundy coat. He had a bald pate and a most powerful baritone voice. I tell you upon hearing the strains of that stirring melody for the first time, I was overcome with a sense of our noble destiny.

As we made our way through the streets that evening, we could hear that hymn over and over. As Lincoln would remark, we of the North. now possessed an anthem that rivaled *Dixie* and a cause that would bring us glory.

Before we were to make our return back to the battle front, the twelve of us made the most of our last night in the City. After dinner at the Metropolitan Hotel and a series of fiery speeches and fond remembrances at the Hibernian Hall, we traveled to the Bowery to observe a display of the manly art of self-defense.

It was a November thaw and a bare knuckled prize fight that brought us to the docks overlooking a torch-lit barge. There, stripped to the waist, amid a crowd in formal attire, stood two willing participants in a fight to the finish.

The combatants were Jerry McRory, back from his enlistment with the Fifty First New York and a dark, hair covered specimen known simply as Bulldog. I tell you they went at it with a vengeance, until our twelve became embroiled in a much more encompassing display. It was a matter of respect and honor that brought our delegation to center stage on that night.

I believe I advised you that the one we called William Herbert was in reality a Russian Jew who had once made his living by his wits, under a myriad of aliases. Herbert was a dashingly handsome devil with an insatiable appetite for ladies of questionable reputation.

It seems that while we were engaged in the placing of a pooled wager, Herbert had come across a comely acquaintance who had gained some respectability by taking up with one of the Bowery's more notorious hoodlums. Having been engaged in far more pressing matters over the previous two years, Herbert was unaware that this lady fair was not only spoken for, but jealously watched over by this aging former convict.

It was not Herbert's practice, nor his preference to throw himself at any member of the fairer gender. He, like Meagher, displayed a certain reserve and grace that enhanced their manly charms and enticed the kind of creature who found such traits irresistible. Such was the case on that evening.

Of course, all of our number were in civilian attire and thus without the protection that patriotic fervor might allow. It began when a gang of burly hooligans surrounded Herbert, while he was standing inexcusably close to the object of their leader's affection. In truth, we may have had the opportunity to avoid this engagement, but the surly manner of those bastards and the intemperate nature of their address to one of our number made our blood boil. The drink, of course, contributed to our pugnacity on that occasion.

I suppose they believed that Herbert was alone and therefore vulnerable to their bullying ways. They seemed quite determined to deliver a memorable lesson in manners to our rakish friend. Their designs, however, would meet with a bold resistance. I am certain they were most unprepared for our response, for we had grown quite accustomed to the most sanguinary of engagements.

When they sought to drag Herbert from that place and tar and feather him, we interceded. It was McGee who inquired where our friend was being taken and received a most ignoble shove from the gang's ringleader, a profane scoundrel with a nose reddened and disfigured by too much of the drink. It was Gosson who lifted this rum pot above the crowd and deposited him head first in the river flowing around the barge.

From that point onward, it was a ferocious brawl, all of our number engaged in a brand of fisticuffs that put McRory's and the Bulldog's minuet to shame. I tell you I never saw such a fight without killing. There was gouging and there was biting. There was the tearing out of hair. There was Gosson taking two lads and running them into two being held by his accomplice, First Lieutenant Charles Lucky.

I saw Lynch kick the shins of at least three and lay them out cold with one punch each. I recall Tracy, taking one, falling upon his back and pitching the bastard with his foot into the freezing river.

I was most proud of Herbert. He was not a large man by any means, but he was sinewy and he was strong. After taking a full measure of three of their number, he fought like a champion and reigned victorious over the lot.

As a final gesture, he grabbed a hold of the lady whose charms occasioned that melee. He lifted her up and then brought her down into his manly arms, kissing her lips.

With our enemies in flight, submerged or knocked senseless, Colonel Kelly called us to attention. With the precision of a finely tuned weapon of war, we marched three abreast from the scene of that Bowery battle, the cheers of the crowd ringing in our ears.

CHAPTER 40

There is much superstition in war. Of those who managed to remain alive within the dwindling ranks of the Brigade before the fearful slaughter that was Fredericksburg, most believed that charms and rituals would aid in their safe return home. Our origins I am sure played a part in this disposition. The Celts were a fierce yet fearful people, who relied upon rites and incantations to light their journey through the Dark Ages.

Legend says that Patrick, our patron saint, was more of a sorcerer than a priest. That he conversed with spirits and used his powers to drive the snakes from Erin's green earth. It was he, they say, who gave the shamrock its significance. Within the towns and villages of our youth, the old ones told of fairies and banshees that dwelt among us. On our march toward the Rappahannock on a cold December morning, an episode occurred that sent a shiver down all of our superstitious spines.

I was again in command of Company B of the Eighty Eighth, as our weary column of blue dragged itself along a winding country road that stretched like a snake toward that river of no return. There was a picket fence in disrepair to our right as we came within sight of a bungalow, ravaged by the blight of war. The men began searching it in a vain attempt at forage.

It was then that we heard her wailing in the distance. She made her way toward us across a barren field, wrapped in a ragged shawl. The mist was thick upon the earth. She was a crazed woman of ancient years, toothless and disheveled. Her whitened hair was in disarray and her boney fingers exhibited blackened nails of noticeable length.

Some said her name was Ashby and her son was a rebel general killed during the Peninsula Campaign. Others insisted she was a witch, whose curses were an omen of a dreaded event about to occur. As we passed, she writhed and shrieked in a most unsettling manner, while none of our number sought to silence her demonic display.

I remember that the lads were spooked by her demonstration and sought to defend against her vile oaths by crossing themselves. Then Meagher rode up on a golden horse and confronted her where she stood. The boom of his voice echoed through that misty morning.

"Be gone woman," he bellowed. "Your curses will not bring your son back to life."

"You're all doomed, doomed," she howled. "Your wives and babes will never set eyes on you again. Your mothers will cry in the night, as I have cried. Goddamn your Yankee souls to hell."

Later on, just before the rebels turned our flank at Chancellorsville, Meagher would speak of this strange and unsettling encounter. It seemed that the appearance of this crone had been foretold to him by that mysterious old woman in New Orleans. It was a premonition that a time of much disaster was at hand.

As we marched onward, Meagher sought to allay the men's fears that the old woman had somehow placed a curse upon them. I remember him snatching a sprig of evergreen from a nearby hedge and affixing it to his forage cap. The lads followed suit and festooned their attire with these emerald boughs. As I have recited, we are a people inclined to superstitious beliefs.

After Fighting Dick Richardson succumbed to his wounds at Antietam, the General Staff placed our division under the command of Winfield Scott Hancock. General Hancock was a feisty, dark featured, fighting gentleman, determined to defeat the rebel generals who were once his friends at West Point. Enamored of Meagher and his Irish Brigade, he was a kindred spirit whom we never hesitated to follow. The men believed in Hancock and cheered him roundly, whenever he appeared in our midst. Such was not the case with Butcher Burnside.

Among the leadership of the Army of the Potomac, there were several Generals who were not fit to lead brave men into battle. Ambrose Burnside was one of these. His military career was derived from political influence. Since his early years, his design had always been to accord his beliefs to the shifting winds of power and authority. Lincoln chose him as "Little Mac's" successor because of his willingness to obey the commands of his President and his professed resolve to attack and defeat the rebels who surrounded Richmond.

It was Burnside who had ordered Crook to attack under a murderous barrage at Antietam. It was he who would forever have the blood of our brave lads on his hands after Fredericksburg.

We came within view of the Rappahannock River on the afternoon of December 10th. As we approached, we could see the engineers constructing pontoon bridges upon the shore. By sunset we had settled into camp and sought shelter from the bristling winter wind that swept across the water from the direction of Fredericksburg.

All night we could hear the rebel army, busy as beavers with the construction of entrenchments, redoubts and rifle pits upon the heights that rose beyond the town. Under the cover of darkness rebel sharpshooters slipped into the houses that stood across the river from our camp. There they would remain until the engineers began positioning their bridges for the attack.

There was a lad who had tossed and turned all night in the camp of the Eighty Eighth. He was a recent recruit with a pink face and a perturbed expression. His curiosity and concern for his survival had provoked him to make inquiry of Colonel Quinlan.

"Colonel," the boy asked, "will the General be asking us to cross that river under the guns of the whole rebel army?"

I remember Quinlan's reassurance. "Have faith in your generals, lad. They'll not be askin' ya to commit suicide."

In the gloom of that frozen dawn we learned of Burnside's design. Suicide was as good a name as any for what that whiskered walrus had in mind.

I remember the embalmers in their black frock coats and stove pipe hats, passing among us as we moved in columns closer to the river. They were handing out their business cards and promising the lads that they could count on a decent burial, by pinning those cards to their tunics. It was St. Claire Mulholland of the One Hundred and Sixteenth who chased that flock of vultures away with the flat of his sword. I tell you he was a man's man that Mulholland. A braver soldier I never knew. He would win the Medal of Honor, before his service to the Union would be through.

In the morning light we waited in columns near the river's edge. Soon we could see the engineers below us, attempting to secure the pontoon bridges for the attack. Over a hundred of our artillery pieces had been drawn into position upon the heights above us, awaiting the signal to commence the assault. Suddenly the rebels who had taken up position in the houses across the river opened up on those brave engineers of the Seventeenth and Fiftieth New York Regiments.

I tell you it was like shooting fish in a barrel. Their planks and boats were riddled by that enemy fusillade. Those brave lads tumbled into that freezing river by the score. Some were shot more than half a dozen times before sinking below the surface. Their blood turned that river red. Finally they were forced to dispense with their endeavor and seek shelter amid the cover of the hills that ran beyond the Rappahannock.

Our artillery soon responded to this slaughter, by focusing their fire upon the houses where the rebel sharpshooters were concealed. We cheered as the shells shook the town and covered its streets in smoke.

We watched as the rebels retreated from that shelling, falling back to the rear of the town, and awaiting the next movement of our brilliant commander.

Soon the call went forth for volunteers. It was decided that a bridge-head could not be achieved without first landing a party across the river to drive out that nest of sharpshooters. That task fell to the Seventh Michigan and the Nineteenth Massachusetts. They numbered no more than two hundred. Into the boats they went with Colonel Hall in the forefront.

With their muskets as oars, they crossed the river under shot and shell from the rebel artillery. We screamed our encouragement as they landed and fixed bayonets. We witnessed their charge toward the rebels who had thrown up barricades in the rear of the Town. We were so proud of those brave lads. They fought like tigers and soon succeeded in securing the streets of Fredericksburg for our arrival.

I must tell you now of Meagher. On the 11th of December he was made aware of Burnside's battle plans, plans that would burn the name of the Irish Brigade into the annals of military disasters. Meagher received our fateful orders from General Hancock and immediately questioned the wisdom of a frontal assault upon entrenched, elevated, positions.

Hancock agreed that the course plotted for that campaign could only result in death and destruction for the Army. The two rode off together to Burnside's headquarters. Their purpose was to petition their commander and force him to reconsider his battle strategy.

Meagher related to us the circumstance of their encounter with Burnside. By that time both he and Hancock had grown tired of political generals and their propensity for getting brave lads killed. They cared little for Burnside's gentility and were determined to speak their minds.

The two of them arrived as the clouds gathered above the Rappahannock. It was a cold dark December afternoon, full of foreboding over commands that would prove fatal in execution.

Burnside's quarters were located within a rambling farmhouse that commanded a majestic view of both the river and the town. From that location one could observe the battlefield in a most particular detail. He was seated in a handcrafted rocking chair, smoking his pipe. Round and soft, with a balding pate and whiskers that ran down both cheeks to his chin, he was attended by three aides de camp.

His riding boots were worn above the knee and polished to an ebony sheen. The urgency of their mission caused Meagher and Hancock to be ushered immediately into the presence of that bloated bastard. Burnside welcomed his visitors and offered to each a libation of Napoleon Brandy. They respectfully declined. He soon discovered that their visit was not a social one. It was the fiery Hancock who delivered first.

"General, we come to you on behalf of the men we command.

May we speak to you in confidence, without military formality?"

"By all means, General," Burnside replied, directing his subordinates to remove themselves, allowing the three of them to confer in confidence, behind a closed door.

"What is it Hancock? Are my orders not clear?" Burnside demanded. "Or is it that they lack subtlety? I trust your men are prepared for a fight"

"They appear only too clear, General." Hancock answered, attempting to conceal his contempt for his commander. "That is what concerns us. Have you calculated the casualties that will come from a river crossing and frontal assault upon entrenched positions?"

"Our artillery will soften the rebel defenses and a bold thrust will carry the day," Burnside insisted, approaching the map that was spread across a long table, detailing his battle formula with the point of his sword.

"Sumner's command will attack upon the right and cross the river at United States Ford. Hooker will move upon the center, and Franklin will cross down river and assault the rebel's flank. If the men do their duty, a glorious victory will be ours, gentlemen. I feel it."

"Lee has moved his artillery to the crest of those heights, General," Meagher offered. "He has had time to secure his defenses and knows well the advantage of the high ground. I saw the effect of rifled muskets and field artillery upon infantry at Malvern Hill. I fear a terrible slaughter will result from this plan of attack."

"This is not the time to speak of your fears, Meagher. This is the time to do your duty," Burnside challenged.

"We know well, what our duty requires," Hancock argued. "We ask that you do your duty General. Put forth a battle plan that will not cause brave men to be murdered by the thousands upon those heights."

"You have your orders, gentlemen," Burnside fumed. I expect you to carry them out." His voice quaked and his hands shook with a tremor that caused him to conceal them within his coat.

"Mark me general," Meagher warned. "This attack is folly and can only result in a most fearful slaughter. I ask you to move the Army away from this place and cross the river nearer toward Falmouth. There we can attack with force on the enemy flank. I ask you to save the lives of my men."

The die had been cast. The future had been foretold to one who would not listen. It was a disastrous future indeed, disclosed to Meagher years before by an old woman with the gift of prophecy. The Butcher's pride would not allow him to change the course of that campaign. Ah, war, it is all hell.

CHAPTER 41

After Manassas, the strength of the three regiments that made up Meagher's Irish Brigade totaled more than two thousand. On the morning of December 13, 1862, General Meagher mustered what was left of that number upon a cobblestoned street in the Town of Fredericksburg.

As Meagher inspected the men, we noticed that he grimaced with pain as he made his way among us. The leg wound he had suffered at Antietam had become infected and he was unable to ride or walk without agony. This would be the first time that he would not lead us into battle. This would be another omen to darken our spirits on that dreadful day.

As our artillery blanketed the hills beyond the town, he spoke to us like a father to his sons. He was subdued by our circumstance, knowing that death awaited us on Marye's Heights.

"Lads, we have been called upon once again to carry the attack to the enemy. Throughout history the Irish have answered the call of distant drums. At Fontenoy, Albueta and Waterloo, the green flags flew above our ancestors' heads, spurring them onward, inspiring them to perform deeds of valor and acts of extreme sacrifice."

"On this day you will carry that heritage into battle. It is your solemn duty to uphold the honor of those who have gone before. Those who have shed their blood in defense of foreign soil now beckon you to shed your blood on behalf of this our adopted soil. Remember that you are engaged in a noble conflict. Your sacrifice on this day will secure the blessings of liberty for our children and our children's children. May God bless you all!"

We stood in battle formation in the center of the town, the rebel guns echoing across the sweeping battlefield that rose above us. Field hospitals had been set up on both sides of that street in grim anticipation of the slaughter that was about to ensue.

Nugent was out in front and telling the men to close up ranks and make their shots count. I passed him and saw in his eyes the sadness of one about to say farewell to so many of his brave lads, lads who had adorned their caps with evergreen sprigs in the manner of their beloved General Meagher.

On that morning the clouds concealed the sun, and the wind blew mercilessly through the basin where Fredericksburg lay. Up to our left, the fighting had become hot and heavy. Smoke and fire was all that could be seen. Through it all sounded the thunderous din of artillery.

There we were, saying prayers, shouting curses and making vain attempts to provoke a laugh or a smile, the drums beating along with our hearts, the commands of our leaders ringing forth, directing our play, sweeping us forward to meet our fate.

There was Meagher, standing beside Hancock, saluting us, urging us on, his wolf like eyes were dim with a grim foreboding, his wounded leg preventing him from leading us into that bloody fray. We would sorely miss his direction. Without his hand to guide us, we were just another brigade about to be sacrificed to the god of war.

There was a clock upon a belfry in the distance. Through the smoke that enveloped the town, our commanders listened for the bells to signal the arrival of noon. Sumner's troops then moved forward with French's Division in the lead of the attacking column. The Brigades of Zooke, Meagher and Caldwell would follow their advance.

The battle raged beyond us. In the distance we watched as French's troops disappeared beneath the smoke of the enemy's barrage. Then it was Zooke who ordered his men forward. They moved upward toward the enemy entrenchments. They too became enveloped by the smoke. Then the command rang out "Irish Brigade Advance". We stood in columns checking our cartridge boxes, examining our muskets. Our throats parched, our hearts throbbing within the temples of our heads.

Again I gazed upon the faces of the lads I had grown to love, wondering whether I would ever set eyes upon them again. At the double quick we advanced, a deafening chorus of shot and shell descending upon us as we climbed. As we came upon Marye's Field we could see the carnage that the rebel batteries had wrought upon those who had gone before us. They had disappeared into the smoke and fire of a terrible engagement. It was a slaughter pen of inconceivable dimension.

Everywhere were men and boys, blown to bits and struggling to move upward beneath a storm of lead. I saw an officer without legs crying for his men to close up ranks. I watched boys struck six and seven times, the minnie balls twisting them to and fro, as they tore into their persons.

Then it was our turn to ascend into the full measure of Lee's fusillade. I tell you they shot us down by the score. Still we attacked, bugles blaring, cannons roaring, brave men falling like flakes of snow.

We crossed a crude bridge under the most horrible fire, the corpses of dozens of brave men impeding our advance. We climbed over the dead from noon to dusk on that dreadful day. I never saw such bravery in all my years. There was no retreat by our lads, despite the fearful toll.

On the crest the rebels stood behind a stone wall, their muskets firing constantly for hours on end. It was Anderson's men and they were methodical in their mayhem. They were four deep behind that wall of granite. Picking their targets, firing their muskets, then moving back to give another Johnny a crack at killing a nameless blue coat. There was many an Irishman among those who defended Marye's Heights. War has made enemies of many who were Irish born.

Among our ranks I saw Nugent fall, while Major Cavanaugh, the bantam rooster of the Brigade, cried to the lads "blaze away and stand it boys!"

Captain Leddy was screaming for the men to take cover among the dead when his left arm was blown apart at the elbow. I watched as Lieutenant Callahan was shot four times and still managed to advance toward the rebels upon that hill.

There was a ravine that ran below the crest of Marye's Heights. It was there that many of our lads sought a refuge from that storm of artillery and musket fire. It was there that we gathered and stripped off our haversacks and bedrolls for the valiant attacks to follow.

I can see the lads' faces still, blackened by the soot and smoke that surrounded us, shaken by the shot and shell that blanketed that terrible hillside, yet bent upon their mission, determined to press on despite the cost.

Below us we saw Caldwell's Brigade crossing Marye's Field, as the enemy batteries tore gaping holes in their ranks. They fought their way upward, then they came to the funnel of that crude bridge. It was there that the rebel muskets focused upon them, decimating their columns of officers and men with a relentless enfilading fire.

We wondered what had become of our artillery. Why the rebel rifle pits and redoubts had not felt their wrath. In truth, our guns had delivered a withering barrage upon the rebel positions at the outset of our advance, but Lee was masterful in making the most of a defensive position. At Marye's Heights, he would deliver another bloody lesson on the advantage of elevated entrenched positions and the effect of rifled muskets on an advancing infantry.

Again and again we attacked that stone wall. Six times we advanced and six times we were thrown back. We could see the faces of the rebels as they shot us down like dogs. Some cheered us on, while others killed us by the score in a bloody frenzy of smoke and fire.

I saw O'Neil shot through the face, while aiming his musket at a rebel in a plumed hat. Burke too, stood screaming for his men to advance with his left shoulder shattered by a blast of enemy grape shot. Major Hogan and Captain Young drew the closest to the stone wall before being cut down. Indeed, never were men so brave.

I cheered as Lucky and Gosson climbed closer to the stone wall, both of their tunics riddled with bullet holes. I tell you to this day I cannot fathom how those two survived that horror unscathed. I saw Kirby fall while leading some lads from the Sixty Third. I called to Herbert as he crawled among the dead, minnie balls whistling all around him like angry bees.

As I moved toward him, I felt a burning in the flesh of my left thigh. It was as if hot soup had been poured upon it. I lay still, unable to move. A scalding fragment from a rebel shell had crippled me.

As dusk turned to darkness, the torrent of death that had been unleashed upon our brave lads slowly subsided. Without the benefit of a blanket and in desperate need of a drink to quench my raging thirst, I remained exposed on that freezing hillside. All around were the dead and dying.

Thousands killed and thousands of moaning wounded to keep them company. In the agony of that place and time, my spirit took flight and my fancy carried me away through a myriad of remembrances.

Again I visited the quay at Waterford and followed a starving mother toward a famine house. Again I saw Thomas upon the stage at Conciliation Hall, speaking of resistance to an ageless tyranny. There I was at Clonmel; only this time I was among the convicted upon whom a sentence of death was to be passed.

Throughout there was Thomas, his eyes, his words, his matchless eloquence calling me home, calling me home across the sea, shivering in the hold of a coffin ship, shivering in the cold of that hillside, fearful of what was to become of me.

Then suddenly I was awakened by another's caring voice. With the light of a match there followed the whine of a minnie ball. There I was back on the field at Fredericksburg, in the company of one who had answered my prayers.

In the dark I could not decipher his features. He was in the company of another who seemed his subordinate. He spoke in words that were melodious and refined. He was a man of learning and compassion. He inquired of my regiment and after my response gave his regards to General Meagher.

From his canteen he quenched my thirst with a most merciful libation and bandaged my screaming leg with a crude tourniquet. I do believe that I would have succumbed to my wound, had that noble soul not endeavored to bestow his loving aid upon my person. It was only later that I learned the name of my Samaritan.

It was he who would save the day at Little Round Top. It was he who would lead the Twentieth Maine so gallantly, sustaining six separate wounds in the fray of battles fought, yet surviving to witness the surrender of Lee. Whenever I hear the name of Joshua Chamberlain, I will always remember his mercy on that horrid night, upon that horrid hillside.

CHAPTER 42

At least two thirds of our officers and men fell on the field at Fredericksburg. An unparalleled disaster had befallen the Irish Brigade and Burnside was to blame. The toll of dead and wounded was evident in the field hospitals that were set up within the town.

I was transported from the battlefield in a gruesome wagon of dead and dying lads. Everywhere there was misery, blood and gore. For hours I remained, lying among hundreds of others, awaiting an examination of my wound. I attempted to offer consolation to those that surrounded me, but to no avail.

I had never seen such dejection among our men. Among the groans and the cries of those who had shed their blood in that engagement, there arose a chorus of insubordinate curses. Again brave men had been murdered and maimed by a battle plan that was momentous in its incompetence.

They said that Burnside had attempted to join in the last of the attacks at Fredericksburg in an effort to cause his suicide. I tell you, if he had been present among those whose wounds turned the streets of Fredericksburg crimson, he would have been strangled by many a pair of vengeful hands.

I recall being brought closer to the entrance of the field hospital while hearing the shrieks and howls of men having limbs amputated. I became possessed by the notion that I too would receive such treatment. It was then that I managed to crawl away from that place of butchery. I must have fallen into an unconscious state at that point, for my next recollection was awaking within a stone edifice with my nostrils singed by the stench of death.

As if in a dream, I spied Kirby. He was walking among the wounded, searching for survivors from the Brigade. I swore I had seen him fall and yet there he stood in the distance. I called his name and he turned toward my entreaty. Both his neck and his left shoulder were wrapped in blood drenched bandages, yet he was able to make his way toward me. That proud son of the South was a blessing indeed. He would bring me to Dr. Reynolds.

After Fredericksburg, Meagher was determined to obtain a furlough for those who remained alive within the Sixty Ninth, Sixty Third and Eighty Eighth. He had walked among the vestiges of those veteran regiments and seen in the eyes of his men that deep and unremitting despair and exhaustion that annihilates the will of even the bravest of the brave.

Meagher was overcome by the tears and outcries of his beseeching lads. They and he had reached a most precarious state, the state of all sane men who have been spent by the depravity of war. Despite their valor, despite their unrivaled camaraderie, the lads had been used up by the rigors of that war and Meagher knew it. He would write to the Secretary of War in an attempt to preserve and replenish the original regiments that comprised his Brigade.

There was a story told of General Hancock passing among the ranks of those who remained after that fearful slaughter. He had commanded that the men fall in for inspection. It was then that he came upon a lost and solitary lad from the Sixty Third, with an evergreen sprig affixed to his cap. He admonished him for standing alone and not joining the ranks of his company. With that, the lad explained that he was all that remained of his company. Hancock could only salute him and pass on.

I never thought that I would return to the White House where the President resided. Yet, I suppose that when you hitch your wagon to a shooting star like Thomas Francis Meagher, you cannot predict what course your path may follow.

Meagher had not yet received a response to his petition for furloughing those who had fought with him since the formation of the Brigade. He was most persistent in his efforts. He prevailed upon Seward to arrange an audience with Lincoln. Since my leg wound was in need of healing, I was allowed to accompany Thomas upon this mission. It was December, 1862 and the slaughter of that war was without an end in sight.

Washington was an armed camp by then, garrisoned with thousands of soldiers and rampant with rumors of a rebel invasion. After much difficulty we managed to obtain a room at Willard's Hotel. It was there that we were to await a summons from the Secretary of State, a summons that would allow Thomas the opportunity of speaking to the President in person.

While we were waiting, we chose to avail ourselves of the Hotel's saloon. By that time the drink had become a necessary antidote for the jitters occasioned by the front. Within that place we were made aware that U.S. Grant was also registered as a hotel guest.

We had heard much of Grant by that time. He had guided his army to victories at Fort Henry and Fort Donelson and engaged his men in a fearful slaughter at Shiloh Church. By then, Hooker had been placed in charge of the Army of the Potomac and Grant had become a casualty to rumor and innuendo.

He was too much of a drinker to lead an army, some said. He was too willing to commit his forces to a bloody engagement. Yet to Lincoln, Grant was a fighter and a man who understood the awful arithmetic of casualties that the War of the Rebellion would require, before a Union victory could be achieved.

Both Meagher and Grant had been subjected to the glare of fame. Both in turn had been tarred with the brush of the drunkard. They were two men of similar size and dimension, yet different in disposition.

Unlike Meagher, Grant was shy and taciturn, choosing to dwell in the shadows, while Thomas was a creature who had courted the light. By then, both had borne painful witness to fleeting victories and ignoble defeats. Those episodes had affected each of them differently. While Grant was determined to detach from the slaughter in order to defeat the enemy, Meagher was determined to safeguard what was left of his men.

We were seated at a small table with sweet meats and crackers at our disposal. Quinlan had returned from the hotel's tonsorial parlor with freshly cut hair and the fragrance of cologne upon his person. It was while he was engaged in this attempt at improvement of his appearance that the barber advised him of Grant's presence within the hotel.

This report caused Meagher to call the concierge and commission a messenger to deliver his salutations to the General, along with an invitation to join our company. Within the hour a response was received from the man who would guide our army to victory. "You are welcome to join my company."

We gathered ourselves and passed through the crowded lobby and made our way to Grant's room, inconspicuously located in the rear of the Hotel's third floor.

Grant answered Meagher's knock with dispatch. He was without the benefit of either an entourage or an aide de camp. He too was awaiting a conference with the President. He appeared a simple, unremarkable soldier with rust colored hair and a neatly trimmed beard that clung to his angular face like an auburn wreath. The smell of cigars permeated his sparsely furnished room.

As I said, he was of the same stature as Meagher, with pale blue eyes and a furrowed brow. He was attired in the worn blue uniform of an officer without commission. He shook each of our hands vigorously and invited us to join him in front of a crackling fireplace. I took him to be confident in manner yet wholly without pretension.

His voice was more rasp than tone and there was a trace of Ohio in his speech. From a smoked glass decanter he poured us three glasses of brandy. His refreshment, however, was derived from a pitcher of spring water. This departure from his purported predilection for the drink was a cause for comment by Thomas.

"Will you not be joining us in a more substantial toast, General?"

"I would enjoy nothing more, General. Yet I must be circumspect when called to Washington. That is the reason I asked you to visit with me here. If I were seen within Willard's Saloon, it would add fuel to the fire of those who care to replace me. The walls in this town have ears, General. Tell me, how fares the Irish Brigade?"

"Our Brigade is little more than a regiment now, General. That is why I have come to speak with Mr. Lincoln. Many of my men are in desperate need of a furlough. I fear they will not last much longer without it."

"Ah, this business has made us all weary. I will be glad to see my sweet Julia once again. I tell you the nights are without end when she is away from my side. Where are you headed from here?"

"Heading Back to New York, in an attempt to recruit more for what lies ahead. I too long for the sound of my wife's laughter and the sight of sunset over Fifth Avenue. You must come and visit with us some time.

Who knows? We may even make you an honorary Irishman. What do you say, O'Keefe? Could we teach the General to sing *Kathleen Mavourneen* at Hibernian Hall?"

"Without much trouble at all," I answered, provoking a hearty laugh from Grant.

I became enamored of the man, long before the newspapers and politicians made him their darling. Of course that was after they crucified him for the loss of so many on the bluffs above Vicksburg. We bade him adieu and returned to the saloon that afternoon. That evening, our summons to meet with the President arrived.

I recall us being ushered into a spacious room, down a wide hallway from the East entrance of the White House. We could see that there were many waiting to speak with Lincoln that evening.

It was a night lacking in stars and the sentimental regard for seasoned soldiers.

There were diplomats, clerks, and ladies in winter finery, coming to beseech their weary leader for favors and appointments both large and small. Upon entering, Lincoln was cordial but not warm. On each of the occasions that I had observed him, I was taken by the manner in which his responsibilities had caused him to age. On that night he seemed particularly distracted with details of defeat and impending disaster. He was aware of Meagher's entreaty and addressed the issue immediately after bidding us welcome.

"General, I am grateful for the sacrifice of your men and I appreciate the need that brings you to me."

"I would not have come, had I not believed that to do otherwise would be to fail in my duty to the men, Sir."

"We are in a fight to the death, General. Make no mistake on it. On every front I am beset with requests such as yours. Everywhere there is death and desperation. Yet, we must muster the strength we have and press on. Those who have fought with you the longest are the best teachers for those who will come after. They will set an example of the will to survive."

"They will be a poor example if they are dead or beyond hope, Sir," Meagher argued, his voice bearing the trace of exasperation. He was standing beside us, his eyes riveted upon Lincoln. "My men are spent and in desperate need of a return home. Give us a month to renew their spirits and to find more recruits to answer the call."

"What shall I tell the others who make the same request? Can I risk a furlough for all of our fighting men, with the enemy pressing us at every turn? You know General, when a polecat has you in a death grip, you better kill him or he'll be killing you."

"My men are worn down from killing, Sir. I ask only for a fortnight's furlough."

"I will review your request again, General. I will speak to General Hooker and the Secretary of War. If we can spare your men, we will allow you your wish. I must tell you once again of my deepest admiration for the Irish Brigade. They have written a glorious chapter within the history of a proud and valiant people. My prayers and my thoughts are with you all. Good evening, gentlemen."

We were escorted from that place of power and history. I could tell that Meagher was disappointed by Lincoln's words, for in them he could detect the seeds of his decision.

He knew that the General Staff had a preference for officers who rose from the ranks of the Regular Army, and resented those like Meagher who were creatures of political power. There were many in Washington who saw Meagher as an upstart, whose sole design was to enhance his reputation and that of his Brigade.

In a sense they were right. For Meagher did feel that the Brigade was a symbol of the Irish themselves, and its success meant success for us all. Within the month, Meagher received a note from Seward that his request had been denied. The Brigade would remain at the ready in winter quarters near Falmouth, Virginia.

Meanwhile, the three of us made a brief return to New York, Quinlan with his fever, I with my leg wound, and Meagher with his ailing heart. There we would spend time with one another and our loved ones. There we would attend a Requiem at St. Patrick's for those who would never return home again.

CHAPTER 43

New York was a most welcome sight when we arrived. I returned to my residence and renewed my devotion to my loving wife and three children. Each morning, I was given my pipe and languished in the love of my family, while recuperating from my leg wound. Soon I began to think of the lads and their Christmas away from home. I had become one with them and longed to be in their company once again.

It was then that a messenger came up the backstairs and delivered a letter from Thomas. It seemed that he too had followed my course, partaking in the care and comfort of his home, then slowly turning to thoughts of the Brigade. He invited both Quinlan and myself to join him for a Christmas toast. I recall traveling by sleigh over crushed snow to his residence located on Fifth Avenue.

The Meagher's lived in the home of his wife's father, a self-made man of the merchant class who had discouraged his only daughter from marrying an Irish exile, without position or property to make her secure. But Elizabeth Townsend was a head strong lass. She had her pick of almost all the eligible bachelors whose families were entrenched within the upper crust of New York Society, and yet she bestowed her love and considerable charms upon Meagher. They met after Thomas had delivered a stirring speech to a boisterous crowd congregated in Washington Square.

At that time Meagher was a handsome widower who had taken employment with the *Irish News*. His caring nature and his ability to weave a spell over those who had gathered, entranced the comely Elizabeth. In truth, Thomas was resigned to the solitary life of an adventurer, until his eyes fell upon her from across the crowd.

Meagher had been a man for the ladies. From his youth he had a weakness for a well turned ankle and the sweet surrender of making love. Since the tragic demise of his beloved Catherine however, he had forgotten how to be in love. It was the self-assured Elizabeth who would touch his heart and give him a reason for falling in love once again.

It was this lovely creature who answered my knock on that crisp December night. She was wearing a crinoline dress of the most magnificent blue and her manner was warm and inviting. Their residence was a brownstone of three stories, elegantly decorated with a breathtaking view of Fifth Avenue from its second floor.

Quinlan had already arrived, attired in a charcoal gray coat with amber trousers. I tell you our old engineer cut a dashing figure on that winter night. His furlough had allowed him to overcome his fever and return the blush to his round, pleasant, face. It was not long before we were summoned. Elizabeth escorted us up a winding stairway to Meagher's study overlooking the City. I tell you there were at least a thousand books of every size and subject within the chestnut cases that lined its walls.

Meagher was dressed in a burgundy smoking jacket with trousers of black silk. Upon his feet he wore a pair of black leather slippers. He was situated in front of a roaring fire with a snifter of brandy. His time away from the front seemed to renew him, and yet his blazing violet eyes bore the trace of a deep and indelible sadness. He embraced us both and kissed his sweet Elizabeth with the golden hair, before she left us alone.

Our night was spent in reminiscence. I suppose the Christmas season causes many to reflect upon life and its moments of mirth and melancholy. The snow began to fall upon the City shortly after our arrival. Having slogged through so much Virginia mud, it was a delight to watch that pristine blanket make a picture postcard of the world outside.

Everywhere there were sleigh bells and carolers. For at least that night the war seemed to be a feature of a far off place. Elizabeth would look in upon us from time to time and inquire as to our needs. We could hear her playing Brahms in the salon below us. She was in the full flower of her womanhood then and Thomas was her gallant knight.

It was while we were taking our leave that Elizabeth beckoned us to join her in the anteroom adjacent to their front door. Thomas had excused himself momentarily from our midst and she took this opportunity to speak with us in confidence. Her lovely face and hazel eyes suddenly bore the trace of a concealed anguish. Her words were derived from a deep devotion to her husband.

"You must take care of my Thomas," she whispered. "For he carries a wounded heart wherever he goes. I fear that when he passes beyond the reach of my love, he will fall into a dark place and lose his way back to me. I have heard him recite the names of the boys he has lost in battle over and over in his sleep. Take care of him, please. For I love him so."

They waved to us from the doorstep of that place, as our carriage made its way through the snow. All the way back to our homes on the West Side, Quinlan and I were silent. We both knew that Elizabeth's words were true. Meagher was a man of extremes. He could love and hate with a fervor beyond that of most men. When he descended into a melancholy, his days and nights were a torment of darkness.

Perhaps this is the burden of those who lead others in times of righteous conflict. Such was the case with Meagher. Such was the case with Lincoln. In those dark days of that merciless war, there were many whose souls were touched by a sorrowful fire.

I must speak to you of the Requiem High Mass that was held at The Cathedral of St. Patrick. For it was an event that spoke of the devotion of our people to those from the Irish Brigade who had fallen on the field of battle.

I can still see the pews and aisles bursting with a vast congregation. By then, Nugent had joined us, following his release from the hospital.

Meagher and Elizabeth led the way in a solemn procession toward the altar. Among those gathered were many old men who had served in the Sixty Ninth New York State Militia before the Rebellion drenched that service in blood.

Nugent, Quinlan and myself were attired in the uniforms of the three original regiments of the Brigade. Green flags, festooned with battles fought and slogans shouted by our brave lads, were unfurled as we filed in precise steps behind the General and his lady fair. Father Ouelette led the clergy in the liturgy.

We gathered together like a bereaved family, mourning the loss of brothers and sons who had made the extreme sacrifice for the cause of freedom. I tell you my heart was full of pride and sorrow as the choir and the regimental band enhanced the solemnity of that occasion with an inspiring rendition of *Mozart's Requiem*. The sermons and the sincere sentiment of those who came to pay their respects etched that event on the tablets of all our memories.

We returned to our encampment outside of Falmouth, Virginia toward the end of January. The men gathered around us and gave us all three cheers of welcome back. It was good to see our brothers in arms once again.

A brutal February accompanied by sleet and snow, discouraged any bold ventures on the part of either Army. Indeed, the war seemed to freeze in place except upon the picket lines. Everywhere the men attempted to keep warm and avoid the influenza that had taken a terrible toll throughout the ranks.

It was said that Hooker was planning a spring campaign that would once again make a run at the gates of Richmond. The men knew that the killing season would soon be upon us and sought to savor those dwindling days before another savage bloodletting.

Beyond the endless drilling, there were rumors and bawdy stories to pass the freezing hours in smoke filled huts. A few of the lads would venture off after lights out and visit the whore wagons that serviced Hooker's Army.

During that interval, I busied myself with letter writing and recollections of joyful times that had gone before. Every Wednesday I would travel to Gosson's hut for a game of cards and a pint or two. Before we broke camp for our march toward Chancellorsville, a most startling event would take place involving The Irish Brigade.

As I have said, our green flags were deemed sacred cloth to be cherished and safeguarded. In all the battles leading up to Fredericksburg, none of the flags of the Brigade had fallen into enemy hands. In truth the dejection of the men following our failed attacks upon Marye's Heights was made more pronounced by the knowledge that the flag of our Twenty Eighth Massachusetts Regiment had been captured by the rebels.

It was a bleak March evening and I was in charge of a picket detail about a mile outside of our camp. All was quiet except for the usual banter between the men of both sides, assigned to that hazardous duty. Suddenly a messenger from C company arrived, informing me that a rebel had been captured and insisted on speaking to General Meagher. Without delay the prisoner was brought to me and to my surprise turned out to be none other than Michael Sullivan.

In the days of the Young Ireland Movement, the Sullivan's from County Kerry were stalwart supporters of our cause. They were a proud, black Irish clan with haunting eyes and a history of opposition to British rule.

In the revolt of 1798 Patrick Sullivan served as a loyal lieutenant to Michael Dwyer. After being wounded at Vinegar Hill, he was hunted down by British Dragoons in County Wexford. There he was taken to a public square in shackles and forced to wear a canvas covering, soaked in pitch, upon his head.

As the crowd watched in horror, that covering was ignited by a British officer, burning Sullivan's head to cinders. A public hanging followed. Patrick Sullivan's legacy was carried on through his nine children. Michael Sullivan, a corporal in McMillan's Georgia Regiment, was his grandson.

At first I did not recognize him, for he was a lad of ten when I fled Erin. I knew his brother, Peter, and they shared a similarity of appearance. It was when I questioned him in the firelight that I became aware of his identity and his heritage.

His person was searched for weapons and he was given food and drink. He advised us that he had taken the wrong path in returning to his camp and found himself amid a dozen boys from the Eighty Eighth. They had given him a rough time of it before he demanded to speak with Meagher. He was in his twenties but seemed older somehow. I and two of my company accompanied him to the General's quarters.

His gray coat and trousers were threadbare and the shoes upon his feet were covered in holes. He wore a brown slouch hat with a torn brim and his face bore a ragged beard. When the General arrived, he snapped to attention and conducted himself with the manner of a seasoned soldier. I could tell that he had endured much fighting and was unafraid.

"General Meagher," Sullivan reported. "I was up behind that wall at Fredericksburg when your boys attacked. I saw one of their color bearers fall after being hit near a dozen times. I tell you General, I was proud of those boys of yours, proud they was so brave and proud they was Irish. That's why I crawled out to that there color bearer. That's why I come to you, General. After so many of your boys died, I could not let their flag be captured."

With that, Sullivan reached beneath his coat and removed the tattered green and gold emblem of the Irish Twenty Eighth. With a salute, he tendered it to Meagher. Each of us who witnessed that admirable act were without words to say. I could not help but recall that night in Waterford when Meagher himself removed the tricolor concealed beneath his coat.

Sullivan received the General's heartfelt thanks, before being escorted back to his lines. The news of his mission soon spread throughout our camp. Years after the war ended, I was informed that he had been killed in the Battle of the Wilderness. What a perfect name for such a place of war.

CHAPTER 44

espite the terrible toll taken by the war, despite the fear that stayed with us and made us ashamed of our own humanity, despite cowardly cries by armchair generals for peace without honor, those who remained within the ranks of the Brigade continued to serve as the spring of another year began to awaken the world that surrounded us.

Perhaps it is the promise of spring that causes us to believe in the hope of redemption. It is a season when the birds and the budding flowers teach us of things natural yet profound, urging us to persevere somehow, to muddle through the misery of winter. For life is like unto a circle, turning round like the earth upon its axis, teaching the wise that growth is life and growth is often painful. In the spring of 1863 the flower of America the free began to grow within our hearts.

Through it all there was Meagher, expanding with the hurt of almost forty winters. The years had shown him to be flawed, reminding us that he was mortal, for he had dared and he had failed. Yet when he walked among us in the woodlands of Virginia, as that spring began its rise from beneath that blood drenched ground, we knew he was our one and only chieftain and we were what remained of his proud and valiant clan. In that there was a solace beyond the reach of the grave.

Before we took the field at Chancellorsville, we reveled in the respite of one last Saint Patrick's celebration. I shall always remember that occasion, for it was our last as Meagher's Brigade.

Invitations were sent to generals and dignitaries alike. All the previous day, the men were engaged in preparations of the finest detail. Meagher was a master at organizing such an event. A pasture was selected with a grand view of the countryside. In the forefront flowed the river, while in the distance stood the mountains. Those who attended were treated to games of chance, and contests of strength and agility.

Like a Celtic festival of old, there were jugglers, tumblers and a recent recruit from the Twenty Eighth whose stock in trade were tricks of a magical variety. At every turn there was music; fifes and fiddles, pipes and drums, songs to sing and tunes to have a dance. Little Johnny Fleming serenaded the ladies and brought a tear to those who remembered times and companions lost forever, since our last St. Patrick's Day.

Somehow the loss of so much and so many had made us more aware of the need to live in the magic of that moment. Thomas stood upon a grassy knoll that overlooked the pasture and welcomed all who had made the journey to attend. There were at least fifty banquet tables with twenty place settings upon them, arranged in rows that ran along the ridge beside that pasture.

As always, the center piece of that occasion was a steeple chase over a two and a half mile course. Quinlan again had been called upon to construct hurtles, ditch fences and hazardous water jumps that tested both the courage and horsemanship of the race's participants.

On that occasion the purse for a first place finish was $500. A crowd of nearly a thousand was in attendance and situated in strategic locations that offered the best vantage points for observation. In the grandstand there were generals and commissioned officers, along with a score of the finest ladies.

After Hooker and his aides arrived to a chorus of cheers, Meagher ascended the reviewing platform and with much comedy introduced the riders and their mounts. As usual, the costumes worn by the participants were outrageous in their appearance. After receiving Father Oulette's blessing, the men climbed into their saddles and took their place at the starting line. With a noble flourish and a report from his Colt, Meagher commenced the contest.

Over the course they flew like knights of old, their horses galloping and leaping. The crowd roared, as each of the gaily clad riders displayed his prowess in the saddle. A fine chestnut mare would carry the day, as well as the wages of the entire Sixty Third Regiment.

All those present seemed elated before the dinner bells were rung. The food was delectable and the drink was most refreshing. More festivities would follow, including foot races and the hilarious pursuit of a soaped pig.

With nightfall there were theatrical performances and recitations, toasts and flirtations. There was whiskey, rum and champagne a plenty. Gosson and Hogan were commissioned to create a most memorable punch. Both were overcome by that duty before the night was done.

At the last was a reading by Dr. Reynolds, the poet laureate of the Brigade. Beneath a star filled sky, with what remained of the crowd in rapt attention, he delivered a poem especially written for that occasion. I can still recite from memory much of what he wrote. I am most enamored of these lines.

> Now we're pledged to free this land,
> So long the exile's resting place;
> To crush for aye a traitorous band.
> And wipe out treason's deep disgrace.
> Then let us pledge Columbia's cause,
> God prosper dear old Ireland too!
> We'll trample on all tyrant laws;
> Hurrah for our old land and our new!

It rained for much of that April, making life in camp muddy and miserable. As the warmth and sun arrived, we knew that our waiting was coming to an end. The daily drilling was done in earnest, for lives and battles could be lost by a breach of discipline.

Suddenly we were on the march again, miles and miles of men and wagons wending their way like a blue and white river southward toward another reckoning. The men had faith in Hooker and believed the only way home was through the gates of Richmond. It was in the forest outside of Chancellorsville that another chapter in the history of the Brigade would be written.

The plans of that campaign were deliberate and detailed. Our army numbered one hundred and thirty thousand. We were, we believed, an unbreakable chain of men and weaponry that would encircle the rebels somewhere outside of Richmond and bring an end to the rebellion once and for all.

It was the end of April 1863. Sedgewick's forces were supposed to keep the enemy occupied in front of Fredericksburg while the rest of the army was to make a crossing up river and come in behind the rebels encamped along the Plank Road.

As we marched across the Rappahannock in the moonlight, we saw ourselves as invincible and destined to win a great victory. With the arrival of May we were camped in the forest in front of Chancellorsville, awaiting the commands of Hooker to commence the attack. Our lines stretched for miles through that dark and dismal wood. Our right flank was guarded by Howard's Eleventh Corps. A corps composed of mostly German recruits.

I must speak to you of the Germans who fought and died in the cause of freedom during the War of the Rebellion. The revolutions that swept across Europe in 1848 caused many a brave German, Austrian and Hungarian lad to seek the overthrow of the old ways, the ways of the privileged few who controlled the many.

Like those engaged in the Young Ireland Movement, most were educated and inspired by the examples of Jefferson, Washington and Adams. They too, had become disciples of freedom, seeking an end to the oppression that made prisons of their homelands. They too, were stalwart rebels, yet lacking in the means of defeating tyranny. They too, became exiles who came to America in search of liberty. There were thousands who joined the Union army after Fort Sumter.

In our ranks they were called Dutchies. They were made to suffer much for their difference in speech and manner. On the battlefield they served with Siegel, Steinwehr and Schurz, proving themselves brave soldiers when the cannons roared.

At Chancellorsville they were under the command of General Oliver Otis Howard, a man of learning and limited military experience. At Chancellorsville, The Eleventh Corps was no match for Jackson and the hellfire of his seasoned scarecrows.

Neither Howard nor Hooker had inspected our right flank on that fateful day. There were no entrenchments, no rifle pits, no fortifications; only two cannons curled around facing west, while the men frolicked and slaughtered steers for dinner. Reports had told of a rebel force moving south from the town of Catherine Furnace. Hooker, confident in the chain of his army, believed that Lee was retreating toward Gordonsville. A chain however, is only as strong as its weakest link. In the bloody slaughter of Chancellorsville that link was the Eleventh Corps.

In truth, Lee was engaged in another desperate gamble. While he remained in Chancellorsville, he divided his army once again and ordered Stonewall Jackson to move off to the south, as a feint.

Jackson's aim was to then circle north, then east through impenetrable woods toward the exposed right flank of Howard's German troops. Those once brave Dutchies were caught completely by surprise when Jackson's men emerged like wild beasts from the thickets and swarmed around and over them. It was not long before the rout was on, as Jackson's troops began rolling up our right flank.

The wilderness muffled the noise of this engagement from Hooker's command. It sounded as if the battle was raging closer to Chancellorsville and not to the West. When the truth of the matter was discovered, Hooker sought to defend his army from annihilation rather than attack the divided forces of the rebels in detail. This would prove a most sanguinary strategy for seventeen-thousand of our lads in blue.

Everywhere we were upon the defensive. Surprise and ferocity were the allies of Lee's forces, as they pressed their attack. Fear and retreat were our enemies. For the next three days we fell back and attempted to regroup. All the while the shells fell around us.

I saw Lynch blown to bits before my eyes. One moment he was rallying the men to stand and fire. In the next, he was gone, only vapor left where human flesh once stood.

Again Meagher was leading us through another valley of death. He was riding a golden mare and utterly without concern for his well-being. The air around us was riddled with lead as he calmly called upon the lads to "fire and hold fast, fire and hold fast." The men called to him to take cover, as shells landed, killing those around him. Still he refused to come in from the storm. I too was the recipient of a divine providence.

We had retrieved two cannons that the rebels could well have used to slaughter more of our lads, when a barrage descended upon us from the heights of Hazel Grove. I recall the ground shaking, as if in an earthquake, and the branches and limbs of toppling trees becoming deadly missiles that added to the terror of that moment. On the ground surrounding me lay the dismembered remains of at least a score of brave lads. I and a drummer boy were all that remained of Company B.

As night fell, I remember making my way through the wilderness in the darkness. There I heard the ceaseless screams of the wounded and dying who had been trapped amid the flames and suffocating heat that enveloped that forest. Shells landed and minnie balls whined, while brave men cried and died all around. I felt so alone in that hellish place. In the woods outside of Chancellorsville Lee would achieve his greatest victory.

As we retreated across the Rappahannock, we were a beaten lot for sure. I recall asking the Almighty how He could allow such a defeat. I remember wondering whether God truly wanted men to be free, whether He was a good and just God, or vengeful and cruel. I resolved that it was not the will of God that brought evil into the world of men. Evil has its own force upon earth.

CHAPTER 45

After Chancellorsville, Meagher would tender his resignation to the General Staff. He had petitioned Washington to replenish our decimated ranks with recruits who possessed the fire of those who had fallen like autumn leaves beneath the green flags. General Halleck and Secretary of War, Stanton, had turned a deaf ear to these entreaties.

By then, Meagher had become a clanging symbol to those who whispered to Lincoln within the corridors and back rooms of a war torn Washington. The fiery reputation that had once rallied thousands to seek enlistment within the Irish Brigade had now become an impediment to discipline and decorum within the Army.

Although he had helped turn the tide at Malvern Hill and Antietam, leaders without loyalty labeled him a political general, an inebriate, and an embarrassment to the regular officer corps.

By then, the tenor of the war had made Meagher and the Brigade an anachronism. His gallantry and his devotion to his men were of a nobler time. He was a knight who had stayed too long at Court, a *chevalier* in a world of locomotives. He had become the chieftain of a dying clan and saw the handwriting upon the wall. He bade farewell to those who remained his brothers, rather than have his family torn from him.

It was May 19, 1863. We had returned to our camp outside of Falmouth, Virginia. The toll of the Brigade's dead and wounded in the defeat at Chancellorsville was enormous. Those would be the last letters to mothers and wives that Thomas Meagher would write. It was a day of blinding sunlight when the bugler sounded boots and saddles. In a hollow square we mustered upon the parade grounds that overlooked the river.

There were fewer than five hundred of us left when Meagher, Nugent, Colonel Kelly and Colonel Caldwell marched to the center of that saddened stage. The green flags rippled in the warmth of the breeze, as Meagher snapped to attention and stepped forward to address the Brigade for the last time. He was in his fortieth year and the tribulations of his life had given him a weary, careworn look.

His hair was almost entirely gray, his figure full and his eyes were dim and filled with tears, as that melodious voice rose above us one more time. I recall him looking straight ahead as he spoke, not wishing to rest his gaze upon the lads he loved. His words, as always, bore the imprint of his classical education. On that occasion he held all of us within his tender grasp. I recall the last of the lines he recited.

"Not less vivid, not less ineffaceable will be the recollection of my companionship with the Irish Brigade in the service of the United States. The graves of many hundred devoted soldiers, who went to death with all the radiance and enthusiasm of the noblest chivalry, are so many guarantees and pledges that, as long as there remains one officer or soldier of the Irish Brigade, so long shall there be found for him, for his family and little ones if any there be, a devoted friend in Thomas Francis Meagher."

His voice quaked at the last, as the men streamed forth in a spontaneous torrent of love and appreciation, cheering him, touching him, bestowing their manly affection upon him. To each of us he spoke, calling us by name, caressing us as a beloved father would his sons. Gosson, Lucky, Herbert, Nugent, Quinlan and Kirby, all of them were moved to tears, as he happened upon them.

Upon my cheek he placed a kiss, beseeching me to remember the times we spent together. I told him from my heart of my devotion and vowed that I would never forget. Colonel Kelly assumed command as Meagher mounted a chestnut charger. With a formal salute and the doffing of his forage cap he galloped from that place. It would be an eternity before I would see him again.

At the commencement of the war, Sherman had prophesied upon the course it would follow and the havoc it would wreak upon both the North and the South. For this he was dismissed as a madman and transferred to a command where his views would not be sought. As the frightful image of that conflict appeared through a glass and darkly, the madman became a sage and warfare as the world knew it was forever transformed. Meagher and the Brigade became casualties of this transformation.

Thomas would return to New York and live for a time in relative anonymity, waiting and wondering where the river of his life would carry him. A year would pass before he knew.

Lincoln and Grant knew the truth. They could read the tea leaves. Victory could only be achieved by means of an awful arithmetic, the infliction of casualties that would cause the Confederacy to wither and die. In such determinations there is little call for gallantry.

After Chancellorsville, we had fallen into darkness. Yet it is always darkest before the dawn. As the summer arrived, we sweltered in the Virginia heat. Then Lee was on the move again. In a bold maneuver, his Army of Northern Virginia moved northward into Pennsylvania. Outside a tiny hamlet by the name of Gettysburg, the sun of a decisive Union victory at last began to rise.

By July 1, 1863, the Army was under the command of General Gordon Meade, a tall, gaunt graduate of West Point and the Mexican War, whom the men called a damn goggle-eyed snapping turtle. He was a soldier without an ounce of spit and polish, frequently displaying a mud spattered uniform and boots that extended above his knees. Despite this appearance he was a man of decisive disposition and Irish descent, who had won the admiration of brave men in the field. It was he who ordered us to stand at Gettysburg.

On the second day of that battle we took up position along the left of a rise known to history as Cemetery Ridge. To our left rose Culp's Hill and the Round Tops. Before us lay a wheat field, a peach orchard and a gathering of boulders they called the Devil's Den.

Across a rolling plain waited Lee and his Army of Northern Virginia. All of us knew that our gathering hosts would clash as never before in a struggle of Biblical dimensions. For those who fought at Gettysburg and survived, words alone can never capture the torrent of killing that erupted over that field of battle.

Our troops were fanned out over a three mile arc. There were eighty thousand who wore blue and at least fifty thousand rebels poised to wade into us on that steamy summer day. Both sides had positioned their batteries in strategic locations to deliver withering barrages upon one another.

As at Malvern Hill, we had command of the high ground. All of us who had seen the effect of rifled muskets and artillery upon advancing infantry were content to remain in place and await the enemy onslaught that was certain to occur.

It was mid-afternoon when the impulsive Sickles sallied forth with his forces and extended a salient toward the enemy beyond the peach orchard. I can tell you that many an experienced soldier cursed that cuckold as he advanced toward that field of fire. There Longstreet's men would serve him a slice of hell.

Colonel Patrick Kelly was a Galway man who had assumed command of the Brigade after Meagher's resignation. He was much admired by the lads for his gentle spirit and courage under fire. His handsome face had suffered a disfigurement when a rebel bullet had torn through his jaw at Antietam.

He was a devoted father and husband who performed his duty above and beyond its call. Hancock ordered Kelly to lead all but the Twenty Eighth into the wheat field in order to assist Sickles against a series of fierce rebel assaults. At close quarters our smoothbore muskets took a toll upon the advancing enemy. They fell in ranks like cord wood.

It was then that Kelly ordered us to fix bayonets and charge into them. The slaughter that ensued was terrible. It was a killing frenzy for sure. I recall being surrounded on all sides by men intent upon a bloody chore. I fired my Colt into faces no more than a foot away. With the sword of the Papal Brigade I became a butcher of men and boys.

All the while the shells fell, killing men and horses and making a bloody mess of God's creation. The slaughter spread across that entire field of fire. Thousands were locked in a death struggle. In the peach orchard, upon the wheat field, amid the ravines and boulders of the Devil's Den, men clubbed, shot and bayoneted each other like never before.

On Little Round Top, history was written in the blood and gore of brave young men. Our own Twenty Eighth provided close support for Chamberlain's Twentieth Maine, as they held the line against savage enemy thrusts designed to turn our left flank. In a desperate measure that arose from the depletion of their ammunition, those valiant Maine boys swung down like a gate from hell, killing and capturing the beaten rebels before them. This would prove to be the turning point of that epic struggle. It was that God man Chamberlain who helped stem that Confederate tide.

If ever there was a reckoning it was at Gettysburg on that second day. Like Antietam before it, the sun seemed to fix in the heavens as the slaughter spread and spread some more. In other engagements I was able to witness the valorous deeds of my comrades in arms. At Gettysburg on that second day, I was too immersed in killing to pay heed to the details of its ordeal.

In truth, I cannot recollect the means of my disengagement, for I was beyond the reach of reason by that time. I only remember a profound weariness, as I reclined within a field near to a cemetery, overlooking that field of slaughter. I was so grateful to God that I would live to witness another dawn.

I do recall awaking in the dead of night and looking out over that killing field as the surgeons' lamps flickered like a swarm of fireflies before me. In the distance on Seminary Ridge I could see the rebel campfires spread out like an incandescent sea. There was no retreat by either side. The dogs of war were still untethered. The following day would bring the climactic, titanic end to that fateful battle.

On the Eve of our Independence Day, Lee would order Pickett and his thousands out from the wood yonder and across the valley toward our fortifications, a valley that would soon become a graveyard for so many gallant sons of the South.

CHAPTER 46

On the third day Lee focused his final thrust at the center of our lines. For all gamblers there comes the time to lose and leave the game, chastened by bitter defeat. For the rebels and Robert E. Lee, that time arrived on the bloody afternoon of July 3, 1863.

Since first light, upon the heights of Cemetery Ridge, we watched and awaited a ferocious enemy attack. As the day wore on we heard skirmishing to our left near Culp's Hill. We would learn later that Custer had confronted Stuart's cavalry to our rear and carried the day with a reckless charge.

Still we on Cemetery Ridge wondered what the rebels were up to. It was unlike the Confederates to give us time to prepare and repair our ranks for their savage storm. All who wore blue were at the ready, sensing that this would be our day for retribution. Suddenly two rebel field guns marked the commencement of the most terrible artillery barrage of the entire war. For those who endured its deafening terror, there will always remain the memory.

The shells shook the earth like the wrath of God. I crawled into a ditch filled with a score of our lads, muffling my ears against the fury of that cannonade. To the rear I saw three caissons explode and fly into the air in fragments, like leaves in a whirlwind.

Everywhere men were taking cover from that horrible storm. After what seemed an eternity the guns grew silent. I found a place among the men of the Sixty Ninth and prayed with Father Corby that the Lord would grant us a victory on that day. Then the call to arms rang forth down the line. Lee's long awaited attack was about to begin.

Lee's boldness had finally run the course of fortune. Perhaps he believed that he was beyond the pale of defeat by that time, I do not know. All I can say is that the charge carried forth by Pickett and Pettigrew on that torrid afternoon was a study in gallant suicide.

This time we were upon the high ground behind our breastworks. This time our muskets and cannons were loaded and ready to kill and dismember their brave infantry.

We watched in hushed silence as the rebel columns emerged from the wood and began their deliberate march into the annals of military disasters. There were thousands arrayed in lines stretching more than half a mile. I borrowed Quinlan's glass and observed those gray backs in detail.

They were young and old, some proud, some petrified with fear, all intent upon their mission, a ragged sea of gray and butternut, many without shoes. Their colors showed us that scores of their regiments were engaged.

There was a rider on a pale horse out in front. He wore golden curls that touched his shoulders and a gray and red forage cap. I drew a bead on him and waited until he came within range of my rifle.

As they drew closer their multitude of bayonets glistened in the summer sun. That entire field seemed to fall into a terrifying silence, broken only by the rhythm of marching feet. It seemed that all who wore blue held their breath in awe as that martial spectacle made its way toward us like a terrible tidal wave.

They were half the distance across that rolling field when our cannons began once more to roar and rain bloody death upon them. From their ranks rose a rumble of regret, as shot and shell tore gaping holes into their lines of march, Men and horses blown to bits, the flower of the Confederacy dying on the vine. And still they came.

In rows we waited behind hay bales and sundry cover, some kneeling, some lying prone, some standing above, cannons with their elevation screws lowering to fire at point blank range.

I saw a rebel general with his hat upon his saber, urging his men forward while the shells took their toll around him. Down the line to our right I could see the green flags of the Sixty Ninth Pennsylvania. It was upon their shore that the brunt of that enemy wave would break.

My heart pounded as I checked my cartridge box. My throat grew parched as Colonel Kelly warned us to hold our fire until they drew within range. There was a drummer boy beside me to my left. He had taken up the rifle of a fallen sergeant. I listened as he whispered the *Our Father* over and over. I told him to cease his praying and aim low for the kill. I could see tears rolling down his pink hairless cheek.

Then they drew near enough for a rifle to reach. Sporadic pops soon turned into a rolling thunder. They volleyed and surged forward at the double quick. Their screams and yelps were met with our shouts and cries. The heavens rang out with an unmerciful din. Now the entire field was aflame and covered in smoke.

All around me men were firing and falling, the attacking enemy driving closer to our barricades as they scaled a rail fence. There were some of our number who ventured forth from behind their fortifications. They had grown accustomed to killing that was hand to hand. I fired my smoothbore and made every shot count. It seemed an instant before I had emptied my box of cartridges. By then I could kill at close range with my Colt.

There seemed to be a sea of rebels surging toward us. I fired and fired and still they came. I tell you I thought for sure they would overwhelm us on their last charge. Then the command was given to fall back behind our cannons.

This was a master stroke. For in an instant our entire line seemed to recede like the tide. Then up and down the line lanyards were pulled and entire enemy regiments were blown away. It was a fearful sight indeed, to see brave young men destroyed.

My last recollection was watching the remnants of those proud rebel regiments retreating all along the line, beaten by the Army that they chased from the Peninsula, slaughtered by soldiers who had witnessed the slaughter of their brothers in blue at places like Savage's Station, Chancellorsville and most especially Fredericksburg.

All who watched those decimated rebel ranks retire from the battlefield at Gettysburg could not help but recall the sights and sounds of that preceding December. The cries began beneath the green flags of the Sixty Ninth Pennsylvania and spread along the line to those who remained standing from the Irish Brigade. The cries became a chorus and the chorus a haunting chant that rang across that valley where so many brave lads had fallen. The chant resounded over and over like an echo in a canyon of death, Fredericksburg! Fredericksburg! Fredericksburg!

It was said that Meade was in error for not closing in upon Lee's Army for a righteous kill. The armchair generals and history writers that sat in the comfort of their offices and parlors were not the ones who witnessed the terrible fury of those momentous three days. Battle exhausts its participants like no other expense of energy.

I recollect simply sitting with my back against the wall of a graveyard. Too tired to speak, too wrought to raise my head from the aftermath of that battle. They say that the sky on the night of that third day was magnificent in its splendor. For all of our lads who fought and were blessed just to breath in the Lord's air, there was naught left but a deep mournful silence of the heart. We seemed to sense that the ordeal of those three days had transformed us. We now knew that we would win the war.

You see, our nation had been stained by the shame of human bondage. Like some indelible, original sin it remained in the very core of our spirit and made a mockery of noble words and righteous revolution.

The fire of Gettysburg marked the true beginning of our redemption, as an army, as a people, and I suppose as a nation. The titanic nature of that three day struggle was like unto a crucifixion and from that sacrifice the America of Jefferson's Declaration would be resurrected. Dawn brought the 4th of July.

Over these many years I have thought much of that time of slaughter. The fire of that time made me blind with the rage of the warrior, then burned into my soul with the promise that one nation under God's grace would emerge from that warfare.

Perhaps it was necessary for the warriors on both sides to return to their home fires and deliver the righteous news, time for the warrior who had been vanquished and the warrior who had been victorious to set about turning their swords into ploughshares and bringing forth a nation of freedom.

The promise remains. The struggle continues. Through it all we must prevail. Yes, I have meditated upon these subjects and with this meditation comes this solace. I and others of The Irish Brigade served America well.

CHAPTER 47

Twilight spread its mantle across the farms and fields of the English countryside as the serpentine train rumbled onward toward Southampton and my departure upon a troop ship for the war in France.

My hand had grown weary with the transcription of O'Keefe's recitation. I marveled at the detail of his recollection and the ease in which it poured forth from his person. It was as if I had accompanied him back through the years of his storied life and attended to the occurrences described firsthand.

I had become enthralled by the history the old man related and most enamored of the person that was Thomas Meagher. I was submerged in a wild dark river of adventure and deeply curious as to its outcome.

O'Keefe arrested my dictation with the wave of his hand and advised me that it was his custom to perambulate the train before the sun could set. He explained that the sight of young men heading off to war was one to which he had long grown accustomed and it presented him with the opportunity of reliving his youth and delivering his comfort to those in need. He excused himself from my presence and promised that we would share a delightful repast upon his return.

I soon fell into a deep slumber in which my reverie reenacted the sights and sounds that O'Keefe had recited. Then suddenly I was running across

"No Man's Land" as the *rat tat tat* of a German machine gun resounded in my brain. I awoke to find O'Keefe across from me.

He was immersed once again in his cherished crimson text. His manly face and silver hair and mustache appeared almost radiant as the darkness descended within his compartment. In the glow of that cabin's gaslight, his eyes seemed aflame.

Soon the steward arrived and presented us with a most delectable selection of dinner entrees. I was famished by that time and much in need of a drink. The old man inquired as to the quality of the roasted duckling and with my permission ordered it prepared for two. He complemented this request with a bottle of the very finest Bordeaux. I offered to contribute to my host's expenditures in this regard, but he rebuked me gently for even suggesting such a course of action.

He seemed to be sincerely taken with my company, as I was of his, and he had chosen to bestow both his largesse and his wisdom upon one such as me. For this I was eternally grateful.

Following our meal, we finished off that vintage wine and savored a pair of cigars. It was my intent to follow the old man's lead and learn as much as I could of the remainder of his life and that of Thomas Meagher. As usual, he perceived my intentions and did not disappoint with his dictation.

Again I took up my pen and positioned myself at the table beneath the cabin's window. From my valise I retrieved my final bottle of ink and the last of my paper. The old man simply smiled and commented that he was always available for a student who was eager in his quest for knowledge.

O'KEEFE RESUMES HIS RECITATION

After Gettysburg, those who remained standing beneath the green flags of the Brigade were determined to see the war through to its bitter end. In New York, however, the sentiment of many of our people was much to the contrary.

The sights and losses of the war's destruction had become commonplace throughout Brooklyn, Manhattan and the Bronx. Convalescent veterans with amputated arms and legs were everywhere. The passing of the poor box for the widows and children of husbands and fathers who had fallen, was a weekly occurrence at Sunday Mass. Many of our ward bosses spoke of the need for an armistice and peace at any price.

As enlistments fell, Lincoln was forced to institute a draft that would fall heaviest upon the poor and the powerless. The sight of young, able-bodied members of the gentry avoiding military service through wealth and social station instilled in many of the Irish a deep resentment for the government and its laws.

While the Brigade was licking its wounds in Virginia after a bloody engagement outside Bristow Station, anarchy reigned in many parts of New York City, anarchy that took the forms of race hatred and draft riots. It was Meagher who wrote to me of these things. By then he had returned to his domicile on Fifth Avenue. He would always remember the outrages he witnessed during that summer of 1863.

Meagher had hoped that the notoriety and sacrifice of the Irish Brigade would open the doors of opportunity to our people in the cities of the North. In this he was bitterly mistaken. He had returned to New York City and traveled frequently to Boston and Philadelphia, the City of Brotherly Love.

During these sojourns he was made painfully aware that he was now just another member of the Irish immigrant class, just another Irish interloper, without a band of brothers to lead or a noble cause to follow.

In this state he wandered and wondered where he and his people could truly find freedom. It was then that the draft riots sent a shock through his soul. I suppose that is when he began his romance with the West, a romance that would once again incite the wanderlust within his restless heart.

He described the occasion to me in detail. He had gone to the Hibernian Hall for a meeting of the Fenian Brotherhood and was making his way back home in a hansom carriage. That was when his driver saw them up ahead, setting fire to a police wagon and pelting the authorities with bottles and rocks.

There were at least a hundred of them and they were blind with rage and the drink. To Meagher's shame they were mostly Irish and against all that he and his Brigade had stood and died for.

In truth, the draft was sometimes used as a tool of oppression. It could sweep the streets and mines clean of Irish troublemakers, trying to change the old ways of doing business. In the coal fields of Pennsylvania the ringleaders who sought to better the lives of those who went down into the hole were often conscripted and dragged from their homes as a means of quelling unrest.

On more than one occasion their secret society, known as the Molly Maguire's, would fall upon the wagons carrying their brothers away to war and deliver a painful lesson to the powers that be. In New York, arson and murder were the fruits of these frightful rampages, often claiming the lives of unsuspecting blacks caught in the crossfire of war and bigotry.

In order to avoid a confrontation with this mob, Meagher's driver applied the whip to his horse and directed her through a labyrinth of back alleys and lanes off the main thoroughfares. Along the way they caught glimpses of burning buildings and bloody encounters with freedmen whose misfortune was to be about at the hour of that mindless destruction. That is when they came upon a most outrageous example of that mindless rampage.

There before them was a black soldier, dressed in his Union blue, beaten and hanging from a lamp post with a crude sign dangling from the rope that surrounded his strangled neck. Below him upon the ground was a black boy child with his throat slashed.

Meagher had no excuse or explanation for this outrage. He detested cruelty more than any man I knew, and forever raged at the injustice of that senseless act. From that day forward he would speak out on behalf of the black soldiers who fought with distinction in the Grand Army of the Republic.

He and the driver would take the dead to an undertaker and make the arrangements for a decent burial. For months thereafter Meagher remained a festering sore, removed from his loving wife and once more soothing his doleful mood with the drink.

As another winter of war approached, the tide of battle shifted westward toward Tennessee. At Chickamauga Creek, Braxton Bragg drove Rosecrans and his forces back into Chattanooga and laid siege to the City with twenty thousand Federal soldiers trapped within.

It was there that Grant came to the rescue, using Hooker to open up a lifeline to those besieged troops and deploying his forces toward Lookout Mountain and Missionary Ridge. With the assistance of Sherman's troops and Sheridan's cavalry, he was able to defeat the rebels and establish Chattanooga as a base for future forays eastward into Georgia and South Carolina.

Just before Christmas, Meagher had accepted the invitation of his devoted friend, Michael Corcoran, to visit the camp of Corcoran's Legion, located near Fairfax Courthouse. By that time the Legion had distinguished itself in a series of bloody engagements that enhanced the reputation of Irish soldiers under fire.

Chapter 47

On December 22, 1863, after a festive celebration, General Corcoran was thrown from Meagher's spirited stallion while the two were returning to camp at the gallop. He lingered for a while, before succumbing to his injuries. The loss of his cherished friend and comrade in arms caused Meagher to fall into a deep melancholy.

That January, Meade's Army of the Potomac moved its camp north of the Rapidan River and settled down for a cold, cruel season of skirmishes and sharpshooting. By then, many of the Brigade who had reenlisted for the duration of the war were granted a month long furlough. That was when I would see Meagher again. By then he was in dire need of manly companionship and the saving grace of a new assignment.

This time the return to New York of the men serving within the Irish Brigade was an event of little significance to those managing the affairs of the City. Meagher in turn was determined to honor his gallant lads, despite the Copperhead sentiment that swirled around us. I had been breveted a Colonel and placed in charge of the Eighty Eighth Regiment. By formal invitation I was asked to appear for a luncheon at the Whitney House in the center of Manhattan.

The purpose of this affair was to arrange a commemorative banquet for the men of the Brigade at Irving Hall. All the superior officers who had survived the bloody sacrifice of the previous two years were in attendance. It was at that time that confidential conversations revealed the depths of Meagher's distress.

His outward appearance was much the same as he passed among the likes of Nugent, Bentley, Maroney and Kelly. Dr. Reynolds, as always, brought his particular brand of dignified cheer to all in attendance. Father Corby delivered a most heartfelt prayer before the meal was served and memories and stories were shared and savored. Together we took account of those who were not there.

I remember sitting between Colonel Bentley and Dr. Reynolds while we reminisced upon Duffy, Kavanaugh, and Michael Corcoran. Then Meagher approached and bestowed his manly welcome upon me. I tell you it was always an occasion to be in his presence.

After the dinner Thomas spoke of the need for us to close ranks as in battle and cherish the memory of times and valiant comrades past. We knew that he had thrown in with the Fenians by then and wondered whether he would ever return to the command of soldiers in service to the Union.

I learned through those in attendance that he had rescinded his resignation and petitioned the President, himself, to provide him with a posting that would further the cause of winning the war.

From the depths of despair arising from blood drenched battles lost, he had acted upon impulse with his resignation. After months of lassitude at home, he had come to the conclusion that he was now a man without station or purpose, searching for a way back to fulfillment.

Despite his courageous service, despite the desperate need for commanders who could lead and inspire raw recruits in times of terror, Thomas Meagher was a wasted resource, suddenly shunned by his superiors. He had become a leader without a following. It was this and the lack of a steady income that occasioned disputes with his father in law and long lonely nights apart from his beloved Elizabeth, sleeping in the bed beside him.

These circumstances caused him to cherish the memory of the Irish Brigade even more and to retrieve a forsaken sense of himself from his recent past. When all in attendance had departed, he asked if his carriage could carry me to my residence. I accepted his generosity because I could sense that he was in need of my company. The day was bitter cold as we made our way out toward the West Side.

"Cornelius," he began, "it is a pleasure to see your smiling face once again."

"Likewise, Thomas," I replied.

"We must not let them forget us. We must keep the deeds of the Brigade alive. Too many of our lads have given their lives and limbs for them to be forgotten. I should have been with the Brigade at Gettysburg. I regret my resignation. I must return to the field before it is too late. I must, or I fear I will go mad."

"Nonsense Thomas," I protested, "you have done more than your fair share. You have done nothing that merits regret. Enjoy your life. You need not sacrifice further. Besides, you are in the camp of the Fenians now. Is their cause not enough for you?"

"It is a cause with many factions, my friend. I am not altogether certain that it is the right cause for me. I have seen too much of war to believe in the hopes and plans of the Fenians. I am in need of a command in the Army. I pray it is not too late."

With that, we rode in silence toward my residence. When we finally arrived, I invited him in to visit with my family. He respectfully declined, offering the excuse that he would be late for a previous engagement. I could tell by his manner that there was no such engagement, and he knew it. I would see him again at the Irving Hall Banquet.

That commemoration was attended by almost all of our lads who had served and survived. Many were still convalescing from the amputation of limbs. It was a most memorable affair in which all who followed Meagher into battle stood and cheered as he entered. For at least that night he was once again our chieftain and we his devoted clan.

With the spring, Grant assumed command of the entire Army. His victories at Vicksburg, Lookout Mountain and Missionary Ridge had made of him an icon, a hero with a growing following riding the crest of a precarious wave.

As always, Grant sought to distance himself from this adulation, recognizing it for what it was, and understanding fully that his task was a daunting one. He must destroy Lee's Army in whatever way he could. In May of 1864 he set about that bloody endeavor in earnest.

Grant and Sherman devised a plan to act in concert in the final year of that blood drenched struggle. Grant would engage Lee's dwindling forces over and over again in the Wilderness of Virginia, then lay siege to Petersburg and finally surround Richmond itself.

Meanwhile, Sherman would turn his sights upon Johnston's Army and march from Chattanooga to Atlanta, then from Atlanta to the sea; all the while destroying the Confederacy's capacity for waging war. Then the design was to turn his war hardened troops loose on South Carolina, the despised cradle of the Confederacy.

I suppose I should speak to you of my final service within the Brigade and the manner in which I was reunited with Meagher.

After furious fighting at The Bloody Angle, our Second Corps made its camp outside of Spotsylvania Courthouse, Virginia. We were under orders from Hancock to keep up the hot pursuit of the retreating enemy. Recruits arrived daily and were sent to the slaughter by the thousands. It was a dreadful butcher's yard for weeks on end. By then, General Thomas Smythe, a brave and gentlemanly soldier, had been placed in charge of the dwindling ranks of the Brigade.

It was the 15th of May, a warm cloudless day, when we happened upon rebel fortifications within a pine forest. I was leading my lads through a hailstorm of enemy fire when I fell wounded. I recall seeing Blake waving the colors, urging the lads onward when minnie balls tore into my right shoulder and left side. It was Kirby who carried me from the field. The loss of blood had made me weak and weary enough to give up the ghost. It was the Brigade's son of the South who gave me the will to endure.

Receiving shrapnel wounds to his neck and back, Kirby would also be transported by a wounded wagon to the Army hospital outside of Fredericksburg. There the two of us became inseparable, spending many an hour of convalescence, conversing about times past in Waterford and Tipperary. His tales of service within the Papal Brigade and his loving depictions of the bayous and Baton Rouge thrilled me with delight.

I will always remember the sweet sound of his Louisiana speech and its role in our engagement with Forrest's raiders. I have given many thanks to the Lord for the person of Lieutenant Daniel Kirby, many thanks that he chose to change the color of his coat from Confederate gray to Union blue.

CHAPTER 48

The endless hours of my convalescence occasioned a steady correspondence to my wife and children in New York. For months I was unable to move without agony, requiring Kirby's hand to put pen to paper, thereby relaying the most heartfelt sentiments to my loved ones, mustering through life without me in New York.

The wounds to my shoulder and side were slow in healing, while a steady stream of the maimed and dying came and went around us. Between the dread of gangrene and the danger of a spreading fever, Kirby and I bore witness to a relentless procession of misery, begotten by the storm of war. It was a blistering August afternoon when we each received letters from Meagher.

Thomas had been speaking out within the Boroughs of New York on the Union's pressing need for Lincoln's reelection. Our old friend, McClellan, had taken up the gauntlet and become the Democratic Party's choice to unseat the President and bring about a negotiated peace with Davis and his band of traitors.

Meagher was once again the orator of an unpopular cause. Among the Irish and within the political circles of New York, Lincoln had become the subject of violent opposition and ridicule. Despite his allegiance, General Halleck and Secretary of War, Stanton, were unwilling to find a posting for the once troublesome leader of the Irish Brigade. It was Grant who would release his kindred spirit from the depths of his despair.

Despite the opposition of Sherman, Grant had arranged for a posting for Meagher within the Army of the Cumberland, under the command of General George Thomas. By that September, Meagher was on his way to Nashville, Tennessee and in need of two aides de camp of demonstrated loyalty and proven leadership.

Since both Kirby and I had recuperated from our wounds, we accepted a transfer to his command. As the troop train pulled into the Nashville station, I began another chapter in service to the Union and the person of Thomas Francis Meagher.

Nashville had not felt the lash of conquest, like some other Southern cities. Its commerce had remained intact and its railroad lines had been redirected toward the accomplishment of Sherman's objectives. It had become a depot for the defeat of the crumbling Confederacy.

With the razing of Atlanta, the rebel forces of Hood and Forrest were determined to make of Nashville a diversion to deter Sherman from his march to Savannah and the sea. It was around Nashville and Chattanooga that we would engage bands of Confederate raiders in the give and take of ambush and terror. It was a brand of warfare without glamour or glory. It was a time of retreat and reprisal and the tactic of the hit and run. In that bloody theater, its most accomplished player was Nathan Bedford Forrest

Forrest was a tall, rough-hewn slave trader in his middle years. He had the most murderous brown eyes that peered out from behind high cheekbones. His hair was the darkest brown and the contours of his long thin mouth were enclosed within a close cropped beard and mustache.

Far from a gentleman, he could spit and curse with the meanest soldier. When the air was thick with lead, he was at his best in bringing hellfire to his enemies. When Kirby and I arrived at Nashville, we were taken to Meagher's quarters and soon put to the task of combating this demon in his own country.

Like Meagher, Forrest was a born leader. In the first year of the Rebellion he formed a brigade of volunteers from those who dwelled and hunted in the backwoods and hollows of the Deep South. They were a fierce collection of men and boys who could ride, shoot and kill Yankees by the score. To such as these, Forrest was lord and master.

He was at home in the saddle and at his most lethal when wielding a saber at the gallop. In the ferocity of battle, he would be wounded on four occasions and have more than a score of horses shot from under him. Through it all, his terror remained legendary. His legacy would linger among all who despised the black and believed they were a lesser form of being. In Thomas Meagher, he would confront an enemy whose courage was soon surpassed by his cunning in the give and take of that peculiar brand of warfare.

Meagher was put in charge of the Fifteenth and Seventeenth Corps of the Army of the Tennessee, a rag tag collection of convalescents, bummers and garrison soldiers, gathered from a number of Union regiments. Despite the questionable caliber of his men, Meagher was determined to demonstrate his ability as a general officer, to both his superiors and his subordinates.

The duties of his new command seemed to rejuvenate him. Once more I saw that unmistakable fire in his eyes. It fell to Kirby and me to carry his commands down through those ragged ranks. Many of the men assigned to the Fifteenth and Seventeenth had spent months foraging and wreaking havoc with the citizenry of Georgia. Their first inspection manifested a lost respect for themselves and the Army that had nearly forgotten they existed.

It was Meagher who would restore their dignity and make of them a force to be feared. He knew that spit and polish among men such as these was a hopeless aspiration. Instead, he molded them into guerillas and won their admiration with his dash and his caring.

The task at hand was to safeguard the Chattanooga and Knoxville Railroad from destruction by Forrest's raiders and to watch and wait for the approach of Hood's forces. The necessity was to drill and train a portion of the men in the art of ambush and the terror of the night attack.

Meagher was determined to take the initiative and bring his own brand of hellfire to that devil Forrest. To do so, we needed horses and a cavalry that could live off the land. It was here that Kirby with his Louisiana roots would prove a most valuable asset. He chose two hundred who could ride and shoot the eyes from an owl on horseback. Meagher and I trained the rest. After almost a month, all were ready and able to meet the enemy.

It was then that Meagher called us to his quarters in the dead of night and gave to us a mission that was beyond the boundaries of war as we knew it. He was seated on a sofa in the parlor of a Chattanooga rooming house, his graying hair falling to his shoulders. Candles gave to the room a dim, eerie glow.

He was attired in a cavalry jacket and trousers. His boots were muddy and his sheathed sword rested upon the pine of the floor. Wearing two colts in his belt, his manly figure had lost most of its girth in those torrid days and weeks away from home cooking. He appeared once again the Thomas of old.

We three were alone and removed from ears that could betray our confidence, when he spoke to us of a clandestine venture that would beard the devil in his den.

"Daniel," he began, directing his attention to Kirby. "A long time ago an old woman spoke to me in New Orleans. I am certain our friend, O'Keefe, will remember the occasion. I believe she had the power, for too many of her predictions have become occurrences."

"It was she who told me of this place near a railroad, where I would lead two hundred gray horsemen against the devil himself. I know now of which she spoke. I recollect that bloody day at Antietam, when Hill's forces routed our own, while wearing Union blue. In my dreams I have seen a vision and your face and that of O'Keefe appearing beside me. This is the reason I sought both of you for this command. In the colors of the enemy, we will give the devil his due."

Together we listened to Meagher's strategy. We knew that the penalty for such a masquerade was the hangman's noose and yet we believed in its merit. From a captured enemy storehouse we dressed and equipped our cavalry. Through the countryside we rode as rebel raiders with Kirby in the lead. From those still loyal to the Stars and Bars we learned of Forrest's movements south of Chattanooga.

It was not long after the battle of Franklin. We waited in a wood where the railroad crossed the Tennessee River. Across the water lay Forrest's camp. On that December night the wind whistled and carried the scent of our horses away from the watch fires of the rebels. Meagher made us muffle the sound of their hoof beats with rags of muslin.

There was a full moon gleaming over that roaring river, when Thomas removed a green and gold silken flag from his saddlebag and gave it to our color bearer to fly. At that moment, he drew his saber while astride a chestnut mare and gathered our band of renegades around him. It was in this manner that he spoke.

"Lads, all your training and all your sacrifice will serve you well this night. Across that river is the son of a bitch who put Fort Pillow to the sword. Across that river are the bloody bastards who have killed your friends and poisoned the streams so that our lads would die from the thirst and the fever. Vengeance is yours on this night. Beneath the green flag that covered the casket of General Corcoran, I will lead you against the enemy. May God guide you and protect you in the righteous killing that lies ahead."

We followed Meagher's lead and dismounted as we approached the railroad bridge. In the distance, on the other side, we knew that their sentries were waiting.

Our hope was to catch them by surprise and sweep over them while they slept. I could tell that Meagher wanted Forrest for himself, like some vengeful knight bent upon trial by combat.

We made our way slowly over the bridge, all the while keeping our mounts as quiet as could be. Once across, Meagher formed us in a column of fours and called upon Kirby and myself to lead the charge.

My heart was pounding within my chest as we drew our sabers. That was when Meagher smiled at us in the moonlight of that night. In an instant we were among them.

Surprise and our disguise proved to be worthy allies. Their sentries hesitated long enough to die where they stood. I had never taken part in a cavalry charge before that night. The fury that comes with horse-borne combat was beyond comparison. The rebels fought with the desperation of men who knew their time had come.

We slashed and shot them as they emerged from their tents. To my right in the moonlight, I spied Meagher. His mare leaped over the rail fence of the enemy's corral, while a report from his Colt began a stampede of their horses. To my left I saw Kirby, firing and cutting, while surrounded by shirt tailed Johnnies. I took my eyes from him and aimed my Colt at a fleeing rebel. He fell face forward in a stream; my bullet exploded the back of his head like an egg.

Then there were three up ahead, sprinting toward a knoll where their rifles were stacked. At the crest Meagher appeared and chased them back toward me. I drew a bead upon them and they surrendered. Then from our right, on a coal black charger, came Lucifer, himself. It was Forrest and a score of his officers.

Their camp was in a grove of trees above that of the enlisted men. Like lightning shooting across the night sky, he struck. His saber poised above his hellish head, his fiendish face bent upon a bloodletting. He rode full stride into a dozen of our men, killing and maiming as he drove through them.

Again and again they tried to unhorse him, but he was a fiend possessed and protected by the force of evil.

I saw Meagher rear back upon his horse and make for the place where Forrest was killing his men. He too bore the look of a creature possessed.

I leaped at the opportunity before me, as did Kirby. One of us, I was certain, would kill that rebel bastard on that moonlit night. It was then that Forrest pulled his pistol and shot my horse from under me, while riding at Kirby with saber slashing. That was when Meagher fired and killed two raiders to his left. Sensing the game was lost, Forrest fled toward the wood.

From my fallen horse I retrieved a rifle and fired at him as he roared past. He slashed at me; the "woosh" of his saber narrowly missing my ducking skull. I fired twice more in his wake, as did Meagher and the rest of our number.

In all, twelve of his officers fell, but not Forrest. Amid that fusillade, he reached and grabbed one of our men by his belt, hoisting him up behind him as a shield. Meagher and Kirby gave chase with the skill of trained *chevaliers*.

Along the trail they found our man; his throat cut from ear to ear. There was hide nor hair of Forrest. Under the cover of darkness, the devil had disappeared.

CHAPTER 49

*I*n January of 1865, Meagher received orders to transport roughly six thousand provisional soldiers to New Berne North Carolina. There he was to assist in Sherman's movement toward Richmond and Petersburg. Attrition and blockade had taken their toll upon the enemy army. Rebel desertions soared, as their homes fell beneath the heel of the ever encircling Federals. In the last months of that brutal struggle, there was naught but misery and mercilessness upon the land.

By then, Meagher had grown weary of the role he was told to play. Brigadier General to a motley aggregation of volunteers was an unworthy assignment for one who had helped turn the tide at Malvern Hill and Antietam. Without the occupation of a fighting command, he resorted to days passed in reminiscence and nights devoted to more worldly pursuits.

It is an exaggeration to say that he became a hopeless drunkard, for I was in his company and knew his methods and his manners well. Like many of our generals, he would release his passions with the aid of the drink. During those final days, after so much misery and bloodshed, most of our finest fighting men engaged in like behavior. When killing becomes commonplace and life itself hangs in the balance, there are few who wear a saint's halo.

Rather than return through New York and make our way by ship to North Carolina, ice upon the Ohio River would cause us to travel by railroad to Pittsburgh. From there we were to travel to Annapolis then find our way to New Berne.

I must confess that the men did become rowdy after days vainly awaiting the arrival of a troop train. Yes, we did commandeer three trains to Cincinnati and displace certain of Ohio's leading citizens. Yet, it was a slander to say that we behaved as if we were still in enemy territory. For none of that rolling stock was put to the torch and none of those rails were fashioned into Sherman's neckties.

After all, Lincoln had defeated McLellan and we were soldiers in Mr. Lincoln's army, about to achieve a noble victory. Of course we took some liberties, but none that were lethal to my knowledge. Perhaps discipline should have been more the order of the day. But those were desperate times and we were creatures of that desperation, in transit to another theater of that bloody war.

In truth, Meagher removed himself from all responsibility for disciplining his troops and failed to delegate that duty to a sure and sober subordinate. Yet, whenever he passed among those ragged, ranks, he was cheered and revered. There were few generals who still commanded the affection of the men. Meagher was always one.

It was at Annapolis upon the *Ariel* that he was discovered by his superiors to be down with the drink. This information was soon telegraphed to certain of his sworn enemies in Washington. A slander was then perpetrated upon him by certain spineless political beings. They said Meagher had lost control of his command and spent his days and nights abusing the enlisted men, by catering to the whims and outrages of his officers.

I who witnessed those events can attest that Thomas was our unquestioned leader and no transgressions were committed that merited his removal from command. The armchair generals and petty politicians however, would exact their revenge upon one whose courage and exploits rose to the level of the legend.

On the twenty fourth of February, 1865, General Thomas Francis Meagher was relieved of duty at New Berne, North Carolina and sent home to New York in disgrace. There he was to await word on the convening of his Court Martial.

For one who had fought and led the Irish Brigade with such distinction, this was indeed a shameful episode. Yet Meagher would rise from the dead once more and take the lead in ushering many of his brethren to an unbridled promised land.

In the final days of the war, I was assigned to Sheridan's command, as a Colonel in charge of infantry. We were encamped west of Appomattox, Virginia, when Lee ordered Gordon and eight thousand men to cut their way through our lines in a desperate attempt to preserve what was left of his army.

This was Lee's last hope of escaping the complete annihilation of his forces. At first, Sheridan's cavalry was forced to fall back under the duress of that attack. Then that feisty bantam rooster regrouped and appeared among us, riding his black stallion, Rienzi.

He ordered us up into the breach; then led his cavalry against the enemy's left flank. That was the last engagement I would witness in that bloody conflict. For it was then that a party with a flag of truce emerged from the Confederate lines. Lee had decided to meet Grant at Appomattox Court House in order to negotiate the terms of his army's surrender.

The day of jubilation had at last arrived. It was Palm Sunday 1865. The peace would bring our Army back through a vanquished Richmond on our way toward Alexandria, Virginia. I shall never forget the sight and sound of our brave men as they marched through the Confederate Capitol, fervently singing the Battle Hymn of the Republic.

The eyes of all my soldiers were filled with the tears of a joyous exultation.

Those last few days were a time of triumph and a time of reconciliation. With the peace, my heart and those of my comrades in arms harbored no animus toward those who had fought so bravely wearing gray and butternut. That is the way with war, I suppose. When one's duty is to kill the enemy or be killed by him, there is no place for a merciful heart. Yet, when the pale of war has passed, enemies in battle soon become allies in staying alive. Such is the way of men in this world. Such is history.

The priest and the minister tell us that Christ died for our sins on Good Friday. I was seated at a table in my hut overlooking the Potomac, when a messenger rode his lathered horse into our camp, announcing to all who would listen that Lincoln had been shot at Ford's Theater. I emerged into the darkness of that April night and observed a congregation of my soldiers, kneeling next to the campfire, praying the Our Father.

It cannot be; I remember thinking. Not after the war was won, not our Father Abraham. For those who truly believed in the promise that was America, the cowardly act of that mad assassin was the cruelest blow of all.

I can see Lincoln still, watching at the window of his White House, waving to me with that sorrowful countenance. On Good Friday, Abraham Lincoln became the last and most damaging casualty of that war.

He was laid in state within that house of white. I came to pay my respects, bearing a heart brimming with grief. I waited for hours in a line of mourners as the rain pelted the City of Washington. All around me, men and women were weeping, weeping for their fallen President, weeping for their tortured nation, weeping for a world that had gone mad with the poison of human hatred.

It seemed that a circle had somehow been made complete. The man who had devoted himself to the preservation of the Union and the liberation of those who had been enslaved, had now passed beyond the bondage of this world and been set free from a life of sorrow. As I was descending the White House stairway, I heard the call of that unmistakable voice that had brought me to that place in my life.

The sight of Meagher making his way toward me in the attire of a country gentleman made my heart leap within my chest. His face bore the signs of one who had been crying, for more than any other, he was enamored of Lincoln, and saw in him the lasting hope of a free tomorrow. He embraced me warmly without uttering a word. We made our way to Willard's Hotel and secured an alcove away from the eyes and ears of irksome and inquiring personages.

Meagher was shattered by the circumstance of Lincoln's death. To him Booth's deed was beyond comparison in its treachery. He believed that death on the field of battle was a foreseeable consequence of warfare. But death at the hand of a sniveling non-combatant was without any semblance of justice.

I suppose it was the injustice of that assassination that bothered him most, after all that Lincoln had done. After all that he had meant to the Union and its struggle to remain united, it was an outrage that one such as Booth could bring an end to Lincoln's time upon earth.

Meagher was one who believed that certain of us are ordained to lead and blaze the trail for others to follow. This was the precept by which he conducted his life. This was the dogma instilled in him by those who shaped his being. Men like Smith O'Brien, Brother Edmund and Mitchel fashioned his mind and his soul. They challenged him to rise to the occasion of leadership. They invoked a sense of honor and valor from within him that caused others to gravitate toward his person.

I know this is the case, for I was one who saw in Meagher something more than that which moved other men. He seemed to have in mind a nobler mission, a greater design that others were unable to perceive. So too did Lincoln. Yet the angel of death is blind to the heroic deeds of those it embraces. Both the prince and the pauper are humbled by the grave.

In an alcove at Willard's Hotel, after the most sorrowful Easter that I can recall, Meagher and I spoke of such things. In the end, we were uncertain of the answers to our questions. In the end, we remained confused. Perhaps our faith was all we had to reassure us, in the end.

I recollect returning to the lessons taught us of the Christ in childhood. In my solitude I prayed upon these things and by that faithful discourse partook in small measure of that kingdom beyond the realm of men. It is there, I believe, that the Christ and Lincoln await us all.

CHAPTER 50

T he Army marched proudly up Pennsylvania Avenue on the day of the Grand Review. Bands played and the flags of the regiments passed by the bunting draped platforms upon which President Johnson and the Cabinet stood and saluted.

I rode a golden mare on that wondrous occasion. My uniform of blue with gold braid was resplendent in the warmth of the spring sunshine. The women and children showered us with praise and rose petals; just as they had done in New York on the day of our departure for war, a lifetime before. There was just the hint of the melancholy that was to come.

The summer of my thirty-seventh year was at hand and I was uncertain as to the course my life would take beyond my service in the Grand Army of the Republic. I was hopeful that the civilian life would be to my liking and offer me the chance of earning a living for myself and my family. After mustering out in the middle of June, I soon discovered that opportunity for Irish born veterans was a futile aspiration.

Having once learned my way in the Irish banking trade, I traveled day after day into the City and sought a position keeping books of account within the financial houses that prospered there. Again and again, I would see "NO IRISH NEED APPLY" in the windows of shops and manufactories that flourished, while I was shedding my blood in the service of the Union. Again and again, I was advised that there was no place or occupation for one with a name such as Cornelius O'Keefe.

I then sought a return to the newspaper business; only to learn that the need for reporters and copy printers did not exist, for worthy applicants were as plentiful as blades of grass. Even the ward bosses were overwhelmed with demands for employment by those returning from the war. On the West Side, Martin O'Loughlin and those of his ilk, exacted a hefty tribute for empty promises.

It seemed that time and circumstance had passed me by. At every turn, the Nativist and the Know Nothing appeared to obstruct my way. It was then that Quinlan came calling up the backstairs and advised me of a position in charge of a crew of sand hogs. The work was hard and the wages were low, but by that time beggars could not be choosers. I swallowed my pride and resolved to make the best of burrowing beneath the streets of New York.

Quinlan also advised me that there was to be a celebration for the Fourth of July and that those who served within the Irish Brigade were to parade up Fifth Avenue. I recall retrieving my cherished uniform from the recesses of the attic, shining its buttons, creasing its trousers, making straight its epaulettes and traveling to the Metropolitan Hotel. It was there that I would be reunited with those who had been my brothers in battle.

Since his removal from command, Meagher had been petitioning his political allies to use their influence to prevent the convening of his Court Martial. Charged with a dereliction of duty in New Berne, North Carolina, became a phrase that attached itself to his noble name, like some blood sucking parasite. There are always those who believe the worst of the ones who lead. There are always the critics who stand away from the fray, offering opinions from a safe and secure distance.

I believe it was Grant who determined that the entire affair was a misplaced exercise of a soldier's prerogative and brought it to a final rest. That was his way of repaying a brave and battered general for valorous deeds on the field of battle. After all, the War of the Rebellion had already destroyed far too many who were good and far too many who were courageous. There was neither reason nor justification for adding Thomas Meagher's name to that list.

A respite from their company brought a yearning to see the faces of those with whom I had served. As I walked through the ornate golden and glass doors to the lobby of the Metropolitan Hotel, I could not help but recall the night of my initiation during the Harvest Ball.

As I walked up the crimson, carpeted stairway toward the spacious second floor ballroom, I swear I could almost see and hear the one we called William Herbert, eyeing every lovely that passed by him, while playing a Mozart Sonata upon his violin.

For an instant they were all there, as if the war had never taken them from me. There was Duffy with the devil in his wild Irish eyes and Michael Corcoran's manly figure rising above us all, speaking of Fenians and the future of Erin. Again I saw young Johnny Kavanaugh, whirling with the dance, before giving his tired leg a rest next to the double doors leading out upon the veranda. All the while the music played, above the sounds of fifes and drums, beyond the roar of cannons and the blaze of guns. It was a flight of fancy so real, that I prayed it would remain with me forever.

Suddenly, I felt as if the walls and ceiling were closing in around me. The scars upon my neck and side began to throb without mercy. I could not catch my breath. I found myself falling into a wild dark river, being swept away, giving myself up to the liberation of the deep.

It was Gosson and Lucky who rescued me from my malaise. They were coming from the saloon when they spied me. I was stumbling toward the refuge of a nearby divan, in need of a place to recline. They assumed I was taken with the drink and carried me across the ballroom and out upon the veranda, where they had trained recruits in the give and take of hand to hand fighting. That was where I became reunited with the ones who had served beside me in the ranks of the Irish Brigade.

The summer sun blazed down upon Broadway on that most memorable day. My guardians had placed me in a white wicker chair to the left of the doors leading from the veranda. They commanded a dutiful waiter with a red mustache and chin whiskers to bring me a tall glass of beer and told him to follow it with the very finest Irish whiskey. In truth, this refreshment was just what the doctor ordered; Doctor Lawrence Reynolds, that is.

His hair by that time was as white and fine as a swan's feathers. His face was a florid pink and his pale blue eyes peered from beneath a pair of silver spectacles. The blue of his uniform had faded and his voice seemed to lack the vigor of the past.

He was draining the remains from a glass of Irish when my eyes fell upon his. A look of bewilderment soon came over him as he drew closer. It was as if he had seen a ghost. I spoke to reassure him that I was still a creature of flesh and blood.

"Do you not recognize me, Doctor? Come and sit a while with an old friend."

"By God," he cried. "I thought you were killed with Kirby at Spotsylvania."

"I trust I've not disappointed you. You can check for a pulse if you'd like."

"By God, O'Keefe, you are a welcome sight. By God, I am glad you're alive. By God," he repeated, while nearly wrenching my hand from my wrist. "What of Kirby? Is he alive as well?"

"As far as I know, I'm told he's taken up with a widow over in Brooklyn. She's trying to make a suitable husband of him. She must be daft. I expect we'll be seeing him before the day is through. What have you been up to, Doctor?

He sat across from me in an oversized rocking chair and advised me of his service with the Sanitary Commission and his dreams of assisting Father Corby in the establishment of a Jesuit institution of learning known as Notre Dame College. I asked him about his poetry and he assured me that he was still making rhyme.

As we conversed the others started to gather within the ballroom. Slowly they began to make their way out toward the fresh air of that veranda.

I have already spoken of Gosson and Lucky. It seems that those two rascals were among the first to arrive. Whenever a celebration was in order, they were always ready to report for duty. Their appearance was all but unchanged. Each was wearing their Union blue. Gosson's muscled shoulders bore captain's bars, while Lucky's jacket displayed the stripes of a lieutenant. Gosson was still a burly bear with black wavy hair, while Lucky remained the slender dark featured son of a Milanese nobleman.

Together they had fought and survived the worst of times and returned to New York City. Like most of us, they were in need of a stake to make their start. It was their design to become partners in the running of a saloon and bawdy house.

There were close to four hundred who marched beneath the green flags of the Brigade on that last occasion. I had almost forgotten the reassuring comfort of that camaraderie. There were many whose faces I did not remember, many who had taken the places of those who had fallen at Antietam and Fredericksburg. Many, too young to have fled from the field at Manassas. There were but a few who had managed to serve from the start.

There was Quinlan, with his proud, portly figure, marching ramrod straight to the sounds of *Garryowen*. He would build many a bridge within the employ of the railroads, before his days were through.

There was Nugent, with his forage cap tied to his slender head, looking into the crowd in search of his wife and children. His angular face was now clean shaven and without the unruly beard that once concealed a boyish chin from his men. He would study for the law and argue many a compelling case for the widows of those who had fallen in service to the Union. His quiet courage and unswerving devotion to justice would cause his name to be remembered long after he had departed from this earth.

As we approached Saint Patrick's Cathedral, I observed William Herbert near the rear of our number. His face was no longer that of the rakish lady's man. He had grown so much older. As I watched, I understood the reason for this transformation. A perusal of his person revealed that the right sleeve of his blue and gold jacket was now empty and pinned to his side. The sweet strains of his violin would never grace another celebration.

He had come to the shores of his adopted land for the promise of freedom. Now he was a reminder of those who had suffered so much in service to the Union. He had saved my life in battle. I was blessed to have been his friend. That would not be our last time together.

At the end of our procession there walked a solitary figure in civilian attire. His face was forlorn and his eyes were wet with tears. The crowd that cheered our passing paid no heed to the one who walked alone.

Once he had been their darling. Once he had been a part of their dreams. Now he had no use for their adulation, for he had come to understand that fame is a faithless mistress. There in the rear of those who had served beneath the green flags walked the one who led us along paths of glory.

As the parade continued along Fifth Avenue beyond Saint Patrick's Cathedral, the person of Thomas Meagher quietly broke from our ranks and disappeared into the jubilant crowd.

CHAPTER 51

It was at the tail end of an eighteen hour day. My nostrils and eyelids were caked with the soot of another excavation beneath the streets of New York. My throat and lungs ached with every breath, as I waited outside the offices of Montgomery & Son for the appearance of Carlisle, the superintendent of labor.

My crew of 40 sand hogs waited in line behind me, upon a boardwalk that led along an alley to the company's back entrance. As a relentless rain soaked us to the bone, I was reminded of those dreadful days upon the Peninsula. The mood of the men was as dark as the night sky, for that was the time when our wages and costs were figured and paid by those who believed they were our masters.

Carlisle arrived in a carriage with two of his hooligans. All three were well armed and of Welch extraction. He was a squat, dark featured bastard with thick black eyebrows that knitted together atop a pock marked face. His associates were straight from the gutter; one more surly and imposing than the other. Both wore dark, unruly beards, and yellow dusters.

It was said that all three had come to the employ of Montgomery & Sons after working for a coal mine operator in Pennsylvania. There they made their living from the misery of Irish miners, working them like slaves and hiring informers to spy upon their secret societies.

Carlisle passed by us without greeting and unlocked the door to the back room where we were summoned one by one. I was the first to be called. Carlisle was seated at a rectangular wooden table with his companions standing on either side of him, like two trained mastiffs. I could see the pearl handle of a revolver protruding from the waistband of the hairy hound on the right. I suppose I was meant to.

It was then that my hours and wages were announced and counted out on the table before me. I recall being charged for three shovels and a pick that had been damaged during my watch. These expenses left me with a pittance to provide food and shelter for my family. I could feel the rage welling up inside of me, like lava within a volcano. I attempted to explain that the tools we were provided were decrepit and could not withstand the rigors of burrowing through rock and shale.

That was when the dog on the right smirked at me, while Carlisle questioned whether I was fit to supervise a crew of men. He spoke with a Welch accent, reminding me of a detested landlord.

"You Irish, you're always making excuses for not doing your work. You're not in the army anymore, O'Keefe. You had better toe the line around here or we will find somebody who will. Now get on with ya', before I have them throw you out on your arse."

There was no holding back for me at that point. I had my fill of bosses and landlords and doors being slammed in my face. The evil I despised was sitting before me. He had taken away my wages and now threatened my dignity. I had fought and killed too many whose designs included the bondage of other men, to accept his insults.

In a flash, I overturned the table upon him and kicked the dog on his right squarely in the belly, snatching his pistol as he doubled up on the floor. Toward the other I whirled, training the pistol upon him. I had all I could do to stop myself from killing all three.

Instead, I called to my crew and had them hold the bastards at bay, while I, who knew only too well how to calculate in books of account, dispensed our wages fairly and without fanciful subtractions on behalf of Montgomery & Sons.

My mind was a jumble as I emerged from the alleyway on to Eleventh Avenue. I was thankful the rain had finally subsided. I knew that it was only a matter of time before they would come for me and resolved to return to my home. I hired a horse and galloped first to Quinlan's and advised him of what I had done. He told me he would seek out Meagher and arrange for a lawyer through the friends of the Brigade.

I will always remember the sight of my sobbing wife and three small children as they gathered around me. I delivered the news through angry tears. I explained that I could no longer endure the damning circumstance of my present situation. I would have sooner taken up the criminal trade than become a man without hope or respect.

Two nights later I was brought to the precinct house in shackles. From there I was thrown into a miserable cell among drunkards, vagrants and petty criminals. The following morning I was brought by wagon to the courthouse. It was there that I would meet my barrister.

He had been a friend of the Brigade from the beginning. It was Meagher who engaged his services. His name was James Brady and his reputation for defending those accused of high crimes and misdemeanors was exceptional.

He was a bear of a man in his fifties with at least three chins and an enormous head of silver hair. His fiery green eyes, booming voice and command of the language caused the courtrooms to be filled whenever he was on display. To my astonishment he had managed to enlist Greeley's *Tribune* in my cause.

Having fought and bled in the cause of liberty, I was grateful for an advocate who could use his wiles and his words in my defense. After six weeks beneath the heel of my indictment, I came to trial in the Manhattan Courthouse.

In all, nine witnesses were called. All the while the *Tribune* advised the world that my actions were justified, that I was a misused veteran who should be commended for his deeds, and not condemned. These were the same words used by Brady in his summation. They were the means by which I was set free.

My confinement had indeed been painful to endure, yet it gave to me an opportunity for earnest reflection. I could no longer remain in a place where I had been a prisoner. I had resolved to follow in the footsteps of another. I would make my way westward toward the frontier and there once again be reunited with my chieftain, Thomas Francis Meagher.

You see, Meagher had fallen into disfavor among many of his New York brethren. His support for the reelection of Lincoln had made him an enemy to those who voted the Democratic ticket. His orations upon the sacrifices of our black soldiers and the need to afford them the opportunity to live and work in a free nation had eroded his reputation even further among the Irish.

Even within his own home, his father in law referred to him as an upstart and an idle pretender, without the name or the means of being accepted into New York society. Meagher grew tired of his surroundings and the criticism of compromised men. He resolved to make his way to the Western Frontier. That was where he could finally be free.

His design was to secure a position in the West and win his fortune from the mining of silver and gold. It was a dream that consumed him and caused him to petition President Johnson for a posting as Governor of one of the western territories. Johnson had been the Governor of Tennessee before Meagher was stationed in Nashville. The two had become enamored of each other during Meagher's speech in support of Lincoln's policies, before the Tennessee House of Representatives.

I recall reading of Meagher's appointment as Secretary to the Territory of Montana while I awaited trial. At that moment, I too began to dream of majestic mountains and the unbridled promise of life and liberty in an untamed West.

After my acquittal I returned to the loving arms of my wife and children. There a letter was waiting. I recognized the handwriting as Meagher's. He had anticipated my release and forwarded a draft in an amount sufficient to meet the immediate needs of my family. He had also included a precise sum for booking passage by rail and stage to the Montana Territory.

Within the letter he spoke of his dreams and enlisted me as his ally in another bold adventure. Once again, as at Waterford, he challenged me to be courageous. By the 14th of September, 1865, I was making my way westward with the hope of a bright and prosperous tomorrow.

Like a light bearer, Meagher would lead me and thousands of others up into the majesty of that wilderness. There we would meet people who were at one with that wild land. The coming of our ways would change their world forever.

PART THREE
THE WEST

CHAPTER 52

The way westward was an avenue taken by many who had fought beneath the green flags of the Irish Brigade. The War of the Rebellion had touched our souls with the fire of freedom's promise. Its ordeal had fashioned us into tempered steel. Having endured the sights and sounds of hell itself, we developed a supreme sense of the significant. It gave us an insight into the hearts and minds of those who wielded power.

I suppose it was Lewis and Clark who showed us the way at first. Then came the trappers, the hunters and the mountain men. There followed the early settlers who buried their dead beside the Oregon and Mormon trails; all of them searching for satisfaction beyond the blaze of the next setting sun.

After the war they came, from both North and South. They fled from the cities and the soot of civilization. They fled from the farms and their ceaseless chores. They fled from the ruins of the plantations and their shattered way of life. By rail, stage, steamboat, ship and covered wagon they traveled, seeking a new beginning, a fresh start, a bright tomorrow.

It seemed that all who had overcome their fear of the unknown, all who had reached the end of opportunity back home, now looked upon the West as a place of salvation. It was the same yearning and the same hope as before.

I, who had crossed the North Atlantic in the bowels of a coffin ship, now embarked upon another quest, another passage in search of liberty. I had been smitten by the siren wanderlust. She had beckoned me to pursue her beyond the wild Missouri. There I would be reunited with Meagher.

I followed the route Thomas ascribed for me, and heard tell of his exploits all along the way. He and a stalwart wagon master by the name of James Fisk had embarked from New York during the first week of August. Fisk was a giant in stature and reputation who had trapped and lived among the Crow and Shoshone. He had broken bread with Bridger along the Musselshell and survived many a winter within the wilderness of the Bitterroot and Cabinet Mountains. He would lead many an expedition westward. Of all the places where Fisk made his bed, Montana captured his heart the most.

Like Meagher, I traveled by rail to Saint Louis. This was the departure point for most who had made the decision to go west. I had packed a haversack with sufficient supplies and belongings to meet my needs. From Saint Louis, the Missouri River wound its way north westward through endless mountains and valleys toward the territory of Montana.

Some chose to book passage upon a steamboat bound for the trading post at Fort Benton, while others sought a quicker course by overland stagecoach through Kansas, Colorado, and Utah. Either way had its share of danger and hardship.

I chose the stagecoach. It was a rough and tumble journey within a creaking, comfortless, carriage that sat atop high wooden wheels.

There were six passengers, a driver and a guard to protect against attacks by road agents. Within the coach we sat three across, facing each other from leather covered benches.

Our haversacks and suitcases were lashed to the wood and canvas roof. There were two doors and four rectangular slots that served as windows. These were covered with canvas curtains that provided little relief from the dust and the sweltering heat.

With an eye for detail, I made note of those who were my companions upon the trail. The driver was the captain of that land bound schooner and the last word on any disputes that arose upon the journey. He was a burly man in his forties who wore a blood red shirt and brown leather vest. His belly spilled over a silver buckled belt and stove pipe trousers. A gray beard stained with the residue of chewing tobacco covered his broad weather worn face. He wore a six shooter and a black slouch hat pulled down tightly around a large balding head. He answered to the name of Ned Schofield.

Seated directly across from me was a tall white haired preacher with ferret-like eyes of brown, who read constantly from the Good Book. He was on a mission to save souls in Topeka, Kansas. I made it a point to steer clear of such personages, whenever possible.

Along-side him was a spinster bound for Minneapolis. She wore a paisley bonnet and a plain gray dress, buttoned all the way to the neck. Throughout the journey she spoke little and knitted much. I recall a cameo broach that was fastened to the area of her right collar. It seemed that her wrinkled, plain face would shatter, should she manage to crack a smile.

Beside her sat a perspiring, portly drummer, bound for Denver to ply his wares. His speech was rapid and bore the trace of a Polish accent. A derby hat covered his silver hair and his bespectacled hazel eyes seemed to peer from the recesses of his large round head. Throughout our time together he recited many a story and yarn. I grew quite fond of that aging huckster before we parted company.

The remaining passengers were two brothers from Virginia by the name of Slocumb. Both had golden hair and sky blue eyes. The older of the two appeared close to twenty five years of age. He had a jagged scar running alongside his bearded cheek and the haggard look of so many who had suffered starvation and the destruction of all that was near and dear. His manner was taciturn and surly.

His younger brother was no more than seventeen. He too bore the trace of the defeated and yet there was a courtly way about him. He wore a wispy yellow mustache and the trace of a Mansfield below his lip. He was polite in his manner and inclined to be pleasant.

I would later learn that these two had returned to their home within the Shenandoah Valley, after serving under Longstreet. There they discovered that their farm had been burned, their livestock slaughtered and their folks nowhere to be found. Both were heading West with nothing left to lose.

Throughout the journey, I carried a pistol concealed in my coat and a knife in my waistband. I had heard tell of slit purses and road agents that lurked among the hills and draws of Kansas and Colorado. I knew that the frontier was wild and without mercy for those who failed to protect themselves from harm.

There was much spoken about Indians and wild beasts that roamed the frontier. I understood that a journey by stagecoach was not for the faint of heart, as did my companions. For there were many back East who had written in vain to relatives whose bones lie bleaching along trails leading West.

From Missouri we crossed the prairies and plains of Kansas. I remember gazing from the rear window as far as the eye could see. There were few farms and signs of civilization, only an endless expanse of arid land that seemed unfit for man or beast. We came to the Town of Topeka on the afternoon of the fifth day. By then the six of us had been bruised and battered by the rocking of that merciless coach and become acquainted with each other's smell. We rolled down the main street bordered by wood frame buildings under the watchful eyes of several of the Town's citizenry. I recall that a gang of ragged children ran after us, shouting to those who cared that the stage had arrived.

The guard descended from his post, seated beside the driver, and directed us toward a rooming house with a white sign above the door reading Overland Stage Company.

He was a young, arrow-thin sullen sort, with leather breeches, a brown fedora and a Sharp's rifle. His skin was the color of cowhide and his shirt was tawny buckskin. He had dark hair that touched his broad shoulders and a prominent nose that gave him the appearance of a large bird of prey. His name was Lemuel and he spoke with a slight stammer. We learned that he was the driver's nephew and his family had been killed during one of Quantrill's raids.

The accommodations in Topeka were superior to those of the way stations along the trail. After a shave and a bath, I once again began to look and smell like a man of some refinement. I inquired as to a suitable location for a meal and was advised by the hotel clerk that Slattery's Saloon would meet my needs. On the way I took up company with the drummer bound for Denver. His name was Harry Roth.

Topeka's main street was alive with the bustle of wagons and horses. As we walked along its crowded boardwalk, we passed a mercantile bank and a dry goods store with sacks of feed and grain on display out front. There was a livery stable, a lawyer's office, a boarding house, a doctor's office at the top of a set of rickety stairs, and finally Slattery's Saloon. It was an oasis in an otherwise threatening landscape. I was dying for a decent meal and a glass of cold beer.

Through a set of double doors we entered and observed the interior of Topeka's finest restaurant and drinking emporium. It was a long narrow place with a bar that ran all the way down its right side. There were a dozen or so tables, each surrounded by six cane back chairs. From the center of a seven foot ceiling hung a small chandelier. Its uneven floor was covered with sawdust and alive with a midday crowd.

While inside, we soon encountered the Slocumb brothers and our guardian, Lemuel. Soon all of us were seated around a spacious table covered in a red and white cloth. To my delight the beer was cold and a treat to the taste. It was the drummer bound for Denver who brought us together with his curiosity and his nimble conversation. It was the first time we spoke without the dust of the trail flying into our faces.

"Lemuel, does our driver, Mr. Schofield, call Kansas his home?"

"When it suits him, I r'reckon," he muttered, while hovered over a bowl of rabbit stew.

"He seems to be a fair man, and not afraid to take a risk or right a wrong. That's exactly the kind of man the West needs," the drummer observed. "What about you boys, are you Montana bound or is Denver more to your liking?"

"We ain't decided yet," the younger Slocumb responded. "We just looking for a place to make our way. That's all. We was wondering about you, mister. My brother here says you look like a Yankee officer. Is he right?"

"As right as rain, son," I said. "I was a colonel in the Irish Brigade."

With that the older Slocumb focused his piercing eyes upon me and studied my face and figure before whispering to his brother.

"Were you at Antietam?" the younger asked.

"That I was, and will not soon forget the occasion. Many brave lads on both sides fell on that fateful day."

It was then that I raised my glass and offered a toast to their memory. All at the table joined in that commemoration. I can still see the older Slocumb, staring across at me with sadness and the hint of suspicion in his sky blue eyes.

With the departure of the preacher and the spinster switching stages for Minneapolis, we picked up two new passengers before making our way across the wilds of Colorado toward the mining town of Denver.

One was an aged prospector by the name of Matthews and the other was an itinerant actor who called himself Edwin Roberts. Matthews claimed to be a forty-niner who struck it rich near Sacramento then lived high off the hog for almost ten years. He spoke of life in the mining camps and the sight of gold nuggets glistening in the summer sun. He was on his way to Colorado in search of one last strike. I tell you the way that old man talked of prospecting made me wonder if I should take up the trade.

Roberts was another story altogether. He wore a faded brown frock coat and a broad brimmed yellow hat, tilted rakishly toward his right eye. His hair and beard appeared to be an unnatural ebony and his brown eyes glistened with a distant stare.

He was a tall, effeminate man with an elaborate way of speaking and gesturing. He appeared out of place beyond the confines of the theater. It seemed that he had passed his prime and was in dire need of retrieving it. From his valise he produced two yellowed reviews, praising his performance of Macbeth in Cincinnati. He told us he was on his way to San Francisco and asked at each depot whether a letter had been left for him.

I recall the first time I saw them, rising from a golden plane and resting their rugged shoulders against an array of gigantic silver clouds. The driver brought the stage to a halt and summoned us forth to partake in the panorama before us. Ahead, we observed the Rocky Mountains and the expanse of Colorado.

The terrain was far different from Kansas. The endless expanse of brown prairie and dusty plain had given way to verdant forest and sparkling rivers. I marveled at the majesty of it all and recall giving thanks to the Almighty for allowing me to witness such masterful creations.

I knew then that I had made the right decision in striking out for the frontier. No matter what the peril, no matter what the penalty, I would never regret the choice of risking all in search of freedom. We would make our way into Denver by the following night.

CHAPTER 53

The promise of gold and riches had enticed thousands to travel west. It began in California and spread like wildfire across Nevada and into Colorado. By 1860 Denver had become a raucous, lawless way station for prospectors, miners, thieves and cutthroats.

At the time of our arrival in September of 1865, Denver was a frontier town wrestling with the need for law and order. While spending two days in this respite along the trail, I would witness a brand of frontier justice that chilled me to my bones.

By that time, I had become better acquainted with the Slocumbs and spoken to them of Erin and my passage upon the coffin ships. They in turn told me of their life before the war and the beauty of the Shenandoah Valley. Although those two had been my sworn enemies less than six short months before, the ending of hostilities had given me a broader outlook, a more peaceable view.

I had never seen lynch mob justice before that episode in Denver. There we were, passing a sweltering afternoon beneath the shade of a rooming house porch, when our attention was drawn toward an angry crowd making its way up the dusty street. It was our driver, Ned, who advised us that a hanging was about to occur. The matter of fact manner of his observation told us that this was a common occurrence in that place.

As the crowd drew nearer, I could see the faces of two terror filled lads, surrounded by a gang of hooligans who called themselves a vigilance committee. One lad had a copper color to his skin and wore curled brown hair to his shoulder. The other had the features of a dim wit and cried like a child to be released from the clutches of his captors.

Nearby was an enormous chestnut tree that provided two sturdy limbs for that mob's dirty work. Ropes were thrown over its boughs and nooses fashioned for the event. By then it seemed as if the entire town had turned out to witness the spectacle.

I recall seeing children of tender years, chewing on licorice sticks, as a gaunt man dressed in shirt sleeves and suspenders attempted to intercede on behalf of the condemned. He kept telling the crowd that the boys deserved a fair trial before being hanged and that the marshal would be coming back soon.

He was shouted down by the crowd and told to leave that place or he would suffer a similar fate. As he retired from their midst in disgust, the older Slocumb asked him what crime the boys had committed.

He told us that the darker of the two was a half-breed, wanted for stealing horses. The dim wit was assumed to be his accomplice in crime. He shook his head and vowed to bring the matter to the attention of the marshal, upon his return from the territory.

It was then that a wagon was drawn up and the boys hoisted upon it. A minister of sorts read from the scriptures and the boys were asked if they had any last words. The dim wit simply sobbed as the noose was tightened around his neck. The half-breed, told the crowd that he would see them in hell.

Then suddenly the wagon lurched forward leaving them dangling; the nooses snapping each of their necks with a horrid crack, their bodies and their legs shaking furiously, as if in a spasm. Then their corpses grew still. I had never seen men hanged before that occasion. I pray to God I will never see such a sight ever again.

We were pleased to take our leave of Denver on the morning of the following day. We were now accompanied by a widow and her boy, headed for the Mormon settlement in Ogden.

Along the trail Edwin Roberts recited his Shakespeare, while we observed the most magnificent country through the stage's windows. There were endless valleys and mountains that reached into the heavens. There were rushing rivers and herds of antelope and deer running wild in the distance.

All the while, Lemuel and Ned were on the lookout for the approach of road agents, for that was a territory where the outlaw ruled and many a life was ended in the blaze of a six gun.

At night we slept in way stations that smelled of coal tar and kerosene. In a week we were a days' travel from the Salt Lake. The dust was everywhere and the food left much to be desired.

The Town of Salt Lake was governed by those who followed the teachings of Joseph Smith and Brigham Young. Like the Pilgrims, the Mormons fled from a world that despised their beliefs. In a place of desert heat and merciless landscape, they made their home and raised their families. To one and all they gave the name brother and they worked and prospered like the Israelites in the land of Canaan.

Ned, our driver, told us that the Mormons were the most honest people he had ever run across. From what I saw, I had no cause to dispute his assertion.

It was in Salt Lake that I secured a month old newspaper from Minneapolis, in Minnesota, and read with great interest of Meagher's sojourn there. It seems that he and Fisk had arrived to a hero's welcome and that Meagher had delivered a courageous speech to that city's Irish Immigration Society on the plight of the black soldier and the injustice of denying him liberty.

In a way station on the trail to the Montana Territory, I read the words he spoke to an audience of Irish exiles over and over again. Words reprinted in the Irish newspapers back East. Words that made me search my own soul, words that made of him an exile among many of his own people. These were the words he spoke:

"The black heroes of the Union Army have not only entitled themselves to liberty but to citizenship. The democrat who would deny them the rights for which their wounds and glorified colors so eloquently plead is unworthy to participate in the greatness of the Nation."

I remember envisioning Meagher, as he spoke those words. With his eloquence and his presence before the crowd, he had the capacity of reaching into their hearts and touching that which sets man apart from the beast. This was his great gift and his calling. I longed to see my chieftain once again.

We drew near to a trading post on the trail that led along a rim of mountains toward Virginia City. It was there that we came upon a band of Crow Indians, seeking to barter buffalo hides for guns.

At that time, there was peace along the plains and the Crows were admired for their skill as hunters. Heading westward, I had heard many a tale of vicious savages who preyed upon women and children. In truth, these Crows seemed the opposite of those depictions. I could not help but admire the manner in which they groomed their persons and conducted their affairs.

There were six who stood beside their horses and two who spoke in signs to the proprietor of the establishment, seeking to strike a worthy bargain. My attention was drawn to one of their number who stood above the rest. He was tall and muscular with ebony hair that shone like a raven's wing. His skin was the color of a copper kettle and his dark eyes possessed the look of a warrior chief. If I were required to guess, I would say he was no more than twenty five years of age and a man of great respect among his people.

He wore a shirt and leggings of tawny buckskin and eagle feathers upon his head. His feet were encased in moccasins and a necklace of bear claws encircled his manly neck. It was apparent, as the bargaining continued, that the proprietor, a small, sturdy, old man with coiled white hair and a Swedish accent, had great respect for the Indians with whom he spoke.

I believe he called the tall one, Dark Wolf, and the other who stood beside him, Brave Elk. That night I spoke to Ned, our driver, about the Indians we had seen and the manner of his dealings with them. I can still recollect his reply and his sentiments towards those whose lives we changed forever with our coming.

"I've seen my share of Indians, alright, Blackfeet, Shoshone, Crow, Sioux. Hell, I was married to a Flathead squaw for nearly four years. A finer woman I never met. She stuck by me through thick and thin. Then she came down with the smallpox; caught it from some settlers' kids down along the Judith. One night she just up and crawled away and died. Goddamn, I miss that there gal. I surely do."

"I tell y'a, I never met an Indian who would lie to y'er face, nor turn tail and run from a fight. Course I ain't made a study of such things, but I s'pose, if we could learn their ways and teach 'em ours without preachin' to 'em, like they was damned sinners, this whole damned country would be a damned site better off."

After suffering through five more days in another merciless coach, we made our way over a rise and caught sight of Virginia City, Montana. We had arrived just as the winter winds began to howl in the mountains, and find their way down into the camps where men came to make their fortunes.

It seemed so strange to me. There I was, thousands of miles from New York and thousands more from the green fields of Erin, beginning a novel adventure. I spoke to the Slocumbs of the promise of Montana. The rest I would leave to Meagher.

CHAPTER 54

*M*eagher had arrived nearly a month before. He had come with the wagon master, John Liberty Fisk and reported to the man he was supposed to serve, Sidney Edgerton, the Governor of the Territory. Edgerton called Ohio his home and despised the loneliness and hardship of the mining frontier. It seemed that as soon as Meagher arrived, Edgerton hightailed it back East. Instead of Montana's Secretary, Meagher soon became its Acting Governor. As the "Acting One", Thomas would make his mark and once again present a problem for those who feared the fearless and the free.

Just a few months after amber nuggets were discovered at Alder Gulch, Virginia City became one of the great gold camps of the West, drawing prospectors to it like bees to honey. By the time of my arrival, its population had swelled to more than ten thousand hearty souls. It was set within the mountains and was nearly a mile in length.

There were four wind-swept muddy streets in all, with two ramshackle hotels, three saloons, a dry goods store and a cathouse that did a brisk business, day or night. There was an opera house that rang with the sounds of Shakespeare and a library with a sundry collection of dilapidated, dog eared texts upon its makeshift shelves. There were shacks and tents for drummers and merchants, Chinese laundries and opium dens.

Within the year it would possess both a Catholic and a Methodist Church, along with hundreds of settlers' cabins and a public school. It was the place where I would make my fortune.

As I walked up Main Street in the company of my Confederate companions, searching for a place to lay my head and quench my desperate thirst, I saw Meagher coming toward me in the company of two men carrying rifles sheathed in fringed buckskin.

He was wearing a brown slouch hat and an unbuttoned yellow duster. It was early October and the wind howled like a beast in the wild. It seemed that he had once again transformed himself, changing with his surroundings and the times. He had the unmistakable cut of a man of the West, wearing a pair of striped trousers and a blue woolen shirt. A holstered Colt hung from his broad, black leather belt.

He was Meagher of the Sword, now twenty years older. His eyes still shone like English violets and his hair was almost entirely silver. Upon his face was a broad gray mustache with a manicured Mansfield beneath his lip. His cry rang out and gave me a sense of comfort and joy. I was once again within the province of my chieftain and once again he would make me feel at home.

"O'Keefe, you are a sight these eyes have longed to see. Welcome to Virginia City, Welcome to all of you."

"So good to see you Thomas," I cried, meeting his manly embrace with my own. I then introduced him to the Slocumbs. The genuine warmth of his greeting seemed to dispel their misgivings, arising from the war.

Meagher in turn introduced his companions. It was as if he had known them all his days. It seemed they had served with Fisk in bringing wagon trains across from Minnesota. After weeks of observing their skill and loyalty along the trail, Meagher enlisted them to serve as his aides and his bodyguards.

Both were mountain men. Both wore pistols and knives upon their imposing persons. Both became my devoted companions through a mutual respect and regard for Thomas Meagher.

The tall one was a grizzled bear from Hudson's Bay with coal black hair and a flowing beard, who called himself Jean DeSault. He knew Father DeSmet and the ways of the beaver and the elk. The other one had the look of a Spaniard, with olive colored skin, close cropped, graying hair and hooded brown eyes. He was named Francis Joseph and Shoshone blood ran through his veins.

It was he who would lead us among the Peigan and Kootenay Indians. It was he who told us of Crazy Horse and Chief Joseph. Through him we learned the ways of the people who were one with the sky and the earth. Through him we would meet the one they called Michel.

Meagher guided us down along a boardwalk in the company of his protectors. It seemed as if the entire town had turned out and was traveling upon that dusty street. To every passing face he nodded a greeting. To the ladies he gave the special salutation of a tip of the hat. He seemed entirely at ease and among his element. Virginia City was a hurly, burly place and Meagher would become its leading citizen.

We came to a halt in front of the gilded, glass windows of the Gem Saloon. This was Meagher's favorite watering hole; run by a blonde, broad shouldered, blue eyed Austrian whose name was Striemer. Striemer had manned the barricades of Salzburg during the rebellion of 1848 and received a jagged scar across his massive forehead for his trouble. He would prove a loyal friend and shrewd investor in matters of mutual interest and benefit.

His drinking establishment was the scene of many a festive occasion. Soon we were seated at a spacious wooden table, our eager lips submerged in the foamy delight of a mug of home brewed beer, a rowdy crowd filling the place from wall to wall.

"You're in for a treat this afternoon, gentlemen," Meagher announced. "It's Sunday, a day when all in Virginia City take a well-deserved rest. After you've had the chance to lift the dust from yourselves, I would welcome your company at a glorious game of ball."

By then the game of baseball was wildly popular across the length and breadth of the country, In New York every beer hall and fraternal organization fielded a team. During the war, it was rumored that the Battle of Chantilly was postponed until the boys on both sides could finish their ball games.

In St Louis, Minneapolis and Denver there were fields and games of ball to be played upon them. It was an up and coming pastime in an up and coming land and we were much enamored of its pace and its play.

After making sure that we were well situated with both bed and bath, Thomas departed in the company of his guardians. I was overjoyed to be in his presence once again. I was certain that he had made a most favorable impression upon my southern companions, for they were much disposed to accept his invitation and join in the festivity that was to follow.

I longed for the chance to speak with Thomas in confidence and receive his guidance as to the proper path to follow. After paying the landlady of my boarding house a week's rent, I was left with a solitary, silver dollar to my name. I suppose that was the predicament of many who made their way West.

In a golden field upon a hill overlooking the expanse of Virginia City, the *Bannock Badgers* gave their all against some local lads, calling themselves the *Silver Dollar Bunch*. There must have been at least three hundred spectators who cheered wildly from the sidelines.

I remember that the Bannock boys seemed older and more skilled in the manner of their play. They wore grey uniforms with the name *Bannock* stitched across their chests. Their pitcher, a long legged, handsome lad with auburn hair and beard, was able to hurl the ball with great power and deception.

The boys from Virginia City were a different lot. They first seemed overmatched; dressed like miners and without any appearance of organization. Yet as the day wore on toward sunset the worm began to turn. The score became knotted at three a piece, while the contest passed into its eleventh inning.

All in attendance waited on every pitch. I was seated next to Thomas and I remember him nibbling upon his fingernails, as he focused intently upon the spectacle before us.

I recall thinking how different it all seemed, there in the wilderness in the company of my devoted friend. On this occasion there were no shells or minnie balls whizzing over our heads. I wondered how many of the lads engaged before us had served beneath Old Glory or the Stars and Bars. I am certain there were a few.

As the Virginia City lads were batting, the setting sun was beginning to bring matters to a close. There was a portly man in a brown overcoat and chin whiskers who declared that it was to be the last at bat for the home team. If the score remained even, after three were out, that would be the end of it.

I remember there were many who voiced their disapproval with this pronouncement. Then, one of our boys was hit in the head by a pitch and awarded his base. At that, those who had traveled with their team from Bannock began to act unruly. I am certain that the drink played a part in their behavior.

I recall Meagher becoming uneasy at this display, signaling us with the wave of his hand to be at the ready for what might happen. It was then that one of our lads got a hold of one, driving it over the heads of those on guard in the outer field.

The lad who had been awarded first, rounded third base sprinting like the devil himself was upon his tail. Then the ball was retrieved and relayed back toward the formidable presence of a bow legged catcher. As the lad arrived at the catcher like a runaway steer, so too did the ball. In a cloud of dust, with arms and legs askew, they collided. All of us strained to see what the outcome was of that melee.

Suddenly, the umpire gave us the signal. Our lad had knocked Bannock's catcher into a stupor and the ball loose. Virginia City was victorious, as the crowd erupted into a stampede.

At first there was much jostling and then open fisticuffs broke out. Soon many in the crowd began selecting a suitable combatant and delivering a blow. Then the entire field was enveloped in a brawling mass, fighting for the sake of fighting's release.

I must admit that I too entered the fray, delivering a couple of roundhouse blows before being set upon by two who were younger and stronger than me. I can still see the Slocumbs; their backs to one another, wrestling and thrashing.

At first, Meagher tried to be the peacemaker, shouting to any who listened, that all fighting should stop. A blow to his nose caused him to cease in this capacity. He then spat upon his hands and joined in the fracas. After a while, a truce was declared and order somehow restored. I tell you, those were wild times.

CHAPTER 55

The following morning a boy came calling for me at the rooming house. I had been invited to breakfast at the Acting Governor's home. In an instant, I was accompanying the child up the street, toward a long, log house with Old Glory flapping over it in the mountain wind.

It was a crisp October day and I was filled with the anticipation of beginning a new chapter in my life. I recall feeling absolutely certain that I was meant to be in that place at that time. Meagher and I had finally found a place where even rebels could live free.

The boy approached the heavy wooden door that marked the entrance to the Governor's domicile and availed himself of its brass knocker. As the door opened, an aged Chinese, dressed in an emerald silk coat and trousers, bade us welcome.

His name was Cheng Lin and he was a Mandarin of nearly four score years and five. He was small of stature with white, wispy hair and beard. His wire spectacles assisted his tiny gray eyes in observing life in the very finest detail.

He was Meagher's man servant, as well as his cook and confidante. His spirit and his sayings were most instructive in leading Thomas to follow a righteous course in matters both public and private. Through him I would learn much of the ancient Chinese civilization.

Before me was a large fireplace of quarried stone with the head of a bull bison staring down from above it. The floor was constructed of hickory logs and there was a long pine table running almost the length of the room, framed by a score of cane backed chairs. There were four spacious windows with formidable, wooden shutters upon either side. These could be closed in a hurry, in the event of an attack by hostile invaders.

Upon its walls were murals of mountains and valleys and Indian blankets of many a colorful display. This was the grand room for meetings and dinners. This along with four bedrooms, a study, and two out buildings constituted a most proper place for the Acting Governor to make his residence. It was the place where Meagher would conduct the business of a booming territory.

Our breakfast of bacon, eggs and apple dumplings was a most delicious affair. As we dined together, drinking our coffee, we shared the remembrance of days and deeds gone by. I could not help but inquire as to Meagher's impressions of our circumstance and his aspirations for his life upon the frontier.

His responses were those of a man who believed that destiny was his ally and dreams of glory his stock in trade. I remember him telling me of his plans for Montana and his conviction that the paths he had chosen in his life were righteous ones indeed.

"I will endeavor to make of this territory a place for all men to live and work in peace and prosperity. I see a precious opportunity up here, amid the mountains and the clouds. I know now why I have been traveling upon this path for so long. Do you see it, O'Keefe? Can you feel it deep within your heart? We are meant to make of Montana an Eden, where all men, no matter the place of their birth or the shade of their skin, are treated as equals. Do you remember Brother Edmund and that night at the famine house?"

"Indeed I do."

"That night, he set me upon my journey, challenging me and awakening my soul. As I've told you, he appeared to me later, lifting me up from the depths of the dead and the dying. It was a vision and yet it was as real as real could be. He rescued me and gave me a purpose. I am meant to lead others to freedom. That was the reason for my imprisonment and my escape to America. The old woman in New Orleans, do you remember her?"

"I do."

"She had the gift of prophecy for sure. She foresaw the killing of Fredericksburg and the curse of the witch at the gate. She told me of that night in Tennessee, when we gave chase to that devil, Forrest. She saw me in this place and spoke to me of a river to freedom. Will you assist me, my friend? Will you accompany me along this path, wherever it may lead?"

"I will, Thomas. You know I will."

Through his intercession, I was able to secure a position within Virginia City's Assay Office. There I would learn of locations where gold would be discovered and mined. With the help of certain prospectors and with funds provided by our friend Striemer at the Gem Saloon, it was not long before Thomas and I were silent partners in The Liberty Mining Company.

With funds sufficient to more than meet our needs, Thomas and I embarked upon a course of attracting others to the freedom and opportunity to be found in the Montana Territory. In the newspapers of New York, Philadelphia, and Boston, cities where the Irish were still under the heel of the Nativists, we placed advertisements, telling of Montana's promise.

In New Orleans, Nashville and Savannah, southern cities with many who admired Thomas Meagher, the word was spread that the Montana Territory was a place where land and liberty could be had. I was charged with answering all of the letters of inquiry that arrived.

It was our belief that land was a precious commodity that afforded man his freedom. In the Montana Territory, there were endless miles of plains and prairie, wood and forest. These could more than accommodate the teeming masses, choking in the cities of the East.

By the thousands they would come, Irish from the North and the South, Germans and Swedes, former soldiers who had worn Union blue and Confederate gray; freedmen and those who had once enslaved them, all of them searching for hope and the chance to escape from the burden of their desperate lives.

Our's was a noble dream and a valiant effort. Yet there are always those whose dreams are of the selfish kind, those who believe that the few should control and oppress the many. Those whose greed and lust for power will not permit them to share their table with those they look down upon. They are the ones who seek to make of this world a prison house; where they are the masters and those of a different country, those of a different color; those of a different upbringing become their slaves. They are the ones who fear the fearless and the free. They were the ones who saw in Thomas Meagher an enemy.

The war had sown seeds of hatred that took root deep within the Montana legislature. Meagher's choice as Territorial Secretary seemed at first a master stroke, for he was acceptable to both of the factions vying for control of that bounteous territory. On every issue, at every turn, Montana's Council and its House of Representatives snarled and fought along partisan lines.

If you were a Montana Republican, you waved the bloody shirt of those who had fought and died for the Union and called your Democratic opposition, traitors and Copperheads. If you were a Democrat, you despised the dogma of those who despised you.

As Acting Governor, Meagher was thrust squarely into this pit of snakes. He was unaccustomed to the treachery of the political arena and openly uninterested in those who sought acclaim within its confines.

Meagher wished to open the territory to all those wanting to live free. The immigrants, the blacks, the Chinese, the Confederates, all were invited to partake in a noble experiment. All were beckoned to live in an Eden of freedom amid the mountains and the clouds. His position as Acting Governor allowed him to test his theories concerning the natural rights of man.

I remember on more than one occasion, searching for him in some secluded place, far removed from the clamoring demands of his office. Often, I would find him, reading his Jefferson and his Paine, ablaze with his aspirations. In a way, he had always been a dreamer. I suppose that all who truly believe in the promise of freedom must be.

I should speak to you of one by the name of Wilbur Fisk Sanders, who drew close to Thomas upon his arrival in the Territory. He was an ambitious, young lawyer with hopes of one day becoming Montana's Senator. A member of the Vigilantes, he made his mark in the prosecution of the notorious Plummer Gang. Never one to miss a political opportunity, it was Sanders who officiated as Plummer and his boys were left dangling from a hanging tree.

I remember the first time I met him. He was a tall, slender man in his early thirties with a high forehead and a prominent nose and chin. Meagher and I were eating dinner at the Gem Saloon in the company of his bodyguards, when Fisk introduced himself. His manner was fawning and his deep set brown eyes shifted back and forth, away from my probing stare. In truth, I never trusted him and my misgivings would prove prophetic, as time and circumstance would show.

I remember when we were loading up the mules and horses for our venture northward to Fort Benton. It was not long after my arrival and Thomas had insisted that I accompany him to an encounter with the Piegan Indians. There were ten in our company and I for one was reluctant to embark upon a journey to that treacherous trading post, situated upon the wild, dark Missouri River.

Francis Joseph, Meagher's guardian, had warned us of that lawless outpost, telling us that traders from as far north as Saskatchewan and as far south as St. Louis traveled there to peddle guns, liquor and pelts. He said that many a white man had lost his life, while trading in that place, and many an innocent Indian had been blamed and hanged for his death.

I recall that Sanders was standing nearby, wearing a derby hat and Sunday suit. I suppose he felt we needed his good wishes, before we departed on our six day journey. After Francis Joseph spoke, Sanders offered his own opinions on the subject.

"I hear tell there's many a white scalp been taken up in that region, and that any hanging done, was much deserved. Course I could be wrong about the situation, General. I surely could."

"Mebbe someday, somebody put rope 'round your neck," I remember Francis Joseph muttering. "Then mebbe we see how you like it, huh? Until the fox is trapped, he no' learn to cry."

"It seems, we all have much to learn." Meagher said.

CHAPTER 56

*I*nto the snow covered Rockies we traveled, where winter arrived early and the elk and antelope roamed free. Across frozen rivers and along treacherous gorges, our party of ten horsemen and three pack mules trekked, passing the lair of a mountain lion and observing a herd of buffalo that moved like some great dark presence over the whitened landscape.

After passing the Great Falls and crossing wind-swept plains that rose to meet endless sky, we came upon the Missouri River. For two days we followed its winding course northward toward Fort Benton. At night we sought shelter in mountain caves or amid gigantic ferns and feasted upon freshly killed game.

The purpose of our venture was to secure a treaty of peace with the Piegan Indians and prevent open warfare from breaking out across the territory. Through Gad Upson, the Indian agent for the Northern region, Meagher had arranged a rendezvous with Mountain Chief, the leader of the Piegans, and a man of great respect among the Blackfeet.

It was a sun filled, frigid, November afternoon when we came upon the Piegan village. It was located in the hills that overlooked Fort Benton, amid a scenic stretch of the Missouri. From our party of ten, Meagher selected a delegation that included Francis Joseph, DeSeault and myself. Into the gaping jaws of danger I once again followed Meagher.

As our horses made their way closer to the village, I counted nearly fifty tepees arranged in a series of circles throughout the snow covered hills. Soon the Indian Agent, Upson, appeared on horseback in the company of two Piegan braves. He was a smallish man in his fifties with a ruddy, wrinkled, impish face. His hair and beard were gray and he wore a broad brimmed slouch hat and buffalo coat.

Upson had served under Grant at Shiloh and come to the territory as an able servant of the Government's Interior Department. Through his honesty and his concern for the Indian, he had become a trusted envoy to both the Blackfeet and Gros Ventre Nations.

Since the Fort Laramie Treaty, the Northwest had been divided into areas that were supposed to safeguard the tribal lands of the Plains Indians. The history of the Government's dealings with the Indians however, would be full of broken promises, the betrayal of blind trust and the slaughter of a primitive people in the name of progress.

The Piegans were a proud and fierce people, whose tribal lands extended over the hills and plains surrounding Fort Benton. Since the signing of the Fort Laramie Treaty, the quest for gold and the travel of steamboats upon the Missouri River had made of Fort Benton an outpost of unbridled commerce. The Indian and his sacred lands had become obstacles in the path of progress.

All who had eyes and a sense of history could see that a bloodletting was approaching. It was Meagher who sought to prevent the outbreak of war within the territory he governed. It was he who saw the flame drawing near the powder keg of a proud people.

I recall riding a bay horse beside Meagher's buckskin as we entered the kingdom of Mountain Chief. The women and children watched us in silence as we passed. The men were unarmed yet seemed at the ready to deliver a deadly lesson, should our mission prove a pretext for an attack.

Upson had told us of the events that had caused the men of the tribe to speak openly of taking the warpath against the white eyes. The beaten bodies of two Piegan boys had been discovered floating face down in the river. Both had been scalped. One was the age of fourteen and the other twelve. It seemed that they had strayed too close to a camp of white traders and were falsely accused of trying to steal horses.

Only Mountain Chief counseled against vengeance. He summoned Upson to his lodge and warned him that many white scalps would be taken, if the Father in Washington did nothing to right the wrong committed.

Meagher called upon President Johnson to make the peace. He was given full authority by the President to negotiate on behalf of the American Government. Of course, any treaty signed required the approval of the Senate. A Senate whose members considered the western expansion a righteous crusade and the Indians savages to be subdued.

Mountain Chief was the first Indian I grew to know. In all my years, I have met few who could match his wisdom. He appeared to us in the company of six fearsome braves. He was a powerfully built member of the Piegan's warrior class. He was not as tall as Meagher but broader along the shoulder and back. His dress was that of a long buckskin shirt and leggings.

Upon his magnificent head of flowing raven hair he wore a head dress of feathers. Around his neck hung a necklace of beads, claws and stone. He wore finely crafted moccasins upon his wide feet and his copper colored skin was wrinkled with age. He had a long slender nose and piercing brown eyes that bore a trace of sadness within their gaze. I was never able to determine his age, yet I know that he had seen many a moon appear over his beloved Mother Earth.

He raised his hands above his head upon greeting us, then swept them downward toward his heart in a gesture of welcome. We had been told that he was schooled in the religion of the missionaries and spoke French and English with deliberate yet near perfect diction.

We would accompany him and his braves through the entrance of an enormous teepee. There we sat in a circle upon buffalo robes and partook of a long smoking pipe that signaled our hopes for peace among all people. The taste of the herbs within the pipe occasioned a warm sensation to pass over me. It was Upson, the Indian agent, who spoke of the matters that brought us together.

"Mountain Chief, leader of the Piegan people, warrior of the Blackfoot Nation, I bring with me Meagher of the Sword, leader of the white eyes that live below the Great Falls. He comes in peace and brings with him gifts to make the way straight between our people."

"I welcome him to our village, Upson, and I pray the Great Spirit will bless our words and bring peace to the hearts that cry for war."

Francis Joseph then spread a blanket full of gifts before the Indians. There were hats with feathers, a spyglass of great strength, many blankets, a ticking clock, three swords, a goblet of silver and a compass.

A brave examined this cache approvingly then returned to his seat beside his chief. At that point, Upson motioned to Meagher to address Mountain Chief.

"Great Chief of the Piegan people, I come to hear of your sorrows from the Father in Washington. My heart was wounded when Upson told me of the death of your young sons. I know that the Great Spirit watches over them and holds them close to his heart. I promise you that those who have caused your people this pain will be punished. I promise that no more will your people suffer at the hands of those who violate your land and your people. This is my word to you and the word of the Great Father that sends me to the Piegan Chief."

"I too pray that the hearts that cry for war will hear the song of peace, ringing in their ears, like the cry of a child being born. I have seen the face of war, Great Chief, and I have buried many brave young sons who have fallen in battle. We must not have war. We must have peace. We must have peace."

Meagher's words were heartfelt. His years as a warrior and his participation in the scourge of battle had transformed him into an advocate of peace. The obstacle lay in his powerlessness to control the untamed territory he had sworn to govern. All of his good intentions and all of his noble beliefs could not invest him with the authority to make his promises hold true. Just as in Ireland, he spoke in vain with the wisdom of one with a clearer vision, a more encompassing view.

Like a pilgrim venturing forth in a world that was not of his making, Meagher would run afoul of those who wielded power, without concern for the powerless. It was their design that would determine the drift of history. It was their power that would spread death and disease among the Indians, forcing them from their lands and corralling them like cattle upon barren reservations. It was their power that would one day be turned against Meagher.

That night we stayed in Fort Benton as the guests of an up and coming entrepreneur by the name of I.G. Baker. He would make us welcome within his three room cabin that bordered Front Street.

Upon this narrow, muddy thoroughfare that ran along the Missouri River stood a series of saloons, cathouses and dance halls. All of them catered to the trappers and traders that traveled up from St. Louis or down the "Woop Up Trail" from Canada, in search of gold, whiskey, or other worldly pleasures.

This lawless, frontier outpost had arisen from the trade of pelts and whiskey some years after Lewis and Clark's Expedition. To the North of Front Street stood a square stockade, two hundred yards along each of its four sides. This was supposed to be the outpost's refuge from savage Indians. In truth it was the white and not the Indian who were the savages in that dangerous place.

Most of Fort Benton's denizens seemed to be armed and desperate. Murder and mayhem were common place occurrences within its confines and vigilante justice was the order of the day. The week before our arrival a gunfight had broken out upon one of the steamboats moored alongside the river, leaving three dead and two to be hanged. Our arrival was cause for a memorable celebration.

The Last Chance Saloon was a notorious haven of gambling, and drinking within the settlement of Fort Benton. It was run by a bleary-eyed French Canadian whore who called herself Madame Mustache. Within its spacious backroom we were treated to a festive occasion that caused us to forget the rigors of the trail and the troubles that brought us to that place.

I.G. Baker had arranged for a superb dinner of venison and the dispensing of enough wine and whiskey to cause even Francis Joseph to join us in song. The music was supplied by a blind fiddler from Saskatchewan. In truth, he was no Johnny Fleming, yet his jigs and reels brought us to our feet on more than one occasion.

I remember sitting next to Meagher, as a steady stream of well-wishers made their way toward us from the adjoining saloon. There were at least twenty who spoke to us of friends and relations within the Irish Brigade.

To all, Meagher displayed a geniality that seemed to warm their hearts. It was then that I accommodated DeSeault by accompanying him into the saloon. He was inclined to participate in a game of chance and because of his inebriation sought my assistance in keeping a lookout for card sharps and cutpurses.

Within my coat was concealed both a knife and a pistol. With these weapons at my fingertips, I felt more secure in those perilous surroundings.

I cannot remember the exact manner of the encounter. I know that we were seated at a round table along with a customary collection of riff raff, when a tall, dignified black with peculiar scars upon his forehead asked permission to sit in on a hand or two.

The dealer, a dandy in a waistcoat and tie, inquired whether there was any opposition to having a black join their game. Hearing none, he dealt him in.

The saloon that surrounded us was filled with a notable variety of personages. There were prospectors and whores, fur traders and steamboat captains, card sharps and drunkards. It was a way station for those seeking an escape from lives that had been without hope or faith in the future. I recall that the Acting Governor, himself, soon made his way to our table, accompanied by a bevy of drunken hangers on.

While standing beside DeSeault, smoking his cigar, Meagher suddenly focused his eyes upon the black with the scarred forehead, busy gathering his winnings from the last hand. When their eyes met, a flash of recognition and remembrance appeared upon both of their faces.

The black then sat back and stared at Meagher momentarily, a faint smile appearing upon his angular face. As he dealt the next hand, he made his inquiry in the manner of one who had been reared on the Dark Continent.

"Excuse me, Sir. Have your travels ever taken you to the port of Cape Town?"

"They have," Meagher answered.

"And while there, did you kneel upon a sacred place in the Mosque of Thalasaam?"

"I did."

"Then Allah has crossed our paths once again. I was a servant to my Master Burton when he bade me to make your acquaintance so many years ago. Do you remember such a time, Sir?"

"I remember that time and that place. And I remember your face."

"I was called Matuto then, but now my name is Matthew. It brings my heart joy to see you in this place."

That was the time when a former slave who had changed his name and his station became a companion to Meagher. I have never met a man more loyal to a friend than Matthew. By the spring that would follow, he would come to work for the Liberty Mining Company. Through his labors he too would become a man of property.

CHAPTER 57

efore we departed from Fort Benton, we bade farewell to Mountain Chief and his people. By then, Meagher had devised a treaty of peace by which he would make good his promises.

The names of the traders who had murdered the young Piegans had been discovered and warrants of arrest along with a reward had been issued. By order of the Acting Governor, there would be no more trespassing upon the tribal lands of the Piegans, and the sale of whiskey and guns to all Indians was forbidden.

Meagher appointed Gad Upson as his representative for the granting of licenses of commerce for all those seeking to trade with the Piegans. This measure was meant to prevent contaminated goods from causing disease and death among the Piegan people.

Meagher believed that this treaty would prevent war within the territory. He believed that the keeping of promises made to the Indians would insure a lasting peace. Perhaps he was right in this belief. Before Crazy Horse and Sitting Bull surrounded and slaughtered Custer and his soldiers at the Little Big Horn, countless promises were made and broken by the Government to almost all of the Indian peoples.

I recall standing on a hillside overlooking the Piegan village. I was in the company of Mountain Chief and Meagher. At least for a while war had been avoided and Mountain Chief sought to show both his appreciation and his brotherhood by presenting Meagher with gifts.

These included buffalo robes, blankets and several handsome ponies. As Meagher stood across from the Chief, he spoke of his abiding concern for the Piegan people.

"I thank you, but cannot accept your presents. I am paid by the Government for my services and have no right to your property. Keep it for yourselves and your children, who else may go cold and hungry this winter."

I can still see the outpouring of the village, as we rode away on that blustery winter morning. Scores of braves stood proudly by their tepees in the company of their wives and children, bidding farewell as we passed.

Mountain Chief, splendid in his buckskin and feathers, repeated the gesture of raising his hands to the heavens and returning them to rest across his heart. Meagher and our band of ten waved goodbye, believing to a man that there would be peace in the future between the white and Indian people.

I am glad that none of our company possessed the gift of prophesy on that day. For the hope of peace would have never filled our hearts. Instead, we would have foreseen the brutality and bloodshed that would occur in the future.

We would have foreseen regiments of blue coats, mercilessly slaughtering Indian women and children. We would have foreseen savage war parties, descending upon the camps of terrified settlers. Indeed, I am thankful that none of us was able to foretell that which would become a most sorrowful chapter in the history of America.

Before we departed from Fort Benton, Meagher invited Matthew Johnson, the former slave, to accompany us back to Virginia City. He readily accepted with grace and gratitude.

After two days upon that snow covered trail, he became a valued member of our party. His cooking was a considerable improvement over that of DeSeault and his talent for telling stories and making us laugh was most appreciated, during that hazardous trek through that frozen mountain wilderness.

Three days out from Fort Benton we ran into a merciless blizzard. I believe we were about one hundred miles north of the Great Falls at the time. Shivering and wondering whether we would ever see our loved ones again, we sought refuge in a tiny log cabin used by the mountain men who broke trail through that country. It was then that two of our pack mules became blind from the driving snow and fled into the mouth of the storm with most of our food and drinking water upon their backs.

It was Meagher, myself and Francis Joseph who followed after them, fearing our party would starve to death in that God forsaken place and not be discovered until the spring.

We trudged through the drifting snow, attempting to follow the tracks of those errant jackasses. Soon we were lost, finding ourselves upon a narrow mountain trail that wended its way along the edge of a bottomless gorge. Behind us and to our left, we could make out the shapes of those snow-blind mules through that blinding storm.

Suddenly there appeared before us a bull elk, blocking our path and bent upon hurling us into eternity with the thrust of his formidable antlers. It seemed that our approach was a threat to his young, who were huddled in a nearby mountain cave.

There was no time for deliberation. As we stood one behind the other, perched along that treacherous precipice, the bull lowered his head and made straight for us, freezing both Francis Joseph and me in our tracks. I am certain that the brunt of that attack would have driven both of us over the edge, if Meagher had not acted with characteristic dispatch by drawing a pistol from beneath his coat.

"Get down," he commanded. His voice nearly muffled by the bite of the howling wind.

We complied as he fired twice, bringing that charging elk to a dead stop just paces from where we cringed.

Over the years I had seen much of Meagher's grace under fire. On that mountain pass, suspended over certain death, he saved my life and that of Francis Joseph. Never once did he mention this episode to our party upon our return. That was the way of Meagher.

When we arrived back in Virginia City, Wilbur Sanders had arranged a homecoming for us at the Gem Saloon. It was there that Meagher, in the company of both his Chinese man servant and a former slave whom he had befriended, spoke of his plans for convening a Constitutional Convention and seeking statehood for the territory of Montana.

In stirring words, he promised a state government that would fulfill the promise of Jefferson's Declaration, a government that would provide a home of equality for all men. With the confidence that he had brought about a lasting peace with the Piegans, Meagher told all who would listen of his hopes for a truly free Montana, thereby making those who opposed these aspirations his enemies.

Thereafter, the battle lines became clearly drawn. Upon his arrival in the territory, Meagher believed that the Republicans were the ones who would assist him in the creation of his Eden. As time passed, he began to see the true nature of their convictions and sought to turn his favor upon his fellow Democrats. For those were the roots of his political persuasion.

By this shifting of allegiance, Meagher was perceived as a traitor by the Vigilantes and others who wielded power within the territory. As a man of ideals and dreams, he was a threat to those whose business pursuits fired the furnace of their political power.

The Vigilantes were a band that was quick to take offense and slow to forgive. At first they had accepted Meagher, believing that a Union General would be a proper representative of their burgeoning territory. It was only after they began to see the company Meagher kept and the blasphemy of unbridled liberty that he preached, that they began to plot against him.

They would use the newspapers to portray him in unflattering ways and false lights. They would gather at secret locations and conspire in bringing an end to Meagher's tenure as the Acting Governor. They chose the opportunistic Wilbur Sanders as an envoy to their powerful friends in Washington. His ambition would prove him a most willing and able servant of their designs.

Still, Meagher persisted with his plans. Still, he endeavored to attract those in search of liberty, calling to them across the miles. Montana, he promised, was a place where all men could live free.

Of the hopeful thousands who responded to his call, there were many who served under Meagher's command. One of these was William Herbert. In the spring of 1866, he reappeared among us.

CHAPTER 58

*W*illiam Herbert was a living breathing reminder of the suffering occasioned by the War of the Rebellion. The amputation of his right arm just below the shoulder was a gruesome reminder of his bloody service within the ranks of the Irish Brigade.

He arrived by stage during a thaw in the spring of 1866. He was haggard and without the means of making his own way. Like a wastrel he had come to Meagher's doorstep. His ordeal in reaching the destination of Virginia City had threatened his very existence, for he had grown terribly ill from the drink and the desperation of his life.

Following his arrival, Herbert passed beyond all caring. Crawling into the alleyway outside of the Palace Saloon in a drunken stupor, he was content to die alone and unknown. Had he not been wearing a ragged tunic that bore the insignia of Meagher's Irish Brigade, a pauper's grave would surely have been his final resting place.

It was this talisman that caused him to be carried to a ramshackle rooming house. Thereafter, word was sent that a drunkard was dying who had served within the "Acting One's" Command. I was dispatched to investigate this circumstance and must confess that I did not recognize the dissolute figure, lying on a cot before me.

"Does anybody know who he is?" I shouted, to those who inhabited that miserable way station.

There was no reply.

As I drew near with a lantern, I began to make out his once handsome face from beneath the filth and hair that covered it. In truth, it was the empty right sleeve of his faded tunic that made me certain.

I was standing before the man who had guided me to my reunion with Thomas at the Metropolitan Hotel and had saved my life in battle. This now pathetic figure had once accompanied me over the bloody landscape that remained after Antietam. I had last seen him marching down Fifth Avenue. Through the care of two nurses, the one we called William Herbert remained among us.

We soon learned that he was wanted by the authorities in both Missouri and Kansas. It seems that he had used his skill with a knife to carve his way across those territories, wreaking revenge upon those who had given offense. It became the endeavor of Meagher and I to save our once proud comrade from the demons that had taken possession of his soul.

Once Herbert was able to walk, Meagher enlisted him as an aide and bodyguard. Frequent run-ins with bitter political enemies had made us all concerned for Meagher's well-being, when traveling in a crowd. Despite his position, Herbert continued to drown in the drink and visit the cathouses and opium dens located in the Chinese end of Town.

I recall many a time when he would be among the missing and Meagher would send me out to search for him within the darkest of Virginia City's dens of iniquity. On those occasions I would take along either DeSeault or Francis Joseph, for Herbert was more than one man could handle, when engaged in these dark pursuits.

There was a time in a raging thunder storm when we had not seen hide nor hair of him for days. Meagher had been awaiting the arrival of his beloved Elizabeth, and was most disturbed by the timing of Herbert's wandering. In truth, Thomas was starting to lose patience with being his brother's keeper.

A merciless downpour made the streets and alleyways a quagmire, as bolts of lightning tore across the night sky. We acted like a posse in pursuit of an outlaw. In a way we were, for Herbert had departed from the straight and narrow long before that night. It was as if we were descending into hell itself. A toothless whore provided assistance in following Herbert's trail.

I remember coming upon a canvas tent where rotgut was sold and poker played. Inside were a gang of desperados who had come to Virginia City in search of gold. It was there that DeSeault delivered a lesson in manners to one who had spoken to Meagher without the proper respect. A skull cracked in two by the butt of a Sharp's Rife was his reward for talking out of turn.

Lower and lower we descended, down into the dens where opium took all cares away. There among a score of others, lost in a haze of smoke, subdued by the poppy that steals the soul, we found him.

He was lying on a bed of filthy straw, beside an ancient prospector who had made of that shack his final resting place. The stench of the old man's corpse had been eclipsed by the odor that hovered there. To see Herbert upon his back, in the throes of that hellish habit, so hopeless and pitiful, was more than Meagher could stand.

You see, Meagher refused to sit in judgment upon those he called his friends. In light of his own worldly ways, he refrained from focusing upon the faults of men he chose as allies. Over the years he had tasted much that was forbidden fruit and sought not to condemn others of like appetites. An abiding concern for William Herbert's welfare however, caused him to depart from his usual course and assume the mantle of a disappointed father.

I tell you it was as if he had been stricken speechless by the fallen state of his once proud lieutenant. He beckoned us to carry him away, out into the downpour of that night. He ordered us to lock him in the jail until he was no longer within the grasp of his iniquity.

During this confinement he howled like a hound from hell. His tormented state caused us to bind him hand and foot and watch as he wrestled with the demons in possession of his soul.

I cannot recall another time where Meagher prayed openly for the salvation of one he loved. While anxiously awaiting the arrival of his Elizabeth, and managing the affairs of his office, he took time from each day to look in on Herbert and to attempt to bring comfort to his pitiful predicament.

By that time Herbert's fitful state had subsided and been replaced by a biting malevolence directed toward one and all. He was attired in a filthy nightshirt and his hateful eyes and haggard figure gave him the look of one who had become depraved. Francis Joseph and I were keeping vigil in the room adjacent to his place of confinement, when Meagher arrived and asked how his errant lieutenant was faring.

Despite ample notice of Herbert's foul temperament, Meagher insisted that he be allowed in to see the demon who had once been his friend. He asked us to go and have a drink at the Gem Saloon, while he spoke to Herbert man to man.

I suppose Meagher believed it was best to make this approach alone. We feigned our departure and kept watch through an inconspicuous aperture, near the top of the jailhouse door. The scene we observed touched both of our hearts and filled our eyes with tears.

"Let me out of this place, Meagher. I beg you," Herbert implored with his Ukrainian accent, as he knelt and thrust a beseeching left hand through the bars that kept him at bay. "Why do you keep me in cage like some beast?"

"It's for your own good, my friend. I could not stand by and watch you destroy yourself. I care too much to allow such a fate to befall you."

"My fate is my affair. I have won the right to live as I desire and die in way I choose."

"Not on my doorstep," Meagher replied, drawing close to the bars behind which Herbert knelt. "I remember a man of promise. A man who defied the fates pitted against him. I called this man my friend. Together we met all that was thrown against us. I still see that man, even now."

"Want to know what I see and what I feel, Meagher? I see cripple who causes children to laugh and ladies to turn away. I dream of standing before welcome crowd and feeling caress of violin against my cheek, just to make once more a melody most beautiful. Then I wake and know my fate, again feel loss that will end only with death."

"We are all cripples of one sort or another," Meagher counseled. "Life is full of loss and the change of cherished circumstance. With the years, we all grow infirm and fall out of step, in this dance before the grave. It is this that makes us men. Yes, you are no longer what you were. You have sacrificed much and been forsaken. But it is your soul that I cherish. Please, return to us, before it is too late."

As Meagher spoke these words, he unlocked the cell that had imprisoned his friend. The tearful embrace of these devoted men was more than I or Francis Joseph could longer observe. Later that evening, Meagher's beloved Elizabeth arrived, bringing with her a charm and a grace that warmed us all and made Meagher whole, at least for a while, at least until the wanderlust took hold of him and brought him to a river of no return.

CHAPTER 59

The presence of Meagher's beloved in our midst made me long for a reunion with my own wife and children. It had always been my intention to earn enough from my endeavors at The Liberty Mining Company to send for my loved ones and bring them westward with the prospect of a suitable homestead, and the promise of a boundless future.

It had been my ritual to write home twice every week, forwarding the funds necessary for my family's support in New York. It was my belief that Virginia City was a proper place to gain a fortune and live my life as a man of the frontier, yet it was wholly unsuited for the raising of children. The arrival of Elizabeth Meagher and our company's exploration of a mine near Helena, Montana, would allow me to make plans for a home in the city that would one day become the state capitol.

From the time that I first beheld Thomas and his elegant Elizabeth, in the lobby of the Metropolitan Hotel, I knew that he had been blessed with her love and affection. She was a beauty for sure, with golden hair, sea green eyes and an enchanting smile that beguiled with its innocence. When she spoke, it was as if an angel had bestowed her grace upon you and when she laughed, it made you forget your cares and revel in the sweetness of her company.

As a member of one of New York's finest families, she had attended the very best finishing schools. Yet on the frontier, she never treated others as being beneath her station. Her manner to all who made her acquaintance was both warm and inviting. In truth, all of Virginia City fell in love with Meagher's lady fair.

I recall many a lonely night, when I would make my way to the Meagher homestead for dinner. As soon as Elizabeth would greet me with her joyful ways and fine womanly figure, my solitariness would melt away and I would find myself once again in rapt admiration of that enchanting creature.

To say that she was devoted to her husband was to do an injustice to that lasting union. Pure and simple, Meagher and Elizabeth were kindred spirits with a love that transcended both time and space. Their passion was fashioned in the fire of a first glance and persisted through the travail of war and the separation of distance.

I recall a time along the trail, when Meagher and I were returning from a mission that took us to the mining town of Missoula. While Francis Joseph was out tending to the horses, he and I were seated by the campfire. At that moment he seemed lost in his reverie, while puffing upon a finely crafted Swedish pipe. There was a serenity about him, a marked contentment. It arose from the knowledge that his Elizabeth would be waiting for him when he returned.

As he gazed into the fire, his wolf-like eyes seemed to be passing over the landscape of his memory, while a solitary wolf howled in the distance. It was then that he spoke to me with much affection, beneath a spectacular starlit sky.

"We have come a long way together you and I. Tell me... do you have any regrets of what might have been in your life?"

"I cannot think of any, Thomas."

"Nor can I. I suppose a life can be measured by such as this. I am grateful that our paths crossed while we were young. I often wonder how all this will turn out?"

"What do you mean?"

"I wonder what lies in store for us and this nation."

At first, I offered no reply. Instead, I focused upon the past. For it is true that we live only in the moment, that the present is the past of what will be. With the wonder of our minds, we can revisit the region that has gone before or spin dreams from hopes for the future.

"I know this Thomas," I replied, "I would not have lived a life as full, had it not been for you."

"Do you believe in providence?" he asked, staring like an avid astronomer into the night sky.

"I do."

"With all of this to take care of, can we expect that the Almighty watches over all that we say and do? Perhaps we are like the stars; distant lights that spin in the space of our lives; placed here with the hope that we will follow a proper design. The Jesuits taught us that we are beings of free will, exalted above all of God's creations. Yet I believe that only a few are truly free."

"We have witnessed much that was unjust. Trials and troubles heaped upon the weak and the innocent, dying children with their mouths stained green from attempting to fill their empty bellies with blades of grass. Men like Kavanaugh, Duffy and Richardson, killed in battle, while others of lesser moment live on and care not. I wonder what lies in store for us, my friend. I wonder."

To this I could offer no response. I simply stared at the sky and wondered as well, grateful to have accompanied Thomas Francis Meagher during much of his journey upon this earth.

It was a time of political turmoil, when we returned to Virginia City. The factions that had been clawing at each other since Meagher's arrival and appointment were now vying for outright control of the territory. In the vain hope of bringing harmony to the discord, Meagher would attempt to align himself with one side and then the other.

As the Acting Governor, he had called the legislature into session and set about the passage of laws and ordinances that would bring some semblance of order to that wild, untamed territory. In all of these attempts he was opposed by the Vigilantes.

By the autumn of 1866, Wilbur Sanders had been dispatched by them to travel to Washington and seek out Meagher's enemies in the hope of having him replaced. It was their desire to have all that he had accomplished in Montana set aside.

As before, Meagher was portrayed as an Irish brigand and drunkard who had surrounded himself with a lawless band of freebooters and former Confederates. There were many who had made fortunes in Washington, while Meagher was leading brave men in battle. These were the ones who would lend their support to Meagher's restraint and removal.

Both The *Montana Post* and the *Helena Herald* made no secret of their politics and their opposition to Meagher. He had come to represent all that was threatening and hostile to their dominion. Whenever the territorial legislature would meet, filibuster and ferocious disagreements would arise. More and more, Meagher would become disillusioned with this spectacle and long for the camaraderie of his Irish Brigade.

Eventually, all the laws that were passed by the Montana legislature while Meagher was Acting Governor and all of the actions of his Constitutional Convention were declared null and void by a Republican Congress.

Thereafter, all of the agreements that Meagher made, including the treaty with the Piegans, were deemed of no force and effect. He had become an Acting Governor in name only. That was when the Daniels affair came across his desk.

It seemed that a gunfight had erupted over a game of poker at Helena's Phoenix Saloon and James Daniels had been charged with attempting to murder the establishment's proprietor. After a hasty trial in which Daniels was prevented from presenting evidence to support a case of self-defense, he was sentenced to ten years at hard labor in the territorial prison.

It was the outcry of Daniels' family and friends that captured Meagher's attention. He'd been railroaded, they claimed, convicted by a rigged jury, just as Meagher had been convicted at Clonmel.

Meagher summoned me to his residence and directed me to depart for Helena on the next stage. I was to investigate the matter and determine whether justice had been done. I took William Herbert along for company.

Once we arrived in Helena, it did not take long before we became convinced that young Daniels had indeed been convicted by a jury that was far from impartial.

Using the skills I had acquired while reporting for the *Tribune*, I spoke with those who sat as Daniels' jury. I found that most were friends and acquaintances of the dealer. Men who had made their minds up before the trial began. We then met with the convicted, shackled in a putrid cell, facing a decade of confinement.

He was a round, squat lad with a pock marked face and a large head of unruly brown hair. His age was no more than twenty and he, like many others, had come to Montana in search of gold and a brighter future.

At first, he was taciturn, unwilling to converse about the matters that had caused his imprisonment. It was Herbert who advised him of our purpose and discovered that he had served with the black hats of Wisconsin's Iron Brigade.

That experience had schooled him in the handling of a knife and pistol and doing so at the drop of a hat. His version of the episode in the saloon was a far cry from that related by the five witnesses who testified against him.

The accusation of bottom dealing against one who made his living by the gambling trade could prove a most hazardous event.

Daniels insisted that the dealer had been cheating him and others at the table, when he caught his sleight of hand.

From a former bartender who had turned his calling to prospecting, I learned that the gambler had been accused before of being a card sharp, and both he and Daniels were taken with the drink before their gun play. The gambler had only recently become the saloon's proprietor.

Daniels swore on his mother's grave that the dealer made the first move, reaching for a derringer beneath the ruffled cuff of his left sleeve. Before he could shoot, the thunder of Daniels' six shooter blew a gaping hole into the gambler's shoulder, disabling him for the remainder of his days.

On the way out of town, a mob caught up with Daniels and delivered a beating he would not soon forget. Helena's Vigilantes soon came to his rescue, promising the blood thirsty crowd that their vengeance would be satisfied after Daniels was convicted. His trial was little more than a charade.

In the same saloon where the shooting occurred, frontier justice would soon be put on display. The judge was a drunkard with no legal training, who had never presided over an acquittal. The accused was denied the benefit of counsel, and was not allowed to call witnesses to contradict the testimony of the gambler's companions. The *Helena Herald* spoke openly of the dealer, as if he were a fine, upstanding citizen. Daniels, in turn, was labeled an outlaw, long before sworn testimony was given.

All of this was weighed by Meagher, before he decided to commute Daniels' sentence. In an act of conscience and defiance, Meagher sent an unmistakable message to the likes of Sanders and his Vigilante handlers. By setting Daniels free, Thomas advised all in the territory that he was still the Acting Governor and still possessed of the rebel's will.

Rather than get, while the getting was good and make tracks for a new territory, Daniels chose to remain in Helena. After a day of drinking and telling those who would listen that he would get even with the ones who had testified against him, he returned to the Phoenix Saloon with gun in hand.

In his drunken state he was soon overpowered and dragged to a hanging tree by a band of Vigilantes. After his corpse swung for two whole days, it was finally cut down. Thereafter, a piece of the rope used to stretch his neck was delivered by a rider to the Governor's residence. The note that accompanied it read, "It don't take a stronger rope to hang a governor."

The signal was sent. The message was received. Meagher was a marked man and an enemy of the ones who called themselves the Vigilantes.

CHAPTER 60

From the turmoil that surrounded him, Thomas sought a refuge. He and Elizabeth would spend their days riding into the mountains and dreaming of a home that was removed from partisan politics and public outcries. They sought and secured a homestead in a quiet section of Helena and attempted to live their lives apart from those determined to destroy their happiness.

With the appointment of Green Clay Smith as Governor, Meagher's political obligations were temporarily diminished. This caused him to look for other avenues of adventure and fulfillment. Upon Elizabeth's return to her ailing father in New York, Meagher decided to travel once more to San Francisco.

As I may have told you, Meagher and William Herbert had become acquainted in San Francisco. It was there that they shared an interest in a certain saloon by the name of *The Barbary Coast*. It was indeed a pleasure to accompany them on their return to that worldly venue and visit the sights that made that City a place for all the world to see.

We arrived by stage in October of 1866. The magnificent setting of the City, rising above the clouds and a most exquisite bay that opened on to the Pacific Ocean, gave to it a character and a prominence that rivaled our beloved New York. Our band consisted of Meagher, Herbert, myself and Matthew Johnson, the freedman who by then had become a foreman in The Liberty Mining Company. The mission was devoted in part to the pursuit of business opportunities, for our mining company had begun to prosper and Meagher was intent upon establishing a working relationship with the Bank of San Francisco.

Thomas was likewise interested in securing financing for the purchase of a restaurant and drinking establishment in that fair city. This venture could provide additional income and allow he and his wife to partake in a life removed from the frontier. I too explored the possibilities available there.

News of Meagher's arrival spread throughout the Irish sections of the City, for there were many from Erin who had made a home there and many more who would do so with the building of the railroad. A flood of invitations had been received, along with requests for speaking engagements. It seemed that the leader of the Irish Brigade had many a faithful admirer in that City by the Bay.

The Archbishop of the San Francisco Diocese had even requested that Meagher come and address his predominantly Hibernian congregation, following the nine o'clock Mass. To all of these flattering entreaties Meagher turned a deaf ear. You see, by that time he had partaken of the public life to such a degree that he had grown weary of its fulsome adulation. Although he never tired of hearing the sound of his name, he had grown to prefer a less public profile.

It was while we were dining together at Delmonico's that we once again encountered a despised envoy from the past. The years had not been kind to John O'Connell.

Revenge and retribution can on occasion taste sweet. To savor a reckoning and then have it come to fruition can bring a profound satisfaction. On occasion however, the grace of forgiveness will erase past transgressions and allow one an avenue to break free of bitter recollection.

Of all the creatures who played their part in our painful days in Erin, there was none more despised by Meagher than John O'Connell. While Meagher fought the British and their cruel domination of all that was Irish, O'Connell did business with them and informed upon his countrymen in loyalty to their rule. There were times when Meagher would rock himself to sleep at night with thoughts of vengeance toward John O'Connell.

At first his face and figure were barely recognizable. His once statuesque form had become bent and bloated from the drink and years of groveling before his betters. His dark hair and sinister expression had been replaced by a wispy pate and a fawning gaze.

We saw him across the expanse of Delmonico's dining hall. He was attired in kitchen linen, clearing tables and scraping to the commands of a haughty Maître De. That was when he turned, while carrying a tray of dishes, and spied Thomas.

The clatter of his burden, crashing to the floor, attracted the ire of his superiors and the attention of Meagher of the Sword. It was the whine of his voice that made his identification certain.

At once Thomas rose and rambled across the spacious dining hall, filled with the admiring glances of those who were gathered there. His approach caused O'Connell to cringe like a lap dog in fear of his life. I rushed to Meagher's side in anticipation of a bloody encounter; only to observe his face soften with pity. Suddenly saddened by the state of Daniel O'Connell's nephew, he derived no pleasure from the shame of a man bereft of dignity.

In the gesture of a gentleman, Meagher suddenly offered to pay for all of the shattered porcelain, advising one and all within the sound of his voice, that even the best of us make mistakes. In a kindly way, he pressed a fifty dollar gold piece into O'Connell's palm, whispering to him in Gaelic, "Long live the spirit of Daniel O'Connell."

The remainder of our visit to San Francisco was marked by a rekindling of old acquaintances on the part of Meagher and a rejuvenated William Herbert. There were so many fascinating characters that inhabited that storied City during those unbridled times.

The saloon formerly known as *The Barbary Coast* had burned to the ground and a new establishment bearing the name of *The Gilded Cage* had taken its place. We dined to the music of its twelve piece orchestra and delighted in the sight of the most comely chorus lines.

During our time together a warm and lasting friendship developed between William Herbert and the freedman, Matthew Johnson. It seemed that each shared a kinship, arising from the suffering in their lives.

Our last night in San Francisco was spent in each other's company. We four were a varied collection. All of us had been caused to travel far in search of liberty and we had witnessed many deeds of kindness and acts of cruelty along the way. We knew that the twist of our days rested in fate's grasp and we accepted that uncertainty with a bold resolve.

It was a blustery October night and the wind rattled the windows of Meagher's elegant suite at the Union Hotel. We had lifted our glasses to fallen comrades and noble sentiments. The discussion then turned to other matters.

It was I who provoked the conversation with a reference to that episode in New Orleans and the old woman who spoke of Meagher's future from a selection of peculiar playing cards. At first, Thomas ignored my invitation to elaborate upon the matter. As the night wore on, however, and the drink brought more intimacy to our conversation, our chieftain pried open the mysterious chest of his memory and offered us all a glimpse inside.

We were seated in chairs throughout the room; candlelight lamps providing an ethereal glow to the ornately decorated interior. In the distance through the windows shone the moon and the stars over San Francisco Bay.

Meagher was standing with his back to us, smoking a cigar and holding a glass of fine Irish whiskey. His body bore the burden of his years by then. He was wearing a ruffled white shirt and striped gray trousers.

As he turned, his face seemed care worn and weary, yet his eyes gleamed as before in the candlelight. He addressed his remarks to us all, seeking to disclose a secret that had altered the ways of his life.

"In Waterford, on a dismal night in the rain, with death and starvation stalking us all, I was dispatched by Brother Edmund to retrieve an infant from the cottage of a peasant family that had succumbed to the fever. My reluctance to march into another valley of death was apparent, for I believed that I had more than fulfilled my promise to the wretched and sought to avoid another brush with the fever. Sensing my fear, Brother Edmund confronted me with his words."

"Be not afraid, Thomas, for death is not an ending but a beginning and we are marked by the light of our caring hearts. I see in you a man who will rise in two worlds, one of the flesh and the other of the Spirit. You will be torn by these worlds, for they will each seek to have and to hold one such as you."

"Do you know lads? I traveled to that cottage and met with an aged spinster who had been caring for that poor peasant lot. It was she who gave to me the infant. It was she who would tell me of my destiny in New Orleans. There is indeed much that is, and makes a difference in the world we cannot see."

We listened intently to Meagher's tale of times past and worlds apart from that in which we make our living. At that moment, Meagher's words made us ponder matters beyond the boundaries of heaven and earth.

CHAPTER 61

*U*pon our return from San Francisco, Meagher received a proposal from *Harper's Magazine* to submit an article for publication that would depict in words and illustrations the majesty and mystery to be discovered within the Montana Territory. Before our last journey together, I accompanied him and Francis Joseph up into the northwestern corner of the Territory. There we would make an expedition into the land of the Kootenay.

Meagher believed that the publicity derived from such an article would succeed in attracting more men and women of grit to our Eden amid the mountains and the clouds. By the middle of April 1867 our band was wending its way across Thompson's Falls toward the sacred lands of that mystical tribe known to the mountain men as the owl people. It was Francis Joseph who told us of them and their legendary holy man, Michel.

On this escapade we were accompanied by a gifted artist named Peter Toffts and a retired cavalry quartermaster who called himself William Bowdrey. Francis Joseph knew Bowdrey from his days as a young scout and enlisted him as a man of his word who had lived through two winters along the Jocko River. Our travel along the Pend D'Orielle Lake and past the Elizabeth Cascade, offered sights that few white men had witnessed.

We beheld crystal clear streams that turned to raging rivers with the melting snow, thunderous waterfalls and picturesque mountain springs that sparkled in the blaze of sunlight. We witnessed enormous herds of buffalo spreading like an enormous shadow over majestic hills and herds of big horned sheep cavorting along the very steepest cliffs.

Along the trail I could see Meagher's spirit soar, for he loved the quest of adventure and became one with unconquered wilds. Toftts was called upon time and time again to illustrate the breathtaking vistas we encountered.

On many a day, Meagher and I would ride out from our camp at dawn and gaze admiringly upon the lands that Bridger and others explored. It was a fitting sojourn for two Irish rebels who had dreamed so long of land and liberty.

On a misty morning, in a glade that bordered a bubbling mountain creek, we came upon the Mission of St. Ignatius and the kindly Father Hoecken. Since few white men had made their way to that place over the years, the good padre was starved for manly conversation. He was a tall man, adorned in a brown cassock and leather sandals. His head was without the trace of hair, while his muscular forearms were covered with a reddish fur. Although he was past his prime, he was still a figure of strength and grace.

It was said that he had been tortured by a band of Blackfeet for nearly four days, before his fearless nature caused them to set him free. The following winter his tormenters returned to receive his teachings, and become baptized in the waters of a mountain lake. He was a man of God who loved the Flathead and Kootenay as he would his own children. I considered it a privilege to have made his acquaintance in my lifetime.

Behind his white washed mission stood a grist mill. This supplied the Indians with ample corn and meal to help them make their way through the merciless winters that blew down from the frigid North. On a sunny, Spring Sunday, Meagher and myself attended Mass at this mission and marveled at the devotion demonstrated by families of what once were savage Indians.

That afternoon our band partook of a festive celebration before heading off toward the lands of the Kootenay. I recall Meagher making inquiry of Father Hoecken as to whether he had made the acquaintance of Michel, the mystical chief of the Kootenay.

"Is he a follower of Jesus, Father?"

"If loving one's fellow man makes him so, I would say that Michel is indeed a Christian."

"We have been told that he works miracles, Father," I recall remarking, while the three of us stood near to our horses, loaded and waiting for our departure.

"Many who have known him, insist that he has wondrous powers. I know he was once a warrior and is now a holy man. Tell him I bid him well. Farewell, my friends. May God go with you!"

I often wondered what became of Father Hoecken. Whether he continued to live in harmony with the Indians, or whether he fell victim to the bloodshed that was to come.

Two days ride beyond the Mission of St Ignatius brought us into the tribal lands of the Kootenay. Along the way, Toffts drew scene after majestic scene in his note pad and Bowdrey told us tales of Bridger and the other mountain men who had blazed the trail that we would follow.

Toffts was an educated man who studied at Harvard and enlisted with the Sanitary Commission during the War. He had bright blue eyes and a constant smile, with dark brown hair that touched his shoulders. He was in his early thirties and would go on to make a name for himself as an artist of some renown in New York.

Bowdrey was a toothless old devil with a ragged gray beard, a gleam in his green eyes and an oath upon his lips. He served the most delectable rabbit stew and could spit tobacco juice farther than any man I ever knew. On many a night the song of his flute would remind us of days gone by in Erin and usher us into a dream filled sleep.

On the night that the owls and the wolves joined in a haunting chorus, we knew we had arrived in the land of the Kootenay. It was Francis Joseph, the son of a Shoshone mother, who ventured forth in his buckskin to tell the owl people and their holy man that we came in peace. It seemed that a regiment of braves had already surrounded us before he sallied forth.

In the stained glass of most every cathedral there are images of saints and holy personages whose heads are bathed in a blessed light. Upon our first encounter with the one the French monks named Michel, we were captured by the warming glow that seemed to surround his person and signal his abiding love.

He was not a tall man, nor did he possess a robust figure that set him off from the rest. Instead, it was a certain indefinable spirit that shone through him, touching our hearts and soothing our souls.

His hair was the shade of freshly fallen snow and his body was slight and sinewy like the antelope. When we first caught glimpse of him, he stood surrounded by a score of Kootenay warriors whose dark features were fierce in apprehension. All wore feathers and cloth that seemed to blend into the forest and cause them to be unseen, even when near enough to touch. It was the power of Michel's person that told us he was the one we had been looking for.

Their village commanded a view of the majestic mountains and valleys below. In the stately trees that surrounded their place of refuge, dwelled hundreds of owls, much larger and more accessible than any I had ever seen. To view hundreds of these golden and chestnut creatures soaring in the clouds with the sweeping spread of eagles' wings, was indeed a sight to behold.

Before we had ever set eyes upon that mystical place, it was Francis Joseph who had spoken to us of Michel. He was a legend among the Shoshone, the Blackfeet and the Crow. It was said that his mother was the wind and his father the sky; that he could appear first in one place and then another, like a spirit, and take the form of a deer or an owl; that he could heal the sick and make the blind see. He knew of our coming long before our journey commenced.

We received the warmest of welcomes from the Kootenay. While a score of handsome braves cavorted to the sound of beating drums in costumes that resembled the elk and bear, their women and children chanted and sang. After a customary exchange of gifts, an elaborate dinner was arranged.

Upon partaking of the most delectable venison I have ever eaten and drinking of the waters drawn from the sparkling pools that existed in that place, we soon found ourselves in a deep slumber. When we awoke, it was within a magnificent lodge house with the fragrance of a thousand flowers bringing us to. It was then that Michel appeared and spoke through Francis Joseph.

His skin was as smooth as a child's cheek and his eyes were that of the owl burning through to the marrow of our beings. His manner was both gentle and harmless and his voice was as sonorous and soothing as a breeze in spring.

I cannot recollect how long we were in his company or the nature of what was said. I know we talked of war and peace, love and hatred, and the meaning of men's lives in this world. I remember a sense of complete belonging, of being in a state that was one with the mountains and the clouds that surrounded us.

In truth, our visitation with Michel of the Kootenay made us believe that he was indeed an envoy from a majestic kingdom, beyond the boundaries of earth.

CHAPTER 62

The bloody harvest that would grow from the seeds of broken promises began to make itself manifest when Red Cloud and four thousand fighting Sioux threatened the farming settlements of the Gallatin Valley. With the departure of Governor Green Clay Smith for Washington, Meagher once again resumed his duties as the Acting Governor. Once again he was situated in the eye of the storm, now made even more foreboding by reports of impending massacres along the Bozeman Trail.

It was John Bozeman, himself, who wrote to Meagher repeatedly, telling him that he had received reports from trusted Indian trackers that Red Cloud had vowed to begin his attacks in the spring of 1867. It was said that he was intent upon ridding all the Indian lands of the curse of the white eyes. Meagher in turn sent word to Washington and the General in charge of the Federal Army, Tecumseh Sherman. His request was that more troops be sent to the Territory in hopes of avoiding a savage bloodletting.

Sherman rejected this request, calling it a figment of Meagher's imagination and the panic of an alarmist who saw savage Indians in his sleep. To one who had witnessed Sherman's panic during his flight from the field at Manassas, this rebuff was a burning insult.

When Bozeman and others were found murdered and scalped along the Yellowstone River, Meagher again warned Washington of the troubles to come. This time Sherman was unable to dismiss these warnings so readily and authorized Meagher to enlist and equip six hundred volunteers in defense of life and land within the Montana Territory. Once again, Meagher would be called upon to become a man of the sword, and I was called upon to assist in this enlistment.

Just as before, I reviewed gatherings of eager young men in search of adventure, to determine whether they had the makings for courage under fire. Just as before, those selected were trained and drilled by men experienced in bloody warfare.

Many former Confederates who had served with General Sterling Price beneath the Stars and Bars enlisted. Many more, who had worn Union blue during the Rebellion recently passed, likewise answered the call. One who had worn both butternut and blue was Daniel Kirby. He rejoined his chieftain during the spring of that final year.

It seemed that the wanderlust had once again taken hold of our devoted friend from Louisiana. He had tried his hand as a family man and a drummer of medicinal ointments in the villages and towns along the Hudson. He had even attempted to accommodate the demands of a querulous mother in law, who had taken up residence with his family and made his life a living, breathing hell on earth. A deep dissatisfaction with the course of his life caused him to rendezvous once again with us.

I should speak to you of that final episode when Meagher set off for Fort Benton. He had received a telegraph from Sherman which advised him that a cache of 2500 rifles was being shipped from the garrison at St. Louis and would arrive in Fort Benton during the first week in July. Meagher believed these arms were needed in order to make the Montana Volunteers a militia to be reckoned with. His aim was to create a fighting force that would discourage Red Cloud and preserve the peace.

Having made the six day journey from Virginia City to Fort Benton the year before, we knew that it was a trek that tested the mettle of both man and beast, particularly during the summer months. There were but three way stations for shelter and supply along the trail.

The summer sun had made a waste land of the plains and prairie and dried up the creeks and streams that could provide water for our canteens. There were six of us who accompanied Meagher upon that fateful final passage. We were a band garnered from the adventures of his life, bent upon securing enough rifles to equip a regiment of 600 cavalry. Along with our ten horses, we brought three wagons, each drawn by a team of two mules.

In that select circle stood William Herbert, the cripple now consumed with rebuilding his life, Francis Joseph, the son of a Shoshone mother and Spanish father, who had proven his worth and his loyalty on many a treacherous journey, DeSeault, the French Canadian trapper whose skill in surviving the wilderness was without equal, Matthew Johnson, the freedman who had become a trusted friend, Daniel Kirby, the former Confederate, who had once served in the Papal Brigade, and myself. This would be Meagher's last command.

The relentless heat and a blazing sun began its oppression upon us, soon after our departure from Virginia City. News of our leaving and our destination spread throughout the crowds that waved farewell to the Acting Governor and his band. It was meant to be a mission of military importance. Instead, it afforded those who despised Meagher an opportunity to strike him down in a remote outpost.

After four days upon the trail, the horses were spent and in need of a respite from their human burdens. For miles we walked them across endless plain and prairie until the sun began to set. That night we reached the welcome of a way station and took a well-deserved rest. All of our canteens were in need of replenishment, since the Missouri River was still a day's ride away.

The coyotes howled, as we passed a pint or two of whiskey around the campfire. The skin of all except DeSeault was baked and blistered from the sun and our back sides bled from days spent in the saddle. It seemed that DeSeault had treated his skin and posterior with a concoction derived from tree bark, and juniper leaves, thus avoiding the misery we endured. Finally, the sight of the Missouri River wending its way up into the mountains renewed our resolve to reach our destination.

While making our descent into a valley that embraced that wild, dark river, Meagher suddenly succumbed to sunstroke and began to talk in a rambling, disjointed way.

In response, Kirby removed a bottle of elderberry from his saddlebag and gave it to Thomas, as a healing elixir. After draining its contents, Meagher was required to take his rest in the rear of a wagon, beneath a canvas shade.

His cursing and curious recollections while under that spell, made us all wince and wonder how long he would remain in that state. I recall bathing his head with water from the Missouri. All the while, he ranted and raved about bloody landlords and the British bastard who had branded his palm with a T, signifying that he was a traitor to the Crown.

Just before our arrival in Fort Benton, we came to a halt along the Mullan Road just above Helena Hill. There we shaved and bathed in an inlet of the river. It was then that Meagher seemed to regain his senses and once again took command of our expedition. I recall thinking that he did not look well.

His face appeared ashen and his eyes betrayed a distant stare. We entered the town on the afternoon of July 1st, 1867. Three of us galloped behind Meagher, along a dried and dusty Front Street, while Kirby, DeSeault and Matthew Johnson drove the wagons to our rear.

At that time, the residents of that frontier outpost were preparing for a Fourth of July celebration and paid little heed to our arrival. The streets were full of wagons and horses and a bevy of steamboats were unloading their cargo upon the dock that bordered the waters of the Missouri.

It was then that I remember observing two desperadoes, whose attire and manner made me strangely uneasy. One was tall and reed thin, in a black hat and long black coat, while the other was short with dark hair and skin, wearing a sombrero and two six guns.

Unlike the others, they seemed to be paying particular attention to our arrival. I recall the tall, hard looking one remarking "that's him", as we rode by. I would later learn that Meagher had also taken notice of their manner and would remove himself to different sleeping quarters that evening, as a precaution.

We were able to secure accommodations in a hotel at the end of Front Street. It was not long before certain leading citizens of that untamed town learned of our arrival and dropped by to pay their respects to Meagher. They would invite our party to the dance being held that night at the Fort. After six days upon the trail, a night of celebration was a welcome event.

I recall that Thomas retired to his room about six that evening, telling us that he felt out of sorts and in need of a few hours rest. He asked that we meet later for dinner at the home of I.G. Baker, a man who had become a trusted friend to Meagher's Administration. Little did any of us suspect, but this would be our last dinner together upon this earth.

At nine o'clock, a table for eight was set in the backroom of Baker's single story home, bordering Front Street. The meal was barely adequate and marked by a series of champagne toasts. Again, I noticed a certain distance in Meagher's demeanor. It was as if he was unable to shake the bonds of his malaise from his person.

I recall William Herbert inquiring as to the state of his health on more than one occasion during that meal. When the table was cleared and cigars distributed, Baker invited us all to accompany him up to the Fort.

Meagher respectfully declined this invitation, yet insisted that we continue on with our celebration. If Thomas had not been left alone on that night, perhaps a far different ending would have been written to his life.

Outside, we were joined by Johnny Doran, an acquaintance of Meagher, who had learned he was in town and sought him out for a drink. He was an old navy man, who had sunk his share of confederate frigates off the coast of North Carolina.

He and Meagher had met in New York at a Fenian gathering and enjoyed the pleasure of each other's company. Doran was the captain of the steamboat, G.A. Thompson, which had traveled up the Missouri from St. Louis and was set to depart the following morning.

After much coaxing, Meagher was persuaded to accompany Doran on board his vessel and share in one more toast to friends and times they once knew. There on Front Street, Meagher and I parted company, simply saying goodnight, never believing it would be goodbye.

As Doran would recall, he and Meagher stood along the upper deck of the steamboat, sharing a whiskey and staring at the moon and the stars that hovered over the fast moving current of the Missouri River. They spoke of their days during the war.

Doran invited Meagher to spend the night on board and sleep in his cabin. At first, Meagher refused, then he must have remembered the desperadoes whose interest was drawn to his arrival. He must have decided that a night on that steamboat was safer than a night in the town. Before retiring, he asked Doran whether he had any guns on board.

"Why do you ask?" Doran inquired.

"They threaten my life in that town," Meagher answered.

Armed with two Navy Colts, Meagher bid his old friend goodnight and bolted the door to the Captain's cabin behind him. I would run into Doran later that night.

For a while Meagher slept beneath the stars, shining through the porthole of the cabin. The air was filled with the scent of jasmine, growing wild along the river's bank. It was then that his dreams brought him back to Van Diemen's Land and the forsaken love of Catherine Bennet.

In his slumber she touched his heart. She was so young and so alive, as they lay together in the green grass next to their mountain lake. Then, her smiling face suddenly became clouded with sorrow, the sorrow of her husband's agonizing farewell. From the depths of her breaking heart, she cried to him once again. He awoke to a voice calling from outside the cabin.

He unlocks the cabin door and ventures out upon the upper deck of the vessel. There she is, standing there. Her face and form appear, as if in a vision, beckoning him to join her from the shadows of the dock below. A passionate yearning fills his heart.

"Is that you?" he cries, as if in a dream. "Oh Catherine," he sighs.

There she is up ahead now, the soft seductiveness of her body drawing him down the gangway and between the warehouses that stood next to the dock. There she is in the darkness, her feet gliding along the boardwalk that leads along Front Street.

The town is deserted as he follows her. The sounds of a joyous celebration can be heard coming from the Fort in the distance. He passes the Baker House where he partook of his last meal. She ascends a stairway which runs up the side of a near empty saloon and pauses to make certain that he follows.

There is a room at the top of the stairway. That is where their passion can be renewed. That is where his heartache can be relinquished. He is her captive once more. He climbs the stair and enters that darkened room.

A candle burns in the shadows as she begins to disrobe. He can hear his heart pounding. Then from those shadows another appears, armed and deadly. A pistol flashes with a thunderous report. A mortal wound is opened in his right side. The face of the gunman is shadowed in the flickering light.

Thomas feels himself falling, as the light fades away. His power is oozing from him. He feels a knife pierce his person again and again. The pain of his wounds is unbearable. He is being rolled up and tied within the blood drenched rug by two who take him into a boat. They attach stones to hide the deed. They row out into the middle of the river and hurl his dying person into the deep. It is there, where he succumbs and remains, caught upon an underwater bramble, becoming one with the river that would set him free.

CHAPTER 63

THE ARGONNE FOREST
OCTOBER, 1918

he memory of my strange encounter with that mysterious old man still lingers. The dawn of another day's battle will soon be upon us. I stand surrounded by the men of the Fighting Sixty Ninth in the mud and misery of an endless trench. The fertile soil of the Meuse Argonne has been consecrated by the blood of our valiant regiment.

Soon the barrage will begin again. Soon the shrill signal whistles will fill the morning and I will once again lead my company over the top and into the desolation and death of "No Man's Land."

General MacArthur has given us hope. He has said that one more attack along the flank of the enemy will bring about an end to this horrid war. I pray that this is so. For I have had my fill of hearing dying boys crying for their mothers. I have had a belly full of war.

Upon my return to France I was beset by the same fears and tremors that occasioned my convalescence in London. A calming solace could only be found in the words and deeds recited by the one who called himself O'Keefe.

Who was he? Why should he appear so propitiously and provide me with the benefits of his ageless wisdom? Was he a messenger from another world, sent to make straight my path? Or was he simply a dream, a miasma, a creation of my tormented imaginings?

In the midst of so much that is madness, much that transpires is foreign and beyond all proof. Whatever the source, O'Keefe's recitations of Meagher and his times provided me with an abiding conviction that only the dead are without fear, and even the best of us have feet of clay, perhaps the best most of all.

The circumstance of our parting must be described, for it reassures me that there is much beyond our senses that is real and permanent in nature. In light of my encounter with this old man, I am of the belief that history and mystery have walked hand in hand down through the ages.

The train was fast approaching the outskirts of Southampton when O'Keefe once again removed that golden flask from his coat and invited me to join him in one final libation.

"Here's to your health, Captain. May the Good Lord bless and keep you in the palm of his hand."

"Here's to you," I obliged, taking one long, last pull of that enchanting refreshment.

"Did they ever find those responsible for Meagher's death?" I asked, while staring across toward O'Keefe in the gaslight of his cabin.

"No, Captain, his murderers were never apprehended and his body was never retrieved."

"Do you know who they were?" I probed, dissatisfied with this response and sensing that he knew more than he let on.

"I have my suspicions."

"Well tell me then. What do you suspect?"

"There was a cold blooded killer by the name of Jack Diamond. Some years after the disappearance of Thomas, he began shooting his mouth, while down with the drink. He was the one who pulled the trigger on Meagher, he bragged. He said the Vigilantes paid him to do it."

"Did you believe that?"

He stared back at me in the darkness of that cabin, his eyes peering forth like a wolf in his lair, a slight smile playing with his silver mustache.

"We caught up with him outside a livery stable in Missoula. Kirby, Herbert and I went together."

"What happened?"

"Well, he had this other one with him. I believe he called himself, Sanchez. The two of them seemed in an awful hurry to make tracks and refused to give us the time of day. Still, Kirby asked him about Meagher and whether he had done the killing."

"What did he say?"

"He never said he did. He just cursed at us and went for his pistol. He was a dandy of sorts with a black beard and narrow chest. Kirby killed him where he stood, and his partner died before he cleared leather. It was all justified, Captain."

"What became of Meagher's wife?"

"After Thomas disappeared, she came to Fort Benton. There she searched high and low along that river for any sign of her beloved husband's remains. She stayed in Montana for a while, then she returned to New York. She would never remarry. There was no other to whom she would give her love. I was told that she adopted a young boy later on, and traveled the world with him. She passed away some years ago. There were only a few of us who came to pay our respects. I am the only one that remains."

***

Those were the last words that were spoken between us. I recall being awakened by the conductor sometime thereafter. It seemed that I had fallen asleep, just before the train pulled into the station. There was no trace of O'Keefe, only his crimson text lying upon the seat.

I asked the conductor whether he had seen sign of the old man, while making his rounds. He shook his head, advising me that he had not seen anyone matching the description I provided. I thought it strange, that one who seemed so familiar to the waiters and porters upon that train, would not be known to him.

I gathered up my belongings and placed O'Keefe's text in the pocket of my coat. The troop ship taking me to France would be leaving the following morning.

As I was standing upon the platform of the Southampton Station, my head flooded with images of Meagher and his Irish Brigade, I reached into my coat and retrieved the crimson text.

Eagerly I turned its pages in hopes of finding an answer in all that swirled around me. To my surprise there were no words of wisdom to be found there, only empty pages without a trace of transcription.

It was then that I heard my name being whispered and turned to stare across the way toward a train leaving the station. Amid the smoke, I swear I saw O'Keefe, waving to me from a cabin in the London train.

After reporting to headquarters, I returned to the men. All of the Army was in preparation for a final offensive against the Enemy. It was not long before we were marching through bombed out towns and villages. Everywhere was death and devastation.

As we drew closer to the front, my tremors began in earnest. I tried to calm myself, but to no avail. Thoughts of Meagher and the sacrifice of the Irish Brigade no longer brought me solace. I prayed over and over for God to give me the strength to persevere, to lead, to overcome my cowardly fear.

Thereafter, I was enlisted to lead a reconnaissance patrol on the morning of the twenty fifth. The First and Third Army had taken up their positions near the forest and they needed volunteers from the Sixty Ninth to scout the wood ahead for enemy gun emplacements.

I gathered Twomey, Dalton and Callahan beside me and we set off just before dawn. I could not load my pistol in their presence for fear they would observe my trembling hands.

It was not long before we ran into an enemy patrol. In the midst of the horrid melee that ensued, Callahan and Dalton were killed. Twomey and I were crouched within a foxhole with enemy bullets buzzing all around.

At that point, I felt an irresistible urge to turn tail and run. That was when I suddenly felt the calming presence of O'Keefe, himself, right there beside me. That was when I verily resigned myself to dying and finally overcame my fear. Our troops soon arrived in force and drove those Huns away.

I reported to Colonel Donovan the following morning. I had not seen him since my return to France. I found him preoccupied with plans for battle. His manly figure was bent over a map of the Meuse Argonne and he was relaying coordinates to a subordinate.

His handsome Irish face was more wrinkled than I recalled. He asked to be kept informed of developments and led me away to his dugout for a short respite. He inquired of my sojourn in London and my progress in writing the history of the regiment. I gave him my transcription and told him of O'Keefe. He seemed fascinated by my encounter with that mysterious old man.

While I was describing O'Keefe's physical appearance, the Colonel suddenly reached beneath his bunk and removed a trunk filled with his personal belongings.

From inside he retrieved a text and selected a certain passage, then handed it to me. There before me was a portrait of a young man, bearing an uncanny resemblance to the silver haired O'Keefe. Beneath this portrait a name was written. The portrait was that of Thomas Francis Meagher.

At once, I recalled standing upon the platform of the Waterloo Station, watching as that old man first approached. Then, there I was on the platform in Southampton, my attention suddenly drawn by a whispered voice toward a train returning to London.

In a window of that train I remembered seeing that old man's face. He waved farewell with a most benevolent expression. His palm was pressed against the glass of the cabin's window. There upon that palm was the scar of a T, an indelible reminder of the evil that is tyranny.

Made in United States
North Haven, CT
26 August 2022